Andrew McCoy was born in South Africa and educated at the University of Stellenbosch. After a brief sojourn in business he embarked on a life of greater excitement. Since then he has been a crocodile hunter, a military adviser, an industrial intelligence consultant, a professional polo player in South America, a transatlantic racing yachtsman and a political organizer. Andrew McCoy is a bachelor who travels where adventure calls.

GW00640654

By the same author

The Insurrectionist

ANDREW McCOY

Atrocity Week

PANTHER
Granada Publishing

Panther Books
Granada Publishing Ltd
8 Grafton Street, London W1X 3LA

Published by Panther Books 1984

First published in Great Britain by
Sphere Books Ltd 1978

Copyright © Andrew McCoy 1978

ISBN 0-586-06197-5

Printed and bound in Great Britain by
Collins, Glasgow

Set in Intertype Baskerville

All rights reserved. No part of this publication may
be reproduced, stored in a retrieval system, or
transmitted, in any form, or by any means, electronic,
mechanical, photocopying, recording or otherwise,
without the prior permission of the publishers.

This book is sold subject to the conditions that it
shall not, by way of trade or otherwise, be lent,
re-sold, hired out or otherwise circulated
without the publisher's prior consent in any
form of binding or cover other than that in
which it is published and without a similar
condition including this condition being imposed
on the subsequent purchaser.

What is set down in these pages is the truth.
It happened to real people. Names have
been changed but the men were alive once;
they are dead now and dead men cannot
sue for libel. Nor will their surviving women,
who have to protect the growing children
who bear the names of their men, wish to
sully the memories of their late husbands.

The events described did not cease with the
men who originated and inspired them,
but continue on the vast bosom of Africa.

‖ Master Map

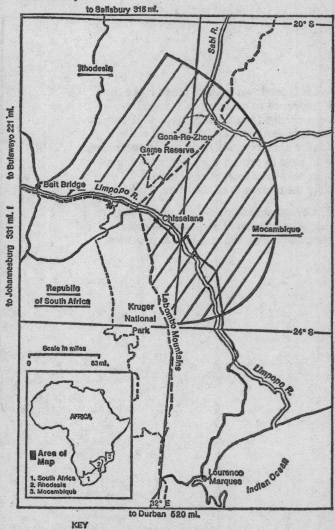

to Salisbury 315 ml.

20° S

to Butawayo 221 ml.

Rhodesia

Sabi R.

to Johannesburg 331 ml. ‖

Gona-Re-Zhou
Game Reserve

Belt Bridge

Limpopo R.

Chisselane

Mocambique

Republic
of South Africa

Kruger
National
Park

Lebombo Mountains

24° S

Scale in miles

0   63 ml.

Limpopo R.

AFRICA

Area of
Map

1. South Africa
2. Rhodesia
3. Mocambique

Lourenco
Marques

Indian Ocean

32° E

to Durban 520 ml.

KEY

- - - - National borders   ▧ Hunting Area

——— Main Roads   ✳ Ultimate Test Inc Base Camp

═══ Major Rivers   ∘∘∘∘ Game Reserve Enclosures

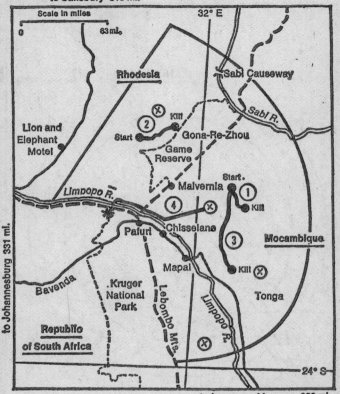

II Map of Hunts

to Salisbury 315 mi.

Scale in miles

0   63 mi.

32° E

Rhodesia

Sabi Causeway

Sabi R.

Lion and
Elephant
Motel

② ⊗ Kill

Start

Gona-Re-Zhou
Game
Reserve

Start. ①
⊗ Kill

Limpopo R.

Malvernia

④ ⊗

Chisselane

③

Mocambique

Pafuri

Mapai

Kill ⊗

to Johannesburg 331 mi.

Lebombo Mts.

Limpopo R.

Tonga

Bavenda

.Kruger
National
Park

Republic
of South Africa

⊗

24° S

to Lourenco Marques 268 mi.

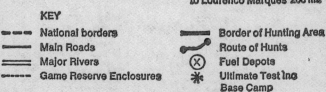

KEY

– – – National borders   ▬▬ Border of Hunting Area

——— Main Roads   ●—● Route of Hunts

═══ Major Rivers   ⊗ Fuel Depots

········ Game Reserve Enclosures   ✳ Ultimate Test Inc
                                                 Base Camp

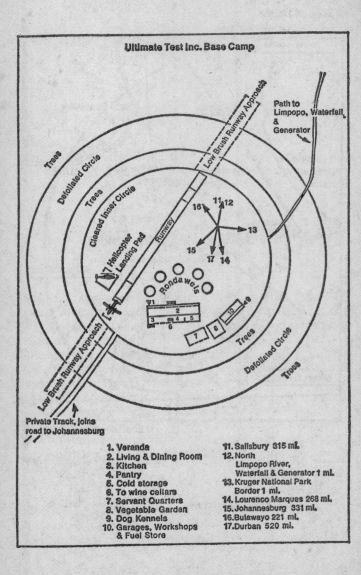

Ultimate Test Inc. Base Camp

Trees

Defoliated Circle

Trees

Cleared Inner Circle

Runway

Low Brush Runway Approach

Path to Limpopo, Waterfall & Generator

11 12
16
13
15
17 14

7 Helicopter Landing Pad

Rondavels

7 1
2
3 4 5
6
7 8
10
9

Trees

Defoliated Circle

Trees

Low Brush Runway Approach

Private Track, joins road to Johannesburg

1. Veranda
2. Living & Dining Room
3. Kitchen
4. Pantry
5. Cold storage
6. To wine cellars
7. Servant Quarters
8. Vegetable Garden
9. Dog Kennels
10. Garages, Workshops & Fuel Store

11. Salisbury 315 ml.
12. North Limpopo River, Waterfall & Generator 1 ml.
13. Kruger National Park Border 1 ml.
14. Lourenco Marques 268 ml.
15. Johannesburg 331 ml.
16. Bulawayo 221 ml.
17. Durban 520 ml.

Death was not far now and defeat certain but he kept lifting his feet rhythmically, chanting in his mind, mouthing the words but not expelling breath to give them life:

> Our men are brave
> our fields are green
> the buttocks of our women rounded
> their wombs fertile
> with more brave men.

His feet were pummelling the hardened earth, his head and knees parting the sharp edged high grass with water ripple wave but he was aware only of the beauty of challenge. At last his breath was starting to rasp in his throat, his chest expanding and contracting now a syncopation through his nose and mouth where earlier he had breathed with the mechanical ease of a steam locomotive. He noted these things and considered them and came to a conclusion: he would be dead soon. Very soon. As soon as the big bird caught up with him once more. He did not panic, nor change the rhythm of his pounding feet, nor breathe quicker. He had seen death before, administered it himself to enemies, watched their dying with interest. He did not doubt that he would die with the dignity befitting one of his ancestry. The words of the induna, *the elder councillor, who had sponsored him and advised and coached him for his initiation rang clearly in his head:* It is not the time of your leaving which is important, you who have so recently become a man. It is the manner of your leaving in which you must make your ancestors and, aye, your sons who will come after you, proud of your valour and your dignity in the face of adversity.

He heard the clop of the big bird behind him but did not look around. The men who had hunted him since an hour after sunrise followed an invariable pattern, had done so for fourteen hours. They would come from behind or from the front, sight and shoot at him. This would take a while. He would run on straight, turning sharply aside at the last moment. He had learnt very quickly not to take evasive action too soon; it would waste his energy, they wouldn't waste a shot but would simply bring the big bird around in a big circle to line him up again in his new direction. He said to himself, in his mind, saving his breath, Wait!

A cool drop fell on his shoulder. He looked up, not breaking his stride. The sky was a clear blue, not a single cloud. His hand touched his ear where the missing lobe had been, brought the blood into his vision as the sound of the shot reached him and he turned sharply in the direction in which the movements of his arm had already unbalanced him. A whipcrack snapped angrily past his head and the sound of another shot followed. Strange that warm blood should feel cool on my body. Oh, first wife, could I but slip into the cool of your body, the warmth of your womb now. *All day he had turned away from the village, the circle of huts. But now he had turned towards it, unbalanced by the movement of his hand to the missing earlobe which, another strangeness, he could still feel in his head as if it didn't lie on the ground somewhere behind him to rot. No matter this once. He would be dead from exhaustion, fall down on the caress of the soil to gasp his last, long before he could complete even part of the return journey. He tried not to think of his thirst, glanced at the sun now directly in front of him. An hour to darkness. Perhaps the men in the big bird would not hunt at night. Then he would live. They would probably find him again, as they had found him each time, every two hours or so, when they had to take the big bird away to eat or drink or whatever it did, perhaps relieve itself, by making searches in large* circles. But if they stopped hunting at sunset, would they find him again at dawn? *In the cool of the night, tired as he was, he would still cover at least half the distance he had covered in the daylight hours.* He had some idea of the distance the big bird would travel before it had to go away: perhaps twice as far as he could go on foot in a day when sorely pressed, as he had been today. And half that distance, exactly the distance he could travel during the hours of darkness, would take him safely into the foothills of the Lebombo Mountains, where he could hide under a rock like a frightened marmot. Also, it was still further away from the circle of huts, his wives and children, whom he held dear above all, even life. Several times he had tried to hide, but the big bird would flatten the grass with its wings and expose him and he would have to run again. *Why do they not shoot at me when I am near each time that has happened? Does the big bird object to blood too close to it? On the savannah was only grass.* In vain he had searched for a foxhole to crawl into or an anthill to hide behind.

The big bird came between him and the sun, now touching the horizon with yellow orange red blue above shading into deep royal blue then purple deeper than black. *Very shortly he would be safe.* He turned sharply to the right, an instant before the bullet sang its fatal song behind him. *Ah, so now they hurry. They can see the sun deserting them.* Another shot rang out and he changed direction to run across the line of fire rather than towards it. He had never handled a firearm but it seemed obvious to him, after this day's experience, that this way he would make a more difficult target. It was the same hunting animals, those running away or charging made the most constant targets, those running across your vision from side to side, though larger targets and exposing more of themselves, would be in the same place a much shorter time. The big bird hung in the sky, sliding towards him, lessening the distance, no longer bothering to go around to give the hunter a constant, no-layoff shot. *They fear they will lose their prey. They wish to conclude their hunt.*

The implication, that he was being hunted for sport by

other men, much in the same way as he hunted animals for sport or food, did not disturb him. The induna had told him of a time when his ancestors, worthy warriors all, had hunted with the Zulu for sport, annihilating the cowardly Matabele. And there had been skirmishes, even in his own time, with the smelling Tsonga, which he had greatly enjoyed. He was in the land of the Tsonga now; the thought gave him a certain grim satisfaction, wondering whether a Tsonga would survive the big bird and the men it carried, even in his own land. Most certainly not.

He kept an eye on the big bird, changing direction constantly to keep parallel to it. It was now within a hundred paces of him and shots rang out continuously. The dangerous urgency pleased him, it confirmed that the big bird could not fly at night. The shots were close but none struck him. Only his head would be visible above the grass and the bird's wings were causing tidal waves in the grass which must surely confound the eye and judgement of the hunters. Two more circles around the futile flapping wings of the bird and it would be dark. They would fly away to roost for the night and he would penetrate even deeper into the land of the Tsonga. He was glad now he had carried his assegai — short stabbing spear — and his shield with him all these weary leagues, even after it had become obvious they would be useless against this new enemy, an enemy who hunted men with the help of a very big and hungry bird. One more turn. The sun was laying its red head to rest. The guns were getting the range, the bullets closer. It was nearly dark. Before he set off for the Lebombos he would rest briefly, he had earned a rest.

His foot struck the anthill he had searched for fervently earlier in the day and he described a graceful parabola through the last rays of a dying sun, crashing to earth at the moment of darkness. He rolled and tried to stand but the pain was excruciating and he fell down again. If he had only rolled and not tried to stand up, the bird would not have seen him. But now it came over him.

He grinned as he gritted his teeth together, rose without

any pain, cast the assegai with all his might at the maw of the bird where the men sat on the tongue, aiming their guns at him. He missed but the metal and hardwood assegai hit the blades, was somehow not deflected but dragged towards the central driveshaft. The blades stopped their chop, the big bird turned crazily as it fell, landed upright, the maw still facing the man who had vanquished it.

He had brought down the big bird, defeated it or at least wounded it seriously enough so that it couldn't fly. Now he only had to deal with the men. The ones sitting on the bird's tongue seemed to have lost their nerve, were looking around wildly, the guns useless in their hands. He had their measure now. They were not his kind. Not hunters. No, they were trappers, diggers of holes for unwary animals, tiers of sliding knots. Not men. He would deal with them easily. He dragged his weary body, now suddenly so exultant, forward on his broken leg to attack the less-than-men who had tormented him all day, even if in the beginning he had been interested and amused.

Another man appeared behind the halfmen sitting indecisively on the large bird's tongue. The wounded man in the grass could not make him out clearly but imagined him to look something like the Jesú of the white man's books: slim, tanned, intense with clear blue guileless eyes. What he could make out was the calm way the man shot the bolt of the rifle and took aim. He thought: If they live in the stomach, no wonder the bird has to eat so often. There cannot be much space for food. Now the poachers of the night, the halfmen, were also raising their rifles but they did not count. Only the calm man counted.

The wounded man in the grass straightened to his full height and raised his shield half in salute, half in defiance. Then the bullets took him in the chest.

The burly florid-faced man sitting on the floor of the helicopter with his feet dangling released the harness holding him and jumped out of the machine on to the land and ran to where the man lay dead, now a pathetic bundle of flesh and bone and a cowhide shield and a loincloth of lionskin from a lion he had killed singlehanded with his assegai when he was fifteen years old.

'Finally got the bastard,' he yelled at the veld at large.

The two equally beefy, equally outdoors-type-and-proud-of-it-faced men who had flanked him on the footplate followed a couple of paces behind, secure in the knowledge that tomorrow or the day after it would be their turn to play the central role in the drama of literal life.

'Never seen such sport in a lifetime of hunting,' one said loudly to the other two. 'Worth every cent and double.'

They grunted their approval and the first man out turned to the photographer standing beside the helicopter, his camera wilting at his side, flaccidly peering at the ground with the zoom lens which dominated the assembly. 'Did you get all that?' the man demanded in a voice even louder than before, afraid it wouldn't carry the intervening fifteen yards. He could be heard three hundred yards away.

A slim man, tanned, intense with clear blue guileless eyes, jumped down from the helicopter as the photographer shook his head in the dark. The slim man was shorter than the beefy men by four inches. He was over middle height but the florid faces were all over six feet and three inches. Yet he seemed to exude command and they made a place for him beside the dead man. The three big men had all carried their rifles with them; the slim man had left his neatly racked in the helicopter.

'Did you get it all?' The man had not seen the photographer's shake of head in the dark which had fallen so suddenly.

'No. The light had gone.'

'I told you we should have brought our own American photographer,' God-for-a-day voiced his aggravation to the other two, glancing slyly at the slim man to gauge his reaction.

The slim man turned the corpse over on its back. He bent down to do so with his hands in the full knowledge that any one of the three hunters would have done it with the tip of an Abercrombie & Fitch boot. He took their money for services; it did not buy his respect.

'If your fucking photographer didn't get it all I want another go.' The aggrieved whine did not match the aggressive content.

The slim man seemed not to hear him. In the light of the helicopter's spotlight he looked at the bone angling whitely skywards through the ragged flesh of the thigh and considered the courage required to stand on that leg in order to attack armed enemies with your bare hands and a cowhide shield.

'He was a brave man,' he said reflectively, almost to himself. And, in truth, he had forgotten the presence of the others.

'He was black,' replied a loud mouth dismissively.

The slim man did not reply. He stared at the three of them with unconcealed contempt.

'Some white hunters think elephant or rhino or tiger is the most dangerous animal a man can hunt. Other big game hunters think the blou wildebeest [Cape buffalo] is even more dangerous. A few Americans give pride of place to the grizzly bear. All of these are dangerous but none is the most dangerous.

'I think the most dangerous animal a man can hunt is another man.'

James (Big Jim) Sylvester-Salmson
Nairobi, 1972

SATURDAY

One

Chris Decker pulled the girl's head away from him by her tangled blonde hair and gazed with the fondness of long familiarity at his erect penis over the rippling muscles of his stomach.

'It stands seventeen centimetres tall,' he told her.

Her tongue flickered around the pout of her lips. 'How much is that? I think in inches.'

Still holding her by her hair he pulled her over on her back. He put a forefinger in her wet moss and traced it damply across her stomach through the valley between her breasts to the base of her throat. 'That long. Long enough to taste.'

She giggled as he rolled over on her and entered her. 'That'll be right.'

Her large breasts rose precipitously from her chest, leaning to the sides to form a small fold on the corrugations of her ribs. He wriggled his toes under the bar standing an inch proud over the foot of the mattress on his oversize bed, dug his knees in and raised his trunk off the bed with this purchase, his hands free to knead her breasts.

'Eighty candlepower headlights,' he rated them and started counting as he swooped down into her. 'One, two, three, four, five –'

'What's best?'

' – six – hundred candlepower – ten, eleven, twelve, thirteen –'

'Ever had a pair that good?'

' – fourteen – no – sixteen, seventeen, eighteen –'

'What's the best you ever had?'

19

'– nineteen, twenty, twenty-one – ninety-two candlepower – twenty-six, twenty-seven, twenty-eight –'

'Ninety-two candlepower.'

'– twenty-nine, thirty, thirty-one –'

'I bet her nipples played tag with her navel.'

'– thirty-two – shut up and just fuck – thirty-eight – thirty-nine . . .'

She screamed on 'fifty-nine' and he squeezed her breasts. She screamed again at 'eighty-one' and at 'eighty-six' and at 'ninety' and then continued screaming while he never let her breasts go once, his fingers closing inexorably into her flesh until it seemed they would meet. He came at the stroke of 'hundred' and rolled off her. He walked into the bathroom and showered while she lay gasping for breath, cruel red marks heralding the advent of the bruises on her breasts like the hand of some avenging angel singling her out to bear the punishment for all the promiscuous.

He came from the bathroom, dropped the towel on the floor in front of the built-in cupboards and started dressing.

'I thought you said we had all day.'

'Sure. But my partner is coming. We have to have a talk. It won't take long. You just stay here and rest and before we go to lunch Uncle Chris will give you another hundred strokes, huh?' The doorbell rang and he started towards the bedroom door.

'For an oldie you're not bad,' she called after him.

His smile didn't alter but there was even less warmth in his voice. 'Just talk sweet, huh, or you can piss off.' He closed the door behind him, leaving her staring at the spreading bruises on her chest and wondering what she had done wrong. Forty-three wasn't that old when you were as fit as he was and so blondly handsome and tanned.

Chris Decker opened the door for his partner. 'Curtis Bill Bonham, welcome to my humble home!' He spread his arms wide but the slim tanned man of average height and a bit simply looked up at him until he stood aside. 'Come in. Come in. Drink?'

'Hello, Chris. No thanks, a bit early for me.'

20

'Suit yourself. I haven't got any coffee or tea or anything like that. Bachelor household, you know. But perhaps we can rob the liquor cabinet of some bitter lemon or tonic or something.'

'No, nothing, thanks. You wanted to talk to me?'

'Yes. Sit down. Right to the point, eh?'

'Yes.'

'Well, I'll match you for straightforwardness. I'll come right to the point.' He looked around until he found a box of panatellas and a kitchen match which he struck on the sole of his shoe to light the cigar. He puffed, inhaled the smoke, blew it out, repeated the little procedure. Curtis Bill Bonham sat patiently, not moving a muscle, looking straight at him. 'It's a bit embarrassing.'

'Come on, Chris. We've been together a long time. Spit it out.'

'Okay. You've been saying for a long time now that the group of hunters starting tomorrow is our last.'

'That's what we agreed when we started Ultimate Test, Incorporated. We'd carry on for five years and then stop.'

'That's just it. We're making a packet. Why stop now?'

'That's what we agreed to do.'

'Yes, dammit man, we have agreed that we agreed then to stop after five years. But this is five years later and I don't want to stop. It's too sweet a racket. Look, nobody makes the kind of dough we do and we only work one week in the month and it's not even hard work. I say we should carry on another year and then make a decision.'

'I've made my decision. But instead of liquidating the land and the equipment and splitting it between the two of us, you could buy me out. I'm sure we can come to some agreement as to price.'

'Shit no. It needs two of us. You for the brain and admin and me for the muscle and daring. I know my limits: I fly aeroplanes and helicopters. You're the organisation whiz. Anyway, I haven't got that kind of money.'

Curtis Bill Bonham's face twitched only slightly, fleetingly, but Chris Decker had known him long enough to be sure it was surprise. He laughed uncomfortably. 'Sure, you're thinking we each made more than half a million tax free over the last five years and even this Hillbrow penthouse and my Ferrari couldn't have cost that much and my women never cost me anything.'

'Expect airfares out of Johannesburg for a few week-ends' skiing in Gstaad and many other week-ends' bullfighting in Lisbon,' Curtis Bill Bonham said drily. 'But still . . .'

'Cards, my friend. Cards. I'm not in debt, mind you, but there's very little in the kitty.'

'I see. Look Chris, if you really want to carry on, I am quite willing to let you have the whole caboodle and you can pay me out as you go.'

Decker squashed the cigar out with more violence than was necessary and leant forward, his voice low. 'Curtis Bill, you know I'm no good with the paperwork. It needs the two of us. I would see a refusal as a betrayal of our friendship.'

Curtis Bill Bonham ignored the threat. 'You could take a partner.'

'No. Where do I find somebody that, one, I can trust with so much money and, two, who will not turn yellow in a crunch?'

'I'll help you.'

'Find a partner?'

'Yes.'

'No.'

'Well, I'm out. I promised Julia five years and then finished. For the sake of our son.'

'A woman and a child!' The scorn in Chris Decker's voice could not be disguised. He did not try.

Curtis Bill Bonham ignored his words and tone of voice. 'There are too many people trying for a slice of the cake. They're crowding us and it's getting dangerous.'

'Since when has killing other men not been dangerous? Shit, you're not telling me you're yellow?'

Curtis Bill Bonham was silent. Nothing showed on his face but Decker knew he had gone too far. 'Of course not!'

'It makes good business sense to get out at the top, quit

22

while you're ahead. Skim the cream, then stop.'

'Christ man, we haven't even made a dent in the pool of guys who want to shoot their very own personal nigger.'

'Perhaps not. But as I explained to you when I invited you to be a partner in Ultimate Test Incorporated, I only went into this business because Africa was all shot out of game and the only thing left was an abundance of men. Now the other safari organisers are finding that out too and with competition springing up all of a sudden, soon this business is going to attract a lot of attention.'

'We're doing nothing illegal!'

'Killing people is illegal wherever you go. But I'm not talking about legal problems. We're not breaking the law of this country. But what about public opinion? What if the newspapers get hold of the story?'

'Fuck me with a stone! Curtis Bill Bonham going on about morality! You steal a Gideon bible somewhere?'

Curtis Bill stood. 'My decision is final. This is my last trip. My offer stands. Find a partner to handle the finances and the rest and you can have all the time in the world to pay for the assets.'

'Fuck you.'

Curtis Bill let himself out. Chris Decker went back into the bedroom to give the girl another hundred strokes.

Two

Curtis Bill Bonham drove the Range Rover to the warehouse at Edenvale near Jan Smuts International Airport. Unlike his partner he saw no reason to buy an expensive car, or a cheap one, while he had the free use of one of the Ultimate

Test, Incorporated Range Rovers. Curtis Bill was not cheap in the least, but he was not extravagant either. His house in the expensive and exclusive Johannesburg suburb of Sandown was not a status symbol; it was a comfortable home with a large garden for his son to play in and his wife Julia felt more at home when not crowded by buildings or people, as he did himself. He drove carefully, with absolute regard for speed limits and consideration of other road users. He had not decided yet what to do once they had sold up the Ultimate Test, Incorporated assets, or once Chris had made arrangements for taking them over. His criteria were few and simple. One, there must be space. Two, there must be no chance of his son ever learning anything about his father's past. Curtis Bill was not ashamed of the manner in which he made his living, now or in the past when he had been a mercenary soldier, but he knew how cruelly suggestive young children could be. He thought of raising cattle in the Argentine. Wide open spaces. Cheap land. And he had never worked in South America, though he had visited several countries there at one time or another, while he was still searching for a place to earn his living conducting big game safaris, before he had concluded that the game was not only shot out in Africa, but all over the world, before he had had his flash of inspiration: Africa has an abundance of very dangerous big game in the form of black men and there must be sportsmen who would pay dearly for the privilege of hunting and killing a black man. But none of the Ultimate Test, Incorporated clients had ever come from South America; mostly they were professional men from European countries, the United States, Canada, Japan and Australia, with a few from the Scandinavian countries. Curtis Bill had once concluded in one of his rare expansive moods that the more civilised the nation, the closer to the skin ran the savagery of its individuals. Chris Decker had dismissed the conclusion with laughter. 'Why we don't get any takers from South America is because they can kill some nigger right there in their own backyard anytime they get the urge.' Curtis Bill reflected without surprise that he would be glad to be done with killers and killing. These 'hunters' were not the kind of people he wanted his son to grow up with. Or like.

He drove through the open door of the warehouse. Like everything else owned by Ultimate Test, Incorporated, it was freshly painted and spotlessly clean. Curtis Bill had no conscious policy of cleanliness being next to godliness; things around him simply arranged themselves in an orderly manner without any additional effort on his part. It was characteristic of Curtis Bill that, a week away from retirement and with his future financially secure at the youthful age of thirty-five, he should come personally to check stores in which the possible shortfall could be no more than a few hundred dollars. He parked the Range Rover out of the way and walked around the refrigerated Mercedes truck.

He took in the scene at a glance, considered the alternatives open to him, and acted. The native driver of the truck stood leaning against its side watching Vincent, Indian chief steward of Ultimate Test, Incorporated, beat a skinny black. The black man wore a patched but cleanly laundered shirt and a pair of wide shorts which flapped around his narrow knees as he moved on his bare feet. He did not try to run, swaying only slightly, his hands protecting his eyes as Vincent repeatedly cut his forehead with a handful of keys. Blood was streaming over the black man's hands, falling on his shirt and splattering the ground around his feet. He made no effort to hit back. Total silence emanated from all three men, the sound of the blows dull thuds with an hypnotic rhythm all their own.

He had only two choices. He could assume that the beating Vincent was administering was just punishment and that Vincent, as the man in charge, should be allowed to proceed. Or he could act out his own superior authority as Vincent's employer and stop the beating. The third alternative, ignoring the whole business as this was the last week he would employ any of them, did not occur to Curtis Bill; it would not have been in character.

'Vincent.'

Vincent struck the black man one last blow with the handful of keys and turned leisurely. He reached into his pocket for a handkerchief, wiped his knuckles and the spots of blood he found on his leather jacket. The beaten black man stood with his hands over his eyes, expecting to be beaten again, blood flowing freely, white bone showing on his forehead.

'Morning, Mr Bonham.'

Curtis Bill looked levelly at the Indian until he dropped his eyes and offered 'I was punishing him.'

'What is his name?'

'Jonas. He helps in the kitchen at the base camp.'

Curtis Bill turned to the driver, who had straightened when he had first spoken and now obviously wished he were elsewhere. 'Take Jonas in the Range Rover to the first aid station at Jan Smuts Airport. Stay with him while they sew him up. Then bring him back here.'

The man unfroze. 'Yes, Master.' He went and stood near the bloodied cook's helper but did not touch him. It was obvious from his clothes and his manner that he was aware of his social superiority to the other black man. 'Come. We are going to the hospital,' he said.

The beaten man took his hands from his eyes, looked uncomprehendingly at Curtis Bill. He had saved his eyes but he would never be handsome again. Shock was clear in his eyes. 'If they say he has to be treated for shock or something else, take him to Baraghwanath Hospital. Tell them to give him a private room and his employers will pay.'

'I understand, Master.' The driver hesitated, then decided to speak when Curtis Bill nodded in a friendly manner. 'He is Bavenda.'

Curtis Bill understood. Jonas had been hired from one of the local tribes near the base camp. He was not one of the urbanised blacks. He would probably prefer to be looked after by his wives at his own hut. The hospital would frighten and disorient him seriously. 'It is good that you tell me. But do as I say and tell them at the hospital, should you have to take him there, to tell him as soon as he can understand that

26

we will send for him on Monday or Tuesday or as soon as the hospital is willing to let him go home.'

'Yes, Master.' The driver walked around the back of the Range Rover and opened the tailgate.

'Let him sit up front.'

'The blood, Master.'

'Let him sit up front.' Curtis Bill took Jonas by the arm and helped him into the front passenger seat. 'Your wife and children will not be hungry while you are in the hospital,' he told him in his own language, adding to the driver, 'Make sure they repeat that to him as well at the hospital. We don't want him to climb out of a window and start walking home.'

When they had gone, he asked Vincent, 'Why did you beat him?'

'He was insolent.'

'How?'

'He called me Vincent.'

'That is your name.'

The Indian looked at his shoes, then defiantly at Curtis Bill. 'He should call me Mr Vincent.'

'And because he did not, you marked him for life?' Curtis Bill kept his own voice even. Losing your temper at stupidity gained nothing, often did a lot of damage.

'You're only frightened the authorities will find out!' Vincent said in an intense whisper. He photographed all the hunting for those hunters who wished a permanent record of their triumph. This was a blatant threat of blackmail.

'I have warned you about brutality to the other servants before. On two occasions. I do not give people a third chance. But since you will be in our employ for only one more week and you have been a loyal servant for five years, I shall make an exception this once and not dismiss you. However, I do not take kindly to insolence either.'

Without further warning, Curtis Bill hit the Indian in the pit of his stomach with a fist from which two knuckles protruded. The Indian sucked in his breath, leant forward holding his stomach. Then he started scuttling backwards, his

27

arms over his aquiline face to protect his handsome features. He made no other attempt to defend himself or to strike back. Curtis Bill rained a merciless storm of blows on his body until he sank to his knees, whimpering. Then Curtis Bill put his foot on the chest of the Indian, pushed him over on the floor. He was sickened by the man's cowardice and sadism.

'I did not mark you this time. But if I ever find you practising this kind of brutality again, I shall smash your face and maim you for life by breaking both your arms in the elbow. Do you understand?'

The Indian had his arms over his face, his knees drawn up to his chest. He seemed not to have heard. He was moaning to himself. Curtis Bill poked him in the back with his shoe. 'Did you hear me, Vincent?'

The Indian slid away on the ground, his panic and fear hiding from him the fact that Curtis Bill was no longer threatening him with immediate pain. 'Please don't beat me any more, Mr Bonham.' His voice was a high scream.

Curtis Bill took his jacket off and started checking that the caterers had delivered everything ordered. When he had finished the tally, he started loading the boxes into the truck. Halfway through he told Vincent, who was still snivelling in a corner, 'Go wash your face. You do not wish to have your subordinates see you like that.'

The driver returned, Jonas with him, the kitchen helper's head turbaned in bandages. The black man had recovered remarkably from his dazed state and insisted on helping with the loading of the truck even though Curtis Bill told him to rest. His strength belied his slender body. The work was finished in an uneasy silence. Before he left for home, Curtis Bill gave instructions for the driver and Jonas to rest while Vincent spent the afternoon fetching the guns and heavy luggage from their clients who would be arriving even now and checking into their hotels. The guns and luggage would go into the big truck and be driven to the safari base camp overnight.

He took his wife and his four-year-old son to the zoo after

lunch. In the early evening, they sat beside their pool and watched the boy swim its length again and again. He had been able to swim before he could walk. Julia was a fine figure of a woman, he thought, smiling fondly at her across the little table between their lounge chairs. She threw him a quick smile before looking back at the child again. It was strange, they had both wanted many children but had been able to suppress their pain when the doctors had told them Julia would never have another; now they had become used to it, no longer mentioned adopting a little brother or sister to round out the family.

'I wish you wouldn't go,' Julia said without preamble.

'Go where?' he asked, startled. 'I thought we were eating in.'

'Go on this last safari.'

He looked at her questioningly. She had not mentioned his work once in five years though she knew what he did for their living. And she was not the kind of woman who spoke idly, expressed vaporous wishes.

'I have a bad feeling about it.'

He was immediately alert. He rose and walked to the edge of their pool. His son looked at him, dived in the middle of the pool. Julia's premonitions were often uncannily and sinisterly justified by events. 'Anything specific?'

'No. Just a discomfort when I think of you going away. So near, yet so far ... that kind of feeling.'

'It will only be from tomorrow, Sunday, till next Saturday. I'll be home for good eight days from today. Then we can plan what to do with the rest of our lives.' His son swam the whole length of the pool underwater and he clasped his hands above his head in a sign of congratulation.

'Can't your partner do it?'

'Let him go alone?'

'Yes.'

'No. I must do my share as I ask him to do his. That is my commitment.'

Julia didn't argue. She was a good wife. She knew her husband. He always met all his commitments. If he said he

29

must go, he would go. He stood at the edge of the pool, looking into it, applauding the antics of their son and she loved him as she had never loved anybody before, not even her parents or her son. But the ill defined feeling of unease persisted.

She smiled at her son and her husband but her eyes were troubled.

Three

The hunters came their several ways to Johannesburg with their wives, arriving from different directions at different times. They struggled their way through Passport and Customs and Immigration Control at Jan Smuts International Airport with their luggage and guns, found taxis, and checked into the hotel suites which they had caused to be reserved by their various travel agencies. Nobody met them, a procedure radically different from that followed when they had been met by wall to wall fawning lackeys on previous safaris to Africa.

Dr Robert J. and Melody Cameron came from New York via Rio de Janeiro and Cape Town to Johannesburg because this route avoided touching down in any of the degenerate European countries. They had been booked into the Carlton Towers, newest of Johannesburg's international hotels and, at fifty-five stories, the tallest building in the southern hemisphere. Dr Robert J. Cameron was not interested in hemisphere records. He was irritated because he had not been met, as he had expected and as was his due when he was paying so much money. When an Indian named Vincent came in the late afternoon and asked for his guns and heavier luggage in order to load these on to a truck which would drive through the night to the safari base camp, he refused to hand the guns over to a 'yellow nigger' and demanded to speak to one of the partners of Ultimate Test, Incorporated. Chris Decker came, listened to his recital of grievances, said:

'Ultimate Test does not conduct safaris for little boys. If you cannot change your own nappies, join the junior chamber of commerce tour or apply at the South African Tourist Bureau.' He turned to go.

Cameron contained his fury. This man controlled the only game in town. He, Cameron, would surely look a fool if he came this far and then turned back. Word would get out. Worse, the word would be 'coward'. 'What about my guns? This yellow nigger of yours —'

'You can either give him the guns or not. If you don't, they'll stay here because there is no space in the plane for them and you can do your hunting with a slingshot.' Decker left without saying good-bye.

Cameron thought of chartering a special plane to carry his guns but he didn't even know the exact location of the safari base. He reluctantly let the waiting Vincent have the gun cases. With his guns gone, he felt naked, unprotected, vulnerable in this brash city which was so richly American in its underlying violence yet so unAmerican in its range of colour and offered experience.

Melody sensed his mood and left for a walk. In Commissioner Street she found a shop specialising in baby wear and spent nearly two hours dreaming with her nose glued to its windows. When she returned her husband made it loudly clear that she had made him late for dinner, then picked desultorily at his food when it was served. She tried to be invisible, which was difficult because she was tall and blonde and people tended to look at her with interest.

Confronted with any kind of officialdom wearing a uniform,

Enoch Pascoe reverted to a totally unintelligible East Cheap accent and grammar. This did not expedite his explanation to a customs official of why he needed such an impressive armoury to shoot the one *eland* for which he had a hunting licence. Judith had her period and had gone off to the ladies' to change her sanitary pad, thinking it safe to leave him to deal with the Customs and Passport and Immigration Control in a country where all the officials were guaranteed to be white and therefore not likely to offend Enoch's sensibilities. She was wrong. When she returned after only fifteen minutes, Enoch was red in the face and shouting in some foreign language. Five minutes later she had the helpful officials, who could see they were rich tourists, understanding her carefully modulated English perfectly and half an hour later they were on their way to the President where they were booked in. But Enoch took a long time to simmer down, which is why she attempted to shield him from a hurtful world to the greatest possible extent, and the events of the day did nothing to soothe his ruffled spirit: first, there was nobody to meet them at the airport and to help with customs; second, a customs official who didn't understand plain English and who became most obstinate when Enoch started raising his voice; third, an Indian sent by the safari organisers to take Enoch's guns away caused him to threaten to take the next plane back to England and to abuse the 'coolie' roundly – fortunately, in this white man's country, the Indian knew his place and wisely let Enoch run down, after which Enoch helped him carry the gun cases and heavy luggage downstairs and asked Judith to tip him well; fourth, the Indian insolently refused the tip, sending Enoch into a renewed rage; fifth, a waiter serving lobster amorocaine splashed a drop onto Enoch's suede shooting jacket with shoulder patches of leather, which on anybody else would have been an affectation but which was Enoch's daily wear, causing him to strike out violently and upset the whole dish over himself; sixth, in the ensuing commotion Enoch somehow gained the idea the hotel's constructors/owners/managers/staff/clientele were Jewish and had entered into a conspiracy

32

against him and he was calling loudly for his bill to be made up when Judith finally persuaded him that this was the height of the season in Johannesburg and there would be no other first class hotel space available; seventh, his stomach rumbled during the night from the effects of not having had dinner and kept him awake; eighth, he reached out for water during the night and pushed over the large travelling photograph of himself standing with his Nitro-Express 600 rifle on a white rhino he had shot, inscribed 'Enoch Pascoe and Friend', breaking the glass and cutting the photograph beyond repair; ninth, he cut his fingers on the glass scrabbling for his photograph on the floor in the dark.

Omo Minowara steered his and Yodoko's luggage and the guns through the formalities at Jan Smuts International with firm good manners and a great deal more expeditiously than either Cameron or Pascoe, using the dignity of his sixty-eight years to good effect. If he was surprised at not being met by the organisers of the safari, he said nothing. They took a taxi for themselves and another two for the luggage to the Rand International Hotel, where he always stayed when he came to South Africa. In the taxi they were silent as usual. Later, while Yodoko unpacked for their overnight stay, he told her about *apartheid*.

'In this country we are "honorary whites" in much the same way as the first Jesuit missionaries to the Japans in the sixteenth century were considered a cut above the other barbarians.'

She understood what he had not said: We must therefore be on our best behaviour, though he was incapable of so shallowly crude a thought. 'It is interesting, Omo-san.'

'Yes, very, Yodoko-san.'

After a bath she dressed for dinner in traditional garments, complete with the ceremonial but exquisitely sharp and brutally functional three-inch dagger in its sheath at her waist. Her husband approved and rewarded her at table with an insight into his mind.

33

'Life is the concomitant of death,' he said without preamble. 'And conversely. The uniquely distinguishing mark of death is that it comes to everyone. Neither money nor purity can buy immortality of the flesh.'

It was a favourite subject of his, the only one he had raised twice before in four years of marriage.

'But the commonplace of death does not make it less threatening nor is it any consolation to those who hear its tread.' The fish was served and he collected his thoughts. Their few conversations were generally in the form of monologues to which she listened attentively, happy in the knowledge that her husband confided his soul to her.

At twenty-two, which she was, death was distant in time but Omo-san talked convincingly from his nearer vantage point, raising a thought: *I shall be most unhappy when he is dead. Perhaps I shall take the old way and commit* seppuku *when he dies.* She wondered fleetingly what the wife of the man Omo-san had come to hunt and kill would do once her husband was dead.

'Death is contrary to the spirit of the twentieth century in that it alone, of all the base everyday commodities, commands the mystique which is the price men are willing to pay for the rare and unique.'

They ate steadily for five minutes while she thought on this. She was certain his logical mind had not come to a conclusion yet. Of all the luxuries and extravagances of the Tulip Room, only the euphoria of her husband's confidence had any meaning or reality for her.

'The mystique of death is the single life each man has to offer.' After a moment he added whimsically, looking at her over the table, 'Cats do not have a mystique of death for they have nine lives.'

It was the supreme accolade of her life, being allowed to laugh inwardly with him at cats who could not appreciate death and its glory. It was almost a shame that it would not be well mannered to laugh aloud at the misfortune of cats.

SUNDAY

One

'What's red on the outside, black on the inside and screams?'

Curtis Bill Bonham had first heard the riddle in 1960 and innumerable times since but he said dutifully, 'No, what?'

'A London Transport bus full of Jamaicans going over a cliff.' Enoch Pascoe roared at his own joke.

Curtis Bill laughed politely. The sparrowlike, nervous woman in the back seat laughed as if she had heard it before too. Enoch Pascoe seemed not to notice, he was enjoying the joke tremendously, gaining sustenance from it. Curtis Bill glanced at him out of the corner of his eye. The English couple were an ill assorted pair, this big teddy bear of a man and the short, bony woman. It was easy to imagine him walking through a room of delicate furniture, creating firewood by his passing without even noticing. He had walked into an expensive leather case while they were loading their luggage, bending its metal inner frame quite visibly, looked at it incuriously and continued with the joke he was telling. She had bent over the case, inspected the damage briefly, thoroughly, and shrugged; broken artifacts around her husband was no surprise to her. She seemed to be in charge of all their arrangements, paying hotel bills, tipping staff, arranging to have a jacket left for the dry cleaners picked up on their return. He stood by, his mouth open, his hands dangling, staring into some electronic dreamland when he was not telling his inane jokes. Curtis Bill wondered whether it was a successful-inventor act or whether the man was really that vague, that unaware. He would watch him, anyway, when it came to handling firearms around people and in the confined quarters of the helicopter. Clumsiness there would bend a great deal more than luggage, might be fatal. For all of them. He remembered the brave black man who six months ago had brought their helicopter down with only an *assegai*; a misplaced shot with a high-powered rifle would send it, and them, up in flames. Curtis Bill Bonham had often wondered, during his years of mercenary soldiering under flags where prisoners were not taken or taken only for the most excruciating torture, whether he would be able to die with dignity. He did not fear death but his mind cringed at the thought of humiliation and the most degrading of all human activities must surely be an undignified dying. For the first time ever he considered an accidental death by fire . . . No, that was not his way. Accidents happened to other people.

To head off further bad jokes he asked Judith Pascoe, 'Do you have any children?' He saw her face light up with a saintly glow as her eye caught his in the driving mirror.

'Two. A boy, Eric. He's twelve. A girl, Joan. She's nine. They're both very clever, like their father.' Her voice was the kind Curtis Bill mentally classified as 'genteelly impoverished', the sort of voice the ladies at orphanages use to differentiate themselves from their even less fortunate charges.

'My brains and their mother's looks, what more can they ask,' Pascoe roared and turned in his seat to blow her a kiss, spraying spittle as he went.

'Joan has a lovely skin and Eric is very sturdy and tall for his age,' Judith Pascoe added for Curtis Bill's benefit. It was clear she did not consider herself the most stunning female in the world.

At Grand Central Airport Chris Decker was standing beside his car, a flat red projectile which did not reach past his kneecaps, leaning forward to listen intently to the burble of the running engine. 'There's oil on the number three spark plug again,' he told them. Curtis Bill made the introductions.

Curtis Bill Bonham and Chris Decker had long since found it more convenient and expeditious to cart their clients to the base camp separately. Many, like the Pascoes, did not understand that 'light luggage' excluded metal framed leather cases. Others were abrasive, a condition aggravated by the close quarters of a small plane; they would have enough opportunity to quarrel at the camp and in the helicopter. Flying an overloaded small plane with quarrelsome passengers was something neither Curtis Bill nor Chris wanted to do and they considered the extra time and fuel consumed by the additional flights to and from the base camp to be well invested in peace of mind. Both had been mercenaries and both were well aware that martial machinery could destroy unalert or distracted users with as much efficiency as those they were supposed to be aimed at; both had seen many good men die horribly through no other adversity than lack of proper respect for the machines which protected or transported them.

Fetching their clients separately to the base camp also gave them a brief opportunity to sum up the men and the women: which of the men would turn out to be dangerous cowards or clumsy fools fatal to themselves and to others, which of the women would be cockteasing ego burnishers trying to exalt their minuscule self images by seeking to set the men against each other. Firearms gave men power, blood added the madness to use them again and again. And at the all-in prices Ultimate Test, Incorporated charged you could hardly refuse to let a man drink as much as he wanted to – another inflammatory factor.

Neither Judith nor Enoch Pascoe was showing any interest in the magnificent scenery they were flying over, even when they flew over the escarpment with its jagged edges and deep green valleys separating the savannah Highveld from the lusher Lowveld. He stared slackly ahead, unseeing, while she flickered her eyes around the plane, to the men in the pilot seats and back to her husband, always back to her husband. Her eyes were never away from him for more than a few seconds at a time.

Curtis Bill wondered whether Judith Pascoe knew what her husband had come to hunt. Probably not. The hunters, with the exception of the Japanese, hardly ever told their wives; most wives left the base camp without finding out the purpose of the hunt.

When they landed at the base camp, which Curtis Bill had purposely never named as a security measure, Pascoe went immediately to check that the 'coolie' had brought his guns to the camp and to his *rondawel* without damage. Immediately the Pascoes' luggage was on the ground, Curtis Bill Bonham turned the plane around and took off for Johannesburg while Chris Decker took off in the helicopter with a load of forty-four-gallon drums of fuel with which he was going to replenish their forward fuel depots. The depots had only been started six months ago, after a black man they had been hunting had brought down the helicopter with his *assegai*. Decker had used so much fuel in various tests before he declared the helicopter safe to fly again with passengers that they had made the base camp on the last smell of fuel from dry tanks. And helicopters do not glide when their engines stop from fuel starvation, they drop out of the sky like so many stones. This was not a happy prospect but even less happy was the prospect of having to fight their way out of a hundred miles of Moçambique on foot, backed only by footsore, snorting and sweating overweight coronary cases who hadn't walked more than a hundred paces at a time in ten years. On ground where the blacks would have the advantage of cover and stealth . . . Curtis Bill had said, 'You and I will make it, Chris, but how do we explain losing three hunters and a helicopter a hundred miles inside another country?' The fuel depots were a bother, but essential for the margin of safety Decker and Bonham considered necessary in the operation of heavier-than-air machines.

At Grand Central the plane was refuelled while Curtis Bill took the Range Rover to pick up the Minowaras at the Rand International. Omo Minowara was not as big as Pascoe but he was definitely much taller than the average Japanese; this Curtis Bill had expected: the hunters were generally big men against the norm of whatever culture they came from. He was dressed in the standard black suit, white shirt and impeccably sober tie, so *shibui*, in good taste, it might as well have been black too. His shoes were highly polished black calfskin, but grained so as not to shine offensively. His posture was martial but his chiselled granite face belied his gleaming black hair; there was more than forty years between him and the doll-like quintessence of the exquisite woman accompanying him. Curtis Bill knew Minowara would have an impeccable shooting jacket and under it he would wear his white shirt and sober tie. His wife was Japanese not only in her traditional dress but in the way she walked to one side and slightly behind him and followed him through doorways, shuffling frantically, yet with innate grace, in the tight kimono to keep up with the long strides he made no effort to modify to accommodate her narrowly bound step. Curtis Bill noticed with approval the fine touch of the short ceremonial dagger at her waist; she was not just copying traditional dress but had probably grown up with it, wore it every day. Their name, Minowara, he knew to be one of the oldest and most highly respected in Japan, not *narrikin*, *nouveau riche*. They said little on the plane, preferring to look attentively at the passing scenery, nodding appreciatively as Curtis Bill pointed out salient landmarks. Curtis Bill did not attempt to draw them out. The Japanese were never any trouble and these would be no exception. At the base camp he showed them to their *rondawel* and instructed Vincent to inform Chris of their arrival the minute he returned from the fuel depots. It was getting on for noon when Curtis Bill headed back to Johannesburg to fetch the Camerons.

Two

' . . . so this nigger, stuck in the ground with only his head sticking out, blood streaming from him where the lion had already bashed him a bit, waited his chance. When the lion next jumped on him he bit its balls right off. As one man the Boers in the arena came to their feet and shouted in outrage: "Fight fair, you lousy nigger!" '

Pascoe held his sides as he walked, laughing at Decker's joke. Already his face and hands were suffused with the glow which by nightfall would be a painful sunburn. Judith walked behind the two men, forgotten. The sun seemed to be powerless against her pasty white skin which had neither reddened nor seemed likely to tan. Omo and Yodoko Minowara rose from where they sat stiffly on the veranda of the dining- and living-room common to all the *rondawels*. Decker introduced himself, then the Pascoes. The Japanese bowed politely but Pascoe grabbed Omo Minowara's hand and shook it vigorously, slapping the older man on the back, saying, 'I'll tell you a good one!' Minowara disengaged himself politely and seemed embarrassed when he spluttered for air to replace that driven from his lungs by the blows. Yodoko looked on expressionlessly. Judith looked on helplessly. Decker pretended not to notice and busied himself offering drinks and relaying the order to Vincent who in turn relayed it to the black wine steward who was standing by.

'Very *pukka*, all these servants,' Judith said in the silence which followed.

'Africa runs on black electricity,' Decker answered, sending Pascoe into renewed fits of laughter. Decker raised his voice.

42

'Manual labour is the cheapest commodity and the one with the highest unit return, as the economists say, and it is very easy here in the bush to get excellent servants.'

'Unlike darkest Kent,' Judith tried but nobody laughed at her joke. The Japanese financier said something which sounded as if he agreed with Decker's economics. Then Vincent announced, 'Lunch is served,' and they went in. After lunch, which each of the Minowaras considered privately to be of a better than general standard for western food though grossly served, Decker led them out on the veranda again.

'There's still one couple and the intrepid leader of our safari, Curtis Bill Bonham, to come,' Decker said as he passed around a box of smuggled Havanas, 'but I think we can start the entertainment. Vincent!'

The Indian, who must have been waiting just inside the door, brought a silver tray on to the veranda and held it out to Decker. On the tray was a wooden box. It gleamed polished walnut. While the Indian leaned forward deferentially to keep the tray at a level comfortable for the white man to work at, Decker opened the gold clips holding the lid down, folding each back on to its retaining pin. Then, while all watched his showmanship with snake-charmed eyes, he opened the lid to show the green baize lining contrasting with the walnut. From the shaped base of the open box he took the firearm lying there. Vincent stepped back with the tray and the empty box, executed a military turn and went inside. He obviously relished his little part in this drama. Decker held the long-barrelled pistol up for them to see.

'Aw, shit,' Pascoe said, 'it's only a Browning twenty-two target. A kiddiecracker toy.'

Decker smiled. 'Accuracy is what we're looking for, not firepower. Too much punch would spoil the fun.'

Around the corner of the cookhouse came two of the 'outside' blacks, distinguished by blue clothes from the white of the 'inside' serving blacks. Between them they carried a twelve foot tree trunk of five-inch diameter. Around the middle of the trunk was rolled a chain with thick links. The

43

end of the chain was attached to the collar around the neck of a fierce looking baboon which growled and bared its teeth at the blacks. The men at the ends of the pole carried it high off the ground, causing the baboon to rear up on its hind feet in an effort not to be strangled. The baboon's rear feet scrabbled in the packed dirt for purchase.

'That baboon weighs more than either of those niggers,' Decker said. 'It would take about twenty-five seconds to kill them both by ripping out their throats or stomachs. Hardly much sport. See those canines? Three inches if they're any. We'll see what it can do with them a minute from now. Watch those niggers jump for their lives!'

One of the blacks had put his end of the pole on the ground in front of the chairs on the veranda and stood well back, his body a scimitar curve to keep his foot firmly on the end of the pole and his body as far away from the roaring baboon as possible. The other black held his end of the pole high to put strain on the baboon's windpipe and so distract his attention.

'There's a hole in the ground where the lower end of the pole is. The idea is to get the pole into the ground and get away before the baboon gets them. It takes quite a bit of co-ordination. If one panics and starts running, or if they're just slow, at least one of them is going to be dead meat. The weight of that pole wouldn't stop even a baboon half that size and, as you will see in a minute, these baboons are incredibly fast. Now!' Decker called to the black men watching him anxiously, one nervous eye on the baboon.

The two black men looked at each other and an imperceptible split second signal passed between them. The one holding the high end of the pole curved his body up and over and shoved the pole with his momentum while at the same time propelling himself away from the snapping jaws. A micromeasure of minimum time later the other one cast himself away from the foot of the pole. The pole slid smoothly into the ground for half its length to stop with a jerk which pulled the baboon over on his back. Incredibly the animal was on its feet and running around the pole while his

44

momentum set it spinning to unwind the chain in time to snap at the black who had been at the foot of the pole before the black stopped rolling. The monstrous jaws closed a fraction of an inch behind the rolling man's back, the baboon brought up choking by its chain and collar. It was obvious it had not been in captivity long enough to become used to these restraints.

'Munch him, munch him!' It was clear where Enoch Pascoe's loyalty – or at least support – lay.

The black men stopped rolling, thumbed their noses in the universal gesture at the enraged baboon which kept trying to jump at its tormentors just beyond the short reach of its chain. After a while they tired of the sport, stood up and dusted their clothing. Then they stood respectfully, eyes cast down, waiting, listening to the silence from the veranda.

After a while Decker, finding his guests insensitive to custom, fumbled in his pocket for a coin, flipped it for one of the black men to catch. Judith Pascoe found coins and cast them clumsily at the servants but the coins fell in the dust from where the black men picked them up with unshakable dignity. At a nod from Omo Minowara, Yodoko went forward to lay two high-denomination notes on the railing. These were greeted with loud gratitude by the black men.

'You'll spoil the silly rotters,' Pascoe said. He took his wife's purse and started casting coins within reach of the baboon but the blacks defeated his purpose by dividing their forces, one to distract the baboon's attention, one to recover the coins. Pascoe was loudly displeased at their 'cowardice'.

'No more,' Decker said shortly. 'That's only a curtain raiser and we don't want to tire the baboon before the main event.' It was going well. He was pleased that Cameron would be missing the fun. It would be the start of his punishment for inconveniencing Chris Decker by calling him away from his screwing because Cameron wouldn't let Vincent take his guns.

They ordered more drinks while Decker refused to tell Pascoe what the 'main event' would be, admonishing him to be patient, to wait and see. When they all had drinks, Decker nodded to Vincent, who ducked inside once more to fetch his silver tray. This time there was a silver whistle on top of a red velvet cushion. Judith applauded the striking arrangement and Decker spared her one of his dazzling sincere smiles. Vincent bowed low with the tray and Decker took the whistle from the cushion. He held it out like a magician at a children's party showing there was nothing trick about it, then put it in his mouth and blew until his cheeks bulged. No sound came from the whistle.

Pascoe was about to pass derogatory comment but Decker held up his hand. 'Listen.' From behind the cookhouse came the sound of dogs, many dogs, ferocious, frightened into viciousness, angered, bloodthirsty. 'The baying of the hounds. We breed them specially for this and let them practise on young baboons. The blacks are dragging a dead baboon through the kennels now. Here they come!'

The sound had heightened, intensified itself to an insensate primal scream. All eyes turned to the corner around which the baboon had been brought. Somewhat comically, anti-climactically, around the corner came the two blacks who had brought the baboon, this time on bicycles, pedalling furiously. Pascoe sniggered. Between the two bicycles on the ground dragged the bloodied and ragged carcass of what may once have been a young baboon, only the muzzle with the staring yellow canines and the red bottom angrily proclaiming the origins of seventy pounds of death.

Judith drew her breath sharply. Into view, its drooling open mouth with its rows of outsize teeth and curved fangs almost snapping into the dead baboon, came the largest dog she had ever seen, its reddened eyes fixed with mono-maniacal purpose on the bloody carcass. Behind it streamed a motley collection of mongrels, all somehow descended from hunting dogs, of all the colours, shapes, sizes and hairlengths an imaginative evolution and indiscriminate interbreeding could conceive of. Their common denominator was the yapping open jaw lined with teeth and fangs to populate a Daliesque nightmare, drooling yellow saliva through their cacophonous snarls.

46

The two bicyclists rounded the baboon at its pole closely but it was no longer paying them any attention, its eyes fixed on its natural enemies, the descendants of the wolf and the hyena; its teeth bared in futile warning to these decimators trained on its young by men and maddened through hunger and collective atavistic regression to bloodlusting, self annihilative destruction; its hair electrified in psychic warning of its straining tendons and ferocious killing jaws and manipulative paws.

Decker blew the whistle again, his cheeks ballooning twice. The leader of the pack stopped within a hairsbreadth of the carcass, the other dogs tumbled over themselves, snapping at each other in their frustration, in their efforts to heed the reflexive call of training. One small fox terrier-derivative rolled against the legs of the large yellow monster and had its head crushed in the fearful jaws for its clumsiness. A few did not seem inclined to heed the call of the dog whistle and were kicked back into line by the half dozen black kennel assistants who had come running around the corner after their charges. Those who seemed about to attack the men were beaten with the *knopkieries*, short knobbed sticks, the blacks wielded with practised ease. The two bicyclists made a flourish in the dust and disappeared behind the cookhouse. The pack had now perceived a live enemy and were hurling vocal rage at it but the black men between the straining baboon and the reaching dogs nimbly numbed the venturesome with a single sharp *knopkierie* blow to the nose.

Decker surveyed the baboon, the howling pack and the Bantu between them. He toyed with the whistle in his hand.

'The big yellow dog is a Rhodesian ridgeback,' he said softly, a fine piece of showmanship for the others had to divert their attention from the engaging spectacle to strain and catch his words over the raucous rage of the dogs.

'Huh?' Pascoe.

'He is the only one capable of killing a baboon that size alone and it would be a close thing, even with the baboon on a chain. Rhodesian ridgebacks are bred to hunt tigers but a big baboon can take on a tiger singly and kill it, though it might perish itself in the venture. But a pack of dogs could tackle a baboon, even-steven, about twenty assorted dogs like we have here. Then it would be an even bet.'

'May I make a suggestion, Mr Decker?'

'Yes, of course, Mr Minowara.' Decker was surprised. The Japanese, in his experience, rarely offered unsolicited advice.

'Would it not be finer sport then if we removed the large yellow dog you call a Rhodesian ridgeback? Or have the large dog take the baboon on alone?'

'Exactly what I was thinking. But it is not as easy as it seems, taking away from the dogs what one has already promised them.'

'Honour in one's dealings, even with dogs, is admirable,' Minowara said non-committally, not wanting to force his wishes on Decker.

'The ridgeback is only a large pup. It has another month to full maturity. Let's see if it wants to hunt another day.' Decker called two of the attendants over, talked to them in their own language. They rolled their eyes until they were all white, shook their heads, fingered the padded leather guards on their arms nervously. Decker insisted and they went reluctantly to the large dog. It would not be led away, growling at them without taking its eyes off the baboon for one second. One of them tried to attach a ring at the end of a long sturdy stick to the ring on its collar and it sank its teeth into the thick leather of the arm guard. While the dog was struggling to free its teeth, the other black quickly attached the ring. When the dog freed its teeth the blacks jumped back out of reach and dragged it away, its feet scraping furrows in the ground, at the end of the stick. It had been on the distancing stick before – it did not try to reach the men again but stared balefully over its shoulder at the baboon until it was dragged out of sight around the cookhouse and then its mournful defeated-defiant howl of frustration drowned the roar of the lesser dogs.

'A fine animal,' Decker said after the howl receded in the distance towards the kennels.

'Get on with it, will you!' Pascoe had saliva dripping down

48

his suede shooting jacket in wide blotches, spreading from a thin line at each corner of his mouth in a triangular pattern towards his jawbone, diverted only slightly by the creases in his flesh. For the first time Decker noted the downturned corners of the English inventor's mouth.

'Give those two men a bonus of a week's pay,' Decker said to Vincent, standing attentively near his chair, his face and eyes on the spectacle to come.

Decker gestured at the kennel keepers, who jumped aside, and blew a long blast on his silver ultra high frequency whistle.

The pack was on the baboon like a solid avalanche of warrior ants raping the territory of a vanquished rival hill. For a moment it seemed as if the baboon would succumb to the weight of snarling, biting enemies, proving Decker's promise of an even contest faithless. There was nothing of the baboon to be seen. But the numbers and lack of organisation of its enemies proved a handicap to them. Dogs were biting other dogs in their eagerness to get at the long awaited prey. Soon there were dogs fighting dogs next to the snarling bee-hive pack swarming on the baboon, the keepers beating them apart and redirecting them to the common objective.

Then a large dog was thrown through the air, its entrails streaming behind it, to land beside the fray, to whimper piteously for none to hear over the din, to try and crawl away to die alone, to be mercifully killed with one well placed blow of a *knopkierie*. Soon another dog, similarly ripped open and with one sturdy leg bitten off in the thickness of the thigh, crawled from under the heaving mass of ferocity to stare with suddenly soft brown eyes at the keeper standing above it. The black man hesitated for a moment, assessed the dog's chances of recovering to even halflife, brought his *knopkierie* down between the appealing eyes. His hesitation caused him to misjudge the blow; the dog was still whimpering and he had to strike it once more between the now reproachful soft brown eyes. This time his club crushed the skull to within a quarter of an inch of the earth.

Then the mêlée sorted itself out. The unscathed dogs and

49

those relatively unhurt, with only an ear missing or a bloody scratch down the side to enrage them still further with the smell of their own blood, retreated from the baboon to re-group, leaving seven dogs lying near the baboon. The baboon picked the nearest up, found it dead, cast it away from him to give him space to move. Next was a dachshund relative with some vital bones broken, unable even to crawl away. The baboon picked it up, looked for a moment at its wriggling form, bit it cleanly in two and cast the two halves in different directions. Two of the other dogs were alive and crawled frantically away from the baboon to be dispatched by their trainers and keepers. The baboon cast the others away too, first smashing the skull of one with a single mighty blow of its clenched paw. All this happened in silence, the spectators not being able to hear the whimpering of the wounded dogs over the roar of the snarling pack and being inured to the con-tinuous sound of the pack.

'You have to stop this!' Judith Pascoe's voice was high, unstable, a mezzo soprano crashing down from an over-ambitious note.

'Shaddup.' Her husband's voice was thick with passion. He might have been making love to her in the privacy of their *rondawel*.

'Soon,' Decker said falsely, 'soon.' She'd had his sincere smile. Women always wanted more than their man – or any man – was prepared to give them.

The zero expression on the two Japanese faces reduced to infinity. *Shiran-kao*, the visage of one who sees nothing. Especially not such blatant bad manners, such self indulgence as Judith Pascoe's, their stolid lack of *seeing* stated quite clearly. Decker, not insensitive to his own values in others, noted their proper stoicism and approved. The Japs were always good on safari.

The baboon surveyed its snarling enemies and, more intel-ligent than the canines, considered the possibility of defeat and looked for a line of retreat. First it tested its chain with teeth and brute-straining strength; the chain held creakingly. It tried crushing the pole against its chest but this too failed.

50

Then it tried climbing the pole but gained no more than twelve inches from the ground before slithering down again; the pole was greased.

'It is beyond its experience to lift the pole out of the pipe, the hole,' Decker murmured. 'But if the same baboon ever came here twice, they would learn . . .'

The dogs milled around for a second, then a small dog darted forward to bite the baboon on its redly exposed rear. The baboon turned around to snap at the dog but it was a planned feint and a couple of much larger dogs attacked it simultaneously from behind, aiming for the jugular with the precision of long scarred experience. Even so the baboon broke the back of one with a single blow of its paw and ripped open the stomach of the other with one long gash of its fearsome curved eyeteeth, the dog's fur rippling a wave bulging with baboon teeth in front of the spurting red line. But the other dogs had piled on again and two small dogs were hanging on the baboon's ears with grim determination, while another, resembling nothing so much as an overgrown white rat complete to albino eyes, lips and nose, but not big enough to be a bull terrier, swung gaily from its testicles. Several large dogs were trying to get a hold on its flanks and it was having difficulty dealing with these distractions while simultaneously fighting off the frontal and diagonal attacks on its throat. The present teamwork of the dogs belied their earlier futile and haphazard attack and credited their breeding with more grace than their appearance suggested. While the baboon had come out of the earlier skirmish almost unbloodied, the dogs inflicting more wounds on other dogs than on the baboon, and while it was killing or maiming and disabling dogs at a prodigious rate in the new attack, it was now streaming with blood. It was a losing battle for the baboon, hampered by the chain and unable to protect its back with anything but a slender pole. Yet it shook its head in the motion of ripping out the throat of something already bloody with Kerry Blue bluntness about the nose, sending one of the little dogs flying with a piece of ear still in its mouth, crushed the other with one blow between its paw and its own head,

51

and simply sat down on the ratlike worrier at its testicles, crushing it squealing to death. Still more dogs flew in to attach themselves to the baboon, to replace those killed. A reserve of three large dogs circled warily, watching, waiting, wishing for a split second exposure of the baboon's jugular, heavy enough to rush in past a blow of the forearm hampered by a middlesize dog attached to the tendon of the wrist and shielded under the body of the baboon from the fatal incisors. Then Decker blew his whistle.

The tableau froze. The sound suddenly died. For a second every animal was still. The keepers were black Rodins. The open mouthed guests at the festival wondered if their dream had turned into an ice floe, drifting away from their grasp. A tan-and-black dog broke the spell by turning its head to stare in anthropomorphic disbelief in the direction the sound had come from.

The baboon disembowelled it in mid-incredulity, crushing its last whimper of surprise at an unequal fate by rolling bodily over it to avoid the unwelcome attentions of still another small dog standing on a larger dead dog and sinking its teeth into the baboon's jugular. With the baboon showing willing, the six live dogs were all prepared to disregard the silent whistle's summons and attack again but Decker waved the keepers forward and they started pulling and prodding the dogs away, taking great care not to put themselves within striking range of the baboon. It was still extremely dangerous and snarled at them from the full extent of its chain. It bit right through the haft of a *knopkierie* stuck at it and hurled the heavy stick at the dogs, causing one to roll over and whinny in pain from the blow across the ribs. Finally all the dogs were restrained by leashes or long rods for the larger, fiercer dogs.

'Whaddaya callem offor?'

'Wait, Pascoe. The main event is still coming.' Decker was smiling but his eyes and his voice and his words carried the coolness of impatience with continued interference. He glanced in passing at Omo Minowara but the Japanese financier's face was blandly lined in smooth granite; if Minowara thought Decker was not dealing so honourably with the dogs now, he also thought it wiser – or, more likely, better manners – to keep his own counsel.

'Feed them well,' Decker called out after the kennel keepers as they led the remaining dogs away. Only two keepers were required to lead and restrain the survivors. The other keepers were throwing what remained of the dogs they had bred and fed and trained and sent into battle on to a cart the first two Bantu, the pole-carriers and bicyclists, had brought up with a minitractor. This was a well planned and fully rehearsed spectacle worthy of any stage in the world, Decker thought with pride. Well, so it should be. He had been doing it for five years and suitable baboons were difficult to find nowadays. But this one was a real humdinger . . . The cart with the dead dogs was taken away and the minitractor brought another cart with a tank on top. The tank had its own pump which the blacks started up. They sprayed the area down thoroughly, then turned the hose on the baboon. The water ran redly from him, revealing several gashes and small pieces missing from extremities but making it abundantly clear that most of the gore had been from the once-living bodies of the dogs.

'Not so even-steven after all,' Pascoe offered judiciously. 'He would have munched the rest of those mingy mongrels for breakfast, eaten them like a snack.'

'You're probably right,' Minowara said softly. 'It would have been of interest to see him against a fully grown Rhodesian ridgeback.'

Decker forestalled Pascoe's imminent suggestion by saying, 'The Rhodesian ridgeback you saw is not adult yet. And he doesn't feature in the main attraction, but the baboon does.' Decker had noted Minowara's use of the past tense about the baboon and once more the man had pleased him: Minowara alone seemed to understand and appreciate the total ruthlessness of his intention, the inexorable conclusion of the steps they had already taken, of the artifacts in view.

Decker picked up the Browning target pistol. He looked at the baboon, which was licking its wounds, its back to the pole, facing the men to be prepared for any threat to come from them.

'Vincent.' The Indian took a pocket mirror from inside his leather jacket, held it casually in his hand while Decker studied the baboon. The time for showmanship was over. 'Hold him just there, eh.'

'Yes, sir.' The Indian licked his lips hungrily. He caught the sun with the mirror, fixed the glaring reflection on the earth, swept it along the ground and up the baboon's body and into the baboon's eyes. The baboon stared at him fixedly, its body rigid, its seated posture almost human.

'This pistol has been specially rifled and I manufacture the bullets and load the cartridges myself to assure a very high velocity but almost no stopping power. The idea is to hit no vital organs and no bones, to have the bullet pass clean through. You need to know a bit of monkey anatomy.' Decker turned in his deep chair to give himself a line of sight down his arm and the length of the barrel sprouting thinly from his massive fist.

Judith pushed her chair back with a grating sound.

'Shaddap 'n' siddown,' Pascoe said softly. She sat down again.

Omo Minowara sighed almost imperceptibly. Decker was not distracted, though he noted the incident for future reference. He squeezed the trigger with loving gentleness. The small crack of the shot did not disturb either the watchers or the baboon. Vincent put his mirror away. The baboon went back to licking its wounds. A minute went by.

Pascoe, who had been leaning forward intently to watch the baboon, crashed back into the depths of his chair. 'You missed.'

'Don't you believe it. I never miss.' Decker laughed softly, confidently. 'It takes a while but it's worth waiting for.'

A minute went by, and another. The baboon licked all its wounds carefully. Having dealt with the longer scratches and the deeper gashes, it started attending to minor wounds. Finally it came to a small round hole in its stomach just under the breastbone.

Vincent expelled his breath endlessly, lasciviously. Decker drank from a glass long empty and put it down again without noticing that no liquid had passed his lips.

The baboon sat on its bare red bottom, its back against the pole, its hindlegs spread out in front of it. It found the hole with the fingers of a forepaw, manually considered the regular shape of the wound, then parted the fur and bent its head to look down at the wound's strangeness. It was not like any other wound the animal had ever seen. It probed the hole with a finger, stared disbelievingly at the fist left outside after the finger had disappeared into its body. It pulled the finger from the wound, held it up in the air in front of it, licked it to taste its own blood. It put another finger into the wound. That also disappeared, came out bloody, tasted the same. It bent its head over as far as it could, tried to see into the hole in its body, frustrated curiosity driving it to convulsive contortions, all to no avail. It could not reach to see into the hole. The animal considered, fingering the wound, then it put two fingers inside the hole in its body to feel the unknown it could not reach to see.

'Aah!' Pascoe expelled his held breath. The British inventor had finally grasped the subtlety of Decker's plan.

The baboon watched its hand as the two fingers groped around inside it, spreading the wound by the weight and motion of the fist outside. It found something with the two fingers, tugged impatiently at it. Through the hole came the two fingers holding a loop of reddish purple intestine. The baboon took both paws away to study the apparition from inside it carefully. Satisfied that the loop was not aggressive, it poked a finger at it, withdrawing the finger to avoid possible painful reaction. The loop remained passive. The baboon put a finger in the curve of the loop and pulled. And pulled. Intestine coiled on the ground in front of it between the hind legs. The intestine stopped sliding smoothly through the hole. The baboon gave one end a tentative pull, then a hard jerk. A bloodied end of the intestine came through the hole. The baboon grabbed at its side, in pain from the tearing loose of the intestine from its bodily anchor. For a moment it sat

55

whimpering, considering the new enemy attacking it from within. With a roar of rage it decided to attack the new enemy as it had vanquished earlier enemies, by main force. Each clawed front paw found purchase in the now much enlarged hole and pulled mightily to expose the enemy within. The baboon roared its pain as skin and flesh and tendon and peritonel lining ripped. But it would not be swayed from its purpose and, still roaring pain and rage and outrage and defiance, it held open the curtains which had once been its stomach to spill the remaining contents of the stomach sac pulsing on to the coiled intestine. The baboon considered the quivering shapelessness carefully. Where were the organs for grasping and pulling or holding and biting which had caused the excruciating pain? This did not look like its enemy. Nevertheless, it smashed the sac with a fore-paw, recoiling from the putrescence of the gas released by bursting the membrane. In the baboon's experience animals who needed offensive smells to keep their enemies away from them were not its mortal enemies, rather its prey in cases of extreme hunger. It looked into the stage of its stomach again for the real enemy, the one which had caused the tearing, burning pain which was still throbbing throughout its body though now slightly subdued.

Judith Pascoe made a gurgling sound deep in her throat, tried to swallow ineffectually and was halfway down the veranda to the steps, away from the baboon and its gore and digestive smell, before her chair crashed to the ground or Pascoe could open his mouth in gruff command. Her hand to her mouth, she ran to the *rondawel* allocated to the Pascoes. Enoch Pascoe exclaimed in annoyance. Before she was at the *rondawel* his eyes had returned to the baboon.

The pilot had not turned his head but his trained peripheral vision noted that Judith had not closed the *rondawel* door after crashing through it. 'Perhaps you'd better go see to her. She may fall and hurt herself.'

'Naw. Send a woman to do a woman's work.' Pascoe did not take his eyes from the baboon.

'We have only male servants,' Decker said patiently, his

eyes also on the baboon. The baboon was inspecting its stomach cavity with great care and circumspection.

Pascoe turned to look at Yodoko Minowara. 'What about her?' he asked Decker.

'She is a guest.' Decker turned reluctantly to look at the Japanese financier's wife. 'Though she may, of course, go if she wishes.'

Yodoko Minowara's face was expressionless. When the men had turned to her she had taken her eyes from the baboon to look at them with negatively polite attention. She said nothing.

'Mrs Pascoe may be embarrassed,' Omo Minowara said for his wife.

'She'll lose even more face if we have to send a black male servant,' Chris Decker said brusquely.

Omo Minowara turned to his wife and said in Japanese, 'It is requested by our host. If you wish.'

She stood and bowed to him. She felt no resentment because it was her duty to obey even her husband's unexpressed wishes but she did think the entertainment, though not as refined in its presentation as would have been managed in the Orient, was infinitely preferable to wiping the dribble from the chins of those who lacked self control. The two uncouth barbarians turned back to the baboon before she could bow to them too.

Decker was furious with the Pascoe woman. If Curtis Bill found out . . . Usually the baboon entertainment was a men-only special which he orchestrated while Curtis Bill gave the women a conducted tour of the premises and the pool near the river. But today he wanted to start punishing Cameron for inconveniencing him, Chris Decker, by concluding the first entertainment before his arrival. And, since there was nobody to escort the women elsewhere, they had perforce to be let into the fun. He should have known one at least would be unappreciatively squeamish. Curtis Bill would . . . Stuff Curtis Bill, this was the last safari.

The baboon, his survey of his stomach cavity completed, had found the offender. The beating heart was obviously

57

alive and had the tentacles with which it had hurt him tentatively curled around it, ready to protect it or to strike out to hurt him again. Besides, this bloated, beating small insolence which had dared attack him from within, hid behind a small forest of regular shaped bones where it thought the baboon could not see it. But its rear was exposed below the bones and the bones themselves did not look too strong. The baboon tried one with both paws and it broke with a snap but the flesh imbedding it negated his advantage. Besides, the bloated insolence sank sharp fangs of pain into him somewhere in his chest for trying to expose it. Once more he roared his pain and defiance. He bent over to look at the rear end of the animal below his rib cage, seeking out its eyes. He could see no eyes but brought his paw near it to make sure, held it there for a minute while watching alertly for signs of retaliation. There was no retaliation, therefore the eyes must be watching for his advent in the other direction. Stupid animal. The baboon brought both paws near to the malicious animal, spread his gross fingers into powerful claws, struck. The baboon screamed his pain as the animal, nearly vanquished, dug its tentacles into his body, hugging close like lice, in an effort not to be cast aside and killed. But the baboon's claws were relentless, cutting, breaking, tearing through each of the tentacles in turn until the animal was free in his claws and, too exhausted to deal with it right away, the baboon cast the still pulsing, still live heart from him.

Vincent, breathing heavily through his mouth, held the silver salver out to Minowara. On it was the red cushion and on the cushion the Browning. Minowara took the pistol, checked that the safety was on, held it loosely, waiting for Decker to speak.

'Any time you are ready, Mr Minowara.'

Minowara clicked the safety off, hefted the pistol to gauge its weight, to imprint its balance on his mind. 'The right testicle, Mr Decker?'

Pascoe said, 'That's one part of a monkey you don't need anatomy lessons to find.' Nobody took any notice of him and he laughed only briefly at his own joke.

'A sound choice, Mr Minowara.' Decker decided he had made the right choice in letting Minowara have the first shot. Pascoe might have chosen the brain, not considering those to come after him . . . Selfish men do not make good hunting partners.

Minowara stood, bowed to each of the men, took the classic stance, feet slightly apart, one foot slightly behind the other, body straight, neck straight, arm straight out, trunk turned into the line of fire. He sighted briefly and fired once. Without looking to see if he had hit his target he turned back to the waiting Vincent and put the pistol back on the velvet cushion, first clicking the safety catch back on. The baboon screamed in pain and a thin red stream from the shattered testicle strove its way into the blood-caked mud surrounding it. Vincent offered the pistol to Pascoe, who did not rise but rested the barrel on one of the lower rungs of the veranda rail. He sighted carefully and fired, shattering the other testicle.

He looked intently at the convulsing body, listening to the now continuous scream while he drooled at the corner of his mouth.

'The pistol, Mr Pascoe,' Vincent reminded him. Pascoe dropped the pistol on the cushion without taking his eyes from the bloodied, heartless but still alive baboon.

'Can't let an animal bleed to death,' Decker said. He took the pistol from Vincent and, without bothering to rise or to sight, put a shot through each of the baboon's maddened eyes. Its last death roar opened the mouth for the final shot he put through the palate into the animal's brain.

Three

The five *rondawels*, one each for Bonham and Decker and three for the hunters, stood in a large circle with the verandaed lounge and the dining-room closing the ring. It was fortunate the Pascoes had been given the nearest *rondawel* or Judith would have disgraced herself further. Each *rondawel* was a large circular hut of thirty feet diameter with thick clay walls neatly whitewashed and small windows and a high reed roof to keep the heat out; at the back, built into the wall, was a very effective air conditioner. Each *rondawel* had a bathroom and a bedroom complete with built-in furniture comprising two single beds which could be converted to a double bed, his and hers wardrobes of immense proportions, a vanity table, a writing table, a barred and lockable gun case with locking cartridge drawers underneath. The floor was lushly carpeted, the walls graced with English hunting prints. In the spacious and airy bedroom there were three leather covered armchairs and a low table with neatly stacked fresh magazines. The headboards of the beds were bookcases and colourful titles filled these. The bathroom was equally well appointed, if a little sterile and lacking in warmth for having been fitted exclusively in white porcelain to some austere male specification.

Judith did not care whether the bowl was white porcelain or black plastic, it was a receptacle for the visible results of her nausea.

The Japanese woman came and stood patiently soaking a small towel under the middle tap of the washbasin; the three taps each had an engraved tile labelling them respectively 'Cold water', 'Iced drinking' and 'Hot water'. When Judith had finished even her dry retching, Yodoko held the refresh-

ingly cold towel out to her. Judith wiped her face and neck
with it. 'It is kind of you to come.'

The Japanese woman nodded expressionlessly. Judith
thought *She is only a girl, perhaps twenty. I am nearly double
her age, why cannot I be as composed as she is?*

'My husband is not always like that. It is the hunting, it
happens once a year.' Judith had wanted to say *Just because
my husband's a buffoon, don't underrate him, he knows what
he's doing.* As always the words came out wrong. Her children, Eric and Joan, were the only people the words came out
right with. And with Enoch in the beginning . . .

Yodoko listened and nodded to show attention but not
agreement or disagreement, thinking *She lacks a sense of
duty to her husband and disgraces him by it.*

Four

Curtis Bill Bonham belonged to the class of pilots who believed in firm landings, holding that a feathery landing was
the signature of an overconfident pilot who could any day be
punished by nature for his bravado performance by being
sent whirling in a cartwheel of flame by the slightest whiff of
air. He was therefore not overly receptive to Dr Robert J.
Cameron's comment on his landing at the base camp airstrip.

'Put her down any harder and you'll make a hole in the
ground.'

Curtis Bill grunted noncommittally. Explaining the reasons
for firm landings would serve no useful purpose. And this
American doctor knew better than anybody else on almost
any subject under the sun. The ugly American, Curtis Bill
had once told Decker after a safari, should always be in

motion, never stationary. And preferably in motion away from reasonable men. Far, far away. But Cameron was so typical, he looked the part and acted it. Curtis Bill, who consciously avoided stereotypical thinking, could have described him exactly before he ever met him, given only the clue that he would be the average American client. He was six foot four, two hundred and fifty pounds and balding. Curtis Bill knew he would be told sooner rather than later that balding men are more virile than others. Curtis Bill did not rate predictability highly as a desirable character trait in humans, he had seen too many men killed by their habits. Cameron also had a loud voice and an insistent manner. Curtis Bill had heard all his opinions before. Sample: 'Jack Kennedy was a nigger lover. Robert Kennedy was the only Attorney General America ever had who refused to protect the rights of American citizens. Ted Kennedy is a fornicator and a womaniser before God and before man. All these sons of a bootlegger, all against the right of the people to defend themselves as if it was a mortal sin to own and use a gun like our father's before us.' His public reasons for choosing to holiday in Africa: 'Where else can I go? To Miami with the flabby Jews and the Cuban runaways? To the Catskills with the longhair pinkos? On a sightseeing tour to Washington with the soft underbelly of America oohing and aahing their halitosis all over me and the White House?' Curtis Bill did not relish being best by elimination.

Cameron's wife was a big blonde girl of about twenty-eight, ten years younger than her husband. In her eyes there was a wistful look. Her composed and not uncompanionable silence compensated for her husband's volubility.

Cameron wondered if the safari organiser could be Jewish but was not going to ask. If the man was not Jewish sooner or later there would be an opportunity for him to deny belonging to the socalled chosen race. Still, his tanned skin and slightly curly hair reminded Cameron of a boy at Groton called Mont d'Or who used to make himself more ridiculous by taking out his penis and flashing his circumcision at Cameron while doing a war dance around him, chanting:

62

My grandfather changed the name
three generations ago.
What's it to you, goy?
Take out your cock, schmuck
and we'll see what's what.

Goldberg. Curtis Bill Bonham was a strange name but then
no Jew would organise safaris like these, they were all a
bunch of nigger lovers and nigger-arse kissers.

Curtis Bill conducted Robert and Melody Cameron to the
veranda to introduce them to Chris Decker, Omo Minowara
and Enoch Pascoe who sat in the shade with drinks near to
hand and attentive stewards standing by to fetch more. In
front of the veranda a number of blacks were sweeping the
earth, picking up minute pieces of fur and bone and flesh,
tamping the earth down solid with their feet.

After the introductions were made Curtis Bill, a little
baffled by the instant antagonism between the American and
Decker, escorted the newcomers to their *rondawel*. The
Bantu brought the Camerons' light luggage which had come
in the plane and added it to the stacked heavy luggage
already waiting in the middle of the floor on the deep carpet.
Curtis Bill showed them where everything was and gave
Cameron the keys to the gun cabinet and cartridge drawers.

'Where are the other keys? To the wardrobes.'

'Our servants don't steal. We only lock gun cabinets and
cartridge drawers because it is a legal requirement.'

'Honest niggers, eh? Or have you made an example of a
couple?'

'Uh-huh,' Curtis Bill said noncommittally. 'Come up to
the lounge for a drink on the veranda as soon as you have
unpacked and freshened up.'

Cameron held the slim man's shoulder. 'What were those
nignogs cleaning up in front of the veran – what you call the
porch?'

'Veranda.'

'It looked like a pig butchery.'

Curtis Bill looked around for Melody but she had silently

disappeared into the bathroom and closed the door. Cameron leant closer to him in male conspiracy. 'Like that, eh, Curtis Bill?' His voice was still startlingly loud.

'Chris Decker, my partner, arranged a fight between some dogs and a baboon. This usually happens later in the afternoon but today he seems to have started early.'

'You mean I missed part of the safari?' Cameron's loud voice was taking on pitch.

'We don't run a scheduled service of events, you know. If Chris does something for his own amusement and wants to invite people, that's his affair. There'll be lots for you to do.'

'Yeah, sure, but I missed a turn he put on for that Jap fanatic and the mad Limey inventor, right? So, is there another turn like that tomorrow or the day after, or at least before I leave?'

'No. Only once a month on the first Sunday of the safari.'

'Look, I'm paying a lot of money. This time, let's just forget it because I'm a new boy here and don't want to start throwing my weight around, but maybe you could just hint to your partner that Robert J. Cameron is to be in on everything, you hear, everything!'

Curtis Bill gently disengaged the hand holding him by the shoulder and stepped back from the face suffused with anger. 'I'll tell him. See you on the veranda in fifteen minutes.'

When Melody came out of the bathroom her husband was looking at the sweep second hand of his solid gold Rolex, holding up his free hand in a restraining gesture. His lips were moving, he was counting.

'That air conditioner,' he told her, pointing at it, 'they got it set to seventy cycles per minute. Listen to it.' He waited for her to listen. 'The same rhythm as the heartbeat which is the first sound the foetus in the womb hears. Very soothing. They probably do it to calm nervous hunters, like that old Jap and the Limey nutter. Very clever, very clever.'

Melody forebore pointing out to him that the air conditioner sported a large dial inviting them to select a different temperature from the one they were enjoying, so causing the machine to run slower or faster to meet their demands; the specific number of cycles per minute or whatever the machine was running now was probably serendipity. But her husband could not be disillusioned of his belief that every cabbie on Fifth Avenue was blowing his horn at Robert J. Cameron, M.D., and it was no use wasting her breath here; she was only too grateful to be away from New York and somewhere exciting for once.

Five

'The sun has not risen only on the new Japan,' Pascoe told Minowara, leaning forward to make his point. 'My 24UW VII-A is exported from Britain to Japan in great numbers.'

'I'm sorry, Mr Pascoe. I am not an engineer. My speciality is financing.'

'Are you calling me a liar?' Pascoe brought his face still closer to the older man.

'No, Mr Pascoe.' Minowara was impassively unruffled. 'I am simply saying that I understand finance better than physics.'

'Well, I made my first million twenty years ago when I was only twenty-four and since –'

Decker raised his voice over Pascoe's as Judith and Yodoko came down the veranda towards them. 'You look much better. Slim, trim and ready to go.'

In the silence Curtis Bill Bonham rose to draw forward chairs for the two women.

'You just keep your hands off my Judith,' Pascoe broke the silence. Decker looked at her thin form and shuddered visibly. Minowara took a handkerchief from his pocket and mopped Pascoe's spittle from his face, pretending he was wiping sweat. The Camerons came up to the veranda and Curtis Bill Bonham introduced the women to each other and Cameron to the other men's wives. He ordered the Camerons a drink each: bourbon and branch water for him, orange juice for her. The silence descended again.

'Is there much to hunt around here?' Judith had turned to Curtis Bill in an effort to break the oppressive silence. She fanned herself in the heat, while she waited for him to answer.

'Ah, yes, quite a number of different animals,' he finally said. Pascoe and Cameron were watching him closely, the two Japanese were paying their usual polite attention, Decker had acquired a sardonic smile from nowhere; only Melody looked out over the landscape and asked:

'What kinds?'

'Kudu, *eland, blou wildebeest, gemsbok*, hippo, crocodiles, you name it, it's there.' This time Curtis Bill spoke immediately and accompanied the statement with a small directional wave of his hand.

'There?' She looked in the direction he was pointing. Then she looked in the other direction. 'Behind us is the area we flew over. There was no game. The game is all in the Kruger National Park over there. That leaves only forward, across the Limpopo, into Rhodesia.'

'You can obviously read a map,' Decker said.

'You're going to hunt over there?'

'Sure. And down the river in Moçambique.'

'But that's illegal!'

Curtis Bill Bonham sent his partner a sharp glance.

Decker said, 'Sheeet!'

'You're not going to hunt illegally, are you, Enoch?' Judith whined at her husband. 'Are you, Enoch?'

Cameron answered for Pascoe while he was still thinking. 'What do you want us to do, lady, shoot the protected animals in the game reserve over there? That would really be against the law.' To his own wife he added, 'That's enough now, honey.'

'But you –' Judith insisted.

66

Pascoe cut his wife off in midwhinge. 'Have you heard the one about what's black and lives in a tree and is learning to fly a jet fighter?'

'Yes, I have.' Decker stood up. 'If you're going to say it's a Nigerian Air Force pilot, don't. I've fought against them and they fly a lot better than any armchair warrior. What's more, they fight a lot better than any armchair warrior.'

Pascoe stared up at Decker's venom, his mouth open, his back teeth visible.

Decker turned away from him. 'I'll take the ladies' tour today. The ladies, and anybody else who wants to come see what the base camp and its surroundings look like are welcome.'

'I'll come,' Melody said brightly. 'Sightseeing, I love it.'

'Judith stays,' Pascoe snapped.

Decker ignored him. 'Anybody else?' The heads shaken lethargically in the heat did not discourage him. 'Just you and I, eh,' he said to Melody and looked defiantly at the big American.

Cameron watched them go. This arrogant Canadian pilot was in for a surprise. Melody might look like a dumb blonde but, like a good dog, she knew only one master. Let Decker do what he, Cameron, was paying him to do: act as a superior and overpaid guide. Let him make his advances. Let him learn his lesson. Her certain rejection of his inevitable lewd suggestion would put him in his place, serve him well for the rude manner in which he had treated the very people who were paying for his bread and butter. Cameron knew that he was far too important to his wife for her to endanger in any way, no matter how small, his affection. It amused him to see other men enviously cracking their heads against the wall of her indifference.

First Decker took Melody to their small airfield. 'The plane,' he said, slapping an engine cowling. 'Cessna 414. Two 310 horse power HP Continental TS10-520-J engines, each with six cylinders. 9400 pounds max take-off. Flat out 290 miles per hour, cruise 278. Range 1294 miles, wingtip tanks available to extend the range. It seats seven passengers and the ceiling is 25,600 feet.'

He took her by the arm and led her to a shapeless mass of tarpaulin standing on a cleared circle of ground. He gestured at the two Bantu in grease-stained overalls standing nearby and they stripped the tarpaulin away.

'The chopper. Aérospatiale SA-316B Alouette III. 870 horse power Turbomeca Artouste IIIB turbine engine to drive the thirty-six point two-foot rotor. Max take-off 4850 pounds. Max speed 132 empeeaitch, cruise 112 for a range of 335 miles. Ceiling 10,660 feet. Six passengers and one crew.'

'Does Curtis Bill fly both the plane and the helicopter?' she asked as he led her towards the kennels, describing as they walked the acreage of their property, the number of servants, the amount of maize and meat necessary to feed the servants, their own electricity generating plant and its capacity, their own water pumping system and its cubic capacity in gallons per hour and other such interesting snippets of mathematical information.

'No. I'm the pilot of the outfit. Curtis Bill stands in for me when I have other things to do. He can't even fly the chopper.'

'Oh. Have you two known each other long?'

'Yeah. Sure. We have about fifty dogs at any one time, all trained to hunt baboon.' They had come to the kennels. 'That large yellow dog is a Rhodesian ridgeback, bred by crossing a great dane with a ridgeback and trained to be ferocious. Christ no!' He grabbed her arm and pulled her back bodily from the kennel. 'You don't pat that dog or any of the dogs in here. They're not pets. That particular one will take your hand off at the wrist as soon as look at you.'

She looked at the snarling dog and shivered. It had looked so innocently attractive when she had put her hand through the fence to pet it, had so suddenly erupted in snarling, jaw-snapping violence. It *would* have bitten her hand off if Decker hadn't acted quickly to pull her away. She looked at the rows of raging jaws spewing bloodlust at her from each dog in the compound and shivered. She held on to Decker's arm until they were well clear of the kennels and the snarls had faded. 'Do you see much of him?'

'I'm up here one week in the month and always spend a little time with my dogs, all of them, not just that one.'

Melody had meant Curtis Bill Bonham, but let the misunderstanding pass. 'Is your partner, Curtis Bill, married?'

'Yes.' Decker was not enthusiastic about this line of questioning. It had been pleasant while she had hung on to his arm after he had saved her from mutilation by the dog but now she had let go. He said shortly, finally, 'He's got a wife and a boy back in Johannesburg but I've never met them. We, Curtis Bill and I, we don't see much of each other when we're not working.'

She asked no further questions about Curtis Bill and Decker was silent too. She wondered if he was sulking.

She squealed with the rapture of the vista which had suddenly opened up to her. Through the short valley of trees still separating them from the river the pool was green and inviting, the tumbling waterfall at one end coolly beckoning, its sussurating song of welcome through the shimmering oppression of heat distinguishing that midsummer African day. They stood silently looking down at the pool, then by unspoken common consent walked around the edge on the paved slate path of indigenous bluestone towards the mystery of the waterfall.

'Can we swim in it?' She was excited, childlike.

'Yes. We built it to swim in, though not many of our guests ever use it.'

'It's artificial?' Little-girl disappointment.

'Christ, yes. Curtis Bill and I built it with a lot of black electricity. It's part of our water supply system. The water is pumped over there, at the rear wall, behind the waterfall, runs over the cobbles here and is syphoned off by gravity through the pipes at the lower end, some for the camp and the surplus back into the river. So you can swim in running fresh water all the time.'

'When you've come this far you may as well swim in the river,' she said without much interest.

69

Decker laughed harshly, abruptly. 'Come. I'll show you the river.' He led her past the waterfall and around the various machines which made the idyll and spoilt it again, for her if not for Decker.

The Limpopo was darkly overhung with trees and growths and even in the middle of the vast expanse of water the sun glinted dully off the top of the turgid blackness, penetrating not one whit into the moribund Abraham's bosom, refracted as from metal to light not within, rejected to glance off in pallid dejection. The most frightening aspect of this flowing death was that it lapped nowhere at a shore or a root or a beer can or an empty milk carton; it was totally silent, like some menacing supernatural force in a B shocker on late night television and therefore quite as unbelievable. Melody laughed shrilly, a predictable response to apparitions beyond the human scale. She had never seen a river like this, an awesome majesty much like that with which architects try to inspire skyscrapers only to fail in the face of the indifference of their inhabitants, such majesty of size and threatened oblivion as needs make no other display.

'Perhaps I wouldn't want to swim in it,' she said inadequately.

Decker smiled cruelly at her admission. 'You have only seen the river. Now let Uncle Chris show you the trimmings.'

She looked at him curiously. What could possibly add to the ominous warning of the blackly moving mortuary before her?

'What do you see over there, where the little birds twitter?'

'Little birds.'

'What else?'

'A brownblack mudgrey beach. Uh, perhaps a log or two buried in the mud.' She took off her sun glasses to see better but put them back on immediately; even under the trees the glare was fierce. 'That's all.'

'It's not all, Melody. It's like that nice puppy in the kennel you wanted to pet. It only looks innocent but it could be fatal to the unwary stranger stumbling on to that muddy river bank. Watch.' He picked up a short log, threw it from hand

70

to hand to measure its weight and cast it overarm on to the beach. The little birds twittered away speedily.

'Eeh, they're nasty!' Melody said in a whisper and started walking backwards. The crocodiles had been baking themselves in the sun only twenty feet from where they stood.

Decker took her firmly by the arm and held her, offered her a one word all inclusive and totally exclusive commentary:

'Africa.'

The single word explained the uniqueness of all she had seen and experienced and all yet to come. She was the Martian in Manhattan here, the total alien. And because of her alienness she could never belong, would forever be the orphan experiencing the joys to be had from understanding only vicariously and unassimilatively. She jerked her arm free.

'Wait.' His voice was sharp. 'There is more.'

She turned back, intrigued, her quick anger at rejection subdued by her curiosity. 'What more could there possibly be?'

'There, in the river, right in front of you.'

The river ran concentric circles of foothigh waves around the enormous dark nostrils. The open jaws seemed to be rising out of the water forever, the measure of their size, the stumpy decayed teeth mammoth relics from a forgotten age but small in the pink jaws fraying around the edges into wrinkled grey hide an inch thick. The ridge of the head broke through a foamy wave two feet high and the piggy eyes sunk in folds of flesh and hide to cover a large he-man's outsize sofa seemed to stare malevolently straight at her. She shivered and would have walked backwards, run backwards, if Chris Decker had not held her arm firmly. The head waved from side to side but the eyes held her as an even higher wave, tons of water, was displaced by the misshapen body waddling out of the water to where the skin of the swinging belly brushed obscenely around the folds of the knees. A convulsive shiver of almost sexual revulsion shook her.

'It's very shortsighted,' Decker said conversationally. 'It's come to see what has disturbed it. Don't move or it will be able to distinguish us from a static background.'

Instinctively, compelled by fear, she disregarded his warning to put the forefinger of her free hand across her lips. 'Shhh!'

Chris Decker laughed. 'No. Its hearing is not directional. Just stand still. It may not look it, and they rarely venture on land, but it can charge a lot faster than you can run. And those jaws can bite a man in two without any extra effort other than closing them naturally.'

'Is it a hippopotamus?'

'Yes. A big bull. A male. There's a cow and a calf in there somewhere. It makes a bad tempered animal even more angry at any disturbances. If we wait we may be lucky and see the calf. Women think hippo calves funny.'

'Thank you, Mr Decker. Perhaps another day. Right now I just want to get away from that . . . that monstrosity staring at me.'

'I told you, it can't see you. Just stand still and it will go away soon enough,' he added soothingly. 'That bull must weigh at least as much as the biggest elephant I ever saw.'

He told her how much the elephant had weighed but she only heard ' – tons, not counting the tusks. They – ' while she stared fixedly at the hippopotamus which was still swaying its head from side to side, the little ear stubs obscene bumps on its malformed nightmare head, as it backed away into the dark death of the Limpopo. The crocodiles were returning to their muddy bank, their sawtooth jaws open in anticipation for the birds already descending on to the teeth to pick scraps of meat from them like so many living toothpicks.

'See the crocodile with his snout closed?' Decker asked, his hand still painfully clutching her arm. 'Watch the side of his mouth.'

She found the crocodile he was pointing at. From its jaws hung the tails and heads of what could only be young crocodiles. She swallowed hard and turned firmly and this time he let her go, catching up with her in two long strides. The wriggling tails and heads were in her mind and would return at random unwelcome times to haunt her, she knew.

'They eat their own young,' Chris Decker informed her needlessly. 'Crocodiles lay eggs in the sand or mud beside the rivers and they are hatched by the sun, hundreds of thousands of them. Crocodiles also grow very old, so all these little wrigglies cannot grow to maturity or they'd have a worse population problem than the Chinese. Their simple solution is to eat them. Since crocodiles do not have jaw structures for chewing, they cannot immediately eat the buck or zebra or man or any of the larger animals they may catch. They drag them under water to drown them and then under the muddy overhangs of the river to rot in the water and later the crocodiles swallow half-rotten sections whole to lie for two weeks or so in the sun after each meal, digesting it and having their teeth cleaned by the birdies. But if they want a snack in between, why, they've bred it and it's swimming right there in front of their nose, small enough to swallow whole and munch, munch they apply their own population control. The Chinks could well learn a lesson from the crocodiles.'

She closed her ears to him, staring at the waterfall and the pool. How inviting even this manmade artifact of nature's beauty looked after the horrors of the river.

'I'll stick to swimming in the pool, Mr Decker,' she said submissively. She knew she would never go past the pool to the river again. She did not see in the river the imprint of eternal beauty which so obviously exhilarated the pilot with its bleak and destructive self discipline.

'Just one thing about the pool. It is a rule of the house that a lady guest is never to come down here unaccompanied.' He smiled engagingly at her quick look. 'The hippos and the crocs won't come up here – the water's too clear for them. It's the *muntu*, the black men. They do not share our civilisation's finer sensibilities and may think a lone white woman fair game. I'm sure Curtis Bill, who usually takes the women's tour, would have put it more delicately but I want to make it quite clear.'

'I understand, Mr Decker. My husband often talks at

length about the depredations Negroes will practise on white women if and when the opportunity arises.'

The sarcasm seemed not to reach him. 'Call me Chris, will you.'

They walked back side by side. Decker told her about a favourite hunting rifle of his, the one he had shot the elephant with. ' . . . 460 Weatherby Magnum with the Mark V bolt action, weight fourteen point one pounds. Overall length 47 inches, barrel 26 inches, drop of stock two and seven-eighths inches. Bullet weight 500 grains, muzzle velocity 2,640 feet per second, muzzle energy –'

' – seven thousand seven hundred and fifty foot pounds. The 460 Weatherby Magnum Mark V is the world's most powerful rifle.'

'You know it!' Insensitive to the divergent moods of others, Chris Decker was perversely delighted. He lowered his voice to a whisper, stopped to face her. 'Would you like to come to my *rondawel* and see mine?'

Woo your women by numbers. Woo? 'I have heard about and seen my husband's 460 Weatherby Magnum often enough to be more than familiar with it.'

'Your husband's?' He was taken off his stroke.

'Bob's. Dr Cameron's. He's had it for years. It is his favourite rifle, too.' She felt sorry for him, the boyish naïveté momentarily overcoming the soullessness of his mind bared to her at the river. She put out her hand to touch him but he had already turned to walk on.

They walked the rest of the way in silence and he delivered her to the veranda where Dr Robert J. Cameron watched their silent return with interest and a smirk. Decker left her there and walked to the airfield, his anger contained in the set of his shoulders and his stride stiffened at the knee to jerk him along viciously.

Six

'I'm sure you ladies want to finish your unpacking and take a rest before dinner.' Curtis Bill stood. To the men he said, 'Chris has gone to start up the plane for our familiarisation flight.'

'Can't we come too?' Melody Cameron asked. 'We promise to sit in the back and be as quiet as mice.'

'No. I'm sorry but there's no space on board the plane for you. And it is the first rule of this safari that women are not allowed on hunts.' Curtis Bill had found quite quickly that it was best to be early, specific and blunt about this rule.

'Aw, come on, just this once.'

'That's enough now, honey,' Dr Robert J. Cameron said gruffly, still watching Curtis Bill's reactions with interest.

'If you get bored at the base camp here, the plane can run you up to Johannesburg for a couple of days' shopping or down Mbabane in Swaziland for some gambling,' Curtis Bill said consolingly but with finality. He led the men from the veranda and across the compound to the airfield. Pascoe and Cameron split off for their *rondawels*. 'Hey, where are you going?'

'To fetch my rifle,' Pascoe said, surprised at the question.

'To fetch some maps so I can know where we are,' Cameron said.

'You won't need either. We're not going shooting, just reconnoitring. And there are maps in the plane.'

They turned back reluctantly and the procession proceeded, the slim and erect shapes of Curtis Bill Bonham and Omo Minowara paradoxically leading the slumped gross forms of the English inventor and the American medico.

'I don't like going out there,' Pascoe waved his arm at the

unknown across the far horizon, 'without any protection.'

Cameron pulled aside his safari jacket to show the butt of a firearm resting in a holster on his hip. 'Relax. I'd never go without at least a handgun out here, no matter what Curtis Bill says.' He unstrapped his belt and put it on again around the outside of his clothing. 'Didn't want to wear it openly up there with the women before the hunting proper had started, so to speak. You know what I mean?'

'Yes. Guns upset women.'

'Right! But now the hunting has started, I reckon it's different. You got a few handguns?' He was inviting friendly conversation.

'No,' Pascoe said reluctantly. He hastened to explain that he had nothing against handguns. 'English law is different, you see. You can have all the sporting guns, rifles and shotguns, you want as long as you have the necessary licences. But a licence for a pistol or a revolver is very difficult to get.'

'Yeah. That's tough.'

'What's that fucking cannon for?' Decker demanded as they came to the plane.

'To defend myself with,' Cameron said stiffly. 'I always carry it.'

Decker started around the plane to do his checks. Curtis Bill started getting the others into the plane. 'Don't step on the wing,' he told Pascoe. 'It's only thin metal. That black step has been reinforced for your weight.'

'Shit, how're we going to shoot anything with a low-wing plane? You need a high wing for shooting out of.'

'We use the helicopter for hunting,' Curtis Bill told him. This bloody Pascoe was a real dodo. 'Mr Minowara, if you'd like to take the copilot's seat. Your friend who recommended you to us said you are a flier.'

'Thank you, Mr Bonham.' The Japanese financier seemed to feel further acknowledgement was called for and turned around in his seat as Curtis Bill settled into the seat behind him. 'I learnt during the war. I was going to be a *kamikaze* pilot but the war ended before I could use my skills.'

'We beat the shit out of you,' Cameron interposed.

76

Minowara ignored him. 'I liked the feeling and after the war I started flying private planes for fun and later for business.'

'If you beat the shit out of the Japs, how come you can't even buy an American transistor anywhere today?' Pascoe asked predictably.

Decker started the engines and no answer was necessary. Cameron said to Curtis Bill, 'Where's the map you promised me?'

'I know where I'm going,' Decker said. Pascoe laughed as if it were a joke.

Curtis Bill leant forward to find a clipboard with several maps on it. The maps were kept specifically for hunters who insisted on knowing exactly where they were at all times.

'The top map shows where we are in the general geography of Southern Africa. The next map shows the point where South Africa, Rhodesia and Moçambique meet. Our base camp is the red star near the junction. Draw a circle with a radius of about a hundred and fifty miles around the star and you'll find it divides into three roughly triangular sections, one each in South Africa, Rhodesia and Moçambique. We never hunt in South Africa. The next two maps are detail maps of the Rhodesian and Moçambique hunting grounds, showing all the usual topographical information plus the towns or settlements.' He had made the set speech so often that he now rattled it off without inflection or pause. He was grateful this would be the last time he would have to repeat it. Each group of cantankerous hunters was getting more tiresome. Once on his *estancia* in the Argentine with his wife and son he would never again have to endure the bad manners money generated in illbred men . . . He pointed out various landmarks, good hunting places, areas to avoid because of possible surveillance or even chance sighting of their activities. Decker flew north by west, then turned directly east to put the sun behind them. The men were silent, each one, including the safari organisers, who had seen it so often, awed before the vast magnitude of even this rigidly defined, narrowed down, fractional section of Africa.

77

'Jesus! It just goes on!' Cameron exclaimed. 'Like the wheat-fields of Nebraska. On and on.' The English inventor and the Japanese financier, both from spaceless cramped countries, nodded their agreement, their earlier taunts and budding antagonisms forgotten in the excitement of surveying the hunting grounds over which soon each would face the ultimate test.

'We're crossing into Moçambique airspace now. What we were flying over was Rhodesia.' Decker's fury at the big blonde with the wet dream body and the angel face who had led him on was abating now he was behind the controls of an aircraft, as he had known it would.

'How'd you know?' Cameron asked, his voice pleasant in recognition of his realisation that his life was for the moment in the pilot's hands.

'There's a town over there. Malvernia. It's almost on the border.'

'Not much of a town.'

'Yeah. The rest too. Really hamlets more than villages even.' Chris Decker turned the plane south, asked Minowara, 'Want to take her now?' Minowara took the controls and they flew on, straight south, in silence but with the stiffness gone in their common aim and their shared vulnerability to detection and punishment.

'I haven't seen any niggers yet,' Pascoe said after a while.

'They're down there all right,' Curtis Bill said. 'We're five hundred feet up – it gets easier to spot them from the chopper at fifty feet.'

'Don't they just go hide in the trees?' Cameron pointed down towards the valley of deep green. They were once more crossing the Limpopo.

'Some do. Then we take the chopper down. Very few get away. For some reason they come out on the other side and head for the mountains.' Curtis Bill pointed south, straight ahead of them. 'The Lebombos. We don't chase them that far or we wouldn't have fuel to get home. Of course, once we see where they're heading, we can finish them off quick and –'

'But that would take the sport out of it,' Cameron said decisively. 'Better to find another one, eh?'

Chris Decker turned from his perusal of the dials in front of him. 'Curtis Bill, tell them about what the ethnologist fellow said.'

'Yes, well. This man, a lecturer at one of the universities, was at Grand Central hitching a lift to come join his family who were already in the Kruger Park on holiday. He told us all kinds of things about the various Bantu tribes around here. One of the things he told us is that certain groups of the Karanga, who stick closely to an ancestral way of life, consider it a disgrace to die in bed. In this attitude, he said, they're probably influenced by their contact with the Tsonga, who are related to South Africa's fierce Zulus, on their southern borders. It's part of their belief that their ancestors, who reside in their version of heaven, will be more pleased with them if they died in combat with some superior enemy.'

'For once I agree with a nigger,' Cameron said and waited for the chuckles to subside. 'Better to go out fighting like a man than snivelling in your bed like an old woman.'

'Our big bird with the men in the belly – that's what they call the chopper with the hunters inside – is the most superior enemy any of them can imagine. So their young men come out to prove their manhood by fighting the big bird.'

'Goddamn stupid niggers.' Pascoe.

'Well, the ones we occasionally let get away, they must be big heroes back in the *kraal*, the circle of huts they live in, because they keep coming, inviting us to attack them.'

'You mean they come looking for you?!' Cameron was incredulous.

'Yes, that's why we have this familiarisation flight, in part so that they can see this is the week of the big bird, which is what they call the full moon now. As you can guess, we only hunt in the week before the full moon. At first it was by accident but later on we planned it that way. It makes it easier for us to know we'll find some healthy specimens who'll make good hunting.'

'And we're performing a public service for them,' Chris

Decker added and turned back to the controls under the laughter.

'Good show, Chris,' Cameron called.

'No, really,' Curtis Bill said. 'Chris is not joking. If one of their men die in battle against another man or our big bird or a lion or whatever, the wife and children burn little fires of gratitude for the man or big bird or lion or whatever, lay out offerings of food in pots overnight, that kind of thing. The man or big bird or lion or whatever becomes a sort of a household deity, according to this ethnologist we gave a lift.'

'I rather fancy being a household god,' Cameron said, pleased with the concept. 'What about you, Mr Minowara?'

'The Minowaras have been deities for many centuries, Doctor Cameron. But a few additional worshippers are always welcome.'

Enoch Pascoe spoilt the easy atmosphere in the plane by demanding, 'I still want to see those niggers you're talking about.'

'Perhaps Mr Minowara would take us down to about a hundred feet,' Curtis Bill suggested equitably.

Chris Decker gave the Japanese a new bearing at the same time and Minowara brought the plane down in a wide turn. It was smoothly executed and Decker nodded his approval.

'Perhaps, at this low level, as the pilot in command, you would like the controls again, Mr Decker,' Minowara suggested politely.

'You're doing fine.'

'What's all this mister business?' Cameron asked jovially. 'I'm Bob and we know Curtis Bill and Chris.'

'Omo,' the Japanese said.

Curtis Bill held his breath to be able to interrupt the inevitable 'whiter than white' washing powder joke but Pascoe had his nose against the window, all his attention centred on the ground blurring past them.

Cameron dug the Englishman in the ribs. 'Hey, I'm Bob and that's Omo. What's your first name?'

'Enoch,' Pascoe said without looking at them. 'There's one over there!'

The black man was loping easily through the grass and the low, spreading trees, looking up at the plane, waving at it.

'Son of a bitch is waving at us!' The suppressed fury in Cameron's voice went unnoticed in the tenseness which had entered the plane. 'Let's take a closer look at him.'

Minowara obligingly turned the plane, resetting the throttles to regain the altitude lost in the turn, then slowing down to give them a look at the man down below. They came up on the running man from behind, moving in the same direction. As they passed him his face was seen for a moment, grinning broadly. He was still waving.

'Again!' Pascoe called out urgently.

Minowara brought the plane around in another large circle and swooped over the running man again. As they passed him his face clouded over as he saw the unsmiling white faces peering through the window of the plane at him and he turned sharply away from them and quickened his pace.

'The motherfucker is showing us his arse!' Cameron said through clenched teeth.

Pascoe said, 'Let's chase him a little.'

Minowara headed the plane into a wide circle and Pascoe said, quite calmly, 'He went the other way.' Minowara ignored him. At the end of half the circle he suddenly put the plane into a very tight turn, losing altitude alarmingly. Minowara's face was calm and the movements of his hands unhurried as he pulled the plane up twenty feet above the tree tops and set the throttles wide open to send them screaming after the running man. They passed thirty feet over the head of the black man, sending him crashing to the ground in a long dive, but their speed made it seem as if they were going to impale him on the nose of the plane.

'That'll teach him,' Pascoe shouted exultantly.

'Maybe we should teach him some more,' Cameron offered judiciously. 'These niggers learn slow.' Minowara took the plane up and around. Cameron continued, 'I should know. I'm Grand Dragon of the New York Fiery Knights of the

81

Ku Klux Klan and we've taught a lot of niggers. We know how slow they learn.'

Minowara completed the stomach-jerking turn followed by the sickening drop and headed the plane back in the direction of the black man who was now standing uncertainly between two trees a hundred yards apart. He looked up at the plane heading towards him, raised an arm and shook his fist at them in anger before falling nimbly backwards when the plane was almost on him.

'The motherless syphilitic nigger bastard gives us the Black Power salute, does he? We'll give him a salute!' Cameron was totally coherent in his contained self-stoking rage, unlike Pascoe who spluttered incomprehensibly.

Curtis Bill was tempted to tell them the black man had probably never even heard of Black Power and was simply shaking his fist in the universal sign of anger, but refrained. It would serve no useful purpose, these men were beyond reason.

This time Minowara needed no prompting. He made an even more sickening and much tighter power turn, the plane seeming to hang on to the propeller by elastic, jerking behind it precariously, about to stall and plummet to the ground. Then they were in a shallow power dive towards the black man. The black man shook his fist at them once more, stood for a moment hesitantly, then started running towards one of the trees. Minowara turned the plane in a low flat surface curve which sent the grass waving away from the propwash in large rolling concentric circles. The running black man saw them coming, heard the scream of the engines and stopped. Then he turned and started for the other tree, now eighty yards away. As the plane passed directly over his head, its shadow engulfed him briefly, evilly, darkly malicious.

'Turn to starboard,' Decker said calmly and Minowara complied instantly. 'And a one eighty to bring us up behind him.'

'Hey!' Pascoe spat his excitement against the window, where it ran down in driblets. 'Why don't we chop him?' He pointed to the propeller whirring its song beside him.

Cameron licked his lips. 'Perhaps after another couple of passes. Make the bastard run first.'

Curtis Bill waited for Chris Decker to squash the suggestion as too dangerous to plane and passengers but Decker said, 'Would you like to chop him, Omo?'

Still Curtis Bill did not speak. He thought Chris Decker was joking, drawing out the suspense for the two non-pilots in the back, Cameron and Pascoe. Omo Minowara completed the tight turn before he spoke.

'He's only a boy.'

'Did you see whether his dong is trimmed?'

'I don't understand.'

Cameron said, 'Circumcised.'

'Yes, he is,' Minowara admitted.

'Then he's a man,' Decker said with finality, leaning forward to close the throttles to lower the speed and give them manoeuvrability should the black man, with whose fleeing form Minowara had once more precisely lined up the plane, try evasive action. 'Chop him.'

'That tree is dead ahead, Chris.'

'Chop him,' Cameron and Pascoe said in one voice, drowning out Curtis Bill's warning, 'Chris!'

'No,' Minowara said firmly. 'I do not kill children. You take the controls.'

They were almost on the black man, the tree thirty yards beyond his running head, squatly dark green and menacing in their path.

Curtis Bill thought, *The Japanese have no compunction about killing children. Minowara either thinks it too dangerous and is ashamed to say so or he doesn't think he can fly that well and is ashamed to say so.* And a moment later, *Nobody can fly that well. We are all dead. There is nothing I can do.*

'Chop him before he gets to the tree!' Pascoe shouted urgently.

'Now! Hurry!' Cameron called simultaneously.

Curtis Bill thought of his wife Julia and his son and his thought was banal and he knew its banality but was un-

83

ashamed: *Julia and the boy will be well provided for.*

'The second I chop him, open the throttles all the way,' Decker told Minowara.

'I understand.' Minowara put his hand on the throttles.

The black man ran for his life, approaching the safety of the tree rapidly. He did not look back to see how near the plane was, perhaps believing they would come round between him and the tree again in an effort to head him off, perhaps just wanting to see where his headlong pace was carrying him. The port propeller sliced neatly through his head like a clean taut wire through cheese. Inside the plane there was no jolt and no sound, only the visual pleasure of the forward spray of blood and bone, splattering on the windows to be almost instantly scoured away by the force of the air passing compressed by their side. Pascoe kept his nose against the glass and the blood and bone, seeming to will it to stay a little longer for his pleasure. Cameron leant over and put his finger over the glass as if to hold down one piece of startling white bone in the middle of splotched blood circled with grey brains on the other side of the window; when he took his finger away the piece of bone had gone and he was childishly disappointed. Curtis Bill noticed that the Englishman and the American were too engrossed to notice the speeding advent of the tree, to understand their danger; he also noticed that the pilots, their eyes on the running black and on the tree, spared a sideways glance for the spectacle as they hit the black man.

Decker spurted in his trousers. He hadn't even known of the erection and the orgasm had been too quick, just a wetness against his leg, an irritation to bother him when he had important things like the tree and their speed and lack of altitude to consider.

'Now!' he said to Minowara in a low voice but the Japanese was already manipulating the throttle calmly. Was there a glint in his eye?

They were heading straight for the spreading tree. It was not a very big tree but it towered over them because they were near it and closing on it rapidly. The extra power would

84

give them some lift but not enough to take them over the top. And they were too low for a sharp turn: the wingtip would strike the ground to send them cartwheeling in flames, consumed in the fuel for their return journey plus ten per cent safety margin. Chris Decker set the plane for the only compromise in his choice. He turned quite gently to starboard and pulled back on the wheel at the same time. The plane lifted sluggishly in the split second eternity, drifted sideways a little, away from the threatening tree but towards its mortal enemy, the hard, unresisting earth. The wingtip brushed the top of the grass, sank into the grass to knife through it. From the other wing came the lawnmower sound of the propeller slicing through the leaves and outer twigs and branches of the tree, the sound of the raw edges scraping the underwing. The wingtip sank deeper into the grass. They were free of the tree but one wing was still only inches from an uneven earth unseen beneath the flowing mantle of grass. Chris Decker gently brought the wings level, aimed the nose upwards at an angle predicated upon a speedy rate of climb just above the stalling point. A tree loomed in front of them and they seemed to be about to fly into its topmost branches but Chris Decker hauled back on the wheel another millimetre and they skimmed over, branches and leaves brushing their frustrated scratchwork upon the underbelly of their escaping prey.

'The fly and the Venus flower,' Decker said to Minowara, who nodded his appreciation of the quip and Decker's piloting skill.

Curtis Bill Bonham let his breath out. How could he have thought of how much money he would leave Julia and the boy when he was near death? What of love and a future? But he did his work for love of them, to build them a future. Still, now he was ashamed of the banality of his only concern in the face of death. It was not truly worthy to think of money, once achieved and secured for them. It was not dignified, not the way he would want to die.

The other two had not noticed their mortal danger, had been engrossed in their pleasure at annihilating their defiant

85

target. Cameron sighed his disappointment when he took his finger away to find the pure white piece of bone gone, his very own splintered trophy taken from him by the wind. Despite the beads of sweat straggling out of his retreating hairline over his broad forehead he was shivering. Pascoe kept his face against the glass, his nose whitely squashed, staring through his own reflection at the relics of what had once been another man. Only when the airstream had removed every last vestige of blood and brain and bone from even the corners and trailing edges of the window's sealing ridge did he reluctantly take his eyes away. Each man sat silently enveloped in his own thoughts until the plane had ascended to five hundred feet. Decker had found their bearings and was directing them homeward along a northeastward route, parallel to the South African-Moçambique border.

'We sure learnt that nigger good,' Cameron said conspiratorially to Pascoe, his hoarsely lowered voice reverberating round the man-silence of the plane, 'didn't we, Enoch?' He had seen it with his own eyes but Pascoe had been closer and it had been all too brief. Sharing and resharing the captivating moment would preserve it, expand it, bring its pleasure and righteous justification back tenfold.

'Yah, we really chopped him.'

'That nigger will never shake his fist at the white man again. I only wish we had some film of it. Who's the photographer?' Cameron demanded of Curtis Bill.

Curtis Bill resented the intrusion into his thoughts but answered levelly, 'Vincent.'

'That yellow nigger!' Cameron.

'Not the coolie!' Pascoe.

'He's had training in the use of motion picture cameras. He makes a good film.'

'You mean he made that movie the dentist from Texas who recommended me to you, the movie he showed me?'

'Yes.'

'I don't much like a coolie knowing too much about my affairs,' Pascoe said.

'He'll swing as high as any of us,' Curtis Bill said shortly. 'He's been at it five years.' He remembered Vincent's threat when he had beaten him at the Edenvale warehouse – was it only yesterday? Vincent was a coward, he would not dare do anything which would call the terrible retribution of Curtis Bill Bonham or Chris Decker upon him.

'Yes, but –'

Curtis Bill cut Pascoe short. 'You need not have your hunt filmed if you don't like the idea.'

'Aw, I don't know about that. You promised a film, so –'

'Right. A film professionally made by Vincent. You don't want something blurred, out of focus and over exposed, in which you can't be recognised, do you?'

'Naw, I guess not.' Pascoe was not entirely convinced.

Curtis Bill wiped the spittle from his face. 'That's it then. A film by Vincent or no film at all.' He was fed up with these overgrown children constantly demanding new flies to pull the wings from.

They flew in silence until they crossed the Limpopo east of Pafuri to turn into the sinking sun on the far, Rhodesian, side of the river. 'Why don't we just cut across, the shortest way?' Cameron asked, holding up his map, tracing a line across it.

'Because that would take us over the Kruger National Park,' Curtis Bill explained. 'If we kept overflying, especially in the chopper, they'd soon get the suspicion we're after their animals. We don't want anybody keeping an eye on us, for any reason whatsoever.'

'Don't they get suspicious anyway?'

'They're only responsible for their own animals. They may think we hunt in Rhodesia or Moçambique but it's none of their business. They'll probably keep quiet about it even if they saw us shooting *game* in Rhodesia or Moçambique, out of gratitude for us not causing them any trouble on their home territory. We try to keep about twenty miles or so between us and them at all times, as a sign of our good faith.'

Chris Decker turned the plane south. They crossed the Limpopo again, upriver from the camp.

'What's that large circle of denuded countryside around the camp?' Minowara asked.

Chris Decker laughed aloud, a startling sound. 'About once a year I spray defoliant on that circle. The leaves drop off and we give the black men who work for us each a bag with some bones in it. We tell them it's the *juju* from the medicine man in the sky. Only those with the *juju* can come through the magic circle. Those who try to pass through the circle without the *juju* will have their balls drop off just like the leaves fell from the trees.'

Decker waited for Pascoe and Cameron to finish their uproarious laughter about this new 'stoopendous stoopidity of the niggers' before he continued. 'It keeps out unwelcome visitors and relations of our servants. It keeps down the numbers of prying eyes and stealing hands around the place.'

'But surely such silly superstition would not deter serious people like the terrorists you hear so much about,' Minowara said to Decker.

'Terrorists venturing this far south would be committing suicide,' Decker said bluntly.

Curtis Bill explained, 'The circle does have its uses but it's not meant as a defence against terrorists. It is mainly a big practical joke.'

'But a good one!' Pascoe laughed, slapping Cameron on the back.

'Yeah,' Cameron spluttered, 'don't spoil it with explanations.'

Decker landed the plane deftly and taxied towards the end of the runway nearest to the living quarters.

They clambered from the plane. Curtis Bill told Decker in a low voice, 'Stay a minute please,' and let the others carry their high spirits towards the bar on the veranda, Minowara the only one with a dignified bearing and mien. Chris Decker stayed reluctantly. Curtis Bill would never start a fight in front of clients or reprimand his pilot in the air. On the ground it was different though, once the clients were out of earshot. Chris Decker watched the white lines of rage bracket Curtis Bill's mouth through his deep tan. He didn't want a fight but there was no avoiding it now.

When the others were well on their way to the veranda Curtis Bill demanded, 'What do you think you're up to?'

Chris Decker put on his most innocent face and looked squarely at his partner. 'Hunting niggers. That's what this organisation is all about, isn't it?'

'With a helicopter and guns. Not with the props of the plane. Not through endangering my life and your life as well as the lives of those fuckwitted morons over there.'

'Are you doubting my ability as a pilot?' A dangerous edge was creeping into Decker's low voice.

'Don't give me that crap, Chris! You know, as I do, that you're a fine pilot. But you also know, as does Minowara, that your fine piloting skills got us out of a scrape that was all your own doing but only by the very short hairs.' He walked towards the propeller, drew his finger along the inside of the nacelle, held the finger, encrusted in blood and chopped leaves, up in the fading light. 'If that stuff had gone into the air intakes we would all be dead now.'

'It didn't. We're all alive and back where we started from. If you want to do the flying, all you have to do is say so.'

'You know I cannot fly the chopper. That's what I have you as a partner for.'

'Until the end of this week.'

'If that's what's bothering you, for Christ's sake don't take it out when I'm in the plane with you. Or any of our clients.'

'Fuck them.'

'Don't do it again, Chris.' Curtis Bill walked away into the twilight.

Chris Decker looked after him. Curtis Bill Bonham was a very dangerous man and, besides, it had been a very good five years. 'Curtis Bill!'

Curtis Bill turned and looked towards him. Chris Decker took a step forward. 'Today I wouldn't let the Rhodesian ridgeback fight the baboon, saving him for another month, forgetting for a while that there wouldn't be another chance.' He paused for a moment, then let the words tumble out. 'Look, can't we go on for just another year?'

Curtis Bill took a step forward. His voice was compassionate. 'Chris, those baboons you have your sport with, they kill themselves by their own greed for more and more. They don't know when to stop and they pay for it with their lives. They destroy themselves through ripping out just one more organ and just one more until they rip their own heart out. Please – ' Curtis Bill took a step forward, his hand stretched out towards Chris Decker in a rare gesture of touching someone besides his wife and son. 'Please, Chris. Let's not be like the baboons. Let's stop while we're ahead.' He put his hand on the pilot's shoulder. 'If it's that you feel you don't want to take over without me and money worries you, I'll stake you in something else. Anything up to a hundred thousand dollars.'

'Fuck you!' For a moment of red rage Chris Decker considered smacking the insult down with an open palm across the tanned face but in midcourse his arm changed direction to cast the hand resting on his shoulder away from him. 'Fuck you!' He turned and stumbled blindly into the plane, found his belt and started the engines.

Curtis Bill stood back and watched the plane take off. Then he walked to the veranda and told Vincent, 'Have the men light the flares for Mr Chris for when he wants to come down. And bring me a large whisky.' Curtis Bill drank very infrequently.

Minowara had also watched the short run-up and dangerously steep take-off of the plane. To Yodoko he murmured softly in Japanese, 'A little education is a fearsome thing in a violent man.'

Seven

Chris Decker came down after ten minutes of flying around the camp, concentrating on not letting a single thought not originating in the lit instrument panel enter his mind. In front of him the instruments smiled their familiar friendly green formulas and calmed him. Later he would have to think of his future, of the insult Curtis Bill had offered him, but not now. Now he would kill somebody if he did not empty his mind of all thought. He set the plane down with his usual neat landing, went up to the veranda wearing his smiling host's face and received a drink which Curtis Bill had ordered for him when he saw the plane come down between the flares.

'Dinner is served,' Vincent said almost immediately.

'A hard day tomorrow and it starts early,' Chris Decker said, 'so we eat early and go to bed early.'

The meal was another of which the hosts could be proud. 'This is lovely food,' Judith said. 'Who's your chef?'

'We stole him from the Hotel Edward in Durban,' Curtis Bill told her.

'Ooh, I stayed there. In 1947 when we came back from the East. Daddy was a brigadier and I was a little girl. A very little girl,' she added wistfully.

Cameron and Pascoe were in high good boyish spirits, inflamed with the life of the man they had urged dead, aided and abetted by the several drinks they had managed to swallow before dinner, extenuated by the good Murati Cabernet Curtis Bill was serving with dinner and which they gulped, slurping it like soda. They laughed at largely incomprehensible jokes, slapped each other on the back often, even raised a smile from Omo Minowara. The women had used the afternoon to become acquainted and now smiled knowingly at each other over the antics of their men; Yodoko did not smile openly but her cheeks dimpled and the effect on her marble face was startling. Curtis Bill and Chris Decker were the finest, most genial, most understanding of hosts, pouring drinks, passing food, wiping up spilt drinks, pouring more wine, ordering food from the servants, filling glasses, telling Vincent to fetch another bottle of the fine wine on his silver salver, listening to a joke, laughingly urging another and still another to be toasted in the fine red wine; they had long since learnt that it was useless to try and restrain their guests – it was far better to get them insensibly drunk before tempers could falsify insults, before neuroses could boil forth into violence.

A 1923 Para Liquer Port was brought, the bottle enveloped in the cobwebs of its age and Vincent's proper respect for its age. Curtis Bill opened it himself, decanted it carefully to a chorus of 'Steady now, partner,' led by Chris Decker. With the port and the nuts and the cigars – illegally imported Havanas, Chris Decker explained – a peaceful semi-quiet descended around the table.

'Should the ladies withdraw?' Judith asked Curtis Bill in an undertone.

Curtis Bill noticed Enoch Pascoe pause in his laughter to glance suspiciously at him. 'No,' he said loudly enough for Pascoe to hear, 'let the ladies stay and enjoy themselves.' Judith Pascoe seemed disappointed; perhaps she had dreamt of leading the ladies out grandly after looking at them meaningfully, commandingly. Curtis Bill would much have preferred the women absent for fear of what Cameron and Pascoe might yet divulge in their cups but he thought Judith Pascoe's chances of conducting an orderly retreat with the other two women in tow to be nil; he didn't want a scene made of her bungling the attempt and so regretfully declined her offer.

Yodoko said something languorous to her husband in Japanese. Minowara saw Curtis Bill looking at them, then looking away quickly for fear of intruding on a private conversation.

92

'Sorry, Curtis Bill, so sorry,' Minowara said. 'We should not speak a foreign language here.' Yodoko hung her head in submission.

'No, no, not at all. This is your home while you are with us.'

'Still . . .' Minowara let the sentence drift away. 'Yodoko-san was telling me a poem.'

'Ah. May I hear it?'

'Yes, indeed.' Minowara looked at his wife, spoke in Japanese. She shook her head. 'Her translation into English is not good. You will have to trust my equally uncertain translation.'

'I'll be delighted. Shh,' he added at Pascoe. 'A poem from Yodoko Minowara.'

'It is *haiku*, Japanese poem of seventeen syllables. But not to worry about number of syllables in English.' Minowara stood, bowed to each person around the table, recited the poem:

> *Death is the beginning of the day,*
> *the afternoon autumn*
> *and winter comes by night.*

He bowed again and resumed his seat. 'Now it is your turn.'

'No. I am flattered by your assumption that I can write poetry and therefore regret all the more to disappoint you with my inadequacy.' Curtis Bill hoped the words did not sound mocking.

'Yodoko-san has given you the first line: *Death is the beginning of the day.*'

'I couldn't manage exactly seventeen syllables.'

'It is not necessary. Please try.'

'Oh, very well. He stood and bowed to each person. He thought for a moment, then recited his lines in an imitation of the flat inflection Minowara had used:

> *Death is the beginning of the day*
> *but does not bear thought*
> *through the long night.*

Minowara nodded his approval. 'Perhaps one of my own in reply.' He stood again, made his bows again, before intoning:

> Death is the beginning of the day:
> after dawn
> the corpse is not alone.

Minowara bowed again and resumed his seat.

'How about this?' Chris Decker did not rise but he bowed from the waist.

> Death is the beginning of the day
> though the final destruction
> comes much later.

'Your turn, Enoch,' he concluded with malicious glee.

The Englishman disappointed him by rising to his feet, bowing solemnly and intoning properly:

> Death is the beginning of the day
> and smells through the hot noon
> to superfluity at dinner.

He bowed again and sat down to stunned silence; nobody had suspected the oafish inventor of having an agile mind or a facility with words. Judith looked at him proudly.

'That leaves only little old me,' Cameron said. Not to be outdone by Pascoe, he rose swaying and nearly fell over as he offered the table a sweeping bow. Melody took his elbow to steady him but he shook her hand off and planted his feet firmly apart to declaim:

> Death is the beginning of the day . . .
> but doesn't know its purpose
> until the sun has set.

He looked lewdly at his wife as his words reverberated around the room. The Minowaras caught his glance, put on their blank looks. Cameron lurched. Over her shoulder Melody said, as she led him away to applause:

> Death is the beginning of the day ...
> is adequate expression;
> more is surplus of sufficiency.

Behind them the sound of the party breaking up receded. Cameron lurched against her.

'What did you mean, putting my friends down like that?' he demanded.

'What do you mean?' Melody asked in consternation.

'That last bit, saying we were frivolous.'

'I did not, but if you think I did, I am sorry. I meant it as a compliment to Yodoko.'

They were at the *rondawel* and she stood back to let him through the door first. Inside he fell back on the bed, raised his legs one at a time to take his boots off and throw them to the floor. He arranged a pillow under his head to watch her undress. She sighed inwardly. The only time he was ever interested was when he had drunk enough to be incapable of having and holding an erection. But she would try. Perhaps this time ... She headed for the bathroom.

'Just take it all off right there, baby.'

'I'm going to brush my teeth. I'll come undress in here.'

'Nope, your breath smells sweet to me. Just take it all off, huh? Give old Lover Bob a treat.'

She was a big girl, five ten in her stockings. She had long slim legs topped by good buttocks which would give any dress a seductive swing if it had even an inch of pleating. Her waist was thin and hourglass curved, her breasts large and firm like the rest of her. Her face was fresh and attractive and neatly framed by blonde hair which matched her pubic hair exactly. The triangle at the apex of her legs had excited Bob in the first days of their marriage. He had made her show him the pink lips pouting through the fair hair in all the positions and taken her twice a day. But after ten years twice

A.W.–D

. . . not even twice a month. She couldn't remember when he had last made love to her in what she thought of in her cornfield-of-middle-America mind as 'the proper way' and she didn't try to remember. Her loyalty was absolute. She took her bra off and he whistled at the sight of her breasts.

'Big tits with lovely pink nipples.'

She blushed and looked down involuntarily to see the blush spread to her breasts, the pink aureola flushing with blood, the nipples rising stiffly an inch forward on the small hillocks of the advancing aureola. She bent over to take off her panties and felt the blush deepen for what she knew was coming.

'Turn a little. Yes, just so. You know I like to see a bit of cunt. Yes, yes! Legs apart a little.' He unbuckled his belt and she went over to the bed. As she leant over him he roared, 'What's that bruise on your arm?'

She looked. There was a spreading dark bruise. 'I must have bumped into something.'

'Decker held you, didn't he? Didn't he?'

'Yes. You're hurting my arm, Bob.'

'He wanted something, huh, didn't he?'

'Yes, he wanted to show me his gun. Please let go of my arm, Bob, or I'll have another bruise.'

'More likely the gun he keeps in his pants,' Cameron crowed. 'He wouldn't just show it to you, he'd want to shoot with it right up your pink pussy. What did you say?'

'What do you think?' This was going a bit too far. If the words excited him, all right, but accusations . . .

'He wanted to fuck you, okay. So did you?' He tightened his grip on her arm.

'You know I didn't!'

'So tell me what you said.'

'I said you'd had a gun like that – like his gun – for years and I knew all about it.'

Cameron let her arm go, threw back his head in laughter. 'That's my baby, that'll tell him!' His hand went between her legs. 'You know what old Lover Bob likes. So give it to him.'

She opened his fly and started pulling his trousers down his legs but he was impatient. 'Just take it out, hurry!' His penis was half erect, a drop of excitement at the end. 'Give it a nice long kiss, come on, kiss it.' His voice was thickening. He tasted of urine and stale semen and sweat and salt. 'More, more, you lovely little cocksucker you, suck it all in!' Once she tried to straddle him, when it appeared his erection was not gaining much through her further ministration, but he was not stiff enough and she was not wet enough and the angle was wrong and he was clumsy in his hurry and too soon he was flaccid again. 'Just suck it, Melody,' he said sharply. 'Just suck old Lover Bob's cock with those nice pink lips of yours.' His hand between her legs had given up the pretence of exciting her, used the fingers to open her for inspection, to turn her to the best light for his visual gratification. Just before he spurted stingily through a curved passage he said, 'Decker would give his right ball to be in my shoes. I'm a lucky man, baby, a lucky man. Aah, suck, don't stop! Yeees!'

She pursed her mouth for the semen, then closed it quickly, sealing her lips as the retracting penis slid out. She rose and ran to the bathroom, not hearing him snore as she closed the door. She hurried to the toilet, turned the seat down, sat on it, the small of her back on the cold flat surface, her legs spread open before her, rising into the air past her face. Her mouth tightly closed, she surveyed the result and decided the angle of her pelvis was not right. She lay down on her back on the floor, lifted her legs to ninety degrees, lifted her buttocks from the cold tiles and was satisfied with the newly acute angle. She sat up, gently let the semen dribble from her mouth to her hand and resumed the pre-determined position. She spread her vulva with one hand, formed a funnel with the hand holding the semen and let it dribble in slowly, careful not to spill any. When it had all rolled off her hand she worked it into the canal with her finger. She felt guilty about the pleasure she felt when her finger touched the clitoris. She was not religious but masturbation had for her a tinge of the unnatural. She lay for an hour, her legs in the

97

air to ensure the correct flow direction of her insertion, before she went to undress her husband and cover him.

First she thought of the stale semen taste on Bob. He tasted that way after the blue movies he sometimes took her to. And after meeting with his buddies in the funny club, the Fiery Knights, he was a big shot in. She wondered what had been so exciting in flying around with a bunch of men. They were probably telling dirty jokes. She remembered clearly how the intimacy of fear had affected her at the river, a sexual quickening. Perhaps Bob's hunting affected him that way; it would be good because then he might get it up and in. The river brought with it the mental picture of the crocodiles eating their own young and it was a few minutes before she could shrug this horror off and give herself over to her favourite daydream, now perhaps nearer to fulfilment than this morning: Melody sitting in a casement window of roughly planed old wood worn smooth with time, set in a whitewashed wall of a thickness no longer built, overlooking a green meadow spreading to the horizon; she unbuttons the top of her dress, shakes out a milkheavy breast with a practised natural shrug of her shoulders and raises the laughing baby from her lap to suck hungrily at the extended life giving nipple. Glugglugglug.

MONDAY

One

Curtis Bill Bonham peered through the uncertain predawn halflight at the sticks the men had drawn from his hand and were now holding up in front of him. He stepped back from the breath of Enoch Pascoe who, woken at four in the morning for muster at four fifteen, had not bothered to brush his teeth. 'Enoch hunts first. Then Omo. You drew short straw, Bob. You hunt last. That okay with everybody?'

''Slong as I don't miss out again like yesterday.' Cameron's voice was slurred with sleep and liquor.

'My forst?' Pascoe's eyes were red, his words almost unintelligible. He had thought of brushing his teeth but decided against the brutal shaking the toothbrush would administer to his hungover head. Now his mouth was furry and dry.

Minowara nodded his head. His eyes were clear and his hangover, if he had one, hid behind his pride. Chris Decker had, for all his gaiety the night before, drunk extremely modestly in preparation for a day of intricate and perhaps dangerous flying; he took his work seriously. Curtis Bill Bonham had had a large whisky and a glass of wine, more than he usually drank, but he was one of those fortunate few who could drink any amount at all and not show the effects the next morning. Minowara, Decker and Curtis Bill ate a hearty breakfast, standing up on the veranda with a plate in one hand, a fork in the other. Cameron and Pascoe picked at their food, leaving plates still loaded with eggs and sausages and bacon and buttered bread, but drank several large mugs of coffee each at Decker's urging. Their hangovers amused him but in the helicopter he wanted them wide awake and

101

alert when they started using firearms.

'It's going to be a fine, hot, sunshiny day,' the pilot said cheerfully. 'You'd better leave those shooting jackets behind, but wear longsleeved shirts. This isn't Acapulco sun, this is Africa.'

'Stop being such an old woman, for chrissake!' Cameron snapped.

Decker refused to take offence. He laughed pleasantly. 'Come ten o'clock, Doc, you're going to think it's high noon in hell with the air conditioning all busted to pieces and you're going to be real thankful for my advice.' He didn't want bulky men trying to struggle out of hot jackets in the confined space of a helicopter flying precariously balanced twenty feet off the ground and he didn't want loose jackets added to the other floating equipment for these clumsy mothers to stumble over.

'Everybody gets to bring one rifle,' Curtis Bill said, 'preferably something not too long in thirty oh six or three oh eight calibre. The hunter – today that's Enoch – gets to bring two rifles, even three if he wants. I'll be gun bearer for him. I'm sure I don't need to tell experienced hunters like you about safety rules.' He nevertheless proceeded to tell them the basic safety rules, adding, 'and in the helicopter these rules count double. So please remember that space is extremely limited and that sudden shifts in weight will throw the hunter's aim off. Give him the same consideration you're going to expect when it's your turn to hunt. And try to give the camera a clear field of view at all times.'

It was four thirty when they came to the helicopter. Black men were taking the tarpaulin away, folding it neatly in sections as they uncovered the helicopter. Curtis Bill sent two with Pascoe to fetch his guns. Two others removed one complete side panel of the helicopter's bubble body and carried it away. Vincent stood to one side and checked the fittings and settings on his camera. Decker passed him as he inspected the exterior of the helicopter thoroughly and said something to him about filters. Vincent nodded and patted his pocket and then the black bag standing at his feet. Pascoe

102

and Minowara came back with their rifles. Both Curtis Bill Bonham and Chris Decker noted with satisfaction that they had chosen medium calibre pieces without excessive length or weight; they also noted Cameron's heavy side arm but said nothing. Minowara said to Curtis Bill, 'I have a folding Armalite type but it is not very accurate . . .' and the safari organiser assured him the rifle in his hand would be all right, thanking him for his consideration.

'Strike me shitless! Matching custom made gun cases!' Decker pointed his disbelief. The others turned. Pascoe was carrying a case in each hand, his size making the exertion effortless. But the weight of the cases could be judged by the manner in which the two black men sagged under the weight of two cases each. The cases were all the same, there was no doubt about it in the strengthening light.

'They're all the same,' Pascoe said, putting the two cases on the floor of the helicopter.

'So we've observed,' Decker said drily. 'You can't bring all those guns and you sure as hell can't bring any of the cases.'

'No, no, no,' Pascoe said irritably, shaking his head, his bloodshot eyes turned a revolting orange by his yellow shooting glasses. 'They're not custom made cases. They're all the same gun with the same gun case. I'm only bringing two or three but I wanted to ask which ones to bring.'

Decker threw up his hands in defeat. 'If they're all the same . . .' He let the sentence trail off and climbed into the helicopter where he sat in the canvas seat behind the gun cases. 'This I have to see. Open the case, please, Enoch.'

Pascoe opened the top case, lifted the rifle out and handed it to Decker much like a child offering teacher an apple. Decker took it and sat stunned.

'What is it?' Cameron demanded. Pascoe's body was blocking his curious view.

'Holland and Holland 600 Nitro Express,' Curtis Bill told him.

'Jesus!'

Decker spoke softly, persuasively. 'Look, you can't hunt niggers with this elephant gun. What I mean is . . . Look, this fucking cannon would blow a nigger into fine bits and there would be nothing left.'

'You wouldn't be able to take photographs afterwards,' Curtis Bill added softly behind Pascoe.

Pascoe turned on him. 'But it's all I have! I got six of them.' He sounded as if he were about to burst into tears, his face crumbling massively, his eyes watery.

Behind Pascoe's back Decker struck his forehead with the palm of his hand. His lips formed the snarling slit but the word was not spoken: Sheeeet!

'You've got six. Okay. So there is something different about each of them. What is it that's different?' Curtis Bill led the English inventor.

Pascoe's face lit up. He looked gratefully at Curtis Bill. 'The scopes. They all have different scopes I designed and built. That one – ' he grabbed the rifle from Decker's hands ' – this one has a heat seeking scope. I built it myself, as well as doing the design,' he added proudly.

Curtis Bill stared at the piece of equipment, neatly encased in moulded plastic, firmly attached to the top of the barrel. It told him little.

'This digital counter at the back here tells you when you're aiming dead centre at a body with a certain temperature, say blood temperature. You set the desired temperature with this knurled wheel here and the windage and the elevation with these two here. Three simple controls. A child can use it.'

'And the others, the other scopes?' Decker asked ominously.

Pascoe explained proudly, showing them his handiwork case by case, rifle by rifle. Besides the heartseeking scope there was: a scope to search out regular rhythmic sounds like a man's heartbeat; a motorised telescopic sight which had its own built-in rangefinder to make automatic adjustments to compensate as the hunter found his prey in the wide angle and zoomed in to the narrow shooting angle; a device for searching out the alpha and beta waves emanating from the brain; an item which Pascoe admitted was still largely experimental, intended to search out certain smells and predicated on the belief that 'niggers smell different to people';

and a completely standard rifle with peep and bead iron sights as a 'scientific control'.

'Maybe you aren't a nutter after all,' Cameron murmured in wonder at the miniaturisation and ingenuity. 'Maybe you got something here.'

'Very ingenious,' Minowara admitted.

'Sun's rising,' Decker said. He ruled, 'You can bring the iron sight and that fancy Takumar based thing with the zoom but none of the others. I don't know whether a chopper puts out alpha and beta waves but I'm not taking the chance. And heat-seeking, or throbbing rhythm-seeking devices, let me tell you a chopper puts out a lot of heat and throbs all the time like a sixteen-year-old prick. As for the smelly thing, no experimental weapons on board my chopper. It might take offence to my underarms.' Decker looked at Curtis Bill; his partner nodded his total agreement, he didn't care for over-sophisticated or experimental weapons either. Pascoe seemed quite satisfied and trotted off with the two blacks to return the four surplus rifles to their cabinet while Decker started up the helicopter and ran the complicated tests and checks necessary before it could take off.

Pascoe returned and Curtis Bill strapped him into his harness between the similarly strapped-in Minowara and Cameron, showed him how to use the throat mike and helped him put on the headset. He showed the Englishman where the quick release button was and hooked his extra safety line up behind him without saying anything about it; if something happened he would remember to undo the English inventor. Curtis Bill simply did not trust Pascoe not to press the quick release to give him more freedom of movement in a moment of stress. He waved an arm at Decker and with a jerk they were airborne and almost immediately crossing the river at an altitude of twenty-five feet.

'Have the stewardess bring me a barf bag,' Cameron said, too loudly. It was a good joke. Even Vincent's mouth curled slightly behind his camera.

Decker turned the volume down, said, 'Just speak softly. The throat mike picks up vibrations, there's no need for volume. And if you want to hurl, hurl downwind from the pilot, huh?' The good spirit, perhaps even the beginning of a team spirit, was back with them, as it had been in the plane the previous afternoon; now oversensitive egos would recognise even a true slander as an uproarious joke, compromise with denigration slight or serious equally politely in the effort to preserve and extend the *camaraderie*. 'Don't worry. We keep a pretty low profile. We don't go higher than about fifty feet and mostly we stay down here at about twenty, twenty-five.'

'That's a relief,' Cameron said. 'I'm not afraid of heights, mind you, but if I fall out this leather harness is sure to hell going to squash my balls. I'll take my chances.' He pressed the quick release button and the clip fell away from him.

Behind him Curtis Bill nodded. He had each of the hunters on an extra line attached to the back of the harness and there was no way the harness could be taken off until they stood full length on the ground. He didn't object to a show of fearlessness on the part of the hunters, though he thought it childish and unproductive, but losing one of the hunters by having him fall out of the chopper would be very bad for his safari's reputation; Curtis Bill would take all the necessary precautions even on the final safari. He tapped Cameron on the shoulder. 'Sorry Bob, but that's another of our rules. You keep the harness hooked up or you don't hunt.'

Pascoe, who had been about to press the release button, jerked his finger away and glanced guiltily at Curtis Bill to see if he had noticed. Cameron exclaimed, 'Aw shit!' in a voice that said clearly what he thought of silly rules. The quickness of his hand in refastening the clip belied his tone, stating loud as words to the trained eye of Curtis Bill that it had been a bravado gesture aimed at impressing the others.

Across the river and five miles into Rhodesia, Chris Decker turned the helicopter eastward, straight into the rising sun. Curtis Bill Bonham leant back in his specially made canvas chair which was bolted to the helicopter floor and stuck his feet in the canvas loops on the floor. His own harness was not attached to the chair but to a running cable in the roof of the helicopter, giving him great manoeuvrability within the confines of the helicopter. Vincent sat with his camera and bag of tricks in a similar chair next to his, his arm around the pole rising between his legs; the pole was to steady the camera against and to lean against when he wanted to stand up for downward angles. Both of them had clear views across the heads of the hunters. Curtis Bill took his own rifle from its rack over the door and checked the action, the clip, the safety and the barrel. Then he racked it again, satisfied it would serve him faithfully in an emergency. He didn't expect an emergency: there had been several small crises during five years of hunting but they were hardly worth remembering. The one debacle worth remembering had been the lone brave black man who had brought the helicopter crashing down with a well aimed cast of his *assegai*. Only Decker's quick wits and piloting skill had saved the helicopter. But the hunters had been slow, had lost their nerve, and the black man was rising to come forward on his broken leg to extract retribution from them with his shield and his bare hands. He had not even had a knife. Curtis Bill had watched the hunters with their weaponry powerless before an unarmed, wounded man and had reached for his own rifle to finish the black man off before he hurt one of the hunters; Curtis Bill had no doubt about the outcome of an unarmed battle between the black man and any one of the three loudmouths who were his clients on that safari. The hunters had sensed his action and raised their rifles belatedly to fire at the defiant hunted man a second after Curtis Bill killed him with a single bullet in the heart, their bullets crashing into his already dead standing corpse. Curtis Bill had let them think they had acted expeditiously to kill this threat to their collective safety because it didn't matter to him; he had nothing to prove and the burnishing of their egos was his business. But Decker had been furious and, back at the base camp, had berated them as 'incompetent cowards' and beaten one, who had dared gainsay the pilot in his terrible wrath, to within an inch of his life; Curtis Bill had only put a stop to it when it was clear his partner was not going to stop of his own will and volition before the American was dead.

Decker's voice through the earphones jerked Curtis Bill out of his reverie. 'We're crossing into Moçambique now. This is your captain speaking. This is black Africa. Beware of terrorists! They are the government here.'

'How do you know?' Cameron asked.

Decker deliberately misunderstood him. 'I read in the papers how these "freedom fighters" got elected after white mercenaries won their "freedom" for them.'

'Yes, that too,' Cameron said carefully, paying the joke a forced chuckle in deference to the bitterness in the pilot's voice undisguised even by the inexact rendition of the helicopter intercom system. 'But I meant about the border. I left my maps in my jacket back at base camp.'

'There's a dirt track down there. It crosses the border just about where we crossed and runs parallel to it the rest of the way.'

Cameron peered back, leaning out in his harness, Pascoe holding him unnecessarily by his belt. Decker turned around to look at the unbalancing weight transfer he could feel in the controls. 'Want me to get back and show you?'

'No. Thanks. I saw it. But you'd have to know where to look or you'd miss it altogether even with a map.'

The flattery pleased Decker. 'I've been flying over here for five years. When you kill your nigger, I'll mark the spot with a cross on one of your own maps.'

'Would you? I'd be damn grateful.'

'Sure. No trouble.'

'Will you do that for me too?' Pascoe asked eagerly.

'And for me, if you please.' Minowara's request surprised both the safari organisers, who had had a number of Japanese clients, mostly stolid and silent men, sometimes uncommunicative to the point of rudeness. The Japanese, in their experience, did not ask favours but nor did they forget to repay any favour or slight received.

'Sure thing. Nothing but a pleasure.'

'I don't see any niggers,' Pascoe offered tentatively. 'And we're a lot lower than the fifty feet Curtis Bill mentioned yesterday. I'm not complaining,' he added quickly, 'just asking.'

'That's all right,' Decker said. 'Ask all you want. We only go up to fifty feet when we lose the nigger we're hunting and have to find him again. The higher you are, the more people can see you.'

'We're heading for a spot where the young braves wait to challenge the big bird with their manhood,' Curtis Bill added. 'We think the place has some religious significance for them, perhaps as a burial ground.'

'Your erudition never ceases to amaze me,' Cameron mocked.

'I'm not so sure I want a nigger to choose me. I'd rather choose my own nigger,' Pascoe cavilled.

'Better sport if they're young and healthy,' Cameron said.

'And game too,' Decker added.

'If you don't like the first one we find, you can always give this hunt to the next man and take your turn another day,' Curtis Bill said, secure in the knowledge that relinquishing his turn was the last thing Pascoe would do. Pascoe confirmed his evaluation by grunting noncommittally, then breathing out explosively.

'That fateful meeting place,' Decker sang in a good country and western imitation, adding seriously, 'Sixty seconds.'

The hunters drew in their collective breath with a shurring sound through the intercom. Decker took the helicopter around in a large circle completely denuded of trees, the long grass waving concentric circles away from the whirring blades of the helicopter. When the hunters saw nothing they let their breath out with a gentle sigh.

'Nothing,' Cameron asserted. 'Sweet fanny fuckall,' he emphasised.

'But you promised!' Pascoe whined. He had already forgotten his dissatisfaction at having to shoot the first black chosen for him by the safari organisers or the first black choosing him, Pascoe, by simple presence at a predetermined place.

Minowara said, 'There he is. The promise was kept.'

109

'Huh?'

'See his head over there above the grass?' Minowara pointed.

'Yuh!' Pascoe raised his rifle.

Curtis Bill leant forward and put a suddenly heavy hand on Pascoe's arm, snapping, 'As you were! No shooting here and no shooting until I say so! Do you all understand?'

Minowara said, 'Yes, of course, Curtis Bill,' and the other two mumbled their acquiescence.

Decker pulled the helicopter into a circle with a diameter of a hundred yards around the black man who stood impassively in the centre of the large cleared space, not turning around to look at them.

'He's praying to his ancestors or gods or whatever for strength,' Curtis Bill said.

'He'll need it,' Decker laughed.

'I don't see any graves,' Cameron noted, petulant at being roughly spoken to.

'I understand,' Minowara answered him, 'they burn the dead and spread the ashes here.'

'Spot on.' The black man paid them attention for the first time and Decker brought the helicopter to hover twenty feet above him and about fifty yards away. 'This is our nigger, all right.'

'What's the goddamn nigger staring at?' Pascoe demanded in a splutter. Curtis Bill Bonham tightened his hold on his arm.

'That one's fullgrown, that's for sure,' Cameron said on a rising inflection. 'And a fine healthy specimen or my doctor's eye has deserted me. He'll run well.' He put his elbow into Pascoe's ribs. 'Lucky bastard, you!'

'Well, why don't we start shooting?' Pascoe snarled at him.

'As soon as he starts running,' Decker said. 'Hold your fucking horses, will you!'

Pascoe's voice rose in emasculation. 'You mean we're letting the nigger choose us, we're letting the nigger decide when to start, we're letting the nigger set the pace, we're letting the nigger – why, you're nothing but a bunch of –'

Curtis Bill cut easily across the tirade, his voice calm but insistent. 'Shoot him now if you like. There'll be no sport then. Chris and I will save our time and our fuel and we can all go sit on the veranda and have a drink and it's not yet seven in the morning.'

Pascoe put his rifle across his knees, mumbling incoherently.

Minowara said, his intention obviously to change the subject and ease the tension, 'Do you want to exchange rifles, Enoch? I should be honoured if you would wish to use my humble firearm.'

'No, thank you. I have become very used to these H and H rifles,' Pascoe said with surprising grace. Once again he had made an amazing recovery from the outer limits of boorishness. 'I think I'll stick with what I know. And I wish to try the gadget I built under field conditions.'

'Do you always find the niggers here?' Cameron asked.

'No. About one in six. The rest we choose elsewhere at random,' Decker said. 'Enoch, I assure you these niggers, the ones who choose us as you say, make the best hunting. Bob's right, you're lucky. But you've got to make up your mind on the spot. Do you want him or can Omo have his go and you get your chance tomorrow?'

Pascoe surprised them once more by turning to Minowara and saying, 'You choose.'

'Luck and the draw of sticks selected you for the first and the finest hunt, Enoch. I would be ashamed to accept such an opportunity from you, knowing that it will never be in my power to repay such a magnificent gift.' Minowara knew Pascoe had made obeisance to good manners, as he had similarly dissimulated in his reply, and admired the Englishman for it exactly as he approved his own tactful self denial.

'He's raising his shield at us,' Cameron said.

'A salute,' Decker replied, frogmarching the helicopter sideways and backwards to a position over the trees at the edge of the burial ground.

'We'll teach him a salute, won't we, Enoch?'

'Sure. That blackfeller's as good as dead. With this scope

111

of mine you can pick the eyeballs out of a fly at a hundred yards.'

'You can fire shots over his head now,' Curtis Bill Bonham started the ballet of death.

Pascoe chuckled. He raised his rifle, then lowered it. 'You chaps care to join me for a few shots?' he enquired in an upper class English accent so obviously fake that he chortled some more. 'Only don't kill my nigger by accident.'

'And don't fire into the air because the chopper's rotor is there,' Decker reminded them. 'Shoot over the nigger's head or into the ground, never upwards.'

The three men sitting on the lip of the helicopter raised their rifles and started firing. Pascoe had only two shots in two barrels and placed each one carefully over the black man's head. Minowara fired his four-shot magazine into the ground in front of him with measured smooth movements of hand to bolt, finger to trigger, hand to bolt, finger to trigger; Curtis Bill watched his familiarity with his weapon and approved. Cameron had an autoloading rifle with a forceful ejector action; he fired only one shot at a selected tree with it before Decker shouted:

'Kill that fucking auto-ejector round my tailplane!'

Cameron's finger had already squeezed the trigger for the second shot into the next tree trunk and the bullet was in the barrel when Curtis Bill's hand closed about the trigger guard and Cameron's hand – Decker not yet at the end of his sentence – and the voice of Curtis Bill said calmly, 'No more.' Cameron noticed without surprise that Curtis Bill had not deflected his aim and that he hit the tree trunk he was aiming at.

'Sorry, Bob,' Curtis Bill said. 'We'll fix you up with another rifle if you're short. But that one's out.'

'It's okay. If you'd told me in advance I wouldn't have fucked up.'

The black man raised his shield once more and set off away from the helicopter. He fell immediately into an easy rhythm bespeaking a lifetime of athletic endeavour. He held

112

his shield and *assegai* easily, appendages and extenuations of his body no longer noticed by him.

'Till this morning he was a fine healthy insurance risk,' Cameron offered his professional opinion once more.

'Right now I wouldn't insure his life for tuppence until tonight,' Pascoe bragged and chuckled richly.

'Is it not likely that a good healthy specimen stands a better chance of survival, of being one of the few that get away?' Minowara asked into his throat mike, watching the black man run. 'No offence or doubt of your marksmanship being implied, Enoch,' he added.

'Strangely enough, no,' Curtis Bill answered. 'A coward runs to a tree and hides or runs into the denser vegetation in the river valleys and survives. But these men, they have a compulsion to test their fitness for survival again and again. That is their undoing.'

'This is the only sport in the world where the fittest does not survive,' Decker said from the pilot's seat.

'Stupid upside down nigger world,' Cameron said.

'What about the few that get away to the mountains as you were telling us yesterday?' Minowara asked Curtis Bill, turning his head to do so.

'They're the really fit ones. They had lasted that far and we then made a mistake of dragging the hunt out too long and consequently we had to return because of low fuel reserves or failing light. They deserve to live as heroes forever. You will see.'

'My nigger's into the trees!' Pascoe called. 'Come on, Chris! You're letting him get away with all this goddamn chat.'

'Nope, I'm not,' Decker said easily. 'Relax your testicles. He's got to come out on the far side of the trees. If he doesn't, then we'll find you another nigger. But I got a hundred quid that says he comes out.'

'No betting,' Curtis Bill said sharply.

'Aw, c'mon. It's taking candy off a baby.'

'That's what I mean. You're robbing Enoch.'

'I don't mind, I got plenty. I'll take that for ten to one.'

Pascoe laughed loudly. 'I'll give that *nigger* a thousand pounds to come on out.'

'I'm with Chris. That nigger was just spoiling for a fight, shaking his shield thing at us. I'll take a hundred too at ten to one in whatever units you're using.'

'Pounds sterling.'

Pascoe said urgently, 'I'll take it all, all! Let's just get going and make sure my nigger doesn't get away!'

Decker laughed cruelly. 'We got all day, man. And I got money riding on making sure he comes out on the other side. I'm not going to risk going over there now and scaring him off. His resolve to fight is sure to strengthen once he's on the far side of the trees in the open grassland.'

Pascoe made a high wailing sound in which ' . . . you bastard . . . ' was the only audible comprehensible sound.

'Buck up,' Decker said. 'I want that nigger as bad as you.' He inched the helicopter forward over the grass circle towards the trees on the far side where the black man had disappeared and Pascoe stopped his wailing – the shiver of the eerie sound crept on the vertebrae of the other men for a few long moments after he stopped – and cheered the minuscule advance. Decker joined him in the cheering. Bonham and Decker had both seen and heard bloodlust do stranger things to men. They were not surprised.

'I'll take a hundred pounds against you too,' Minowara said to Enoch Pascoe beside him. 'I think that black man showed quite clearly that his intention is to fight and fight well.'

'Thank you. I'll take it. I'm glad you think so.' A thought struck Pascoe. His voice turned sly for his question: 'Does the engine burn much fuel to hang in the air like this?'

'Sure. Great big amounts. It just gobbles it up,' Decker told him with tormenting relish.

'Then why don't we sit on the ground and idle or even switch off?' Pascoe asked reasonably. 'If we run short my nigger will get away.'

'See that grass? You could hide an army in it and we'd

never know until they overwhelmed us by pure force of numbers.'

Curtis Bill cut the conversation short. Pascoe was not his favourite person but he did not enjoy Decker's torment of him. Pascoe had paid good money and a great deal of it for the privilege of hunting a black man, this black man. 'We've a fuel depot nearby. We can refuel if we want to. But we cannot land here. It is a point of known reference for any enemies we may have. That is why we come here only very infrequently: we don't want our habits to kill us or our friends.'

'Thank you for including us.' Cameron was quite sincere, though it wasn't clear whether the cause of his gratitude was inclusion in one of the less frequent exclusive hunts or inclusion in an intimate close circle. It would not have entered his head that a man with such apparent common sense, hunting niggers, would knowingly substitute 'friends' for 'clients' simply as a choice of less offensive words in the charged atmosphere of the helicopter.

'We are honoured.' Minowara's tone could take in either meaning and his voice was blandly without emotion or sarcasm. 'But is not the fuel depot also a fixed point?'

'Yes. But we burnt large circles of clear space around each depot. The natives cannot get at us there. If troops or policemen or other official opposition came up it would be no protection against their arms, of course. But in that case we wouldn't fight or hang around – it would be insane. We'd just head straight home with our tail between our legs,' Curtis Bill said bluntly.

'This business is dangerous, isn't it?' Cameron said wonderingly.

'What'd you think it was, a picnic?' Decker sneered. 'If they catch you here – this is Africa – there'll be no trial with platoons of lawyers defending your rights like in New York if you get caught burning some nigger – teaching him good, like you said. Here they'll just cut off your balls and stick them in your mouth.'

'I'll just depend on my gun and my pilot to keep me out of their hands,' Cameron said firmly.

'And don't you forget either!' Decker turned the helicopter through ninety degrees and let it gather speed.

Pascoe screamed.

After a moment he regained his composure to say through clenched teeth, 'My nigger went the other way!'

Curtis Bill soothed him. 'It'll be another twenty minutes before he gets through the tree belt. We're going to refuel so we can chase him further.' It was not true. He and Decker had agreed that, even with the fuel depots, there should always be enough fuel in the tanks to reach the base camp, plus a safety margin. This meant that they could get home even if they found a fuel depot infested with militia or blacks. Since they would burn equally dead with half a tank as a full tank, should they ever become unlucky and drop out of the sky, they had also decided to fill the tanks at each and every opportunity to cater for unforeseen circumstances such as the black man who had brought them down with his *assegai* and the tests Chris Decker had found necessary before he would declare the machine fit to fly; each still had shivers of trepidation when they remembered flying the helicopter into the base camp on what Decker described as 'the whiff of an oily rag'. The extra fuel was therefore not for hunting further afield but for emergencies, though the redundancy of trips back to the base camp for refuelling did in fact allow them to hunt *in the same area* longer; Curtis Bill did not feel Pascoe would be receptive to such sophistry and refrained from explaining.

'It won't take long,' Decker offered an olive branch. 'We'll be waiting for him when he comes out.'

Cameron distracted Pascoe by asking, 'Are you going to let your buddies use those guns of yours with the fancy scopes?'

Pascoe was surprised at the question. 'Sure. Why not?'

'I thought maybe the scopes were secret.'

'Christ, no. The work I sometimes do for the government is secret, sure, but those scopes are just for my own amusement. You and Omo can play with them all you like.'

'Thank you. I was hoping an opportunity would arise but I hesitated to ask,' the Japanese financier said.

'Hell, any time. How's a doctor of medicine and a financier going to nobble my design? Never! Hahahahaha!' Pascoe cackled and the two men flanking him laughed dutifully. Decker turned briefly from the controls to glance meaningfully at Curtis Bill Bonham and turn his finger clockwise beside his ear: a madman. Curtis Bill shrugged; he didn't think Pascoe mad, just a man with a different set of priorities to those held dear by everybody else.

The burnt circle looked small from the air but endless when they were down on it. The hunters helped manhandle the heavy drums a few feet nearer the helicopter after Chris Decker had inspected the seals on the metal stoppers carefully, explaining to Pascoe's inevitable question, 'We don't want some nigger motherfucker putting sand in our fuel and watching us come down from some coward's distance, do we then?' The helicopter had its own pump driven from its own sources and the refuelling was completed very quickly. 'Air to air, five minutes forty seconds,' Decker said with satisfaction. 'Thank you one and all for your help. Next time, let's try for five minutes even, huh?' Such was his magnetism that he evoked a chorus of 'Yes, five minutes even' from Pascoe and Cameron. The *camaraderie* had been restored now that the waiting was over and the hunt on again.

'Here my nigger comes!' Pascoe pressed the button to zoom in on the black man. They were on the far side of the tree belt and the others had to adjust their eyes to discern the black man against the background of the trees he had come from.

'Shall Omo and I put a couple of bracketing shots around him?' Cameron waved his revolver hopefully.

Pascoe ignored the offer. 'The black bastard's not even sweating yet!' the English inventor squealed his fury.

'I told you he is a fine, healthy specimen.' Cameron was irritated by having his professional advice doubted, even inferentially.

Curtis Bill leant forward to put a hand on Pascoe's

117

shoulder. The Englishman had sounded angry enough at the insult offered to his own sweating, overheated hulk by the black man's effortless athleticism to kill the man immediately; later he would claim he had not had the sport he paid for and demand another chance. But Pascoe's hamlike hand was clenched around the trigger guard, none of his fingers inside it. Curtis Bill put his hand on Cameron's shoulder for a brief instant instead. 'Easy with that cannon. At this range you could have an accident and kill or wound him.'

'And it's *my* nigger,' Pascoe grated. 'You just put that wild west relic away, Bob.' Graciously – or as nearly graciously as a man can with clenched teeth – he added, 'We might need it for the coop duh grass.'

It took everybody a minute to work out he meant *coup de grâce*. Cameron said, 'Sure thing,' and holstered his revolver.

'Tell me when you want to start shooting,' Decker said from the pilot seat. 'Everytime you want to shoot I'll give you a steady platform.'

'Yeah. Thanks. Can we make that nigger sweat a little?'

'Sure. I'll take you up beside him and you fire behind him.'

'Yeah.'

Decker headed the helicopter straight towards the black man. 'Let's test his nerve.'

'Yeah. Just don't chop him. And don't make him head back for the trees.'

'No way he's going back into the trees. He's said his prayers and now he'll stick it out as long as he can. You owe me a thousand pounds.'

'My wife will give you all a cheque back at the camp.'

The black man headed straight for the helicopter, looking up at it, but he did not change his easy pace.

'The ones that got away have come back and told the young men that the big bird does not attack immediately,' Curtis Bill said. 'The ones we find at the cemetery always run well. But those we just find somewhere in the veld, we often have to work hard to prevent them from diving into the nearest bolthole and drawing the hole in after them. You'll

118

see when it is your turn,' he added to Minowara and
Cameron.

The helicopter closed with the black man at speed. They
could all make out his features even without Pascoe's mag-
nificatory device. He was tall and thick in the shoulder but
slim in the waist and ran erectly, the shield on the crook of
his arm, the *assegai* pumping an easy rhythm in his other
hand. The gleam of the sun over his shoulder was not reflected from drops of sweat but from the animal fat rubbed
into his body, enlarging the ripple of his muscles. His body
was bare except for a brief loincloth of lion skin. When the
helicopter was thirty yards away the black man raised his
assegai into the air, his arm crooked behind his head for the
throw.

'Fight fair, you dirty nigger,' Chris Decker said calmly and
took the helicopter up perpendicularly. Pascoe laughed at the
remembered joke. His prey held on to the *assegai* at the last
moment and loped on, satisfied that the attack had been
beaten off for the time being, not even bothering to look
around as the helicopter came around in a large quarter
circle to run parallel to him.

Curtis Bill looked at Vincent as the Indian lowered the
camera. Vincent nodded: he had taken several good close-
ups of the hunted man for Pascoe to use in reliving the
premier experience of his life. The Indian changed a setting
on the turret of the camera as Decker said, 'Fifty yards?' and
again when Pascoe answered, 'Hundred would be better,'
and rested the camera high up on the pole designed to steady
it, looping a leather strap around the pole and tightening it
in a reverse friction clip. The rush of the overhead blades
had driven the spittle dribbling from Pascoe's mouth into the
helicopter and Vincent wiped the lens of the camera clean
with a tissue. He held the box of tissues out to Curtis Bill who
took one with a nod of thanks and wiped his face with it.
Vincent didn't wipe his own face: he was used to white men
spitting on him in the figurative sense and had just found the
literal splattering of his face to fire the flame of his maso-
chistic hatred even more furiously. Vincent didn't smile with

119

pleasure – Vincent never smiled – but added the good feeling of being at last spat upon in reality to the other pleasurable contentment of the morning: the black man, his connoisseur's practised eye assured him, would make good hunting, if only this clumsy fool Pascoe didn't shoot him too soon. Vincent enjoyed his job but would never let it be known for fear of losing it for that very reason: white men begrudged all other men not of the same colour even the smallest of pleasures. Even now that he knew he would have to find a new job next week, the habit of reticence was too ingrained for him to show his pleasure.

'I'll hold her here,' Decker informed Pascoe.

'Yeah.' Pascoe fired two shots in rapid succession. Each one went into the ground only a foot behind the running man. He must have felt the breeze with his heels as the bullets closed on him. He certainly felt the sting of earth as each bullet caused a minor crater to erupt in the earth, a force powerful enough to be seen disturbing the tall grass, setting it into violent motion in all directions.

'That's not as pretty as when the grass waves gently,' Cameron said too loudly. 'What weight bullet does that thing throw?'

Pascoe did not answer. He was watching the running black man intently as he reloaded the double barrels by touch.

'Nine hundred grains,' Decker informed him. 'Muzzle velocity 1950 feet per sec. Muzzle energy seventy-six hundred foot pounds.'

'That smartass nigger's not running any faster.'

'Big bullet, low velocity, lot of stopping power. At fifty yards it'll blow a hole in an elephant you can walk through.'

'Doesn't seem to impress Enoch's nigger any.'

Pascoe hadn't heard them. 'Can you hold her again, Chris?' he called anxiously.

'Sure. There.'

Pascoe put his two shots even closer, nine inches behind the running feet. He could get no closer without actually hitting the man because he could not see the feet but had to judge from the position of the head where they would be. The black man kept his pace.

'Those sods of earth must be stinging him on the back of the legs, surely,' Pascoe said. He looked at the running man over his telescope as if willing him to run faster. Silence reigned in the helicopter while he reloaded. He raised the rifle to his shoulder and manipulated the aiming control but did not fire. He lowered the rifle and turned to face Curtis Bill. Cameron and Minowara also turned to face the safari organiser.

'What happens if I fire in front of him?' Pascoe demanded. 'Does he turn back and head for the trees again?'

'He may. It's up to you. It's your hunt.'

Pascoe pursed his mouth while he considered this.

'If they come challenge the big bird as some sort of ritual of survival,' Minowara asked in the silence, 'perhaps they set a time limit before which they will not turn back? Say sunset?'

'Yeah. That's an idea. But I don't want to take the chance of having this one turn back and excusing himself for his cowardice by saying the big bird wanted him to go back.' Pascoe pondered again.

'He might just turn away at ninety degrees,' Cameron offered, 'but that would be stupid like only a nigger can be stupid, giving you a full frontal shot with no layoff.'

'Yeah. That's the same chance though, that he turns back.'

Curtis Bill said, 'He'll either go forwards, towards the mountains, or back towards the trees. He'll know any other way is just a detour to tire him out.'

'You've had these hardarsed niggers before?' Cameron asked incredulously.

'So what did you do then?' Pascoe demanded triumphantly, not waiting for Curtis Bill to answer Cameron's question.

'What I would advise you to do if you had a lighter calibre rifle. Just nick him to show him you mean business. But with that Nitro Express . . .'

Decker finished the sentence for him. 'If you just touched

121

his earlobe with one of those bullets you'd rip his head right off his body. Borrow Omo's rifle, like he offered, and it's on.'

'Naw. It'd take too long to sight it in. Besides –'

'Well, let him take this shot for you then. You saw on the veranda how he shoots. He won't kill your nigger before his time.'

'Naw. I'll do my own shooting. My scope works pretty accurately.'

'Yes, yes, we saw that! I'm talking about the bullet weight and the striking power, not your shooting.' Decker was getting impatient.

'We can't delay the decision too long,' Curtis Bill said, 'or your black man will get the idea he's won a round.'

'Okay.' Pascoe turned back to face the running man and his two companions flanked him facing in the same direction again. 'I'm going to knock that spear out of his hand.'

'You can't even see it through the grass,' Cameron cautioned.

'Sure. But I couldn't see his feet either, could I? You saw where those shots were placed. I'll hit the metal head of that thing,' Pascoe predicted confidently. 'It'll jerk right out of his hand and he'll know I mean business. He'll know I don't let any – he'll know I don't take insolence from niggers.'

'I'll take her over in front of him and give you about ten seconds to judge his speed,' Decker said.

'Can you take me down a bit?' Pascoe was no longer impatient.

'Sure. Tell me when your feet touch the grass.'

'Now.' Pascoe coughed. 'Back to fifty yards, if it isn't too much bother, Chris.'

'Sure.' They skimmed along the grass towards the black man who feinted at them with his *assegai* without breaking his stride. When they came no nearer he seemed satisfied and ran parallel to the helicopter, ignoring it and them.

'Okay, any time now,' Decker sang out and steadied the helicopter in the middle of its circle of rolling grass which reached out to touch the much smaller circle the running

122

man carried with him like so many outsize hoola hoops in perpetual motion.

'Just run smooth, nigger,' Pascoe mumbled, his mouth not opening but the words clearly audible in everybody's headsets through the agency of the throat microphone. He aimed carefully and fired after only the briefest pause. The black man must have felt the wind of the heavy bullet. He looked involuntarily at the helicopter, trying to gauge the form of the next attack, and quickened his pace just as Pascoe fired again.

'Hold your fire,' Curtis Bill said calmly but his voice was drowned out.

'No!' Cameron called loudly.

'Wait!' Decker called urgently.

Minowara drew his breath in sharply and the throat microphone picked up the whistle and magnified it.

'Shit!' Vincent said under his breath and his throat microphone relayed that too.

'Too late,' Pascoe said calmly and started reloading his rifle, 'whatever it was you were telling me.' He'd had his zoom scope down to its narrowest angle, found the black head, measured the speed it moved at, lowered the rifle to give him a view of the grass through which he would have to shoot to hit the running man in the side at the level of the hand, moved forward in a little jerk to allow for the length of the *assegai* shaft, tracked again at the speed the black man was running at, and fired twice while tracking at the constant speed. All the time the black man had not been in his view but he knew he had not hit the spearhead or the others would be shouting jubilantly, pounding him on the back. So, he was getting his rifle ready to fire again.

Curtis Bill Bonham, Chris Decker, Omo Minowara, Robert Cameron and Vincent watched the red spray of blood and bone and gristle fan briefly above the grass and settle like a mist on the last of the concentric waves of rolling grass the black man would make alive. Where the halves of his body fell other waves started a short circle each but the circles ran into confusion and disorder where they met and broke up into

123

random angry ripples; when the body fell in its two halves the black man was already dead. Decker brought the helicopter forward and settled it gently into the grass near the drops of blood forming an irregular circle on the tips of the long blades of grass. The blast of air from the helicopter set the grass in motion again, smoothing out the ragged edges of the bloody circle. The grass grew about the boots of the men sitting on the hunting lip of the helicopter, their feet dangling.

'Hey! Up a bit,' Pascoe said without looking up from his rifle. 'We're sinking into the lawn.' The absence of laughter at his joke from the other men alerted him. He looked up. In seated position, his feet now only inches above the earth, his face was level with a solid wall of golden yellow grass, coarse as a rasp, no longer a smoothly flowing carpet as from the detail-denying heights of flight. 'I missed the short spear thing. That's no need to land though. Chris was holding the chopper perfectly still. And from here I'll be able to see nothing. It's gotta be a downward shot from the chopper.' When there was still no answer he looked at his two companions on the lip of the helicopter, then turned cumbrously to look at Curtis Bill. Cameron leant over to set the Nitro Express on safe. Pascoe swallowed his spittle. 'What're you looking at me like that for? Christ, I've only had two shots from fifty yards at a thing smaller than my hand moving along jerkily where I can't even see it, with waves in the grass to throw off my aim. Christ, anybody can miss under these circumstances. Give me a few more shots and I'll get the nigger, I won't miss.' Tears were coursing along his cheeks to mix with the spittle he still dribbled, to be blown away into the dusty earth and dead seeds or on to the faces of those inside the helicopter by the lazily turning blades. He was pleading now. 'Please! I won't miss.'

'That's the problem, Enoch,' Curtis Bill said. 'You didn't miss. You hit him.'

'So what are we waiting for? Let's go chase that nigger then.' Pascoe turned around eagerly to face outwards again.

'You didn't hit the *assegai*. You hit the man. He's –'

'Impossible!' Pascoe whirled back to face Curtis Bill, digging flying elbows into the ribs of the Japanese and the American flanking him. 'Are you trying to say I can't shoot with my own rifle and my own scope?'

'No, not at all. The man quickened his pace just as you fired.'

'That's what we wanted him to do.'

'Yes. But he ran into your second shot.'

'No. I don't believe it.' Pascoe's voice was cracking between a pleading note guarding against a cruel practical joke and a defiant note distancing the growing truth from him.

'Look for yourself,' Chris Decker said kindly. 'I've brought you down to have a look.'

Pascoe's finger hesitated only momentarily over the quick release button while he looked at the others with calculation: would they leave him here, alone and lost in the veld, without water? Alone with the dangerous black man who knew the veld.

'We can fly over first, to make sure he's dead,' Decker said, the mocking tone back in his voice as soon as he detected Pascoe's distrust. 'But with that cannon . . .'

Pascoe jumped down. Curtis Bill leant forward to unclip the extra safety wire and the headset lead from Pascoe, then did the same for Cameron and Minowara. Vincent passed between the two hunters with his camera and then Curtis Bill jumped down and followed the Englishman and the Indian photographer through the cutting grass. Cameron and Minowara looked at each other for guidance, then followed, carrying their rifles warily, Cameron unholstering his revolver to carry it in his free hand. There was about them the aura of thrill-fear such as children calling up ghosts have: this was Africa and they were sneaking through the dangerous grass to look at a dangerous enemy their hunting companion had just killed with his very dangerous rifle. *Africa!* The word said it all; danger, excitement, rewards for bravery, the sweet companionship of your peers: other brave men, the survival of the fittest. *Africa!*

Pascoe struck aside the razor edges of the grass but it

sprung back perversely to cut his sunburnt face and hands cruelly. He wasted no time looking about furtively for the dangers of Africa, like Cameron and Minowara, but did have time to think that perhaps the black man's body was greased to protect him in some way against the grass. Pascoe found the black man standing in a hole in the ground enveloping him up to his middle, his arm behind him, almost flat on the ground as he contorted to get the maximum throwing force into the *assegai*. Pascoe brought the rifle to his shoulder simply because firing it without a backstop would have his fingers torn out of their roots by the recoil. Still, against his shoulder, the rifle recoiled enough in his hasty hold on it for the rear edge of his telescopic sight to cut his forehead open to the bone above his right eye. He didn't notice. Both hasty shots had missed! Two empty barrels and the black man was staring at him, his eyes unblinking, a grin of deadly rapture spreading his purplish lips wide, showing the bright red gums and the strangely yellowed teeth. The black man was holding his cast, the *assegai* still threateningly on the ground behind him, his arm tensed for the throw. Pascoe became aware of the whirring of the camera close behind him. He turned to find Vincent operating it. Pascoe pointed dumbly to the body and Vincent nodded. If the cowardly coolie could stand there and make a film, Pascoe knew it was only a body. Hesitantly he walked forward and put his foot on the black man's shoulder and toppled the trunk which had been standing up on the ground. There was no hole in the ground. Curtis Bill Bonham came through the grass curtain and followed Pascoe as the Englishman trod the trail of blood to the rest of the body, the other half. Drops of blood fell from Pascoe's brow, pinkish with his sweat and spittle, to mingle freely with that of the late black runner, his precipitous prey. The rest of the body, the lower half, heralded itself with an extended display of human intestine and exploded vital organs. The heavy bullet had struck the man in the curve of the middle, just above the hipbone, and had exploded inside him to blow the top half twenty feet away where Pascoe had already found it. The top half was miraculously unscathed, except for being

126

dead from massive trauma and severance from its lower half, but the lower trunk and legs were a mess. The grass was flattened for five feet around the spot where the bullet had hit the running black man and every inch of it was foul with body parts, blood, bone, gristle, gooey messes fomenting their own nauseous gasses because the biology of the stomach had not ceased life with the host body, all eerily shimmering in the morning sun and swarming with large buzzing multi-coloured flies which had sprung up from nowhere. The shadow coursing across the carnage so lazily was the first vulture, waiting for Pascoe to leave so that it could feed. Not far off a hyena barked, calling the scavenging cleaners of Africa to a late breakfast. Blood dripped in front of Pascoe's eyes and everything came to him through the red mist of his own blood. He did not know he had received a cut. Behind him the camera whirred again.

Enoch Pascoe turned away from the camera before he vomited last night's dinner and liquor and this morning's coffee over the gory remains of the man he had killed by accident before he intended to.

Two

Once awake, Melody knew she would not be able to sleep again but pretended to be fast asleep until Bob had gone. Unless given an opportunity to sleep off his hangovers, he could be exceedingly grouchy. As soon as he left, she went to the window and threw open the wooden shutters to look out at the night. But it was no longer night: the sky was purple and an orange glow was growing slowly on the eastern horizon. She had thought the men were going to get up at

four; she looked and the alarm clock and her watch both
indicated four twenty-five. This was Africa! And first thing,
absolutely first thing, she was going to swim in that pool at
dawn, before the day could bring the nearness of the horrible
river back to her memory. She heard Bob coming and
jumped back into the rumpled bed until he had chosen his
rifle and found the cartridges for it and gone off swearing at
not being allowed to hunt first. Then she changed into her
bathing costume and took a long bathrobe to cover it, remembering what that creepy Chris Decker had said about
the black men and not wishing to tempt them with scanty or
suggestive clothing. Poor things probably had enough problems of their own without Melody Cameron to plant prurient
ideas in their heads. This reminded her that Decker had also
said ladies were not to go to the pool unaccompanied, hinting
that he should do the accompanying. Not that she'd ever go
with him but a rule was a rule and Curtis Bill Bonham looked
like the kind of man who wouldn't think twice about sending somebody away if they broke the rules and hunting with
these particular men had long been the big dream of Bob's
existence and if she interfered with it or caused them to be
sent away he was not likely to forget it for years and she knew
what a long memory he had for things that went wrong.
She'd ask the other two wives and they could all accompany
each other.

Yodoko Minowara was up and dressed and impeccably
ready for the day, having risen before her husband to make
and serve him *cha*: strong bitter black Japanese tea such as
he had every morning at home in Tokyo. She was happy at
the thought of a flowing fresh water pool to swim in and
changed while Melody went to invite Judith Pascoe. Judith
was still in bed, sleepy and irritable and bedraggled and
unable to go back to sleep for fear that Enoch might clump
in one more time with his native bearers to demand of her the
whereabouts of the keys to the gun cabinet and the cartridge
drawer which were found, each time, in their proper key-
holes. She was not enthusiastic about getting up to walk to a
pool to swim but she didn't want to be left alone at the camp

with a lot of black men either. She came reluctantly.

For Melody it was the adventure of Africa, swimming at dawn in a pool which had continuous fresh running water as clear as a Montana stream of Zane Grey vintage. For Yodoko a bath was a part of life, a duty of cleanliness and beauty; this one was cold whereas she was used to warm baths. It was a refreshing change and one she enjoyed tremendously. She decided to come swimming here every morning for the week they would stay. Judith found the water cold but she enjoyed the company of the two younger women. She remembered that Yodoko had been kind to her yesterday when the killing of the baboon – no, not just the killing, the way it was done, the way they had all enjoyed it like the cinema or a play – had upset her. Melody taught her an Australian crawl which soon warmed her up as her genteel and obsolete breaststroke had not. After expending all her breath on the new stroke she dried herself and put her woollen dressing gown back on to sit beside the pool and watch the two younger women sport about in the water like children. It was nice of Yodoko to offer to help her reset her hair, ruined by the Australian crawl and her own honest sweat at the unaccustomed exercise and the splashing playfulness of the other two. A warm glow spread through her, part exercise, part the realisation that she had not had any friends since she left school and now perhaps she would have two all at once.

Melody felt drawn to the silent, self contained Japanese woman. There was no reason, she just was and she didn't mind. This was not Manhattan where people would draw up lists of things in common before even allowing themselves to be introduced. To her surprise she found herself telling the Japanese woman about her false pregnancies, four of them in the ten years since she had married Bob at eighteen, and how the morning illness supported her dreams for months until eventually some or other silly doctor would disillusion her of the phantasy – a good word she'd made up for her phantom fantasy pregnancies – and try to send her to a psychologist or a psychiatrist or an alienist and how she would then change doctors and give false names and pay them in

129

cash. Until the next time, when her longing for a child would again drive her to the toilet in nausea every morning at the appropriate time. And of course you couldn't talk to a real he-man's man like Bob about artificial insemination and the one time she had mentioned adoption he had exploded to say he didn't want other people's cast-off runts and that had been that. Yodoko listened so attentively, not trying to interpose her own great personal tragedy, that Melody, who was normally cast in the role of the listener, instinctively found in her a friend with such *simpatico* as she had never known in anybody. That Yodoko was only being ritually polite to her in a characteristically Japanese manner did not enter Melody's head and it would not have mattered if she had been told; her instinct and intuition drew her inexorably towards Yodoko.

While they were talking at the far end of the pool near the waterfall, Judith rose and called, 'I'm peckish. I'll go up and see to it that the servants prepare a decent English breakfast for us.' The sun was shining warmly and her fears had gone like the mists of the morning. After her swim she felt capable and fresh, certainly up to overseeing someone else's well trained servants in the simple process of preparing bacon, sausages, eggs, toast, tea and coffee. Melody called, 'Give us another hour and we'll eat a horse each,' and they waved at her as she stepped on to the path back to the base camp.

Judith went to her *rondawel* and showered and dressed quickly. Then she went up to the kitchen but the servants had breakfast under control, with kippers, four kinds of sausages, liver, kidneys, bacon and scrambled eggs waiting on warming plates for whoever should want breakfast; the coffee was boiling and so was the water for tea or beef extract drinks and the milk for chocolate. The servants expressed their willingness to perpetrate further wasteful excesses by preparing eggs for anybody in any quantity and manner ordered, indeed to prepare anything anybody could reasonably demand. The cook showed her a pantry where she stood between shelves where smoked oysters brushed shoulders with canned rattlesnake and bottled frog's legs. They could choose from twenty-

130

three different brands of marmalade, he informed her, and he would have all displayed for her if she so wished. The succession of overpaid and truculent butlers who had passed through her home had always managed to sneer at Enoch's accent behind his back and at her lineage in front of her, implying that she was lucky to receive even burnt toast from their hands which had served better personages until a shattering blow of fortune and fate had reduced them to serving the *nouveau riche* Pascoes. Here she was being treated like a queen and she couldn't think of anything to ask for which wasn't already provided and on display, was being mocked by a well meaning cook offering her twenty-three different brands of marmalade. She was glad when she heard the sound of the helicopter and could retreat towards the distraction it offered. She had to will herself not to run. 'You come back whenever you like, Missy,' the cook called after her. 'I make something special for you.'

The helicopter clopped into the circle between the *rondawels* and settled gently on to the hard earth, blowing away wisps of the dust the baboon and the dogs had stirred up, the dust a reddish colour like dried blood even where no animal had bled on it. There were not many wisps and they were soon gone: the Bantu servants had swept the area very clean. Judith peered at the helicopter through the reddish mist and then through the bright morning sunlight as the dust settled further away when the rotors stopped turning. She wondered if the helicopter would be landing in the circle regularly, thinking that it might be dangerous for her and the other wives and certainly the thing made an excess of noise. On the lip she saw Cameron and Minowara strapped in with some kind of wide belted harness and through the plexiglass at the front she could see Decker reaching out to switch off controls. The inside body of the wasplike creature before her was not visible, shadow making it impossible to discern details or even movement. For a moment she felt an anthropomorphic sorrow for the sadly drooping insect, its miserably thin wings hanging in fatigue, its sting standing upright in futile defiance against unseen enemies. Then it struck her: Enoch was a

131

hunter too, just like the obnoxious American and the sinister Japanese. Why wasn't he sitting on the edge of the thing with his feet hanging dangerously over space? He would never let the other men show off alone, not while her Enoch was alive, he would not. If these irresponsible safari organisers Bonham and Decker had let her Enoch fall out over some foreign country where they had never heard of British justice and the gaols were filthy breeding grounds of communicable diseases . . . She started for the helicopter, going down the veranda steps and across the open space at an urgent run.

Cameron saw her coming and said softly into his throat mike, not moving his lips, 'Maybe it's not such a good idea to have women underfoot when men are hunting.'

'It costs the same whether you bring your wife or not,' Decker retorted, 'so most guys naturally bring their wives.'

'Are you calling me a cheapskate?'

'Quiet, both of you,' Curtis Bill said. Chris Decker switched the auxiliary circuit for the headsets off.

Cameron and Minowara pressed their harness release buttons and Curtis Bill unhooked them from his extra safety line. Vincent jumped down to clear away the debris of cartridge belts, tissue box, film cases, running wires, loose shells, and a used hypodermic from under the feet of Curtis Bill Bonham and Decker as they helped the heavy and uncooperative Pascoe from the helicopter. Pascoe seemed a filthy mess of blood and gore and he smelt too but the observer's eye was forcibly drawn to the yellow shooter's glasses still on his face. The frame was bent and one glass was broken and stuck in small pieces to the cut on his forehead, though the blood had stopped flowing.

'What have you done to my Enoch?' Judith Pascoe cried out in pain. But the pain she felt for him didn't prevent her coping with the situation to the extent of reaching up to rip the ridiculous glasses from his face.

'It's what he did to himself,' Cameron whispered. Not hearing himself, he cocked an ear into where the headset had been. 'He did it to himself,' he repeated, too loudly. 'It was his own fault,' he elaborated in his usual loud tone. Satisfied with recovered normalcy, he nodded several times.

Judith stood on tiptoe to pick pieces of glass from the bloody crumpled and lacerated skin of her husband's forehead as he hung slackly between Curtis Bill Bonham and Chris Decker. Cameron pulled her away gently.

'I'll do that and sew him up as soon as we can put him down flat on his back.'

'I'm his wife!' Judith snapped in outrage.

'I'm a doctor,' Cameron said with surprising gentleness. 'Come. He's had a shot of painkiller, ably administered by Curtis Bill, and he's feeling no pain right now. Let them put him to bed and you can assist while I sew him up.' She let him pull her aside.

'He's a heavy mother, isn't he?' Chris Decker asked his partner in a conversational tone. He didn't seem to be labouring under Pascoe's weight and Curtis Bill wasn't breathing heavily either. 'And his feet drag.'

'Well, lift them then, will you,' Judith Pascoe snapped.

Decker ignored her. 'And he smells. Jesus, does he smell!'

Judith preceded them through the *rondawel* door. The black man waiting inside the *rondawel* startled her. 'What are you doing here?'

'Master Curtis Bill send me for doctor bag and accident sheet,' the servant said, holding up Cameron's black bag and a folded rubber sheet. 'Which bed Missy want accident sheet on?'

'Either bed will do,' the pilot said from the door. 'Just make it quick. The bastard's growing heavier by the minute.'

Another black man followed the little group through the door. This one was carrying two enamelled basins in one hand and an outsize medicine chest in the other. Cameron declared, 'I like to see people as well organised as you are.'

'All part of the service.' Decker let go of Pascoe and Curtis Bill lowered him on to the rubber sheet. 'All yours, Doc. I'm going to wash the smell of their blood from me.' He left and the black men followed at a gesture from Curtis Bill.

'Will you telephone for an air ambulance?'

Curtis Bill stopped at the door to answer Judith's question

133

with another, 'Do you really think it necessary?'

'Of course I do!'

Cameron said, his voice professionally authoritative, 'We'll be able to see if he needs hospitalisation as soon as you've helped me clean him up a bit.'

Judith looked at Cameron and Curtis Bill slipped out of the door. When she turned back to insist he make the call anyway she faced a closed door. She took one of the enamel bowls into the bathroom to fetch hot water without having to be told to do so by Cameron. While he was picking the glass out of Enoch Pascoe's forehead and cleaning up around the wound, she found a pair of round tipped scissors in the medicine cabinet, which was really most amazingly complete, and cut the outer clothing from her husband, leaving him in his undershirt and underpants.

The American doctor talked as he worked. 'That medicine cabinet is a bit of a surprise. Curtis Bill looks like the kind of man who's prepared for any eventuality, even practising a little horse doctoring on a sick nigger.' He laughed softly at his own joke, not at all like the loud roar he enjoyed at other times. She wondered whether he could be a good doctor. 'Nasty cut here but easy enough to sew up. Fortunately none of the pieces of glass went into the eye. Looks worse than it really is, much worse. I'll try to leave as little of a scar as possible, just a nice halfmoon. Lots of big game hunters have them.' He threaded the needle at his first try.

'Lots of hunters have their scopes jump back and hit them in the face. But this is the first case of a hunter getting sick, hurling his guts out at the sight or the smell of his own blood that I've heard of.'

'It's the shock of the cut,' Judith said loyally. 'Enoch's done a lot of big, big game hunting.'

'Uh-huh. Maybe it was the nigger's blood or maybe the sight and smell of the busted intestine, worse than that monkey, spread over –'

Judith dropped the enamel basin from which she was sponging the other half of Enoch's face, the half the American doctor wasn't working on. Cameron looked up with a start, his mouth hanging open as he realised what he was saying, but his hands holding the needle and the flaps of skin he was sewing together did not jerk. Judith noticed this and decided he was probably a competent doctor. But it wasn't important any more.

'You mean he killed a man?'

Cameron looked down at his work and made another neat stitch before he answered. 'Of course not.' His joviality rang false. 'I was simply being sarcastic. Forget it. There, all finished. As soon as you've finished swabbing him down I'll give him a good once-over. You know, spectacles, testicles, watch and wallet, just like the Pope when he's been walking among Jews, checking it's all there.' His laughter sounded as false as his joviality. And the pilot Decker had said 'the smell of *their* blood'.

She finished the washing of Pascoe's sunburnt face while the American doctor stood by in the awkward silence. He checked the sleeping man's most obviously important functions as far as he could, prescribed rest and gave her a tube of ointment to rub into the sunburnt flesh. He seemed in a hurry to leave.

'I'll be nearby if you need me,' he said over his shoulder as he left her to clean up the floor and sit watch with her husband.

At noon a black servant wheeled in a trolley with her lunch on it as well as some broth for Enoch. She gave him the liquid over his dozy protests, wiping the dribbles from his chin and covering the sunburnt skin cleared by her ministrations once more with the lotion the American doctor had left with her. Enoch fell back into his stupor and she remembered that she had not had breakfast yet. She ate hungrily. It was fine food, she noticed in passing, but she did not enjoy it consciously; her mind was on other things.

At six in the evening he came awake, totally awake and alert all at once, with no transitional half awareness. 'Where am I?'

135

'At the *rondawel* at base camp. Would you like me to call the doctor back now?'

'Who?'

'The doctor. Cameron.'

'What for?'

'You have a nasty cut in your forehead. You're suffering from shock.'

'Me? I'm all right. I thought you were sick.'

'No, I'm – ' She shook herself to rid herself of the silly charade. 'You shot a man and they brought you back and Dr Cameron sewed up the cut in your forehead.'

It all came back to him and he swallowed bile back from his mouth. 'Can I have some water?' She fetched the water and held the glass for him while he drank thirstily. She wiped the dribbled runnels from his face and automatically applied new ointment over the areas wiped. 'Yeah. Great bigger nigger rubbed all over fat.'

She disregarded the note of relish in his voice, hearing it but having no context to place it in with any degree of credibility. 'It was an accident?' She felt an urgent need to add, *Say it was an accident! Please say it was an accident!*

'Yeah. You could say that. He broke into a gallop when he should have trotted.'

'You were shooting at him on purpose! Oh, my God!' She put her face in her hands, the sobs of cruel reality finally accepted wracking her thin body.

'Hey! No need to cry. I wasn't aiming to kill him.' He put his hand on her shoulder and held her as she tried to jerk away. 'That nigger killed himself this morning.'

'But you shot him!' She had known all the thoughtlessness and careless cruelty of Enoch for years, but maliciously frightening some poor savage with his rifle, that she had not suspected him of. And then being clumsy enough to kill the man . . .

'Aw, come on then! All the others knew where I was aiming and there's the film to show – '

'You had a film made of this – this – this atrocity?'

136

'Yeah. For you and Eric and Joan. To show. Afterwards.' His voice mirrored his confusion. She had never gainsaid him before.

'You had a film made of you shooting at some black man and you want to show it to your son and daughter?' She hadn't believed him, it was clear from her voice.

'Well, to Eric first and later to Joan. It's high time Eric started doing manly things.'

'We'll talk about that once we're back in England,' she said coldly, wiping the tears from her face and looking him straight in the eye. 'But for now I do not know how I can face the other men's wives after what I know and what their husbands will tell them you have done. I want to go home. Now, or if that is not possible, at first light tomorrow.'

'But Enoch doesn't, does Enoch?' Cameron's professional voice slithered towards her from the door. 'Enoch's no cowardly *dik dik* hunter who goes whining home just because he cut himself shaving, is Enoch?'

Enoch Pascoe looked down, away from his wife's accusing stare and said, 'I'm staying the week I paid for and so is my wife.' He didn't notice his wife's departure for the bathroom nor the sounds of vomiting through the imperfectly closed door; he was listening to the soothing voice of respect from another hunter:

'That's a real man speaking! Boy, do you recover fast!' Cameron came to the bed and put his face close. 'Better not tell her too much, eh.' His whisper reverberated around the room.

Pascoe's hoarse whisper was a great deal more purposeful. 'She thinks I killed that nigger by accident. So I did,' he added hurriedly, making it quite clear he was not admitting to a failure of marksmanship. 'But she doesn't know about later, that I would have blasted him anyway.'

'Good. Just keep it that way.' Cameron raised his voice to his normal painful boom. 'Come on, up with you and get dressed. Drinks on the veranda. You don't need my professional care any more, not until the stitches have to come out anyway.' He turned to the bathroom to go see to Judith, his

137

professional habit too strong to break, but she closed the bathroom door firmly in his face just as he arrived on the threshold.

Enoch Pascoe sympathised with him as they breathed the word in one explosion of laughter:

'Women!'

'Mrs Cameron and Mrs Minowara are helping Mrs Pascoe do her hair,' Vincent said in reply to Curtis Bill Bonham's question.

'Send someone over with a tray of drinks for them,' Curtis Bill instructed.

'Christ, if the women want a drink, let them come to the bar,' Cameron said. 'Mohammed came to the mountain, didn't he?'

Vincent waited and Curtis Bill waved a negation of his earlier instruction. It wasn't worth getting into an argument about.

'I want to talk to you,' Pascoe said, leaning forward to put a large hairy paw on Curtis Bill's leg. If anything his breath was even more foul than it had been at dawn. Curtis Bill did not try to escape the foul effluvium; he was a very good host. Pascoe looked at the hovering Vincent. 'Piss him off somewhere first, this is private.'

'I'll go see to dinner,' Vincent said and went inside.

'Want us to go for a walk?' Decker asked. 'I can tell you you're wasting your time, sweetie. Curtis Bill Bonham isn't that way –' he indicated which way with a limp wrist in the gathering darkness ' – at all.'

'No,' Pascoe told Decker bluntly. 'You can listen. It's your neck too. And yours and yours,' he added to Cameron and Minowara.

'What is it?' Curtis Bill Bonham asked.

'It's that coolie of yours and his camera. He's got –'

'You worried because he made a movie of your hurling your guts out over some nigger you shot?' the pilot jeered.

138

'That's enough,' Curtis Bill said calmly.

'Well, I don't like pictures of me hurling a nine foot duke, of course not,' Pascoe said manfully, 'but it's the other business that worries me.'

'There's no need to worry,' Curtis Bill reassured him. 'This morning when I left you in the *rondawel* I went directly and fetched the camera with the film still in it from Vincent. Camera and film are now in my safe in my *rondawel* and you and I will take it out later and you can take the undeveloped film into your own safekeeping. You want to do it now?'

'Yes.'

'Let's go.' Curtis Bill rose and the English inventor lumbered after him, followed by Chris Decker's jeering voice:

'Trusting bastard, aren't you?'

'That's him. What protection do we have?' Cameron asked lazily.

'Same as him. You actually get the undeveloped film straight from the camera the minute the chopper lands. You then have it developed by your own sources when you get back home and you can cut and edit it so it doesn't show you bringing up your breakfast or disgracing yourself in any other way.'

'He's anxious to make up for it, to prove he isn't weak in the head as well as the stomach,' Cameron said with a chuckle.

'We'll see,' Decker allowed reluctantly. 'First his wife, now him. Must run in the family. What do you think, Omo?'

'I'm afraid genetics are totally outside my competence,' the Japanese said blandly. 'Do you have no films at all?'

Decker laughed. 'For advertising, that kind of thing?' Minowara nodded his sleek head gravely. 'No, nothing. How could we without breaking trust with our clients?' Not for Chris Decker the euphemisms of common trade. 'No, we rely entirely on word of mouth. If your friends want to show you their films, if you want to show your film to selected friends, certainly. It is good advertising for us. But we don't really need advertising. We have a waiting list.' He remembered that the waiting list would be worthless with the departure of

Curtis Bill Bonham from Ultimate Test, Incorporated at the end of the week. He looked into his glass in the dark and decided not to have another drink.

Tomorrow would be another day of intricate and perhaps dangerous flying.

Three

The messenger finally found Jomo Iningwe at the Polana where he was making love to a statuesque Greek goddess with a great deal of reddish blonde hair, including a coiled mat of it encroaching on her navel. Jomo was rubbing his nose in it, letting the springy hair tickle his fancy and sneezing deliciously when the knock came timidly at the door. He strode to the door, cursing foully, jerked the door open, bent his head as he passed through to stand naked in the passage and look down on whoever had interrupted him.

'Ah, I found you,' the man said with great satisfaction. It was not really much of a feat, considering that Jomo was an inch short of seven feet and always dressed colourfully while in Lourenço Marques. Also, he was a hero, known to many by sight.

'What is it, little man? Quick, before I pulverise you for interrupting the well earned reward of my labours on behalf of the people.'

The messenger giggled at a mental picture of the 'reward' but stopped immediately he saw Jomo's eyes. 'He wants to see you.'

'Very well. Tell him in one hour, at sunset.'

'Immediately.' The messenger instantly regretted the rash impulse of his statement for he found himself swinging by his throat from one huge hand, his feet scrabbling well clear of the ground. 'For God's sake,' he croaked, 'it is not me speaking. Those were his words, I swear.' He was unceremoniously dropped to the ground, stumbled and fell.

'I shall shower to wash the smell of love from me before I go,' Jomo said calmly. 'You will serve your future better if you carry messages diplomatically.' He waved a hand in dismissal and the messenger scuttled gratefully away. Oh, what a story he would have to tell tonight! What they said about this Iningwe was true and more besides!

The Greek goddess came into the shower to soap and wash him. She was surprised to find he did not use a shower cap over his luxuriant Afro. She had assumed it to be the loving creation of some expensive hairdresser. When it sprung back into shape as he dried it she exclaimed at the wonder of it. He asked her, 'Do you have a thing about black men?'

'No. Are you black?'

'Yes.'

She held her arm against his. 'My tan is darker than your beautiful olive skin. I do not believe you.'

'It is true.'

'Then you are my first black man. Will you return?'

'If I can.'

'When?'

'When I have finished my work.'

'And you don't know when that will be?'

'Don't be sad. There are other men.'

'Do you have a brother?'

'I will send him if I cannot come myself.'

'What is your name?'

'Jomo Iningwe,' he replied as he closed the door behind him.

The man Jomo Iningwe had come to see in a room on an ill lit street was midnight black with purple lips and eyelids. He was also short and squat and cut no fine figure in any kind of clothing whatsoever from bathing trunks through civilian suits. Jomo looked at him in a superior manner because he knew it would irritate him. Jomo had interrupted his education at the Sorbonne to take part in the student riots of 1968 and had been responsible for the deaths of two policemen. Finding it difficult to hide because of his size, he had returned to his home in Dar es Salaam in time to be discriminated against and persecuted with the rest of his family because of the hereditary defect which gave them light skins. They were mistaken for Asians and his mother and sisters were raped and then killed by Tanzanian soldiers as they tried to board a boat which would have taken them to safety. Jomo and his father made their way southward towards the Moçambique border on foot, living off the land or out of his father's money belt and they made it. But at Palma, on the safe, Moçambique side of the Ruvuma River, his father had lain down and died, his will and his spirit broken in his prime. Jomo wandered on, spent six months working on the gold mines in South Africa, another six months in a South African gaol, then wandered north again. That was when Frelimo, a political organisation demanding independence and self rule in Moçambique, employed him as a sharp economist to sniff out those on the fringes of the law who could best be blackmailed into making repeated large contributions to The Cause. Jomo did very well in his often gruesome job. When Moçambique became independent and Frelimo became The Government, he could have had, as a man who was not only dangerously knowledgeable about buried skeletons but also very competent in his own violent right, highly lucrative government favours. Instead, independently rich from his 'tithe' of the blackmail contributions, he decided he liked the old way better and threw in his lot with the more radical, newer groups of terrorists. For a fee, always for a fee. It was not long before Jomo Iningwe found he liked the excitement of violence, of pitting his skill against the skill of other men, with his life the forfeit for misjudgement. Naturally he saw a way of turning this aptitude into cash: Jomo would lead trained men against specific targets for any group who had the cash or would authorise Jomo Iningwe to raise the funds in their name – after all, he was not a common thief.

The squat black man regarded the tall olive god across the

raw table between them with distaste. But his gaze was level and did not fall when Jomo Iningwe scowled at him.

'How goes the nigger mercenary business?'

'Our high purpose . . . ' The squat man stopped when Jomo burst out laughing and added sullenly, '*I* am not a mercenary.'

The obnoxious little shit was probably Sandhurst-trained – bearing and accent and manner spoke loudly of it – but he would cut no finer figure in even the best tailored uniform.

'Perhaps . . . But you have your orders, don't you, *mon colonel*?'

The squat man's shoulders squared but he said nothing. His instructions unfortunately specifically excluded dealing with this terrorist-for-hire in a proper and suitable manner.

'You have the money?'

'Yes.' A stubby finger, black on top, purple at the sides, pushed a thick envelope across the table, jerked back.

Jomo Iningwe opened the envelope, ran a thumb across the notes and put the envelope into his pocket.

'I should much prefer it if you counted the money.'

'You would not dare cheat me.'

'That is not the question!'

Jomo Iningwe smiled his pleasure at breaking the little man's cool. He'd have to watch out for him once the operation was over. 'Let's get on with it. Stop dragging your feet.'

The squat officer drew a deep breath, let it out slowly. He wanted to be quite composed, all his faculties trained on the handsome bastard's reactions, when he told him. 'The job we want you to do is in South Africa.'

Jomo Iningwe stood. His curls were an inch from the beams supporting the smoky ceiling. 'I have waited four weeks for you to raise the money. You have paid me for my time. I shall keep the money.'

'And not complete the operations?'

'Not start it. You cannot pay for my life.'

'You are afraid?'

'Heroism is a posthumous tense.'

'You are admitting to cowardice.'

143

'No. Only fools do not acknowledge the logic of fear and they are soon struck down for their folly.'

'The great Jomo Iningwe—'

'—is alive because he sees to his lines of retreat first. There are no lines of retreat from military action in the white man's South Africa.'

The black officer decided he had gone as far as he could, much as he was enjoying his sport, without losing the freelance terrorist to the night growing outside. 'At least give me a hearing. Sit down and I'll give you a glass of wine.'

'Very well. That much your money will buy you.' Jomo Iningwe sat again, took the glass handed him, sniffed, tasted and surprised the midnight man by identifying it correctly. 'Piesporter Goldtropchen seventy-one. Hardly to be expected in surroundings like these.'

'I brought it with me. The operation is not deep into South Africa. Do you—'

'Let me say that I will listen and drink your fine wine. But understand this: I live in Lourenço Marques. I like living in LM. I never work within the borders of Moçambique. Working in South Africa ... Moçambique is economically almost totally dependent on South Africa. If I were caught, at the very best they would deport me as an undesirable alien. More likely they would hand me over to the South Africans. I have already seen the inside of a South African gaol and have no desire to return.'

'I am empowered to offer you full citizenship of a powerful African nation.'

'I do not like Kampala. It is too provincial for my taste.'

'How did you know?'

'Colonel, you yourself are not unknown and I have eyes and ears everywhere. Besides, who else but the Ugandans would be mad enough to consider mounting an attack on South African soil?'

The black man poured wine to hide his thoughts. He did not like this irresponsible young man knowing his name and his rank and probably the name of his mistress. In this confusion of shame and fear the national insult passed unnoticed. 'I was also authorised to say that all groups enjoying our protection and hospitality would be encouraged to engage you as a fundraiser for them.'

'Kampala is starting to sound like a metropolis.'

'The operation will take place –'

'No, Colonel, first tell me the political motivation. You do not agree with it?'

The man was dangerously acute. It would be a mistake to dismiss him as a violent buffoon. 'I agree with neither its purpose nor the execution by a third party, but I follow my orders. The purpose is simple. It is to show the white South Africans that their policy of keeping Rhodesia and Moçambique as buffer states between their country and black Africa is no longer valid. To prove to them that defences are falling, as they have in Angola. A secondary purpose is to persuade them to start distrusting the Moçambique government, whom our non-military sources consider too close to the South Africans.'

'That's all crap, man! Naïveté of the worst kind. Kindergarten stuff.' Jomo Iningwe laughed aloud in his bitterness at the stupidity. 'But soldiers do not ask questions, they execute orders or they are executed. Speak on.'

The black officer spread his hands. He could not voice agreement with an outsider. 'The desire of the politicians is for an atrocity as close as possible to the meeting of the Organisation for African Unity, the OAU. Towards the end of this week would be a good time. It is not important where it happens, as long as it is on South African soil.'

'They're mad!' Jomo Iningwe held his glass out for more wine. He knew more was coming, his interest was aroused.

'I have worked out a plan. That is where the four weeks went. Also, somebody at home thought perhaps we should try to save your exorbitant fee by using our own resources. We –'

'You sent several groups of homegrown zealots and the best group never even made it to the Rhodesian border.'

'One group crossed the Rhodesian border. The Rhodesian police took them two miles inside the border.'

'A long way from South Africa. I am cheap at any price. You realise I made a compact with you to lead *your* men and you will still have to supply trained men?'

'Yes. The men are waiting for you in a boat on the Limpopo between Fumane and Chisselane.'

'*Jesu!*'

'They came in the boat from Dar es Salaam and up the Limpopo.'

'Trust a mad sergeant to think of the only workable plan.'

The silence was deadly. Jomo Iningwe raised his glass to his lips and lowered it again without drinking. 'Okay, okay! My apologies to General Amin. If you have the men on the spot, why do you still need me?'

'We do not wish a single regular soldier or officers of ours –'

'You're giving me irregular scum!' It was a feral scream.

'No. Trained men. Trained under my supervision, I may add. This project has been going on a year. We had a leader too, but his enthusiasm killed him –'

'Another hero!'

' – in the action I arranged for them to test themselves and to blood the few men unblooded when we received them. Their discipline is good. I do not think you will need be ashamed of them.'

'What is the target?'

'A safari with a base on the Limpopo next to the Kruger National Park. There will be foreigners there. It is important that the story makes the international papers.'

'Men, women and children?'

'Yes. The men have been told there will be white women.' The British-trained officer lowered his head in disgust. 'You must kill all the servants as well: real terrorists would consider them tainted by their masters.'

'Real terrorists would also not be competent against even men with hunting rifles. Real terrorists would leave a lot of their own men lying dead behind them.'

'You will see to that as you leave. The South Africans will

not be able to identify the dead men by either their clothes or their arms.'

'Your hypocrisy sickens me.'

The squat man went on as if he had not heard. 'You will take the boat up the Limpopo at night. The base camp is a mile from the river. They will not hear you when you pass and if they do, it does not matter. Upriver from the base camp you will land and lead your men on foot to the safari base camp. You will attack at dawn. Afterwards you will return to the river and take the boat, which is a planing type capable of forty knots, down the river. Once in Moçambique territory men will get off the boat and make their way overland. This will happen at random intervals but the men will see to it. You will go first, just this side of the border, right after you pass Pafuri. That way you will have the longest walk but there will be less chance of you being caught.'

'And you don't want it known you hired a nigger mercenary to do your dirty work for you, is that it?'

'We take precautions. We try to plan for all eventualities.'

'How many people in the target group?'

'Eight whites. Thirty or forty servants.'

'Armament?'

'None except sporting rifles. I should say they use mostly cameras for their hunting.'

'I would send a sergeant and a brace of men with a mortar.'

'So would I if I had a choice. But that may look like the South African Army had an unfortunate training accident.'

'The South African Army does not have unfortunate training accidents or your ambitious General would have ruled from Pretoria a long time ago.'

The British-trained black officer deliberately ignored his guest's empty glass to pour the last of the wine into his own.

'The South Africans will not hesitate to follow us into Moçambique if they were hot on our heels.'

'True. But you should have at least a four or five hour start. By then it will be too late for them to search.'

'Do the men know who's to lead them?'

147

'They have been told to expect a tall light skinned man, no more. Will you do it?'

Jomo Iningwe stood. He put his empty glass on the table. He spoke reflectively. 'I must go now. I have women to love, white women.'

'When will you do it?'

'Read about it in the papers.'

TUESDAY

One

'Another day, another hunt,' Chris Decker said cheerfully, studying with professional care the light climbing hand over hand over the eastern horizon. 'Another hot sunshiny day.'

'Felt okay to me yesterday,' Cameron mumbled through a mouth full of egg and sausage. 'Was my hangover made me sweat, not the heat.' Both he and Pascoe had drunk more circumspectly at dinner the night before, preparing themselves for an early start to a long day. Today both were in long sleeved shirts but Minowara, who never seemed to be hot, was wearing a suede shooting jacket over a white shirt and a dark tie.

Pascoe grunted his assent, put his plate down on the wide veranda rail. 'I'll go fetch me guns.' He was at the bottom of the veranda steps when Curtis Bill Bonham broke the silence.

'Omo hunts today.'

Pascoe turned with his mouth open. 'Huh?'

'Omo hunts today,' Curtis Bill repeated.

'But – But – ' Pascoe swallowed. 'See here, I haven't had the sport I paid for. That – yesterday – shooting that nigger was an accident!'

'You had your turn, Sport,' Chris Decker said. 'We undertake only to find you a nigger and help you chase him. If you shot the fine healthy nigger we found you before you meant to, that's too bad. We found him, you killed him. That's it!'

'Hey, please!' Pascoe swallowed again. 'There are only three hunters down here and we got six days. Doesn't that mean two days per hunter?'

151

'Chris is right,' Curtis Bill said. 'The spare days are for the odd occasion when we don't find a suitable black to hunt.' He paused for the briefest moment. 'But this time we'll make an exception. You can have another turn.'

'Gee, thanks!' In the halflight it was easy to believe Billy Bunter had inherited the deceased boy's tucker box. Pascoe turned away towards his *rondawel*.

Curtis Bill's voice stopped him. 'When everyone else has had his hunt.'

Pascoe turned, the hurt of disappointment on his face.

'That's only fair,' Curtis Bill added. 'Your extra hunt is a favour. We've found you one black and let you kill him. Anything extra is a bonus and won't cost you a cent.'

'What Curtis Bill means is we're doing you a favour. Giving you something for free. So we don't want to hear any impatient whingeing if it takes a while. And once we get around to it we don't want to hear any crap about the nigger being this or the nigger being that. You understand?'

Pascoe stared at the pilot with hatred on his face and in his swollen eyes for a long moment before he nodded dumbly and turned away to stumble towards his *rondawel*.

'I wouldn't underrate him,' Cameron said easily.

'Oh shit, don't you start on me too,' Decker snapped. Then his face split in a smile. 'Look, even if your assessment is right, this isn't some London laboratory or board room, this is Africa. It's my backyard.'

Cameron nodded. 'If you say so. I'll go fetch a rifle.'

Decker stopped Cameron at the bottom of the steps and Minowara, following Cameron, stopped too. 'They got a description for guys like that at flight training schools. Too stupid to be frightened. Those who get that label stuck on them don't live too long.'

'Just don't you ever tangle with him in a London board room or laboratory,' Cameron laughed. He went off towards the *rondawels* with Minowara.

'That was unnecessary,' Curtis Bill said when they were out of earshot.

'So what?' Decker turned away and walked briskly down

152

the steps and across the airfield to where the Bantu were uncovering the helicopter petal by petal from underneath its tarpaulin blanket.

Curtis Bill Bonham stared after him for a few paces, then turned on his heel to fetch another mug of coffee. He was beginning to regret his decision to promise Pascoe another turn.

'What arrangements have you made for the body of the man I will kill?'

Decker had angled the helicopter north-west, into the grasslands of Rhodesia, and they were ten minutes across the Limpopo with the sun rising a red ball on their right. For a long while none of them looked at Minowara, searching for an acceptable angle in his question.

'What arrangements do you have in mind?' Curtis Bill Bonham finally asked.

'Cremation, burial, some kind of honourable treatment.'

'Christ, they're only niggers!' Cameron exclaimed hotly.

'Digging holes for *muntu*!' Decker laughed. 'Not on your nellie.'

'I would treat any man I killed with equal respect and honour,' Minowara said stiffly.

'You'd treat a white man same as a blackfeller?' Pascoe couldn't believe his ears.

'I would give any man I killed the regard I would expect for myself,' Minowara insisted.

'That sounds like nigger loving talk to me,' Cameron said softly, insinuatingly, the intercom system adding its own sinister note to his words. 'I am disappointed in you, Omo.'

Curtis Bill started, 'We have –' but Decker cut him short.

'Are you saying you'll hunt a white man like we hunt niggers?' He was as incredulous as Pascoe.

'Of course not!' Cameron snapped deprecatingly.

'Let Omo answer for himself!'

The Japanese had been politely silent when Cameron expressed his opinion. Now he said, 'I am afraid that I see no difference between hunting white men or black men or brown men or yellow men or red men.'

'In that case, why don't we make the coolie run for it?' Pascoe asked and turned around to indicate Vincent with a pointed finger so that there could be no misunderstanding. He resented the Indian's presumption in photographing him while he vomited.

'No,' Curtis Bill Bonham said decisively.

'Who's going to take the pictures for you to catch your subsequent cheapies by if you knock off the photographer?' Decker asked rhetorically.

'All of that's irrelevant,' Cameron admonished them sharply. He turned to the Japanese beside him. 'Let's get this clear. You'll kill a white man same as you would a nigger?'

'Yes. A man is a man, especially when he is dead. You seem to be saying a white man differs from all other men in that he should only be shot in unpremeditated anger.'

'Damn right! You can't go around shooting white men for sport.'

'For what, for which reasons do you think one may shoot a white man then?' Minowara asked politely.

'Well, for something serious. Sleeping with your wife. Something serious like that. Like you said yourself, for provocation, in anger. But not for sport.'

'I'd shoot some of the people on the roads who endanger my children with their driving,' Pascoe said and was surprised and then pleased when they laughed, even Cameron joining in.

'But an insult to your honour, a man soiling your wife for example, is an insult regardless of the colour of his skin. For such a dishonour you would react against a white man as you would against any other man, would you not?'

Cameron laughed. 'Yes, but that's an isolated case. You're trying to make the exception prove the rule. And, anyway, I wouldn't react the same way. I'd teach a nigger who fucked around with my wife a lot slower than a white man caught *in flagrante.*'

The discussion seemed to have run its course and after a

154

moment of silence Curtis Bill said, 'Fires for cremation use a lot of wood and make a lot of smoke which can be seen at distances. It would defeat the purpose of our continuous low flying. We carry no shovel for digging holes –'

' – and if we did we would not want to stand at the spot where you killed your nigger for long enough to dig a hole. Let the hyenas feed, I say. They like nigger flesh. Black breakfast,' the pilot answered from the front of the helicopter. 'And we can't carry the body back for cremation at the base camp either because you can't carry corpses across borders without a permit. It would be illegal.' He chuckled joyfully at his own joke and Cameron and Pascoe joined him in the irony of it.

'I'm afraid I must rule against what you have in mind,' Curtis Bill said to the Japanese financier when he could again be heard over the intercom, 'because it would be dangerous to the safety of all of us here.'

Minowara nodded his understanding but it was clear even to the insensitive non-Japanese that he was not satisfied, that he felt he had lost face by being questioned about his motives, by having his reasonable request mockingly refused. In the silence Chris Decker sang softly into his throat microphone:

> *The hunters came over the river*
> *with the intention of killing a nigger*
> *but they'll never bury him*
> *they'll never burn him*

stretching the words to fit *Bonnie Prince Charlie*. Pascoe sniggered. Cameron said:

'If we keep going this way we'll get to the Lion and Elephant Motel just in time for a quick drink before lunch.'

'Been looking at your map again, Yank?'

Cameron laughed. Somehow, there existed between him and Decker a bond which caused Decker's snide cruelty to bounce harmlessly from him: it was Cameron's complete ownership of the delectable Melody. 'God bless the US Army Topographical Command.'

'It helps the Yankees find the way home.' Decker turned the helicopter eastward.

'There's cultivated land ahead,' Pascoe said. 'People.'

'We're flying around the maize patches,' Curtis Bill explained. 'Only the women and children work them. Near the *kraal* is where we'll find the men. Men hunt or fight or tend cattle, they never perform agricultural tasks.'

'The complete male chauvinist society,' Decker said, adding casually, 'What about that nigger over there?' He turned the helicopter so that it was side on to the black man and they could all see. They looked at the man in silence. The black man stopped and looked up at them. He was of medium height and sturdily built. He carried the standard shield and short throwing spear. The shield was of a dull blue-grey colour and shone sinisterly in the morning light. His loincloth, even at this distance, could clearly be seen to have the spots of the tiger. Likewise the curious expression on his flat nosed broad face was clearly visible to the hunters.

'He looks fit to me,' Cameron offered his opinion.

'And not accident prone at all,' Pascoe added but nobody laughed.

Minowara asked, 'What is the shield?'

'*Blou wildebeest*. Cape buffalo. Very dangerous. A shield of the skin probably means he was in a hunting party that killed one. The loincloth of tigerskin definitely means he has killed a tiger singlehanded,' Curtis Bill answered. 'He is a fine specimen of a warrior.'

'I'll take him.'

'A good choice,' the pilot said. 'We're not likely to find finer today.' He sent the helicopter in a circle around the black man, who turned to keep it in sight. 'You want to give Omo the travelogue, Curtis Bill?'

'This will be the first time we have hunted near this village for a year or more. These people do not have an ethic of pitting themselves against superior enemies like yesterday's black man. So he's going to run from fear, not for the reason of trying to prove something. The best –'

'In my personal opinion it makes for better hunting,'

Decker interrupted his partner. 'Especially when we can find a specimen as good as this one.'

The Indian photographer licked his lips. Vincent couldn't agree more: the purpose of the hunt was not to provide some insolent nigger with a challenge to pit his prowess against but to make him run with fear until he shat himself and lay down begging for mercy. And then to make him run dribbling down his legs until his heart gave out or the sport lost its spice and then to wing him to make him run once more until you killed him at dusk.

'The best way to start,' Curtis Bill continued, 'if you want an opinion of course . . .'

'No, please Curtis Bill, your opinion is of the highest value.' Minowara did not dribble like Pascoe, but his voice became sibilant and he had great trouble pronouncing his *r*. His constraint in letting only so much of his excitement declare itself in his manner was observed and approved by Curtis Bill Bonham and Chris Decker, both experts and connoisseurs of men in the grip of bloodlust, of men taken by the impending power of killing another man.

'If you were to bracket him with a few shots.'

Minowara studied the black man's unsmiling countenance carefully while the camera whirred over his head. He bowed to each of his bulky companions in turn, then to the black man who stood uncomprehendingly below him. 'I am Omo Minowara whose lineage is too ancient to enumerate,' he said in English, softly inside his head but the throat mike amplified his words for the ears of the barbarians he shared the helicopter with. 'Be assured though that it is an ancestry of the utmost honour.'

'Huh?' Pascoe's mouth was open again and Cameron looked curiously at the Japanese financier.

'I'll take her back now to give you a bit of a spread,' Chris Decker said.

'Japanese custom,' Minowara explained without letting the indulgence of condescension creep into his tone. 'Before doing battle, one states one's lineage. One cannot fight another whose ancestry is not honourable.'

'Bless me!' Pascoe exclaimed. 'How do you know this isn't a dirt common nigger like all niggers?'

Chris Decker sighed at the tactlessness. Curtis Bill lied, 'The shield. Only the chiefs and the sons of chiefs are allowed to hunt *blou wildebeest* and to carry the shields made from their skins.'

The helicopter steadied. 'Right, I'll hold her here until you give the word. Hundred yards. No wind.'

'Thank you,' Minowara answered gravely. 'Perhaps you gentlemen would like to join me for the opening shots.' They nodded their eager acceptance and checked their rifles.

'Not too near him, if you please,' Curtis Bill said. 'We don't know yet whether he'll run straight or zigzag or which way he'll turn.'

'That means you, Pascoe-limey, and you, Cameron-yank,' Decker added. Pascoe turned around to look at him venomously but Cameron chuckled. 'Don't kill Omo-san's nigger by accident.'

The black man still stood and watched the strange behaviour of the helicopter which had inspected him so closely and now backed off to hover at a distance, dead still in the sky, only the whirring sound of the rotor creating an illusion of movement. When he saw the men on the doorsill of the machine raise their rifles to aim at him an expression of pained disbelief crossed his flat features. He half raised his shield either for protection or in recrimination, then lowered it to stare dumbfounded at the helicopter. After a moment he looked around for a bolthole but the grass rolled in all directions with no bulge of anthill or depression of foxhole or rabbit hutch. He looked up to see the guns still aiming at him and seemed to shrink into himself, his shoulders sinking six inches into the grass.

'That's right, nigger, start sweating,' Pascoe murmured.

'Ready when you are,' Cameron said to Minowara. Pascoe grunted.

Omo Minowara savoured the moment an eternal second longer and squeezed the trigger gently. The bullet threw up dust and seeds and pollen from the grass three feet to the left of the black man. Enoch Pascoe made a minuscule alternation with the joy button on his telescopic sight and placed his heavier bullet in the same spot where Minowara's bullet had struck. Cameron fired and his bullet struck three feet to the right of the incredulous black statue with the shouting face, sending up a similar display of earth and plant matter. Pascoe made another minute adjustment and repeated his fine show of marksmanship by placing his second bullet on top of Cameron's. He was determined to shame the stigma of his accident yesterday by conclusive proof of his competence.

'That's what I call one upmanship,' Decker exclaimed with genuine admiration.

Pascoe said, 'I have to reload.'

Minowara said to Cameron, 'Right?'

Cameron replied, 'Me right, you left.'

When they had emptied their magazines in a neat row of whirlwinds in the grass on either side of the black man, Minowara bowed to the men on the lip of the helicopter beside him. 'Thank you very much, gentlemen. Fine shooting, Enoch.' Pascoe looked a little put out at this clear indication that he was not to fire again but dutifully put his gun up. Curtis Bill leant forward and gently pushed the rifle down across Pascoe's knees so that the barrel pointed past the nose of the helicopter rather than at the rotor blades overhead.

The black man raised his head from his shoulders and looked left and right of him where the bullets had left the grass waving. It was obvious the men in the helicopter had shot to miss. The range was too short to miss with so many bullets. And all the bullets had been precisely placed. The men in the machine were mocking him. He raised his shield above his head, shouted the warcry of his tribe in defiance and charged the men who denigrated him from the safety of their machine.

They watched him coming, his mouth open in screamed defiance, his shield whirling above his head like a badge of pride, his bare feet pounding the earth violently so that they could imagine they felt the shaking of the ground, his *assegai* raised over his shoulder in readiness for the cast which would take at least one of the mockers to his ancestors with him before the others plumbed his measure and hurriedly, fearfully killed him with their guns.

'We have finished shooting,' Minowara said calmly, his fingers not hurrying over the loading of his rifle.

'A good one, I think,' Decker opined.

'Can you hold us till he's about fifty yards away, Chris, and then take us straight up?' Curtis Bill asked without taking his eyes from the running black man.

'Sure.'

Curtis Bill suggested, 'If he could see you laughing, if you could anger him enough to hunt us ...'

Minowara nodded his understanding. Pascoe spluttered, 'I thought the idea was to hunt niggers, not let niggers hunt you.'

Cameron whispered angrily, 'Me too. What's this?'

'It is Omo's hunt. He decides,' the pilot said sharply from the controls. 'You two just shut up.'

'If we let him think he's hunting us, we can lead him away from the huts, which are just over the ridge we crossed two or three miles back —'

'Too damned near for comfort.' Decker.

Curtis Bill continued his explanation. 'We can keep him in the open country, lead him deeper into the savanna. At the same time we're tiring him out for when we turn on him and start hunting him.'

'Oh.' Cameron offered no apology and Pascoe just grunted.

Decker had kept the helicopter dancing backwards to keep fifty yards between it and the black man while the argument was going on. He grunted his disgust at the wasted time.

Minowara smiled at the black man and, after a minute's doubt, Cameron and Pascoe began laughing open mouthed and loudly at him. Decker turned the intercom off. The black man saw their laughter and knew they scorned his manhood on purpose. He quickened his pace and gained on them when Decker held the machine steady. When the black man was forty yards from the hovering helicopter and his arm was already moving backwards one last inch for extra tension in

160

the cast of his *assegai*, Decker took the machine straight up. The *assegai* passed where the helicopter had been seconds before, but the machine had meanwhile ascended twenty feet. The black man danced his rage in the veld under the machine, shaking his shield and his fist at the men disparaging him from their coward's height, inviting them to come down and prove they were men, not mongrel breeds out of asses' arseholes by hyenas. His antics inflamed Cameron and Pascoe's humour, spurred them on to greater laughter. Cameron gathered the spit in his mouth and let fly at the black man on the ground but the thrust of the air blew most of the spittle back into his face and into the body of the helicopter to spray Vincent and Curtis Bill liberally.

Minowara looked over his shoulder to see if Vincent was distracted but Vincent did not even bother to wipe the spittle from his face, though he checked to see that the lens was clear before leaning out to take more footage of the enraged black man hurling the thunderbolts of his libidinous anger skyward at them. Decker switched the intercom on again.

'When he tries to recover the *assegai* I should like to place some shots between him and it,' Minowara said calmly.

'Just say when and I'll hold her still.'

'Thank you.'

The black man on the ground saw his righteous insults have no effect on his enemies other than to enliven their amusement at a safe distance from his wrath and decided he was wasting his energy. He headed for his *assegai* at his usual pace in the veld, a steady trot.

'Now, if you please.'

'Wait, I'll tilt her for you.'

The man on the ground saw the earth spurt in front of him and knew his enemies in the sky had not forgotten him. He stopped and looked up at them: they were fools to mock him when they should kill him. If they were ever to come this way on land, their faces would be printed on his memory like the white man's books. The machine above him was tilted at a crazy angle and he wondered if the white men were glued to the machine by the seats of their trousers but then his sharp

161

eyes discerned the belts holding them in. Another shot spurted and he walked one step forward. Another shot, this time nearer to him but not too much. Another step. He could not leave his *assegai*, that shame was reserved for children. Another shot. His hand reached out for the *assegai* and a shot spurted an inch from the flintstone head. Involuntarily he jerked his hand away.

'Don't destroy the *assegai*,' Curtis Bill warned calmly. 'Without it he will be unarmed and it will all be over, in his mind at least, but he will not run.'

'I understand.'

The black man on the ground snatched up the *assegai* and held it triumphantly over his head. These people did not have the stomach for killing a real man, he knew now. They were shooting at him from their fine machine for sport, because they were too stupid to see the *spoor* of the animals fleeing his hunting prowess in the direction of the Gona-Re-Zhou Game Reserve far in the north-east. They had already interrupted his hunt, so he would pass the time by teasing them as they had mocked him and perhaps he could lure them near enough to kill one of them. Killing a white man would not be as good as killing a Zulu or even hunting a *blou wildebeest* but the helicopter made up for the deficiency to a certain extent. It would be about on a par with killing a Tsonga, cousin to the Zulu, he decided after a moment of thought. An endevour worthy of his time . . .

'What's the nigger doing, just standing there?' Cameron demanded to know, the laughter stilled in his throat.

Decker said, 'Omo knows.'

'I can guess,' Minowara replied modestly. 'He is thinking that we do not have the strength of character to kill him. He is considering ways and means of leading us into a trap so that he can kill us.'

'Hmm,' Cameron murmured with some admiration.

'You know exactly how that nigger thinks!' Pascoe's tone mixed accusation of complicity with an equal amount of incredulous admiration for such insight.

'The hunter and the hunted are but two sides of the same

coin,' Minowara said in a kindly voice, his attention on the black man, his momentary lapse into condescension unnoticed by Cameron and Pascoe.

'Tibullus,' Pascoe said. 'That is a quotation from Tibullus, the Roman poet of the Augustan period.' Into the startled silence he added, 'I learnt that on my scholarship at Manchester Grammar School.'

'Jesus!' Cameron exclaimed. 'Now he tells us!'

'Congratulations,' Decker whispered, too distracted to sneer with his voice as well as the word.

'Perhaps if we could go down to about twenty feet and stay just out of casting range of his *assegai*,' the Japanese suggested. 'Unless there is a better way ... '

'No, that's fine. Here goes. Wheee!' Decker dropped the helicopter straight down with a sickening lurch, straightened it thirty feet above the black man's head and took it down to twenty feet in a shallow dive that ended fifty yards from the black man and in front of him before he could do more than raise his shield reflexively or lift his *assegai* to the level of his elbow. Curtis Bill Bonham drew his breath in sharply but said nothing: Chris Decker was getting very irresponsible, taking risks with all their lives, excellent pilot or not.

'A warrior can cast the *assegai* up to forty yards,' Curtis Bill said as Decker let the black man get to within forty yards before sending the helicopter crabbing along the grass, seemingly supported only by its shadow. Ostensibly the words were directed to their clients, but the intent was to warn Chris Decker that he had noticed the pilot's lapses. 'About six months ago a black man brought us down with an *assegai*.'

'A helicopter? With a spear? He brought you down with a spear? A nigger brought you down with a spear?' Cameron couldn't, wouldn't believe his ears.

'Certainly. As Chris has told you, this is a dangerous business. A lucky cast perhaps, I'll admit that, but it still nearly cost six of us our lives.'

'And I beat the shit out of the guy who let it happen.'

Pascoe and Cameron looked at the black man loping easily after the helicopter with fresh calculation in their eyes.

Minowara's Japanese countenance remained expressionlessly Japanese.

'A nigger like that?' Pascoe asked.

'Yes. A fine specimen like that.' Curtis Bill had lost interest in the subject. Chris Decker was now keeping a good fifty-five yards between the helicopter and the black man, well out of casting range but not far enough to discourage the black man.

'The Texas dentist who recommended me did say it was dangerous, but I didn't think a black man could bring down a chopper with just an *assegai*.' Then Cameron's high spirits returned. 'Mother, I want you! The niggers are closing in with spears on my helicopter and my plastic duck!'

'You're still alive and I bet that nigger ain't,' Pascoe summed up the crux of the matter.

Minowara asked, 'How long do we let my black man follow us?'

'Depends on the fuel situation. Another ten, fifteen minutes. Then we go refuel.'

'We will find him again?' Minowara had to fight not to let his concern show in his tone.

'Sure. He won't hide or try to get away. He's going to think he scared us off or we lost interest.'

Cameron said, 'Boy, is that nigger going to be one surprised motherfucker when we come back and start teaching him for real.'

'Teach him real good, eh, Bob? Teach him not to presume to hunt white men.'

'Too right, Enoch.'

'This thing sure burns fuel like it's halfbrother to an Ay-rab,' Cameron said as he and Minowara turned another hot forty-four gallon drum on its side with brief concerted shoves of their hands. 'And these drums are heavy! Why don't you go sit in the shade and I'll move this one. Younger men have strokes in this heat. Why, I'm half your age and I feel it.'

Minowara looked around. The others had not heard. Cameron had lowered his voice to its professional level. The

American doctor probably meant well. 'I am used to heat in baths, Bob,' he said. 'Thank you for your concern. I shall be as careful as is possible.'

Cameron nodded. They both knew what the Japanese financier meant: once you start hunting you cannot stop to rest or you may lose your prey. Worse, your weakness would lose you the respect of your hunting companions. 'You had a checkup recently?'

Minowara waited to answer until they were rolling the empty drum away to lay it neatly on its side against the other empty drums – the pilot had explained that upright or stacked drums provide ideal hiding places for your enemies but not drums laid down end to end like a pipeline. They rolled the drum forward with their feet, standing upright and goosestepping the empty weight onwards. 'Every six months. I am fit for a man of my age.'

'You understand the qualification?'

'Yes. Not to strain the heart or other vital organs.'

'Good.' Cameron dropped the subject, satisfied that the Japanese knew what he was doing.

'Stop dawdling, you silly motherfuckers,' Decker called to them. 'This isn't a picnic.' The helicopter had been refuelled and they took off as soon as everybody was strapped in, which didn't take long because they wore the harness permanently and only had to clip it in at two points, much like a safety belt in a car. 'Air to air, four minutes fifty-eight seconds,' Decker said with satisfaction.

'So what are you squealing about?'

'Because, if you'd dawdled two seconds longer, we would have gone over five minutes and that's no good.'

'Next time we'll do it in four minutes fifty.'

'Nope. Don't bother. Too much of a strain. Christ, it's a hundred and twelve degrees Fahrenheit inside here in the shade. I'd hate to think what it is out there.' He let them all look out over and into the heat shimmering on the grass. 'Five minutes even is quite an achievement, actually.'

The black man had found the *spoor* he had been tracking earlier when the ignorant white men had interrupted his hunting. But he had only been loping along it for a short while, a handspan and perhaps two fingers of the sun's movement, when he heard the return of their machine. They had come back to redeem their shame at their cowardice, he hoped without hope. Whites, the ones he had met at the mission house, had no concept of manhood, even rejected the will of the ancestors. They were men only by courtesy of having an appendage between their legs. Even so, perhaps he could tease them into providing him with a little excitement, even revenge for their earlier mockery. He knew they would not kill him with their guns because, if that was their purpose, they would have shot to kill when they first found him. To his disappointment, the helicopter came to within a short run from him, then turned away sharply. The white men had not come back to him after all or, if they had seen him, decided he was of no interest. He turned back to the *spoor* and was surprised to hear the sound of the helicopter come nearer again. When he looked up it was hovering in front of him and the men in the belly were laughing and pointing evil fingers at him.

'Square search. Courtesy of the Royal Canadian Air Force. Never fails to find your man.' Decker's five-year-old joke caused uproarious laughter from Pascoe and Cameron.

'What do you want to do now, Omo?' Curtis Bill asked.

'What alternatives are there?'

'You can shoot him, you can start hunting him, you can let him hunt us.'

'What do you suggest?'

'We have all day. Let him hunt us until he decides he's not going to catch us. At that time he will turn away towards water and you can head him off.'

'Ah!' Minowara's satisfaction was evident. 'Yes, let us do that. He carries no water?'

'No. He lives off the land. His fieldcraft is likely to be superior.'

It was the wrong choice of word. Pascoe grunted his disbelief and Cameron explained that the intelligence of a black man was of necessity lower than that of a white man; there-

166

fore the superior fieldcraft of black men was not really superior but only instinctive.

The black man hunted the machine with no clear plan at first. He had noticed that it moved backwards and sideways when he approached. He knew a man controlled it as a man had controlled the similar machine which had come from the white man's hospital to fetch the second wife of his cousin who couldn't get the child out of her belly. But this man was obviously far superior to the other one: he made his machine move with beautiful smoothness, very unlike the jerking and twitching thing it had been in the hands of the man from the hospital. If it moved backwards and sideways each time he approached, the black man reasoned, surely the man giving it its orders must be watching him, as were all the other men and the evil eye of a particularly large machine of the type that stole your image if you were not quick and showed it your back. Therefore, if their rear was unwatched, perhaps he could drive it into something. It would come down and he would deal with the white men one by one on equal footing, their guns notwithstanding, and his name would go from mouth to mouth beside campfires for generations of strong men to come. But finding something to drive it into ... The trees were stunted and far apart and the machine flew at least a man's height and possibly twice a man's height above the highest tree. Then he remembered a particularly deep set of *dongas*, deep gouges cut in the earth by stormwaters. Aah! If they should be pushed into the *dongas*, the whirling circle would catch and they would come down. Perhaps they would prefer to stay above the *dongas* but then he would taunt them. White men did not like being taunted by black men. They would come down to attempt to punish him and they would be at his mercy. He calculated. An hour and a half since they had come back, another hour and a half to the *dongas*. By then it would be noon. In the *dongas* lived *dassies*, stone squirrels. He would pluck a few squealing from their holes, tear them open, eat the livers raw and fresh and still pulsing; the delicacy alone would be worth going to the *dongas* for.

167

'Time to refuel again.'

'That nigger's sweating now,' Pascoe observed with astringent satisfaction.

'It's hard work chasing a chopper,' Decker observed.

At the burnt circle which was the fuel depot, Cameron suggested, 'Let Omo stay in the chopper. Keeps the hunter cool.'

'I'm perfectly willing to do my share,' Minowara protested.

'I'm only thinking of myself. When it is my turn to hunt, I don't want to be hot and bothered with hauling heavy drums around. I want to be cool and collected.'

'Good idea,' Pascoe said. 'We don't want any more accidents.'

'Let's do that then,' Cameron said. Tomorrow he would find another pretext to keep the old man out of the heat. He, himself, and Pascoe, thirty and twenty years younger respectively, were blowing like whales in the sun, much to the amusement of the pilot who, like Curtis Bill, sweated little and breathed normally. Each breath seared their lungs with furnace blown air. 'Can you turn on the fan to keep the workers cool?' He pointed at the rotor overhead.

'Sorry, no. Against safety procedure to run the engine while refuelling. And I can't think of any worse death than by burning.'

'Yeah. Forget I ever asked a stupid question.'

The black man had been a little sorry but not surprised to see the helicopter go. He was not surprised at all when it returned. Like the white man's trucks, it probably had to be fed liquid out of a drum every now and again or it would refuse to work. He had never been able to understand the logic of keeping an animal of flesh or metal that could not carry its own food in addition to the man on its back, especially when the animal was obviously unsuited to eat grass or meat. He started herding the helicopter towards the *dongas* by simply running straight at it and having it back off.

'That nigger ran in a straight line since we left him twenty-five minutes ago,' Chris Decker said. 'What do you think, Omo?'

'He is perhaps going some specific place. We can find out

by changing our direction and seeing if he tries to herd us back.'

Decker took the helicopter forward at a right angle to the black man's path and, true to Minowara's prediction, the black man changed direction so that, if they retreated backwards and away from him as they had been doing, they would be going in the same general direction as before.

Curtis Bill said, 'There are no towns or settlements that way.'

'Perhaps some natural formation he hopes to corner us against?' the Japanese suggested tentatively.

The pilot answered him. 'Nothing higher than these stunted trees for two days of travel at his speed.'

'Well, let's hurry him up!' Pascoe was getting impatient.

'Or we could make it difficult for him,' Cameron suggested.

'I wouldn't mind seeing where he's leading us,' Chris Decker said. 'I know this area pretty well ...'

'Could you take us up parallel to him, Chris?'

The black man changed direction when he saw the helicopter move aside, intending to herd it back but it went too far and he resumed course for the *dongas*. If the white men did not follow him he could at least have a meal. He was gratified when the helicopter stayed with him. When the shots started biting into the ground behind him, snapping clods of earth against the skin of his calves, he was incredulous: a fractional error of judgement could kill him. Involuntarily he ran faster and this seemed to be the intention of the men in the machine for the shots stopped. He was content to keep up the pace for soon they would be at the *dongas* and then the tables would be turned. They shot at him once more when he was only three fingers of the sun from the *dongas* and he quickened his pace again. But then they turned away southward and he was disappointed.

'That nigger should be dead on his feet,' Enoch Pascoe said as they returned from refuelling the helicopter.

'He's like a professional athlete. He trains all day, every day,' Decker said. 'He works with his body like you work with your mind. He's probably just starting to tire.'

169

Omo Minowara leant forward to take the measure of the sameness of the vast country. He searched the horizon for a sign of his prey, consulted his watch. 'Hundred and twelve miles per hour?'

Decker knew what he meant. 'Yes. We should find him in another minute.'

A minute crept around with the second hand. Vincent intuitively caught the tension of the moment on film by starting the camera rolling a second before all three men in front of and below him lifted their arms to consult their watches, one movement as if choreographed eagerness for blood was the theme of a sky ballet. Satisfied that a minute had passed, all three heads lifted over their watches to search the grass and trees. The black man had gone, disappeared without a trace. Not a blade of grass stirred, not a leaf waved except it fitted the symmetric patterns generated by the passing of the helicopter.

'I'll take her up to fifty feet.'

'No! Forward in the same line, if you please, Chris.'

'You think he kept that pace?'

Before Minowara could answer the pilot's question, Pascoe asked, 'Are you sure we're at the right place? This all looks the same to me.'

Everybody ignored the English inventor. Curtis Bill looked at his watch and said, 'Two minutes. Then we'll do a square search. Okay, Chris?'

'He could be hiding in a tree,' Cameron suggested.

'Ten to one,' Pascoe said, 'the nigger just got frightened.'

'I'll take a hundred pounds on that,' Decker said as they skimmed over the treetops.

'And I a thousand,' Minowara said.

Pascoe gulped at the ten thousand pound risk Minowara offered him. The intercom magnified the sound. It could only have one source.

'I'll take all bets half and half with Enoch,' Cameron said. 'I think those last shots Omo put up his arsehole frightened the shit out of him.'

170

'Thanks,' Pascoe said and then he spotted the *dongas* underneath them. 'What's that?'

'The end of the line,' Cameron said. 'Our money's safe. The nigger couldn't have crossed these erosions in time. He's back there in a tree.'

'What are those grey bits against the brown?' the Japanese asked.

'*Dassies*,' Curtis Bill told him. 'Rock squirrels. Your black man passed here, paused here, had time to catch them.'

'What did he do to them?' Pascoe asked, fascinated. 'Tear them open with his bare hands?'

'Yes. He ate their livers.'

'Fucking savage.' Cameron.

Pascoe gulped. 'Raw?'

'Yip. The idea is to tear them open live and rip the liver out and get it in your mouth before it can tighten up. It's like eating oysters,' the pilot informed him.

'Goddamn niggers got no culture,' Cameron elucidated.

'He cannot be far. The blood has not dried yet,' Minowara observed. He was thrilling to the hunt, despite Cameron's earlier oblique warning about straining his heart with excitement.

'These are the *dongas* he was leading us to,' Chris Decker added. 'They weren't here the last time we came by here. They were washed into the earth by the storm rains of the last year. A year ago there was only a cattle path here.'

Cameron whistled. The ravages the water had wrought on the earth spread two hundred feet wide and thirty and forty feet deep in tortuous searching fingers of bare soil and rock. What could be carried away the water had carried away. It was as if a giant hand had scooped out a handful of soil.

'Next year it will be gone, grown over,' Curtis Bill said. 'Your black man is in there somewhere.'

'You'll have to get out and get him on foot,' Pascoe said.

'Nobody gets out of the helicopter until we get back to base camp,' Decker said succinctly. 'It's our first rule.'

The way the black man had found food in this dangerously bland nothing impressed Omo Minowara. Hunting a com-

171

petent man, a survivor, was more exciting than hunting a bumbler. He wondered whether his age would be sufficient excuse for contesting a decision by the safari leaders, whether he would succeed in a demand to be set down so that he could hunt the black man. And kill him or be killed. It would be a fitting end . . .

'Can you go down?' Cameron asked. 'It is wide enough.'

'No,' Curtis Bill answered before the pilot could have a chance to consider it. 'He could be hiding under an overhang and so be able to cast his *assegai* or a rock into the rotor from above. It won't be necessary, anyway. He won't stay there in hiding for the same reason he didn't try to hide in a tree. He wants to get us, destroy us for teasing and mocking him.' He barely stopped himself from adding, *Like the baboons Chris kills with their own greed for the sensation of knowledge.* 'To attack us he must show himself. All we have to do is wait.'

Omo Minowara was glad he had considered slowly. He would have lost face intolerably if he had demanded or even requested to be set down only to be met with such logical exposition and consequent denial.

'And there's no water down there,' Decker added.

Minowara said, 'He drank the blood of the rodent animals.'

'*Dassies.* Sure. But blood's full of salt. His thirst won't be stilled for long.' Decker ran the helicopter the length of the *dongas.* 'I suggest we wait over there, about a hundred yards away. Make him come to us. He's seen us by now and he'll be able to hear us clearly.'

'Very well,' Minowara said and Decker complied.

The black man rested at full length in the shade behind a rock, watching the machine go by, the wind- and sunburnt faces seeming to stare straight at him but not seeing him, he knew, for there were no shots. He knew now that the persistent white men meant to kill him when they had their sport of him. But first they would do what he did with animals when he hunted for sport: make him run. And when he was too tired to run any further they would kill him like a dog, from a distance, never giving him a chance to stand and fight like a man. He was no coward and he had scars and a tigerskin

172

loincloth and a *blou wildebeest* shield to prove his valour but neither was he foolhardy. To allow white men to kill you for sport when you knew your death would be unavenged would be foolhardy and stupid. If there was any chance of taking a white man to his ancestors with him ... but there would be no opportunity, the men in the machine would use their machine to keep them out of his range. He had seen the three men on the lip of the machine and noted their burnt and dishevelled faces – two of them at least, but the third could be dismissed out of hand for his narrow stupid lightbrown countenance and narrow sliteyes – and knew they would not come down to fight like men. He had also seen past them to the neat dark-haired man and the Indian behind the image thieving machine and into the control cockpit where Decker sat at ease, manipulating his controls calmly, and knew these were the men in command and that they would never let the soft ones set foot on the hard earth where he could deal with them. From such odds it would not be cowardly to effect an escape. And escape was becoming urgent. He had had no water since early in the morning, when he had drunk at dawn, and the food had inflamed his thirst almost beyond what a man should be expected to bear. But he lay very still and concentrated on conserving his strength for the long run to the nearest water. The white men were slyly waiting for him to come out of the embracing danger of the *dongas* but he would be like the fox to the hyena and wait for their hungry machine to take them away to its feeding grounds before he ventured into the open.

Minowara's anxiety was reflected only in the frequency with which he consulted his watch. The rotor turned mono-tonously over their heads while the concentric circles of grass waved away hypnotically twenty feet underneath their swinging boots, Minowara's black and highly polished, Cameron's of buckskin with fancy frills and Pascoe's of softly grained wash leather. Pascoe had suggested that they hurry the black man's deliberations by firing fusillades into the *dongas* at random. Minowara had not been enthusiastic: it would show his prey he was not in command of the situation and it could kill the black man by accident. The subject was quietly dropped. Cameron thought the black man might have gone from there but found himself alone in taking bets on it at the now customary odds of ten to one. Even Pascoe believed the black man to be in the *dongas*.

After exactly an hour Curtis Bill said, 'He is waiting for us to leave. He knows we have to refuel.'

'How much fuel do we have left?'

Decker answered the question from Minowara. 'Half an hour.'

Cameron said, 'We could go away for five minutes or so and catch him coming out when we return.'

'Omo?'

Minowara was tempted to assent to Cameron's suggestion but he did not think the black man would be trapped so easily. His restraint in waiting for an hour while the machine beat its threat nearby proved his patience. 'It will not succeed. He will wait for a longer period to make sure. Then we will have only very little fuel and I shall be forced to kill him.'

'How's that?' Cameron asked.

'He will know our purpose and if we lose him once more we do not know where he will go to ground.'

'He can only go one direction for water,' Chris Decker said, rustling a map. 'Straight north.'

'Or south-west, back to where we found him,' Minowara said.

'You are right about losing him if we fail at our next attempt,' Curtis Bill said. 'But he will not go back to the *kraal* because that will lead us to his women and children.'

'Even if he can go only one direction, we do not know if there are more *dongas*.'

'True. It is for you to decide.'

The Japanese thought for only the briefest space of time. 'Please let us refuel now.'

'A wise choice,' the pilot said. 'We can always square search for him later when we will have fuel and time on our hands. If you do not kill your nigger, you get another go.'

'I intend killing this one. I trust we shall find him again.'

'For you, a special effort.' Decker was driving the helicopter towards the fuel depot at full speed because he had fuel in hand and didn't need the economy of the cruising speed. While they refuelled the tanks, the Japanese calmly stripped and cleaned his rifle and reassembled it with nimble fingers. Curtis Bill and Chris Decker both admired his composure; they nodded surreptitiously to each other in the knowledge that the Englishman and the American lacked the strength of character for such care with the final phases of the hunt so tantalisingly close.

The black man listened to the receding clop of the helicopter and measured the sun with his fingers between two rocks he had chosen to mark time. They went early. Were they trying to trick him? He lay back to wait until the shadow reached a point halfway between where he let his fingers rest and the tip of his *assegai*; when the shadow reached the tip of the *assegai*, that was when their machine would have to feed. When the shadow had consumed half the distance between his fingers and the speartip he scanned the sky carefully to assure himself that they were not hiding in its blue depths to dive on him like the sly eagle. The sky was clear except for a vulture which gave him a start: had it smelt his fear and come as a foreboding of birds and hyenas feasting on his flesh? But the vulture passed with a lazy flapping of its wings and he rose and ran to the edge of the *donga* where he crawled on his belly through the long grass already growing down into the cracks of the rocks to hide the wrinkles of age on the skin of Africa. When he had crawled a hundred yards he found a tree and rose carefully behind it to see if perhaps they had put their machine down to wait for him to appear. They were not to be seen or heard. Nevertheless, he put his head down below the level of the grass and headed for the water. The white men would assume he had gone in any direction but the one he had previously held; they would not know where the water was. He ran easily, resisting the temptation to run faster. He could not outrun the machine, he would have to outfox it.

* * *

Once more the helicopter hovered over the *dongas*. Decker angled its tail upwards so that the nosecone in which he sat was tilted towards the rim of the *donga* as he let the helicopter slide smoothly along its edge. The sideways movement of the helicopter petered out so smoothly that only Minowara noticed it. Decker said, 'He headed straight for the water.' He turned the machine sideways on for the hunters to have a look. 'See the green grass growing from the cracks? See how it is bent over and bruised?'

'What's it mean?' Pascoe asked.

'He went over there on his belly,' Curtis Bill said behind him.

Decker took the helicopter up to twenty feet. 'Hundred and twenty miles an hour.'

Minowara looked at his watch, pressed a button on it and said, 'Thank you.'

Decker sent the helicopter skimming forward. 'You can say when.'

Minowara was looking at his watch and did not reply.

'Hey, are you letting us do all the searching for your nigger?' Pascoe exclaimed.

Curtis Bill explained. 'We know the direction he went. We know approximately how fast he runs. We know how fast we travel. It is simple arithmetic to work out when we should be over him if he has not changed direction. Then we need only search the area around the point we have arrived at by dead reckoning.'

'Here,' Minowara said softly and pressed the button to reset the stopwatch.

Decker stopped the forward movement of the helicopter and took it up to fifty feet. 'Watch for every blade of moving grass that does not fit the pattern our own rotor makes,' he said.

'You'd also need to know how long the nigger has been running at this assumed speed of x,' Pascoe said, his eyes scanning the terrain.

'Chris and Omo have been keeping track of time all along,' Curtis Bill replied.

176

'Pilots!'

'Yeah,' Cameron agreed. 'But a good tip all the same. I'll remember tomorrow when it's my turn.'

'No need. It's part of the Ultimate Test Incorporated service.' Decker chuckled. 'Dead spot on. About ninety degrees to your left, four, maybe four hundred fifty yards away.'

'Trust a pilot to find it first. What are we looking for?' Cameron was full of admiration.

'I see it,' Minowara said. 'A wave in the grass. My black man ran there and fell down when he heard us coming.'

'It's not much,' Pascoe said, looking through his telescopic sight, pressing the button to narrow the angle and enlarge the view. 'Could be a breeze.'

'No,' Decker assured him with finality as he sent the helicopter skimming towards the spot. 'Not till much later in the afternoon if at all. He'll be there.' Decker had his hand on the throttle and was sending them forward in a logarithmically ascending climb, the first part shallow, the major section of the ascent very steeply right over the spot where the grass had waved. The grass parted in the downthrust of the engine's power transmuted to the air through the rotor blades and they saw the black man lying on his back between the stalks of the grass, looking up at them past a hand shielding the sun from his eyes.

Omo Minowara sighed softly. Pascoe and Cameron laughed their pleasure. Curtis Bill, Chris Decker and Vincent were quiet.

The black man was not surprised that the white men had found him. He wondered what they would no next, decided he would act as he had always acted, in accordance with his own wishes. He would continue on his way to the water and slake his thirst, let the white men do what they will. He rose and, head erect above the grass, started trotting towards the water.

'Down behind him, please.'

Decker took the helicopter down in silence. The white men watched the black man intently but the black man did not deign to acknowledge their presence by looking around.

'This will do very well.'

Decker steadied the helicopter. Minowara took careful aim in the pregnant silence and squeezed the trigger gently. A moment later the black man clasped the hand in which he carried his *assegai* to his ear. He turned around to stare briefly at them in outrage, then turned and ran on, his movements now jerkily abrupt and much less coordinated. He seemed to be running faster yet covering no more ground.

'Forward for the same range, please.'

Pascoe and Cameron stopped the laughter welling up from their chests at the black man's discomfiture. 'You really mean business, don't you?' Cameron said wonderingly.

Minowara did not answer. He waited until the helicopter was in position again behind the running men, aimed carefully but lowered his rifle. 'He is not running smoothly enough.'

'Give him a few minutes,' Curtis Bill advised. 'Chris will keep the range for you.'

A minute passed, two. They all watched the black man but no one offered comment. Another minute and another. The sweat of irregular movement was growing on the black man. More minutes passed in neat spaced file.

'Now, if you please.'

Decker steadied the helicopter and the Japanese aimed with his customary care. He squeezed the trigger and his companions could almost imagine they heard the shot ring out over the clop of the blades and the whine of the turbine and the innate zing of the intercom in their headsets and the breathing of the others magnified by the throat mikes. The black man fell, his shield swinging through the air.

'Looks like you've had an accident too.' Pascoe.

'No. His hand moving to his ear with the shield overbalanced him. He will rise.'

As if anxious to prove Minowara's theory right, the black man came upright rolling, and resumed his erratic running. The sweat and blood mixed on his shoulders was now stuck

178

with seeds and stalks of grass as well as dust and earth and pollen.

'Steady again, please.'

'What are you going to shoot now?' Cameron asked.

'A shoulder.'

Decker steadied the helicopter. 'Ready.'

This time the black man took longer to rise and his step seemed trudging when he continued stubbornly on his way without paying his tormentors any attention.

'Do you want to do the other shoulder?'

Minowara countered with another question. 'Please, how much fuel is left?'

'Hour and five minutes.'

'And how far to the water?'

'An hour and a half. He will get there by the time we return from refuelling.'

'If we do not head him off now, yes. Will you take me up next to him, please?'

Decker complied readily. Minowara, his two companions on the lip of the helicopter, the safari organisers and the Indian photographer all studied the black man's unsteady progress with great care.

'Difficult,' Curtis Bill summed up for all of them.

'But not impossible,' Cameron added unnecessarily. 'I am glad it is not my choice.'

'Want to have a look from the other side, see him as a silhouette against the light?' the pilot enquired.

'No, thank you.' Minowara raised his rifle and fired one shot in front of the black man. The black man stopped and stared up at the helicopter with bloodflecked eyes bulging forward from his contorted flat face. He took one experimental step forward and Omo Minowara immediately placed another shot in front of him. He stopped again.

To the white men the black man in the veld threw a curse: *May your wives all be barren.* They knew where he was heading. Their intention was not to let him reach water. He tested the assumption by turning away. He ran with the sun behind him for a while and there were no shots. As soon as he started

179

turning ever so slightly towards the water a shot placed so close to his feet but beside him nudged him back to his previous line. He turned in the other direction, even further away from the water and there were no shots. Back towards the water and the shots came uncomfortably close to his feet again. There was no doubt about it in his mind now: they were going to run him into the ground, make him beg for the oblivion of a bullet if he did not die of thirst or exhaustion or loss of blood first. Already he felt weak from the blood he had lost. He had stuffed some wadded grass into the holes in his shoulder, front and back, but there was nothing he could do about the blood flowing from the wounds where his earlobes had been. And the weakness of lost blood was insignificant against the wracking dryness of his mouth and throat and that in turn, he knew, would pale in the shadow of the nausea exhaustion would bring. He slowed down to conserve his strength. When the machine went to be fed, he would change direction and they would have to search for him and so have less time to chase him; he would repeat the procedure until darkness fell and hope the machine could not see in the dark. He did not consider whether he would last until darkness. He only knew he had to. And his change of direction must be away from the water each time, or the white men would find him too quickly and have more time to chase him. But his change of pace had been noticed. No sooner had his breathing evened out its ragged rhythm than the machine came around beside him and the shots started creeping closer to his heels. They would not kill him yet. He kept his pace. The machine came around to face him and he ran straight at it. The shot hit him in the other shoulder and this time it was more serious. The bullet hit bone and broke the bone and splintered the bone before exiting and leaving a large hole on his back. The grass he tried to stuff into the hole simply slipped away on the blood flowing from its gaping maw. He knew he would be dead in two hands of the sun's movement. He would not die like a frantic buck, gasping his last blood and breath, beseeching mercy with his eyes. He would die standing up like a man. He put the shield, which still dangled from his useless arm by the inner thong, on the ground and sat on it. He held his hand over the hole at the back of his shoulder and listened to the angry buzzing of the machine about him but did not look up at it.

'Looks like your nigger's given up,' Pascoe crowed at Minowara.

'Maybe that last shoulder shot was a mistake,' Cameron added.

Minowara did not answer them.

'Why don't you shoot it up around him?' Pascoe suggested.

'It will do no good. You may try if you like.'

Eagerly Cameron and Pascoe raised their rifles and started firing. The black man ignored the shots around him. Minowara did not join in the firing. When they stopped firing he addressed the pilot:

'We will wait here.' He knew, if the English and American barbarians did not, that there was a certain ritual and courtesy in death. If the black man wished to compose himself for his inevitable death, let him have the time to do so.

But the black man disappointed Omo Minowara too. He stood but not to raise his *assegai* or shield in salute to his conqueror. No, he undid his tigerskin loincloth. Then he bent his knees and pointed his hole at the men in the helicopter, spreading the cheeks with both hands, an effort which must have cost him considerable pain in the injured shoulder.

Decker gasped. Pascoe and Cameron spluttered their incomprehensible rage. Vincent whirred his camera happily: let the goddamn Jap with his superior airs – an honorary white! – swallow this supreme insult.

'Kill him,' Cameron finally extricated from his splutter.

'That is what he wants,' Curtis Bill said. Minowara remained silent. He was surprised that Curtis Bill bothered to explain something so obvious to Cameron.

'Maybe we ought to catch him and teach him nice and slow.'

'Yes,' Pascoe breathed enthusiastically. 'Yeees!'

'A couple of shots in the ankles would do that nigger no

181

harm,' the pilot suggested. 'He looked better when he was sitting down.'

As if wishing to comply with Decker's least wish, the black man sat down on his haunches. He looked over his shoulder at the helicopter behind him and the strain was visible on his face. Vincent kept the telelens on his face for a moment, then widened the angle to take in the whole body and then narrowed the angle again to fix the turd slowly squeezing from between the cheeks neatly in centre screen closeup; it was what he had expected and it was beautiful.

'Can you take us up another five feet please and forward a bit, Chris?'

'Sure. What are you going to do?'

'Shoot the turd from his arsehole, of course,' Pascoe said.

'From right here he can see more of it,' the pilot objected.

'And he'd also take the nigger's balls right off and kill him quickly with trauma or massive haemorrhaging,' Cameron snapped.

'I do not intend that he should die for a while yet,' Minowara said, pleased that for once Pascoe and Cameron had discerned for themselves the only proper course to take without having to be told by someone else. 'Please take us up, Chris.'

'How's that?'

'Very good, thank you.' Minowara raised his rifle and aimed carefully.

'Hold her very still,' Cameron said. 'Omo doesn't want to shoot off any of his vertebrae and kill him.'

'I've been flying a chopper longer than you've had your butcher's licence, *Doctor*.'

'Shut up, all of you. Give Omo a chance.'

The Japanese fired one, cut it too fine and missed. He corrected and fired once more. This time the turd was broken off by the bullet an inch from the black man's cheeks and squashed to the ground with impressive force. The black man jumped up as if stung in a sensitive spot by a wasp and ran for the nearest tree. Decker brought the helicopter around

182

quickly to give Minowara time for one shot but the Japanese held his fire.

'He's moving too erratically.'

'And we don't finish niggers just because and when they ask to be finished,' Cameron said proudly.

'We teach them first,' Pascoe added by rote.

An intricate ballet started. The black man would keep the trunk of the tree between himself and the helicopter. The helicopter would whirl around the tree at grasstop height to give the Japanese an opportunity to shoot at the black man under the lowest branches.

'Will you put me down? Then you can drive him towards me.'

'I'm sorry, no,' Decker said compassionately. He really was sorry but he was not putting his helicopter down in adverse circumstances on unknown ground. Besides which Curtis Bill would do his nut, and justifiably so, if he consented to the request.

'If you cannot get this one, we will find you another tomorrow,' Curtis Bill added. 'Our agreement is to find you a black man and let you kill him. Only when you have killed him is our commitment fulfilled. But we do ask that you abide by a few simple rules for your own safety.'

Minowara nodded. He did not trust himself to speak. Despite his injuries and loss of blood the black man was nimble and quick in using the tree trunk for cover, never exposing much of himself for long.

'I can take you up, directly over the tree and you can fire downwards through the branches.'

'No. I wish to see him. What is the fuel reserve, please?'

'Twenty-five minutes. That's cutting it very fine.'

'We will use ten minutes to make him run around the tree. If you gentlemen would join me in firing at the tree trunk I should be grateful. Perhaps we can panic my black man into breaking away from the tree.'

'Why not take the opportunity of another hunt tomorrow?' Cameron asked. 'I know I'd jump at the chance of another nigger to myself all day long.'

'Tomorrow's black man will not be the black man who insulted me today,' Minowara said flatly.

'Around the tree as fast as he can run and no faster?' Decker supposed. 'With the tree between him and us?'

'Yes please.'

The tree shook as the slugs went into the trunk. The black man hurried around it, a flash of arm or heel now and then announcing his continued presence. The helicopter whirred around the tree *ad nauseam*.

'That sure is a stubborn nigger,' Pascoe said. He was feeling pleased with his own honesty in firing only at the tree trunk and not trying to hit the flashes of black flesh he glimpsed. He hoped the Japanese would be as honest with him if he should ask him to help when it was his turn to hunt again in two days. On the second day from today. It was a good feeling, shooting at the tree trunk and knowing there was a nigger behind it and knowing that on the second day it could be your very own nigger to shoot or let go, just as you liked. Except you'd shoot him, of course, because one never lets a nigger go.

'Where'd you learn to speak Southern?' Cameron asked.

'In Manchester, where else?' The question had surprised Pascoe. He had thought Bob to be his friend and friends don't make jokes about your grammar or your accent.

Cameron spent the ten minutes cutting the letters S, E, N, W into the four sides of the tree with his bullets just at the level the nigger's head would be if the bullets went through the tree. Tomorrow it would be his turn and he could only ask for a nigger as game as this one or as fit as the one Pascoe killed yesterday because of his reliance on a fancy scope with too narrow an angle of view and his attempt at fancy shooting after he, Cameron, had warned him against trying for the spearhead where he couldn't even see it.

'Nine minutes,' Chris Decker said.

'When the minute is up,' Minowara instructed, 'please tell us and Bob and Enoch will stop shooting. Then turn us around sharply and go around in the other direction.'

184

'Willco.' Decker gave them a countdown from ten. 'Ten seconds, nine ... eight ...'

The black man's torso appeared beside the tree for half a second as he fell to the ground, jerking spasmodically in mid-air.

'Shit!' Pascoe and Cameron said at the same time. Each immediately assumed the other had been tempted to shoot Omo Minowara's nigger. Minowara knew he had not shot the black man but both Pascoe and Cameron had been firing at the time. He wondered if both had done it or only one of them.

'Okay, which of you clumsy motherfuckers did it this time?' Decker snapped as he brought the helicopter down beside the tree. No one replied to his accusation. There was no reply. Each knew the other had done it and a denial would only be unacceptable finger pointing.

The helicopter had not touched down when Omo Minowara punched the quick release button at the same time as Curtis Bill unhooked him from the safety line. The elderly Japanese jumped nimbly to the ground and walked quickly, very quickly, towards the fallen black that was to have been his prey alone.

Curtis Bill did not wait to undo the extra safety lines on the other two hunters. He grabbed his rifle and ran after Minowara. He had not seen the bullet hit the black man. In the helicopter, Chris Decker saw Curtis Bill run past the bubble carrying his rifle and scratched in his map pocket until he came up with a revolver. He headed for the door as fast as he could, kicking aside impeding belts and jumble.

Minowara stood looking down at the black's body for a second. Behind him Curtis Bill called something but he did not hear in his sorrow that someone else should have dispatched the man he had hunted, the man who had insulted him. Hot tears stung his eyes as he bent down to rest his rifle on the ground and to roll the body over, to have it face up. He put his hands under the bloody shoulder and heaved as Curtis Bill called out once more. Again he did not hear, Curtis Bill's voice drowned by his own startled cry as hands of steel with

185

clawed fingers enclosed his throat. His own frightened rearing brought the greater weight of the black man up with him and then the black man was dominant and forcing him to bend his back as the fingers closed ever more inexorably into his throat. There was a ringing in his ears through which he heard Curtis Bill shout:

'Stand still and I'll come round for my shot.'

But the black man was turning him around, keeping his body between himself and the threat posed by Curtis Bill's rifle. He felt himself swung around and saw Curtis Bill lean over to put the rifle down prior to attacking the black man physically – even in his extremity he had to approve of a man who handled arms with proper care and respect and did not just throw them into the dust with the resulting probable damage to the mechanism – and then he was looking over the black man's shoulder as Cameron raised his rifle to aim and fire. The pilot, Decker, was also on the lip of the helicopter and had a revolver in one hand but it was pointing at the floor while he struck away Pascoe's big-bore rifle with which the fool was aiming at the struggling men.

Cameron's shot took the black man in the back of the head, lifting his skull's top heavenwards in a mushroom of dirty grey brains. A split second later Decker, having dealt with the menace of Pascoe, shot the black man in the back of the knee he had between Minowara's legs: Decker was standing higher than Cameron and carried a heavier firearm; he could neither shoot upwards through the black man's body and hope to miss the Japanese, nor directly at the black man's broad back, because in either case he might have killed the man he was trying to save as the bullet would easily have passed through both men. He shot at the only area of the black man exposed to him behind which he could be sure no part of Minowara rested: the black man's leg between Minowara's legs.

In death the black man nearly took his tormentor with him by convulsively clawing out his throat. Minowara tried to raise his arms to break the black man's hold on his throat and could not. He saw stars and whole galaxies exploding and remembered his father and the fifty men who disembowelled themselves in ritual *seppuku* on the Nijubashi – Double Bridge facing the Imperial Palace in Tokyo – when the war ended and he thought that if the black man killed his executioner even in death he would indeed have died with honour and then he was falling back into Curtis Bill Bonham's arms and the black man's body fell back to Africa, to whom already it seemed to belong. He heard Cameron's voice above the babble.

'I warned him about the danger of a stroke if he over-excited himself.

Two

Yodoko and Melody were sitting on the veranda when the helicopter returned. They had swum before breakfast and after breakfast had the servants prepare a picnic lunch which they'd had beside the pool. Melody had asked Judith twice if she wanted to go with them but the Englishwoman preferred not to take any exercise, she had said. Melody had noted the stiffness in Judith's manner the night before, when she had gone with Yodoko to do her hair, but had ascribed it to natural concern over her husband's injury. Now, after she and Yodoko had come back from the pool in the heat of the afternoon, Judith was still keeping to her *rondawel*. She wondered if they had offended Judith in some way or whether it was the unaccustomed heat keeping the thin woman near the comfort of the air conditioner in her *rondawel*. She did not voice the question to Yodoko; the two of them had fallen into a companionable silence which she found rather pleasant – it was a pity when the urgent clop of the helicopter drowned the sussurous drone of the cicadas and forced them to pay drowsy attention to its approach.

The helicopter came over the furthest *rondawels* low and fast. In front of the Minowara *rondawel* it dropped out of the air and settled firmly on the ground. Curtis Bill jumped out and Enoch Pascoe stepped off the lip where he had been sitting. Vincent jumped out with his camera and pointed it into the helicopter to photograph the events in the interior. Curtis Bill and Pascoe reached into the helicopter and took Omo Minowara from the pilot and the doctor as they handed the Japanese out.

Melody Cameron gave a little cry and started towards the helicopter at a run, bobbing along as fast as the hobble of her kaftan would allow. Yodoko uttered not a sound but she reached the moving group of men before Melody, even though her ankles were tightly constricted in traditional Japanese dress.

Cameron jumped down from the helicopter, told one of the Bantu who had materialised with ubiquitous obsequity or perhaps simple curiosity, 'Fetch my bag. Like yesterday. Understand?' The black man nodded and ran off.

Vincent addressed another black man without taking his eye from the viewfinder of the camera. '*eRedcross box. Hamba!*' The black man raced off and Vincent said to Cameron, 'He'll fetch the medicine chest. There may be something in there you will need.'

'What happened?'

Cameron ignored his wife's question to address himself to Yodoko. 'He over-excited himself and had a stroke, some kind of a haemorrhage of the brain, I think.' He stared at her blank face. Did she speak English? 'Do you understand English?' She turned and went through the door after Pascoe and Curtis Bill as they carried her husband into the *rondawel*.

'She speaks English,' Melody Cameron said to her husband's back as he too went through the door. Then she returned to the veranda. If Bob wanted any help he would ask for it. There was no sense in adding her presence to the congestion in the *rondawel*.

Chris Decker watched them lay the Japanese financier on the bed and straighten his flopping limbs over which he obviously had no control. 'I'll go warm up the plane and keep it on standby. I'll also radio the hospital at Phalaborwa to expect us.'

'Bob may want to send him straight to the General in Johannesburg,' Curtis Bill said.

'No!'

They looked at each other curiously for the source of the croaked whiplash. It took them a minute to realise it was the man on the bed who had spoken. They had already discarded him in their minds as a wilful force, as one who would express wishes and desires. From Minowara the eyes of the men turned to Cameron, the doctor. Only Yodoko Minowara's eyes remained on her husband.

'You are a pretty sick man,' Cameron said. 'I will know more when I have examined you properly. But machines may be necessary for a really thorough examination, machines only a big hospital is likely to have.'

'I have not finished my hunt.'

Cameron turned to Curtis Bill Bonham, Chris Decker and Enoch Pascoe. 'I'll examine him and let you know. There doesn't seem to be any urgency to alert the hospital.' They left, taking the Bantu, who had brought the medical bag and the medicine chest and who were inclined to linger curiously, with them. Cameron examined Minowara thoroughly while Yodoko waited across the *rondawel*. When he had finished, he said, 'All I can tell you is that you have suffered a haemorrhage of the brain and you are paralysed from the neck down. Everything below the neck. Only the neurology department at a major hospital will be able to determine more.'

'How long do I have to live?'

'Does speaking tire you?'

'No. How long?'

'I don't know. It could be many years.'

'In this condition?'

189

'You could recover in ten minutes. Tomorrow. Next year. The major hospital neurology –'

'But it is not likely at my age.'

'It is not impossible.'

'But not probable?'

Cameron was reluctant. 'I don't know enough yet to –'

'Not probable?'

'No, damn it. But anything –'

'I should like to speak to Yodoko-san.'

'Shall I leave? Call the hospital –'

'No, stay. Listen.'

Dr Robert J. Cameron walked with Curtis Bill Bonham and Chris Decker. Enoch Pascoe ambled along behind them, the bandage on his wound a startling white against the sunburn of his skin.

'What it comes down to is this. I think he's a dead man anyway. At his age . . . He could live for months as a thinking and talking vegetable. I do not –'

'So, let's get him out of here!' Chris Decker shuddered. He had never been ill one day in his life.

Cameron smiled at the pilot's revulsion. To Curtis Bill he said, 'Your commitment to Omo, as you told him today, is to find him a nigger and let him teach the bastard good. He didn't teach that nigger today. Chris and I did.'

'So what?' the pilot answered him. 'He's paralysed. There's no way he's going to hunt any niggers.'

'He's not going to do it himself. He has selected a proxy to hunt for him tomorrow.'

'That is fair,' Curtis Bill said.

'Shit, no!' Pascoe exclaimed behind them. 'Bob hunts tomorrow, then me on Thursday. If the Jap or his proxy gets another go I have to wait until Friday. That's not fair.'

'Unless he's selected you as his proxy,' Decker snapped.

'Yes, well, that's different. I would –'

'Shut up and wait your turn. Remember your promise yesterday?'

190

'Yes, but –'

'Just shut up! Who's the Jap selected. You? Me? Curtis Bill?'

'Or me,' Pascoe added for the record.

Cameron walked another ten paces before he answered: 'Yodoko. His wife.'

Yodoko sat beside the bed where her husband lay motionless, only the amplified sound of his breathing indicating that it had been a strain to keep face in front of the American doctor. She was proud that he had asked her to hunt the black man as his proxy even though the American doctor had hinted shamelessly that he, Cameron, should be the one selected. She had no burning desire to kill animals or men but it was her duty to her husband, and a duty she had been trained to as all Japanese children, male and female, are traditionally trained in the martial arts and in ruthless mercilessness to others.

Yodoko's was an old family, not as prominent as the Minowaras but equally honourable in the traditional ways. She had been brought up strictly, patterned to just such a marriage as her family had arranged for her to Omo Minowara, whom it was her duty and privilege to serve as her lord and master. 'Your duty is a pleasure, the greater in its challenge,' her mother had told her.

Yodoko not only honoured her husband, which was her duty, but she loved him, which was considerably more than was expected of her by tradition, family or indeed by him. Omo Minowara was, in his public aspect, quiet and polite but with deadly purpose; he wished for a time now gone when Japan and the Japanese had honour, a goal beyond the coarse grubbing for money which the new Japan had relegated him to as the president of a large finance house. In his home this old worldliness made him an excellent and ideal husband, a stable pillar who gently guided a young wife when she faltered and credited her adequately when she pleased him. Yodoko, who had been taught to regard love of personal youth and beauty – and romantic love itself – as fictional notions from novels, learnt to love him for the warmth she generated in him, so unlike her coldly undemonstrative and feared father. She knew she was the only person in all the world for whom Omo Minowara showed any warmth at all and this made her feel the one great disappointment of his life, that at sixty-eight he had no child, to an even greater extent. Her sensitivity to him was magnified by the contrast of his cold outer public figure and his power of making her glow simply by entering their home. To be truthful, what affection he showed her was very little; as much as a man may show towards his fourth or fifth favourite dog or towards an expensive car which was also comfortable and reliable or towards a servant whose loyalty and longevity of service were both unbroken and unquestionable in the future tense. Yodoko did not know this and, had she been told, would have dismissed the talebearer as both malicious and envious. Happiness is the excess of reality over expectation.

Yodoko had read in the newspapers of the world in the several languages she had mastered of the women's liberation movement and had wondered, on the occasion of International Woman's Year last year or the year before, whether she should feel any of the 'hidden resentment' flowering so grandiloquently from the pages. She had tried hard to find something to resent and failed. Yodoko was not vague, nor was she at all ill-informed; she was simply so perfectly shaped in the image of a society which placed duty above happiness that she had become that genuinely rare person, the one who expects so little that the merest drop of happiness or affection falling into the bucket seems a veritable deluge of joy and love. Minowara Omo-san, said those who observed closely, had in the wisdom of his years picked a jewel beyond price. Yodoko.

Three

eFokoli.

Jomo Iningwe was having his recurring dream. Early in the
morning the dawn had found him saying a fond farewell to
a petite blonde American schoolteacher, promising to return
or, failing that, to send his brother. Creating an addiction to
black cocks among white women, he had told the man he had
brought along to drive the car back to Lourenço Marques, is
not only fair justice but the natural calling of every young
black man. Of course, he added in celebration of the joyful
day and the exhilaration of the suicidal speed he was driving
at, if you need more than one night to addict a white woman,
you were obviously lacking in the essential equipment or
technique and had best devote your entire energies to the
corollary activity, none the less laudable, of killing white
men. His passenger nodded eagerly, staring straight ahead
at the road as if to will the certain disaster awaiting them
to return home, and sank even lower in his seat. Jomo drove
as far as the South African border, then turned back, studying each inch of the road silently and intently. Before they
returned to Chisselane he stopped the car, took his backpack
from the back seat, waved cheerfully at the driver and disappeared almost instantly into the lush vegetation. The driver
rubbed his eyes and looked again but Jomo was gone without
a trace. Jomo went to the river bank and inflated the rubber
raft which constituted most of the bulk of his backpack,
launched it and lay on his back on it as it floated down the
Limpopo, past Chisselane towards Fumane. Three miles past
the well camouflaged boat on which his men had come he
beached the raft and sat with his back to a *marula* tree to
sleep and dream in the heat of the subtropical afternoon. He

was sweating, which was unusual for Jomo Iningwe, but it was the effect of the dream. *eFokoli.*

In his dream he was far away, on the *campong* of the gold mine at Stilfontein, a hundred and twenty miles south of Johannesburg, where the mines' hiring and training office had placed him. He spoke fluent French, a little English, had a degree in Economics from the Sorbonne, had even done some post-graduate work. But he was technically black and manual work on the mines was what he had applied for and got. It would pay any of Africa's poor blacks the fortune they had dreamt of until then, enough to buy cows and wives beyond any man's fondest dreams. A man accepted for work on the mines was indeed a lucky man. He would be fed and housed and clothed and receive free dental and medical care and save all his money and go home to be the richest man in all his tribe. This was both the promise and the reality of the mines. Jomo fitted in well because he was strong and he made a point of assimilating wherever he found himself. Soon he was made a bossboy. For five months he was perfectly happy on the mine, the backbreaking work of the days earning him the heavy sleep of the nights in which he could forget what had happened to his mother and sisters, could forget how his father had laid his head down and turned to the wall and died of hopeless sorrow and shame for his helplessness in the face of Africa's brutality to her own.

After five months of food planned by the nutrition experts to build his strength, he no longer fell into an immediate exhausted sleep but time had done its healing work on the wounds of his memory; he would carry the scars for life but blood no longer flowed from open cuts. It was too good to last. Afterwards, when he could think clearly again, Jomo was ashamed of the savagery with which he had reacted and it took him a long time to realise that savagery was an in- eradicable part of his character.

Jomo, complete with the gang of labourers over whom he was bossboy, was transferred to the command of another

194

white miner. A giant of a man with a skin scarred by acne, he came from the poor white class created by the depression when thousands had to leave their land and find a living in the cities. While no longer poor, this man had taken the mentality of his father as his own, together with the prejudices of a man rich only in pride and his racial affiliations. He blamed 'kaffirs' for what had gone wrong with the 'white man's country' and feared an ill-defined 'black menace' which even the most rightist of South African politicians had long since ceased to expound in public. He referred to Jomo, because of Jomo's light skin, as 'die wit kaffir' – the white nigger – and Jomo, old enough to know that prejudice does not acknowledge logic or reason, ignored him. One day the bigot made a mistake, unwitting but none the less devastating for his ignorance of Jomo's recent history.

'Hey, White Nigger,' he called from where he leant with both hands on a pickaxe handle.

Jomo looked up without stopping the regular rhythm of his shovel shooting the rich ore-bearing gravel on to the pannier at the blasting face. His helmet light glistened on the newly laid rail, sweat dripped from his bare torso and his face; six thousand feet under the surface the air conditioning could do little better than fight a gallant retreat against the all pervading heat. It took a strong man to come down here and stay conscious for extended periods and that Jomo and the other blacks should be able to do strenuous manual work was a tribute to the mines' training scheme.

'Hey, White Nigger, you know I can't stand kaffirs of any colour. But I'd make an exception if you had a sister the same colour as you.'

Jomo stumbled on the rail but was still at the man's throat before he finished the sentence. The bigot was big and strong but he lacked the ferocity of the younger man and he had been taken by surprise; in all the years he had taunted black men none had ever attacked him. He struck at Jomo with the pickaxe handle but Jomo was possessed and did not feel the blow which shattered his collarbone and would have broken his head had it landed squarely. It was the last blow

195

the white man struck. When the other blacks pulled Jomo from him, none too hastily, he had been mauled beyond recognition. After three months in hospital he would emerge with a broken spirit and no mine would have him for the story of his aggravation had by then spread on the mine management grapevine. Jomo was arrested for assault as he came out of the mine hospital with his arm in a sling. The police held him on a charge of attempted manslaughter while they waited for the man in the hospital to die of his injuries.

The mine hired an excellent lawyer to defend Jomo. It was entirely due to his brilliance that Jomo received the cautionary sentence of six months at hard labour to be followed by deportation from South Africa. Gaol had been degrading and more, torture for a man who had slept under the sky so often. But it was the attitude of the court which persuaded Jomo that the colour of one's skin is a partisan matter.

Jomo observed the proceedings keenly. The man on the bench of justice reacted with distaste when it became clear that a high-powered lawyer had been hired to defend a black man in a case of common violence. And when the charge was reduced to assault it was obvious that the representative of justice accepted it with extreme reluctance. All this could have been Jomo's prejudice and fear subjecting his observation but the man's attitude and action in the matter of language confirmed his worst conclusions. He listened to Jomo's English and decided it was not fluent enough. Jomo's lawyer agreed that Jomo should address the court and be addressed only through an interpreter. At first Jomo thought this was evidence of concern for his rights. The language he had in common with the interpreter was Fanegalo, the polyglot mine equivalent of Esperanto. The word itself is derived from 'funny galore' and the language, which is extremely functional, abounds in pidgin and coarse usage from more than thirty European and African languages. The Fanegalo word for 'nothing' is *eFokoli*. The first time Jomo used it he was stopped and told, through the interpreter, not to swear in court. The second time the reprimand was more severe,

196

with a threat of a fine for contempt of court. The interpreter explained that the word was not a swearword in intention but part of the common language between him and the accused. This earned the interpreter a blast from the bench, whence it was claimed the *eFokoli* was obviously the inadmissible Anglo-Saxon *fuckall*. Jomo, who by now had his fear of a biased court confirmed, knew the root given was correct. He burst out laughing. His lawyer demanded an interpreter competent in French or Swahili and was refused. When the sentence came, it was accompanied by a diatribe against the lawyer for technicalities he had raised in Jomo's defence and a statement that Jomo's attitude caused the man on the bench to regret he could not levy a heavier sentence. Afterwards the lawyer came to see Jomo in gaol.

'That man is a bigot.'

'Perhaps. But we did very well, considering that you did in fact damn nearly kill his spiritual brother. Do you want to appeal?'

'I am in your hands. Most gratefully.'

'You are amused?'

'No, sir. Wiser. I smile from sorrow at my earlier innocence.'

'Good. We have grounds for appeal. But it is unlikely that they will release you from custody while the appeal is waiting. Your six-month sentence will be over before your appeal comes to court. The only reason to appeal is to have the deportation order set aside.'

'Thank you but I don't think I want to stay here now.'

The lawyer nodded. 'You are probably wise. You will be tagged a trouble maker. Life could be difficult. Good-bye and good luck.'

In his dream he spent a lifetime in that white courtroom in South Africa waiting to be sentenced to another lifetime of hard labour because his attitude and the colour of his skin were wrong.

* * *

197

He awoke with a start.

'Go away,' he told a multihued bird staring curiously at him from a low branch, 'or I'll wring your silly squawking neck.'

The bird flew away in the same dignified silence it had observed him in. He looked after its receding back with a little regret: it was a bad sign when he started taking out his foul temper, which his dream always left him in, on the nearest living thing. It could lead to errors. Errors in his vocation could cost him his life. He valued his life highly. The litany of logic calmed him. His packing calmed him more. He struck out through the woods without having to consult his wrist compass. He planned on keeping within five hundred yards of the river. When he reached a point which had no reference except inside his head, he sat down against the nearest tree. It was dusk under the trees where he was, but overhead, above the trees, it would still be broad daylight. He sat absolutely still for two hours. Now it would be dusk on the river and over the trees. Underneath the trees the stygian atmosphere could be cut with a knife. The humidity was oppressive but Jomo Iningwe no longer sweated: he was at work and it was work he was used to, work he liked and men do not sweat at what they do well and willingly. He moved slowly from tree to tree, standing still and listening more often than he moved. In an hour he located the guard. In another hour and a half he was sure it was the only guard. He returned to the sole guard and watched him for another hour. The man did not smoke but he made the mistake of looking towards the river and blinding himself with the gleam of the moon's reflection glistening through the trees. He slit the guard's throat while the man peed. The man died while his blood pulsed forth and his water curved a bold stream. He did not struggle or try to scream. Jomo hoped he enjoyed his last relief; there could be no greater pleasure than a good piss. He spent two more hours covering the eighty yards to the river bank and ensuring that there was no guard on the deck of the boat. He boarded the boat and stretched out with his pack as a cushion. His men were probably sweltering below but it indicated good discipline that they should not show themselves even at night. He felt at ease with himself now. Killing the half competent guard had been the catharsis he had hoped for and needed.

He opened his eyes when the first boot prodded him tentatively in the ribs. There were only four of them and they carried their machine pistols with the casual ease of long familiarity. Perhaps the toad-Colonel had not lied, they were trained and disciplined men. Otherwise the whole lot of them would have rushed up here to gawk at the man who had killed the guard and then arrogantly come to take his rest on their boat. It would be a change for the better, working with disciplined men instead of over-zealous stumblebums only too anxious to die for The Cause.

'You killed the guard?'

'Yes. He was incompetent. You are expecting me?'

'There was no need to kill him.'

'You used to give the orders around here until I came?'

'Yes.'

'Then listen carefully. I now give the orders. Your camouflage is excellent. But the fact that you have a guard advertises it as camouflage. You can have camouflage or you can have guards. One or the other, never both. If you have guards, you must check them at least once an hour. It is no good if you have to wait until dawn to find out they were incompetent.'

Jomo Iningwe stood. The machine pistols rose with him. 'I have only a knife. I shall look to you to arm me.'

The man who had been in command nodded at one of his men and the man offered Jomo his machine pistol. The gesture underlined the change of authority. Jomo waved the weapon away. 'Thank you, but I will wait until I can draw from your stores. It would be theft to take a fine soldier's rifle even when he offers it to you. Without it he would be naked.' He knew he had won that man's allegiance for ever. Or at least as long as it mattered.

'Come,' he said to the man who had been in command.

'Perhaps you will offer me breakfast while we talk about what is to be done.' He put his arm around the man's shoulders until they came to the wheelhouse where the man stood aside to let Jomo Iningwe precede him.

WEDNESDAY

One

Yodoko gave her husband his *cha* in their usual morning
ritual. They behaved as if today were like any other day, no
different from all the mornings of their marriage. It was not
only good form, but comforting for both of them not to
recognise the realities of the day openly for a moment: He
was paralysed from the neck down and would probably not
recover, no matter the platitudes the American doctor
mouthed, while she would go out into the African day to kill
a man as his proxy. He lay silent, giving her no instructions
or well wishes or farewells. But she knew his spirit was with
her. At the door she bowed and he turned his head towards
her. Then she left and the temptation of unseemly emotion
was removed.

Yodoko went to the pool to cleanse herself and in the ritual
compose herself to the tasks of the day. Melody had not told
her of Chris Decker's injunction not to visit the pool un-
attended because no opportunity had arisen; Melody herself
had, in fact, misunderstood the pilot, who had meant that
women using the pool should be accompanied by a white
male member of the group carrying arms. On this Wednesday
morning Yodoko did not stop to ask Melody or Judith if they
would like to go swimming with her, partly because she
wanted to be alone, partly because she thought they would
want to attend to their husbands when the black servants
came to wake them at four o'clock for muster at four fifteen,
partly because it was three thirty in the morning, an indeli-
cate time to pay social visits.

'What's keeping that Japanese bitch?' Decker did not take his eyes from the eastern horizon. 'Take-off's at first light.'

'She's putting on her warpaint,' Cameron quipped.

'Her husband's probably giving her tips on nigger hunting,' Pascoe added sourly. The decision to let her hunt had postponed his second chance until Friday at the earliest, an outcome he was not wholly reconciled to.

'Well, she'll get no breakfast if she doesn't get a move on. This safari doesn't hold up anything to wait for women.'

'Perhaps she doesn't want breakfast,' Curtis Bill suggested.

'You can't hunt on an empty stomach!' Cameron's professional sensibilities were outraged.

'Perhaps she's decided not to do it after all,' Pascoe put forward an eager new thought.

Nobody answered him. They watched Yodoko come down the veranda towards them. She carried a rifle negligently in one hand. For the first time since her arrival at the camp she wore slacks and a shirt. She looked like a schoolgirl in the morning light. Decker stepped forward and took the rifle. 'Go on. You'd better gobble some breakfast quickly.'

She walked into the dining-room and through its light towards the kitchen. When she went through the swing doors of the kitchen, Decker took the rifle into the light spilling through a window onto the veranda and inspected it carefully, unloading and reloading it, checking the barrel and the trigger mechanism as well as the safety. The other men waited for him to finish his inspection, their silence bearing testimony to the unease each of them felt about hunting with a woman, especially one so young and frail and . . . foreign. The pilot shrugged and nodded at the other men; there was nothing wrong with the rifle, no cause to send her back to daddy for further instruction.

Yodoko came out of the kitchen, carrying Vincent's silver tray swinging from one hand at her side. In the other hand she carried a box of self-sealing clear stretch plastic used in the kitchen to seal vegetables and prepared dishes and raw meats. She walked past the men, who put down their plates and mugs on the veranda rail for the servants to fetch and followed her through the creeping light to the squat threatening shape of the helicopter.

'If she gets in a clinch with a nigger, like her husband, at least she's got a knife to defend herself with,' Cameron said.

The pilot laughed. 'That thing in the sheath on her waist? It's only about three inches long. It's a ceremonial dagger Japanese women wear with their geisha uniforms.'

They stood beside the helicopter while the Bantu removed the tarpaulin. Yodoko stood quite still and paid polite attention to everything said and done. Vincent stood to one side and clicked the settings on his camera. Pascoe and Cameron stamped their feet on the African summer's morn in parody of the many early mornings they had hunted stag or deer in chillier climes. Curtis Bill Bonham stood by impassively, his head still, his hands at ease. He missed nothing. Decker walked around the helicopter, inspecting it section by section while the Bantu uncovered it. This morning he seemed to be in a hurry to get into the air.

The pilot drew Curtis Bill aside. 'Shall we let her hunt from the cemetery?'

'We have already hunted from there this safari.'

For a moment Chris Decker's heart jumped. Did this mean Curtis Bill had reconsidered, would continue with their partnership? Was he protecting their future hunting grounds by not overhunting them? He framed a word or two with his lips, an oblique question, decided to be blunt instead: 'Does it matter if it's the last time we will be bringing a safari?'

'No. I suppose not. And if we find a black man there it makes the hunting so much easier for her.'

Chris Decker stood stockstill for a moment, an impulse of murder in his heart, adrenalin flowing in his veins. If Curtis Bill had not returned to the helicopter just then, he would have strangled him on the spot for letting his hopes grow and then dashing them to the ground like a cheap earthenware jug.

Yodoko had seen the interchange and noted it in her not-seeing *shiran-kao* manner. Curtis Bill Bonham, she thought, did not know that the massive and violent man he had taken

205

as a partner bore him a grudge. As he leant over her to tighten the straps of the harness, wrapping some straps around her twice before the clips found purchase in a hole at the end of the strap, she concluded that Curtis Bill Bonham and her husband Minowara Omo-san had much in common. Both were observers of rather than participants in life. Both considered life but a slow dying, though only her husband would have a conceptual framework within which to admit his belief. Curtis Bill's hand touched her breast, cupped its fullness from behind; she noted with pleasure at his restraint that he neither jerked his hand away nor quickened the tempo of his work – it was a social accident and merited no further attention. She felt sure that Curtis Bill Bonham's wife was a much honoured woman, though she had no further evidence than what Melody had told her of the safari organiser's wife and son and that he did not keep company with the uncouth pilot when they were not working.

'Ready when you are,' Curtis Bill Bonham said into his throat microphone. 'All strapped in and secure.'

Chris Decker let the turbine rip the helicopter into the air with a jerk and set its head for the river at speed as soon as they reached twenty feet. This morning there was no small talk in the helicopter. Curtis Bill never spoke unless he had something to say. Chris Decker was in a silent rage. Vincent was a servant who knew his place, to speak when spoken to. Yodoko was naturally silent and now she was in the company of her elders. Cameron and Pascoe would have made small-talk to the diminutive woman on the lip of the helicopter between them but they did not trust themselves to avoid the profanity of the hunt and, besides, what do you say to a Japanese woman who has come to shoot (Pascoe), who has come to teach (Cameron), a nigger for her husband? Curtis Bill knew the silence was not comfortable but did nothing to relieve it: any conversation he started Chris would surely escalate to explosion; best to let Chris work off his frustrations through flying as he always did. It would not take long.

'Malvernia's that way,' Cameron said as they crossed the road marking the border. Nobody answered him though

Yodoko nodded her head, knowing the remark was aimed at her.

Pascoe broke the silence next. 'There's a nigger!'

'Use your head, man!' the pilot snapped. 'That greybeard *induna* wouldn't run ten paces before he fell down dead from old age.'

'There's no harm in taking a look,' Cameron said easily.

Chris Decker skimmed the helicopter over the long grass to where the bent old man stood to look up at them with slack-mouthed curiosity. 'Maybe Enoch wants Yodoko to shoot him so's he can hurry his own hunt up, huh, Enoch?'

'Go fuck yourself up the arsehole with a hot stone,' Pascoe said quite clearly, nodding to Yodoko and adding, 'With your pardon, Missus.'

'No swearing when women are present!' Cameron said sharply.

Pascoe ignored him. He raised his rifle and aimed at the old man and squeezed the trigger all in one movement. The helicopter tilted away and Curtis Bill pushed his rifle's barrel down.

'It's Yodoko's hunt!' Chris Decker.

'No indiscriminate killing!' Curtis Bill Bonham.

'What y'do that for?' Pascoe whined his aggravation. 'You made me miss!' He raised his rifle again against the restraint of Curtis Bill's hand.

Chris Decker took the helicopter away at maximum speed. 'You silly motherfucker, how long do you think we'd stay in business if we let every limey Tom, Dick and Harry go around killing everybody they see?'

'He was only an old man.' Sullenly.

'He is probably an *induna*, an elder councillor,' Curtis Bill explained, 'and therefore on a government pension somewhere. They'd miss him.' He had not forgotten, as the pilot had in his anger, that they would only be 'in business' for another three days, counting today as one of the three, but it made no iota of difference: government investigation was the last thing they wanted.

'We ought not to let you hunt again, just for that,' Decker

207

told his throat mike, the threat plainly intended for Pascoe.

After a long silence Pascoe said, 'Sorry.' His insincerity was blatantly manifest. He kept looking back to where the old man with the thinning tight grey curls, still standing there watching the flying machine's antics, had now disappeared over their low speeding horizon. 'You will let me hunt again, keep your promise, won't you, Curtis Bill?' he pleaded.

'Yes.' It was difficult to keep the disgust out of his voice. This goddamn Pascoe was a menace to himself and to anybody who associated with him but a promise was a promise.

'But any more fuckups like that one back there, and you can try flying a Range Rover across the river for your transport because I sure as hell won't be flying you,' Decker said without inflection, then shouted, 'you dangerous fucking limey lunatic!'

The scream startled them all. Pascoe whimpered in sudden fright. Cameron whispered placatingly, 'Okay, okay!' Vincent drew in his breath with relish; he knew how precariously the helicopter was balanced on the edge of disaster and how minute a pilot error by the angry Decker would send them all to a flaming death, something he rather fancied in his mind, telling himself he would hold out until all the others, and especially the Japanese woman, had screamed themselves to an excruciatingly disfigured death before he succumbed in his own good time, savouring every last sensation. Only Curtis Bill Bonham and Yodoko Minowara gave no indication to the sensitive throat microphones that they were startled. Both avoided looking towards the pilot.

Five minutes later, the only sound in their headset-protected ears the slither of electronics and the far off beat of the rotor, felt more through the vibration where they touched the helicopter with their bodies than through their ears, they came to the cemetery, startlingly revealed by the first real daylight as the sun struck across the trees on its rim at the exact moment of their arrival. They flew low over the shadowless place, studying the people who rose from their deliberations to stare at their advent and their strangeness.

'Greybeards and children,' Cameron judged on the second pass. 'Neither are going to satisfy Omo.'

'Not quite,' Curtis Bill corrected him. 'See that group under the tree about twenty–thirty degrees to your left?'

Pascoe found them first. 'Yes. They look all right.'

'Yes, I see them,' Cameron said, a little peeved that the Englishman's eyes had again proved quicker than his own. 'A couple of fine specimens there. The question is, will they run?'

'We'll wait and see,' Decker ruled and withdrew the helicopter to the edge of the circle furthest away from any of the black men.

'Why don't we go over there and cut one out, choose our own nigger?' Cameron asked after a while.

'If you have no respect for their religion, I have,' Decker snapped shortly.

'Huh?'

'That's a religious ceremony down there. We told you last time.'

They watched in silence while the group in the centre of the open area was replaced by the group under the trees. While they studied the new group, Pascoe asked the pilot, partially because he was curious, partially because he considered asking another man questions about himself to be a premier way of ingratiating oneself:

'Are you religious, Chris?'

The pilot thought for a moment before he answered. 'If you mean, do I believe in God, the answer is I don't know. But I sure as hell won't scoff at anybody else's religion, no matter how weird. I have seen what these witchdoctors can do to a man they've never been within a hundred miles of.' He paused, changed the subject: 'Time for a word from America's favourite doctor on your favourite safari station, Radio Ultimate Test. This is your captain, Chris Decker, on location with Dr Robert J. Cameron. Tell me, Dr Bob, do you think that nigger will run?'

'Well now, Chris,' Cameron entered into the spirit of the joke, or perhaps into the shelter it afforded them from their embarrassment of having to conduct a woman to the hunt, 'I

209

would say that one at the right is a fine healthy specimen and will run as well as Enoch's nigger on Monday. So will the second one from the left. Both fine healthy specimens. The question is, of course, whether we can make one of them run. What do you—'

'They're going!' Pascoe interrupted.

They watched in silence as the group of men walked back into the trees. 'Looks like we lost them,' Cameron commented drily.

'Yeah.' Decker let the helicopter drift up and turned it away dispiritedly.

'Wait.' Curtis Bill did not raise his voice.

From the edge of the trees the black man came suddenly out of their shade into the early morning's clear sunlight, raised his shield at the helicopter once and started towards it at an easy lope.

'He's dropped the theatricals,' Chris Decker said. 'So let's show his audience how brave he is.' He let the helicopter ascend slowly. When the black man was in the middle of the clearing, Decker sent the helicopter at him in a screaming powerdive. The black man covered his head with his shield and ran on erect. Decker brought the helicopter up over the small group standing just inside the protection of the tree's shade, raising their shields and *assegais* in appreciation of the running man's bravery.

'He's keen,' Pascoe said, spraying them with spittle by courtesy of the rotor's downthrust swirling the air into the helicopter cabin.

'Little ole Yodoko will teach him keen, won't she?' Cameron enthused.

Yodoko turned to look at Curtis Bill. He said, 'Chris will take you to fifty yards from him and hold the chopper steady for you. Just shoot off a magazine over his head to show him you mean business.'

She nodded. Decker took the helicopter forward and steadied it. The men watched with bated breath, Pascoe even forgetting to complain at not being invited to join in the opening fusillade, as she aimed and fired. Her small hands

210

did not possess the same second nature familiarity with the rifle as her husband's hands but she was sure and smooth in her movements on trigger and bolt. They sighed in unison, a long letout breath. She would do. Speed was not so important if you had calm control of breathing and armament.

When the black man was into the trees, they went to refuel and Curtis Bill explained to Yodoko that they were certain of finding the black man again on the far side of the tree belt. She nodded and did not seem distressed at all by the necessity of letting her prey escape for a short period. But you could never tell with the Japanese . . . Like her husband yesterday, she sat impassively on the lip of the helicopter, checking and reloading her rifle while the men refuelled the helicopter's tanks. On the way to the far side of the tree belt where the black man would next appear, Cameron asked:

'Do you often have trouble? I mean like Enoch cutting himself open to the bone and Omo having a stroke. You two seem to be taking it pretty calmly.'

'Losing your cool can kill you pretty quickly,' Decker said. 'Anyway, those are minor troubles compared to having the chopper brought down and perhaps damaged so it couldn't fly. Do you fancy walking home a hundred miles or more through that?' To emphasise his point, Decker tilted the helicopter so that the hunters on the lip slid forward and would have fallen out had the safety harness not restrained them. The weight of Pascoe and Cameron caused them to sag uncomfortably against the straps. They both sighed with relief when Decker brought the helicopter back to spirit level equilibrium. Cameron said:

'Er, no, I wouldn't care to walk home through that. Not in this heat, thank you. You don't think this safari's jinxed then?' he persisted.

Curtis Bill Bonham thought of his wife Julia's foreboding and her request that he send Chris Decker alone to conduct this final safari and shrugged; it was almost over: only three more days. He opened his mouth to deny superstition and chance any part in the affairs of men who take proper precaution but his partner precluded him by speaking first:

'Christ, no! What are you talking about? A guy cuts his eyebrow with a scope? Just look at how many big game hunters have a halfmoon scar on their foreheads. Man, it's almost a status symbol like sabre cuts from that university in Germany...'

'Heidelberg,' Curtis Bill supplied.

'Yeah. Heidelberg. So, take your other case. An old man has a stroke, if Yodoko will forgive me, so what? You even warned him about it beforehand ... No, I would say what brings on bad luck is talking about it. Sun's shining and the subject's closed.'

'Yes, but –'

'Subject's closed, I said!'

Curtis Bill said, 'Put your scopes on the trees, if you please. He might not come out directly in front of us.' It would distract them sufficiently for a while. It would not do to rile Chris about his superstitions while he was flying a helicopter hanging at most thirty feet above the ground. Curtis Bill decided that he would have no visitors on his *estancia* in the Argentine for the first two years or so, simply to allow the taste of these people to clear from his mouth. The only people he would want to see would be his wife and his son.

Predictably, Pascoe spotted the black man first, before he even cleared the trees.

'That bloody scope of yours gives you an unfair advantage.'

'I'll have one made for you in return for medical services,' Pascoe offered, soothing Cameron's ruffled spirit. 'Is Yodoko going to hurry that nigger a little?' He addressed the question to Curtis Bill; both he and Cameron had ceased to regard the Japanese woman as a volitional entity. She had said not a word and she was her husband's shadow, wasn't she?

'If she wants to.'

Yodoko nodded and Decker took the helicopter up parallel to the easily running black man. Vincent's camera started whirring a second before the black man glanced fearfully at the machine pacing it. The pilot steadied the machine. 'Any time now.'

Yodoko's marksmanship was not in her husband's class but

by any other standard it was superior. She placed her first shot eighteen inches from the black man's pounding heels and her shots crept nearer until her last shot struck the earth twelve inches behind the heel descending on the hardened earth, causing the black man to break into a helter skelter run.

'He got talked into this by the others back there,' Decker opined. 'He wasn't really ready for it.'

'They didn't know we were coming again,' Curtis Bill added.

'All the better,' Cameron said, licking his lips. 'Frightened niggers teach faster.' He slurred his sibilants. 'This is a damn sight better than a nigger that shows you his arse.'

Pascoe spluttered for a moment to gain control of his tongue and the throat microphone amplified the gurgle as he hastily swallowed the spittle in his mouth. 'Maybe little ole Yodoko wants to nip that nigger around the ears a bit, make him think he's at the all-nigger Olympics and he can outrun the white man's chop – chop – chopper!' His voice had risen an octave over the sentence, ending well into the eunuch scale.

'You make him run any faster now and he'll be dead in an hour,' Curtis Bill warned.

'Is that right, Doctor Bob?' Pascoe sought a second opinion.

Cameron was reluctant to give the panicked black man breathing space. 'He looks pretty young and fit to me.'

'Yeah, I don't think he's running full bore yet,' Decker agreed.

Yodoko shook her head. She was in no hurry. If it was over too quickly because she let the two bloodthirsty barbarians and the uncouth pilot hurry her, Omo-san would know from the time of their return and from the developed film. In the back of her mind lurked a thought, and she did not know whether it was welcome: *Omo-san will not wait for the film to be developed.* She would concentrate on the implications of the thought some other time; for now she needed the full extent of her concentration for the hunt. The thing she must do, she told herself, is to hunt as Omo-san would have hunted, to hunt not as a proxy, a stand-in as the American had offensively described her function, but as Omo-san himself. Omo-san, who had laughed inwardly with her at the cats who, with their plethora of lives, could not appreciate the mystique of death. She shook her head again.

'Yodoko says we wait. It's Yodoko's hunt.'

Pascoe turned to face her. He addressed Curtis Bill. 'How do you know? She's said nothing. She never says nothing!'

Yodoko turned to look at the Englishman. His big, jowly, sunburnt, peeling and bandaged face was not a pleasant prospect. It was not long before he looked away.

'Yeah, okay, whatever she wants,' the English inventor mumbled into the throat mike. 'I dunno about women on hunting expeditions though.'

'She should – ' Cameron decided not to complete the sentence: She should hunt like a man if she wants to come hunting with us. Curtis Bill would just say she was hunting according to Omo Minowara's instructions and if she wanted to let the nigger get away once he had the fear of God put in him, that was her business. He was sorry now that he had agreed to carry the incapacitated man's request to substitute a proxy to Curtis Bill but at the time he had thought the Jap would ask him. Who could have dreamt the man would send his wife? It was just simply not natural. The sooner Thursday arrived so that he, Robert J. Cameron M.D. of New York, NY, the Fiery Knights of the KKK and the National Rifle Association, could show them how a man should hunt, the better it would be for all concerned. And when he came back next year he would insist on being in an all-American safari. Or maybe just Enoch and the dentist from Texas and himself, two Americans and a known-quantity no-shit limey; that would be good. No damned Japs who conked out after they had been warned by a proper doctor, none of their stupid Jap women who wouldn't listen to good advice from three truly experienced hunters but instead let the silent Jew Curtis Bill Bonham – funny name – speak for her. None of that. He would see to it that there was none of that.

At the refuelling depot Cameron and Pascoe were sullenly

214

slow and, once back in the air, Decker commented, 'Over six minutes air to air. You guys gone lame? Or just too old for this kind of thing?'

'We pay a lot of money for this safari,' Cameron replied with dignity. 'Why not use some of our money to hire people to refuel your aircraft, or do it yourself?'

'Yeah,' Pascoe jumped in eagerly, 'we pay not to work. We pay you to do the work. We expect service.'

The silence was chilly in the morning's shimmering heat. It dragged until Pascoe could no longer stand it:

'Well?'

'Well what?' Decker asked him calmly.

'Well, what do you say?'

Curtis Bill answered, his voice pleasantly neutral. 'Tomorrow morning Chris will run you and your wives back to Johannesburg in the plane. Your luggage will precede you on the truck through the night. Your money will be refunded to you before you leave. As for today, until Yodoko has finished her hunt, you are advised to remember that you are on board this craft, that we own it, and that Chris is in command of it. Please behave accordingly.' Somehow, unobtrusively, his rifle had appeared in his hands. It lay inoffensively across his lap but his hands were sure and deadly on it.

'Well, I must say you –' Pascoe started.

Cameron, more sensitive to the danger they had placed themselves in, snapped, 'Shut up, you fool. You've done enough damage already. Just shut up!' He turned to face Curtis Bill. 'Look, we didn't mean it like that. It was a joke, hmm?' His voice tailed off before the blank nonunderstanding look on Curtis Bill's face. 'Funny? Haha?'

'I am not open to persuasion.'

'But, just listen to –'

'Shut up, will you,' the pilot snapped. He knew Curtis Bill well enough to know that Cameron and Pascoe were near to disaster. One more push . . . 'Just keep quiet or you'll be walking home.' If they were not dead. 'Shut your idiot faces, that's all we ask of you.' The sound in the earphones was Cameron and Pascoe drawing breath to dig their own graves.

Chris Decker switched the intercom off, consigning their open mouthed shouts to the wind and the air and the noise of engine and rotor.

Vincent started his camera rolling to catch the fury on the faces of the two men flanking the diminutive Japanese woman on the lip of the helicopter. Curtis Bill shook his head at him and the Indian reluctantly stopped the camera. He wished the pilot had not switched off the intercom; it would have been rather jolly to let the two foreigners goad Mr Bonham into killing them both. Strange, he hadn't picked Mr Chris for a spoilsport, not him who was always starting fights off his own bat or promoting them between others.

The black man had disappeared. They square searched until their fuel reserve level was reached, then went back to the depot to refuel. At the depot, Cameron asked Decker:

'Can't you talk to him?'

'No.'

'We'll pay more.'

'Forget it!' *How stubbornly stupid can you get?*

'Look, we'll apologise, both of us. We'll apologise handsomely.'

'Nobody has ever changed Curtis Bill's mind once he made it up. Just shut your mouth and hope he doesn't notice you, friend. You're lucky to be alive.'

Cameron's mouth hung open. He looked towards where Curtis Bill was pulling the fuel feed hose from an empty drum. 'You mean . . .'

'Exactly. He has killed men for less.' A bit of an exaggeration but better a white lie than two dead clients. He had heard how Curtis Bill had shot two policemen in Elizabethville who had asked him to hand over his machine pistol: at twelve noon on a busy street swarming with armed men, Curtis Bill had set his Uzi to single fire, shot each of the policemen once through the heart, stepped over their corpses, walked to his jeep without looking back, and driven away without breaking the speed limit – he had been the last mercenary of whichever side he was on to leave town on that occasion.

Cameron rolled fuel drums with sullen speed after that and Pascoe took his cue from the American.

They found the black man by accident. He had been hiding in a tree and was heading for an even lusher tree a hundred yards away. Chris Decker switched the intercom on and said, 'There's your nigger, Yodoko,' and held the helicopter steady. She fired in front of the running man without further instruction. The black skidded to a halt and looked wildly at the helicopter. Then he turned and tried to race back to the tree he had just left. Decker deftly twostepped the helicopter backwards, held it and said 'Now', just as Yodoko finished reloading and raised the rifle to her shoulder. She sowed a row of bullets in front of the running black man and he turned away at a right angle from the line between the trees, away from the helicopter, away from the threatening bullets.

'Lost his spirit,' Pascoe commented tentatively.

Cameron waited to see if Decker or Bonham slapped Pascoe down before he added his own wisdom. 'No nigger's got any guts.'

Decker kept the helicopter behind the black man, matching his maximum speed constantly. Yodoko fired a neat row of bullets beside the black man every time Decker held the helicopter steady; she needed no prompting on when to fire or where to place the bullets: it was obvious each time that the black man was trying to head for a particular tree or small clump of trees. It pleased her that the hunt was proceeding smoothly; she had not dared hope it would come so easily to her. And it was a boon not to have to listen to the two dangerously insensitive morons beside her: Did they not realise that just before he killed you was when a man like Curtis Bill Bonham's voice would be at its most insidiously polite? Even the pilot, Decker, rationed himself to the necessary operating instructions now that the serious hunting had begun. She would not be surprised if men of honour and earned pride like Curtis Bill Bonham and his pilot found ways and means of revenging themselves upon the American and English buffoons for the unforgivable insults they had offered

217

the safari organisers, addressing them like second rate servants at a third rate inn.

At the end of an hour and ten minutes the black man was stumbling more often, the rhythm gone from his running, sweat flying through the grease on his body with each jerky movement of his limbs. During the last twenty minutes for which they had fuel, Decker herded him around in a large circle by the simple expedient of going up beside the running man, steadying the helicopter and saying 'Now' to the willing Yodoko who fired beside him each time. When they left to refuel the black man was turning away reflexively whenever the helicopter came up beside him. On the way to the fuel depot Curtis Bill explained the manoeuvre to Yodoko:

'The black man might get disoriented and run around in a circle until we come back. It gives us a starting point for our search when we return. It also conditions the black man to run away from the helicopter, giving you a good target for when you start shooting directly at him.' She nodded her understanding.

At the fuel depot, his feet firmly on the scorched earth, Cameron cradled his rifle across his chest and said, 'If I don't get to hunt, I'm not rolling any more fuel drums and you can't make me.'

Decker felt sorry for the sweating American. 'Nobody's forcing you to do anything. But if you want to ride in my chopper, you help fuel it. Otherwise I may just leave you here until I pass this way again on my way home tonight.' The pilot waved at the radius of eight foot high grass growing crazily skywards in the excess of photosynthesis on the edge of the cleared circle. 'If something hasn't come out of the grass by that time . . . Don't be in too much of a hurry to make your decision.'

Pascoe looked at the forbidding green and yellow circle surrounding them and started rolling a drum. After a moment Cameron joined him, mumbling, 'I'm going to get those bastards!'

'Just hold it until we're back in civilisation,' Pascoe

cautioned in a whisper, perfectly under control and not spraying spittle for once. 'Out here they hold the whip hand.'

They found the black man in a tree, not a hundred yards from where they had left him. A few well placed shots from Yodoko quickly had him slithering down the trunk in a panic. He tried to hide behind the trunk but Decker said, 'Hold your fire' and sent the helicopter circling around the tree faster than the black man could run around it. Soon he broke away and stumbled towards a clump of trees two hundred yards away. Chris Decker held the helicopter steady behind him and Yodoko aimed for his earlobe without being told the time had come for that part of the ritual. Not having to be prompted also saved her face when she missed, grazing the black man's neck an inch under the ear as he bobbed and stumbled in his fatigue. Her next shot was more accurate and she correlated the rise of her barrel with the random rhythm of his running. The earlobe came away cleanly with a little spurt of blood and the black man went flying. It took him several long seconds to rise and Decker used the time to take the helicopter over the spot where he lay cowering in the grass, clutching his head and trying to hide under his shield, and to steady the machine at a new position between the black man and the clump of trees.

'If he gets into this group of trees we've lost him,' Decker warned. 'We won't be able to go down low enough to get any clear shots at him.'

The black man rose cumbrously and started away from the helicopter towards the open space around the single tree he had come from. Decker quickly moved the helicopter to a point between the black man and the tree, herding him into the wider spaces.

'He will shortly learn to run parallel to the helicopter and not before or towards it,' Curtis Bill told Yodoko.

She nodded her understanding and waited patiently for Decker to line the helicopter up with the black man's bent running form. When the helicopter provided an absolutely steady platform in the straight line of her prey's precipitous flight, and only then, did she raise her rifle. She aimed carefully, blinked once, squeezed the trigger with a lover's caress, once, twice, three times.

'Jesus, she's as ruthless as her Jap-fanatic husband,' Cameron told Pascoe across her rifle and across her. She and all the others, excluding only the Englishman who was on his side, had ceased to exist for him as people.

Pascoe's mouth was open and he was dribbling continuously onto an already soaked shirtfront. His lips moved but only warm liquid swallowing sounds came through the throat mike, hot thick chocolate being poured from one beaker to another to cool it.

The black man fell and rolled. Then he pulled his shield over him and curled into a foetus cowering in the dust. whimpering his fear and pain to be drowned out by the unrelenting clop of the rotor and the rush of air as Decker brought the helicopter directly over him.

Yodoko knew what to do. Her shots started six inches from the black man's ankles and crept to within an inch before he jumped up and started running again. But she had shot off his other earlobe and put a shot through each shoulder in her single brilliant volley and, though no bone had been touched, the black man was losing blood rapidly and swaying with weakness and fatigue. But he was not so weak and fatigued that the wet weight in his loincloth, where he had fouled himself when he had lost his other earlobe and been shot through both shoulders, did not discomfort him. A hand reached behind him to feel the damp bulge. Then, all dignity gone, he tore the sagging loincloth from his limbs and threw it from him.

'Disgusting savage!' Pascoe.

'Only a nigger would shit himself and then take his pants off in front of a lady.' Cameron.

Vincent ran his camera for the whole sequence, following the loincloth as it curved through the air spilling its soggy contents. When the loincloth sank into the grass out of sight he returned the lens to the stumbling black man and zoomed in on his brown-streaked black buttocks grinding against each other in his laboured forward motion. It was an effort for Vincent to control his own breathing. He had to lean against the pole and rest the camera tightly against it to hold it steady. This was the best film he had ever taken. The Japanese woman might be small and pie-faced but she knew how to hunt.

Their fuel ran out and Decker turned the helicopter back to the depot. The black man fell down in his exhaustion and his own dribbling excretion.

'He'll be lying there when we come back,' Decker said needlessly; even Cameron and Pascoe had suspected as much.

'Doesn't even have the guts to crawl away and hide in a hole.' Cameron sounded disappointed.

'But he hasn't begged for mercy yet,' Pascoe whined wetly.

'He will,' Decker assured them and they worked at the refuelling with gusto, cutting the time to four minutes thirty-four seconds in the blistering heat, much to the pilot's satisfaction.

The black man would not rise, though Yodoko placed one bullet within half an inch of his ankle where he lay hiding under his shield. She looked at Curtis Bill, who shrugged.

'You *gotta* make him run!' Cameron whispered urgently.

'Shut up,' Decker said absently.

'Maybe he frightened himself to death,' Pascoe offered.

'Yeah, it's happened to niggers we were teaching back in the States. But that one's breathing.'

'How'd you know? You can only see his feet and his fingers around the shield.'

'Shield's moving.'

Yodoko shot the first joint from the black man's middle finger where it curled around the side of the shield. Cameron and Pascoe applauded her ingenuity, their earlier prejudicial condemnation of her forgotten. The black man was startled by the pain into running again, running without aim or purpose, knowing only that as long as he ran the shots would not ring out to hurt him as often as when he was still.

Progressively, as the afternoon passed and the refuelling stops blurred into one long pipeline procession of empty drums blistering hasty hands, as the cartons which had once

held cartridges married emptily into the litter on the floor
of the helicopter, as the remnants of food and drink which
Vincent handed out on request were trampled into the mess,
as the smells of sweat and lust and ultra-violet cream and
exploded powder and aero fuel and overheated cheese and
warming orange juice and oil and the crackling metal alloys
blended indistinguishably, as the zing of the intercom and
the clopping vibration of the rotor and the faint explosions
of the gunshots muffled in the headsets and the monotonous
voices of instruction or exclamation became part of the meta-
bolism so that it was strangely discomforting to stand on the
silent solid ground of the fuel depot, it became more difficult
to make the bone weary and increasingly anaemic black man
run. Yodoko had patiently waited for those rare moments of
steady rhythm in his movement to give him a flesh wound in
his upper arm and to score his ribcage with a delicately
placed shot which had Decker whistling and moved Curtis
Bill Bonham to say 'A fine shot,' his highest accolade. But
now, even when the black man was flat on the ground, his
stentorous breathing, though unheard in the artificial en-
vironment of the helicopter's intercom, expanded and shook
his chest and limbs too excessively for accurate shooting. In
addition, the sun was falling rapidly from the sky, seeking a
western horizon to rest behind, making for tricky light situ-
ations. Soon Yodoko would have to finish the black man or
let him go, but it would be a shame to kill him by accident
with the choice so near.

Vincent told Curtis Bill 'The light' and waved his hand at
the opening in which the gross figures of Cameron and Pascoe
crowded the delicate contours of Yodoko Minowara. Usually
he would just let the light recede and say nothing but she
had hunted well and given him much pleasure; she deserved
a record of the end of her hunt. Curtis Bill looked at him and
he added, 'Fifteen minutes, twenty at most.'

'We'll wrap it up in ten minutes and make sure the film's
good,' Curtis Bill said. Pascoe and Cameron sighed their
disappointment, not untinged with anticipation, but said
nothing.

Chris Decker took the helicopter down to grasstop level and headed straight for the black man. The black man did not turn away but fell to his knees in a begging posture, his hands imploring life or a merciful quick death for his broken body, his ashen and drawn face beseechingly upturned. Chris Decker checked the helicopter's advance fifty yards away. Yodoko did not fire. The pilot let the helicopter drift forward another fifteen yards. He held it. Vincent's camera whirled. Yodoko aimed and fired through the grass waving away from the rotor.

Vincent and the pilot both drew a sharp breath and then breathed out languorously. Her shot removed the black man's penis neatly from between his testicles, leaving him a man, unemasculated but impotent. The pilot and the Indian grasped the subtlety of the distinction immediately. Such ruthless mercilessness ... Without asking, Decker turned the helicopter away and Vincent stopped his camera and put the hood on the camera's lens.

'Hey, she hasn't learnt that nigger yet!'

'Isn't she going to shoot the nigger?'

'She's shot him,' Decker told them. They groaned. Decker laughed. Then he turned the helicopter back and let it hover over the black man.

The black man lay in the grass, curling around in pain, his hands between his legs, his shield and *assegai* finally discarded and lying forlorn and useless ten feet away from him.

'Beg for your life, you black bastard,' Cameron crooned.

'Shoot him in the stomach, like the baboon,' Pascoe begged.

Vincent took the hood from the lens.

Yodoko turned between the two bulky buffoons and bowed at Curtis Bill from the waist. She handed him her rifle. He took it, worked the bolt, put it to his shoulder and killed the writhing black man with a single shot to the heart. He handed the rifle back to her with a nod of his head while Cameron and Pascoe emptied their rifles into the broken black body lying beneath them, twitching it to false life with their bullets. When their rifles were empty Cameron fired all the chambers of his revolver at the perforated corpse. Decker waited for them to finish, then set the helicopter down next to the black man. The helicopter's interior lights were a startling reminder of the end of the day as he switched them on to cast their light through the gaping hole in the side of the helicopter on to the riddled body, its bullet-aspirated stomach adding a new stench to the many noxious odours already pervading the helicopter and its inhabitants.

Yodoko pressed the button to release her harness from its moorings on the floor of the helicopter. While Curtis Bill undid the second safety line from her back she found the silver tray under the mess on the floor and wiped it clean with tissues Vincent handed her wordlessly. Cameron and Pascoe stared curiously at her but she ignored them. She stepped down and took two short paces to stand beside the wracked body. She placed the silver platter on the flattened grass, straightened and bowed over the body. She drew the three inches of sharpened steel from the sheath at her waist.

'What's she going to do? Cut out the heart?'

'Maybe she wants you to play Chris Barnard and give her old man a new heart,' Pascoe giggled.

'Shut up!' Decker had left his command post to come watch from the open side of the helicopter.

Yodoko bent over the black body, her face untwitching in the odour emanating from it, and cut into one side of the throat. She held her hand away from the weakly spurting blood.

'Christ, she can borrow my hunting knife,' Cameron exploded and pulled it from his belt. He held it out to her but she ignored him and he sat foolishly with the knife in his hand, arm extended, until Decker said, 'Put it away.'

Yodoko cut the other side of the throat with a single slash, then two more single slashes to lay the vertebrae of the neck bare. She chose her gaps and pressed the point of the knife against it, then tilted the knife sharply to sever the bone and marrow. One more slash and the flesh and sinew and skin behind the backbone was severed and she held the head up dripping, away from her still neatly unspattered clothing.

Vincent jumped down from the helicopter with what was left of their water and poured it over the head and her hand to wash the excess blood from it. Yodoko placed the head on the tray and gave the tray to Vincent to hold. Curtis Bill leant over the quiet and motionless Cameron and Pascoe to hand her the box she had brought from the kitchen in the dawn so many weary hours ago. Yodoko ignored the box while she turned the collar of her shirt and took two pins from behind the collar. She put one pin in her mouth. The other pin she used to pin back the eyelid of the dead head, spreading the eye open first with her other hand, finger and thumb. Then the other eye was similarly spread open and pinned back with the second pin from her mouth. She looked this way and that at the staring head, then took the box Curtis Bill still held out. She pulled out a length of self-sealing household stretch plastic from the box and tore it off against the perforated edge of the box. She gave the box back to Curtis Bill. It took her a moment to straighten the plastic where it had folded over to cling to itself. She took the edges of the plastic carefully in her hands and held it over the head on the silver tray so that the centre of the plastic was exactly over the head. When she was satisfied, she brought the plastic down firmly on the head, exerting equal pressure to both sides so the unstable head should not fall over. She tucked the edges of the self-sealing plastic neatly and nimbly under the tray, her fingers flying to exert the sealing pressure while Vincent turned the tray for her. She took the tray from Vincent and came to the helicopter. Curtis Bill removed her rifle from where she had put it down on her seat, Vincent climbed in and she sat down again, the tray held in her lap. Curtis Bill clipped in her harness catches and the extra safety line and Decker took the helicopter homewards into the sudden night.

Two

One moment the circle of flares lit by the faithful Bantu servants burnt peacefully, the next the helicopter came out of the dark to send the flames bending away backwards from its murderous draught. The hands of a truly experienced pilot set the weary machine dead centre in the circle of flame trying to escape the force of the rotor. The interior light came on and the slim tanned man leant forward in his canvas chair to unclip the three hunters while their own hands pushed quick release buttons. The woman waited for the slim man to push the button to release her harness from the drag of the helicopter, not trusting herself to hold the tray in one hand instead of two. The light gleamed blindingly from the plastic cover of the silver tray. When she was free, she put the tray briefly on her lap and undid the scarf around her hair to drape it across the tray and obscure its contents from curious eyes. She stepped to the ground and walked away, holding the tray ceremonially in front of the thrust of her small breasts. The slim man accompanying her, though only of average height and a hair, towered over her.

The two large men who had flanked her rose and stretched. An Indian jumped down from the interior of the helicopter, carrying an expensive camera in one hand and a leather bag for its accessories in the other. The Indian disappeared towards the lights of the lounge and dining-room. The massive blond pilot came from his plexibubble and jumped down between the two equally bulky men, his unruffled ease a reproach to their dishevelment.

'Are you going to do us a favour and talk him into letting us hunt too?' An aggressive East Cheap whine incongruous in one so well nourished.

226

'Forget it, Enoch. It's not –'

'Hell, now we've seen how good it can be, all we – ' American.

'I told you, forget it!'

The American dropped his hand to the butt of the revolver at his hip. The pilot's voice lost several degrees of non-existent warmth:

'I know you wouldn't even think of threatening me with firearms, Bob, because you know I'll take you apart with my bare hands. But let me give you some advice. Don't even think about threatening Curtis Bill. It would be your last thought and your death warrant.'

'Yeah, so you say.' Solid earth under his feet had given the American some of his confidence back. He took his hand from the revolver, which he had just remembered was not loaded, and put his hand on the pilot's shoulder. 'Look, Chris, you're a good chap. Enoch and I have come all this way and spent a lot of money. All –'

'No. I will not talk to Curtis Bill.'

'What about in the morning? Is it likely he'll have cooled down by then?'

The pilot looked at the Englishman with pity. 'You don't understand. Curtis Bill hasn't been angered yet, or you would not be walking around here asking for the impossible.'

The American doctor took the English inventor by the arm. 'Come. He's not going to help us. Let's go pack our stuff.'

They walked away into the darkness while the blond pilot stared suspiciously after their meek retreat. He was distracted by the reappearance of the slim man.

'Did you get the film from Vincent?'

'No.'

'I'll get it. I don't like him having it for too long. A while ago, when I found it necessary to punish him for brutality to a kitchen servant by the name of Jonas, he threatened to blackmail us with his knowledge.'

'I don't think he would be serious about that.'

'No. Still . . . ' The slim man turned to go as the pilot

227

stared after him. At the edge of the light the slim man turned and faced the pilot. 'About the money we'll lose by repaying Cameron and Pascoe, I'll carry it all. I'll pay out your share for this safari.'

'Ten thousand dollars won't make much difference one way or the other.'

'They were becoming an irritant.'

'Yeah. They're getting on my tits too.'

'Still, it's a bad business, finishing our last safari like this.'

'We can always carry on, have many more safaris.' The words tumbled out under their own volition before he could stop himself. Immediately he hated himself for his weakness.

'No. I am sorry.' The slim man rubbed his eyes. 'Look, think about what I said. I'll stake you in any business of your choice. Up to a hundred grand. Or you can still find a partner and take over Ultimate Test, Incorporated with repayments spread over a term to suit you.'

The pilot listened to his partner with an impassive face. But inside him the turbulence was building up and when it burst his voice was thin and dangerous. 'I don't need charity. I won't take charity. Fuck you for offering charity.'

He whirled so that the other man should not see the contortion of his face. He stalked away to where the plane rested under its tarpaulin and sat down on the edge of the tarp on the far side from the helicopter and its circle of flares and his partner.

The slim man looked after him for a minute, took a step forward as if to follow him, turned on his heel and retreated to where the lights of the building spelled out a welcome.

The pilot leant back against the tautness of the canvas. He considered taking the plane up, knowing it would calm him, but conversely he was in such a state as to doubt the ability in his shaking hands to take off without doing himself or the plane irreparable harm. And the plane would use a certain amount of fuel and fuel cost money. It was a long time since he'd had to worry about fuel bills or spending money in almost any denomination he could desire to spend it in.

228

Money. Curtis Bill was being very unreasonable in not continuing with their arrangement until he, Decker, could build up another nest egg. He didn't know enough about the business end of the safaris to run the whole thing by himself. And the idea of a partner – laughable! Unless you had known a man for a long time, you wouldn't want him in this business with you. It was not a diaper service. Anyway, Decker couldn't even think of anybody he'd go into even a diaper service with except Curtis Bill. The kind of people Decker had known long enough to go into business with – this kind of business – would all kill their grandmothers for some assured amount of folding green and Decker for considerably less: killing was their business and Decker was alive simply because he was very good at it. But there was no sense in bluffing himself he could deal with accountants on equal footing. Curtis Bill had once explained to him the mechanism of the 'Lichtenstein holding company through which they channelled funds in order to avoid paying taxes. Decker understood the difference between tax avoidance and tax evasion, one being legal and the other illegal, but anything more complicated stumped him. Curtis Bill was different, he thrived on that kind of thing, suggested things the lawyers themselves had not thought of, astounding even some very fly Lichtenstein types.

Chris Decker chewed a stem of sweet green grass and added up their assets in Ultimate Test, Incorporated, half of which would come to him. He knew to a penny what the plane and chopper would fetch. Not all that much because both were five years old with a lot of hours behind them. He had a shrewd idea what their three Range Rovers and refrigerated Mercedes truck would realise. A greater percentage of their replacement value than the aircraft because their useful life was longer. Curtis Bill had told him recently their base camp and the land around it as well as the warehouse at Edenvale had doubled in value over the five years and, after a while, he remembered what they had paid for it. He added it all up, divided by two. Thrice as much as he had put in five years ago when he and Curtis Bill had first teamed up; he had come freshly paid from Biafra and Bangladesh then and had felt rich but now several years of inflation had eroded the buying power of his money. His penthouse was rented and his Ferrari paid for but he would drop a packet if he sold it now. Even so, if he took the loss and added the money to his share of Ultimate Test, Incorporated, he would have enough to live on for two years at a much reduced rate of expenditure.

Prospects? He knew nothing but flying and killing. Aging pilots with their own ramshackle little airlines were two a penny and none rich. Licking arses for smelly cargoes was not for him. He was not a businessman who could invest his capital – plus Curtis Bill's hundred grand insult – in something else and make it pay. Forty-three-year-old mercenaries were not in great demand and after five years of penthouse life he was not the man he had been at thirty-eight. Of course, any of the outfits newly arrived to compete with Ultimate Test, Incorporated, would snap him up but he did not relish the idea of being an employee when he had been a partner in the top concern in the field. It would be too much of a comedown. People who had envied him only yesterday would be able to order him around. Security work somewhere? Not with his record and certainly not if he had to keep office hours.

Conclusion? He chewed at a fresh stem of sweet green grass and decided he had left nothing out of his calculations. There was only one conclusion.

Curtis Bill Bonham, to whom he had offered his friendship, was wilfully condemning him to a life of poverty.

Three

With Yodoko gone and Judith unenthusiastic about swimming, Melody had perforce to spend most of the day at the base camp. If Yodoko had persuaded the men to break their own rule and take her with them on their hunt, good for her! Melody was not envious. But that was no reason to break another rule made in good faith for her own protection: not going to the pool unaccompanied. She spent much of the day reading to Omo Minowara, much to his annoyance, tiring him with the effort of keeping face before the American doctor's wife. An additional irritation to the sick man was the continual pantrymaster's delight Judith insisted on sending from the kitchen. Melody helped him taste each dish and by the time a rich broth, the only thing he would have wanted and could digest, came in the afternoon he had lost the appetite to do more than taste it politely. Melody tried conversation a few times but the Japanese was so silent that she seemed to chatter a one-sided inanity to herself and resumed reading. Once she went to the kitchen and suggested that Judith could spend some time with the sick man but Judith obviously preferred to do her duty from a distance. Melody resumed reading, not willing to admit even to herself that the short declarative sentences sounded dull in their rolling infinity: they were never meant to be read aloud but she had chosen the book because it was a man's book. She was glad when the helicopter returned and thought Omo Minowara showed signs of interest too. She would wait until Yodoko returned to the *rondawel* before she left.

'Sounds like they're back,' she said brightly.

'Yes. Thank you for looking after me. You read well.'

Melody suppressed a ridiculous urge to say something

231

about only doing her Christian duty. Who knew what religion the Japanese adhere to? She closed the book and stood to one side, not too near the bed, to wait for Yodoko to come so that she could go. Not knowing what to say, she nodded attentively at the Japanese as she had seen Yodoko do.

There was a knock on the door and then it swung inwards to reveal Curtis Bill holding it open, looking back at Yodoko as she came past him. She was carrying a tray, covered with some coloured cloth. Melody was surprised she'd had time to stop off at the kitchen in the short time since the helicopter had landed. Curtis Bill did not enter; he closed the door behind Yodoko and they heard him crunch away on the gravel path.

Yodoko placed the tray on the card table Melody had erected beside the bed and stepped aside. Melody took a pace forward from the other side of the bed, moving into the light, to say her good-byes. Yodoko had eyes only for her husband as she pulled the coloured cloth away from the tray and its contents.

The clear plastic glinted in the light of the single reading lamp and at first Melody thought the reflection had deceived her. But no, the head of a man stared at her from the silver tray, light glinting dully from his eyeballs, brightly from the pinpoint slivers of steel holding his eyelids open. Drops of water or sweat still trickled from his hair on to the tray, to run a pinkish moat around his truncated neck. Somebody had cut his head from his body! But she clearly saw the aura of his body, neck and shoulders, torso and narrow curving waist, hips and thighs and calves and ankles and feet, underneath the head, through the table and through the floor; the silver tray, which she now recognised as Vincent's serving platter, a guillotine through a living man's neck. Melody gasped and Yodoko turned her blank face towards her, seeing her for the first time. The Japanese woman gave no sign of recognising her but turned back and bowed at her husband, who nodded his head. They both ignored Melody and she knew she was intruding into the intimacy and the privacy of their home, family and marriage, into a culture

232

alien to her. It was the river and the hippopotamus and the crocodiles all over again: she was the outsider, the one who was all wrong, who looked different and thought different and did nothing right. She swallowed a small scream, looked at the head wrapped up on the silver tray like a bouquet of flowers once more to assure herself she was not having a nightmare – knowing that the nightmare would not relent simply because she wished it to – to find the aura gone but the eyes still staring balefully straight at her. Her little scream, scarcely more than an intense gasp, escaped her lips and she rushed out of the door, knowing the two Japanese would not notice her in their rapt attention to the part-man on the tray and ashamed at herself for judging their disregard more important than the life of the man on the tray.

She wandered blindly towards the *rondawel* she shared with Bob. He must have known what was going on. How involved was he in this business? The door of their *rondawel* stood open, warm safe light streaming from it. On the threshold she stepped back, eavesdropping intentionally for the first time in her life. Her husband and the English inventor sent their loud voices drifting out into the night. Melody realised with a start that they were attempting confidential low tones; she even smiled briefly at their self delusion before she recollected with a sob the reason for her eavesdropping.

' . . . so it's his ball and his bat, okay. But that doesn't mean he can say who's to pitch *and* who's to bat. One or the other.'

'Bob, that pilot feller may be a stuffed Canadian shit, but he means us well and if he –'

'Yeah, sure. But he's playing up the melodrama bit, how these ex-mercenaries will slit your throat for a nickel, sure, it makes him seem big too if his partner is dangerous. But Curtis Bill's a Jew and he'll listen to reason, the kind that comes straight out of a cheque book.'

'I didn't know he was Jewish. If I –'

'Of course he is! Just look at his tan and his hair. And who's got a name like that if he isn't Jewish? Tell me, have you heard him deny being Jewish?'

'No. But –'

'Well, what more proof do you need?'

'Have you looked?'

'Sure, when we were having a piss at the fuel depot. The rabbi's been at his dong all right. Look, all I'm asking is just a little moral support from you while I give him a smell of the good ole Yankee dollar, right there under his nose. There's no risk in it.'

'I don't know. I think Curtis Bill's dangerous.'

'Sure. But have you actually seen him do anything? It's all talk. Why, he couldn't even help that poor old Jap! I had to do it, didn't I, save that old man's life? And have you looked at him, really looked at him? He's only a runt, not even six feet. Look, just listen to me for a minute.'

'Okay, I'll listen.'

'What we'll do is to talk to him again in the morning, offer him a real humbly handsome apology, our cheque books real conspicuous-like in our hands. We'll say we'll pay more.'

'It's damned expensive anyway.'

'You want to go back and count your money now you know how good it can be?'

'We still won't be able to shoot anything if we have no guns. It'll be a day wasted while the guns come back from Johannesburg on the truck.'

'How much of the local cash money do you have?'

'I don't know. Judith looks after money. Why?'

'That Vincent's in charge of the niggers, including the truck driver. I'm going to offer him an incentive to have the truck break down before it can leave tonight.'

'I'll go fetch it. What about traveller's cheques?'

'Naw. I got those myself. He'll want the local clamshells, being no brighter than a nigger, just lighter. Lightskinned niggers aren't necessarily cleverer than their black brothers.'

'I know. Like Jamaicans.'

The English inventor passed Melody without noticing her, his head down, his mouth open, his hands swinging slackly at his sides.

'Where the hell have you been?' her husband demanded as she entered the door.

234

'Over at the Minowara *rondawel* and then waiting outside until you finished talking to Enoch,' she said in her usual meek manner, force of habit protecting her for a moment longer from the truth to be faced.

'Oh. Well, look, I want you to pretend to pack. Like we're leaving. Only we won't be leaving.'

'I will be.'

'What?'

'I will be leaving.'

A slow smile broke over his sunburned face, drawing his lips away from his teeth in a hideous ultra-violet fantasy. 'So you were over at the Minowara *rondawel*, were you?' he gloated.

'I saw the head. Who killed the man?'

For a moment the question startled him, then he laughed. 'Why, she did, of course. And cut it off with a neat little knife. And then covered it in gladwrap just like any joint in the kitchen.'

If he thought he was going to make her sick, he was mistaken. 'Why?'

'Why what?'

'Why did she cut the head off and wrap it in plastic?'

'To show to Omo, of course. She was hunting as his stand-in. Would that you were as dutiful and loyal and capable as she.'

She noticed the glass in his hand. It was a large tumbler and it was half full of straight bourbon. She was sure he had originally filled it to the brim. 'What is he going to do with the head?'

'Catch a thrill, mount it, cook it, how should I know! All I want you to do is to appear to pack.'

'Do you kill your man before Enoch or after?'

'Before! Now stick the questions and get on with the packing. I have important things to do.' He gulped the liquor in his glass and headed for the bottle on the windowsill to his right.

'Just one more question, please Bob. Why do we have to appear to pack?'

235

'Because that nigger-loving Jew Curtis Bill Bonham is throwing Enoch and I out as if we were mad dogs.' He held the tumbler up in one hand and hurled the empty bottle against the wall. 'Now pack!'

She looked at the shattered pieces of glass on the floor and saw again the head wrapped in household plastic, standing on a silver serving tray. Her control snapped but she kept her voice calm. 'I shall pack, Bob. But not for make-believe. For real. If you do not come tomorrow when we have the chance to leave, I shall go alone.'

'You'll do as I say!' He took a large draught of his bourbon. *Would that you were as dutiful and loyal and capable as she.* 'And next you'll say Go kill a man and cut his head off and bring it to me on a tray.'

'You're hysterical,' he said, putting his glass down on the windowsill. 'There's only one sure cure for hysterical women.' The return of his hand across her face sent her staggering, her knees buckling with the force of the blow, but he caught her before she could fall, holding her up by the front of her blouse and held her while he struck her: palm, backhand, palm, backhand, palm, backhand, palm, backhand, palm –

Enoch Pascoe came through the door. He gaped at the tableau for a moment, then closed his mouth firmly and sank into a boxing stance, chin tucked into his shoulder and protected by his right fist, left fist circling, punching air threateningly as he shuffled around without taking his eyes from Cameron's massive open hand cracking into Melody's lolling face again and again. 'Bash her,' he burbled. 'A left and a right and a left and a right.'

Cameron became aware of Pascoe. He threw Melody from him. The bed caught her behind the knees and she fell, gasping for air. Pascoe gazed pop-eyed at her large bosom heaving against the thin material of the blouse.

'Give it to me.' Cameron's chest was heaving at the end of the arm he held out for the money.

Pascoe's eyes were fixed on Melody's form spread across the bed. He fumbled in his pocket for the roll of notes, found it and waved it in the air until Cameron took it impatiently and started ushering him towards the door.

'Tell them to send our dinner down here. And a bottle of bourbon. Understand?'

'Huh? Yeah. Dinner and bourbon.'

'And make your wife pretend to pack.' Cameron closed the door in Pascoe's face as the Englishman stared over his shoulder at Melody on the bed. He stood with his back to the door and folded his arms. 'You think I don't know about all those lies you've been telling other doctors about me, about how I'm sterile, don't you? Well, tonight we'll see.' He advanced on her. 'And you can scream all you want. They probably won't hear you. And if they do, they'll probably enjoy it even more than I do. But you can just put any thoughts that they'll interfere between a man and his wife when the man's rightfully punishing the wife for disobedience right out of your mind.'

She rose from the bed and tried to put it between them but he applied his enormous reach and grabbed the front of her blouse again and slammed her back with his free hand. The blouse ripped and she fell but he caught her in mid-air by the strength of her bra and pulled her upright to hit her again. And again and again. Still holding her upright by the bra between her bulging breasts, his knuckles digging cruelly into her flesh, he let her sag away from him while his free hand unbuckled his belt and ripped it free of the loops around his waist. He spun her around and pushed her over on the bed. She fell face down and bounced. He put his hands into the waistband of her slacks and pulled, ripping the slacks and her panties open around the curve of her buttocks and into her crotch.

'Now we'll teach your pink pussy to fuck around with overpaid tourist guide pilots!'

Melody had never been beaten before. She lay perfectly still while the belt blows rained down on her, hoping that if she did not scream or resist or try to protect her buttocks, he would lose interest in her torment and stop. She gritted her teeth through the tears on her face and concentrated on the new experience of hating him.

Four

Vincent held his arm out in front of him and admired the
solid gold Rolex. He now had three, all the same. His own,
which he had bought, and one each which had belonged to
those lumbering idiots Pascoe and Cameron. He also had
nearly three thousand *rand,* the equivalent of four thousand
American dollars, of their money in cash. All for nothing.
In his room at the end of the servants' bungalow Vincent
giggled. All for nothing. He'd taken all the money and sent
Cameron back to get Pascoe's watch as well before he had
given his considered opinion: Mr Bonham was likely to catch
on quick smart if the truck was either in working condition
and simply claimed to be out of operation or if the truck
was sabotaged – in either case he'd ask Mr Chris to look at
it and Mr Chris was a mechanical genius and couldn't be
bluffed. What they should do, Cameron and Pascoe, Vincent told them, was to pack and load their stuff on to the
truck as if they were taking their expulsion meekly but to
keep their guns under their beds. 'Put your shoes or your
after-shave or your wife's cosmetics in the gun cases to give
them weight,' he had told them (Pascoe having come along
to get the expensive advice at first hand). Vincent giggled
uncontrollably. If those two idiots thought Mr Bonham
could be persuaded to change his mind by offers of money
or threats or any other means, they were going to be sadly
or brutally disillusioned, depending on their choice of suasive
medium. Vincent hoped it would be brutally or, failing
terminal violence, at least painfully.

The mental picture of Mr Bonham beating another man
reminded Vincent of his beating at the Edenvale warehouse
and the score still unsettled arising from that occasion. If

there were going to be no further safaris, if tomorrow was going to be the last day of Ultimate Test, Incorporated, tonight was not too early to start settling his debts of pain without any fear of Mr Bonham's retribution simply because Mr Bonham would never find out. He went to his desk and sat down behind it. He pressed the button on the corner and his orderly came in. Vincent said, 'Send Jonas, the kitchen helper, to me.'

'Yes, Mr Vincent,' the man said and left.

Vincent searched around for a newspaper and found one about six months old. He paced the room, discarding pages as he coursed through it. He found an article headed 'New Atrocities' and tore it from the paper, using the straight edge of his desk to ensure square tearing. He folded the article and placed it in a strong manila envelope from a desk drawer. Then he addressed the envelope to the Chief of Police, Lourenço Marques with the aid of a Portuguese-English dictionary.

Jonas was shown in by the orderly. Vincent sent the orderly to fetch a messenger stick. He regarded the black man standing nervously in front of his desk. The bandage around his head was now soiled but his clothing was as clean as ever. He looked frightened. Vincent smiled broadly at him but closed his lips quickly; he was not accustomed to smiling.

'You cannot work in the kitchen while your head is healing.'

The black man's face paled at the threat to his livelihood. He shuffled his feet and looked down at them but did not speak.

Vincent pressed the stopwatch button on the gold Rolex and let him wait a full sixty seconds. The joyous sensation of power over the wellbeing of others would never fade for Vincent.

'Until you can return to the kitchen, you're messenger.' He pressed the bell again and the orderly brought in the newly cut messenger stick, a trimmed branch split at one end. Vincent took the stick and stuck the manila envelope in the split. 'Tomorrow, before the sun rises, you will cross the river and turn towards the sun. Run along the river until you reach the big water, then turn away from the sun until you come to a city as big as *eGoldi*.' The stupid Bavenda was not likely to know the difference between a city of one and a half million people, like Johannesburg, and a city of less than two hundred thousand, like Lourenço Marques. 'There you will find the person this important letter from Mr Bonham is addressed to. Show the envelope to anybody who can read and they will direct you. Is that clear?'

Vincent considered. If the animals or the hostile people did not get the dumb Bavenda on his run of several weeks to the sea and along the coast to Lourenço Marques, the LM police would arrest him for being in their country with an obviously bogus message addressed to the chief of police. With no papers he would stand no chance, even if the LM police went to the trouble, which was not likely, of trying to contact his employers. Both Mr Bonham and Mr Chris would be long gone from the base camp and the warehouse at Edenvale, the only other reference point the Bavenda knew, would be sold. The idiot nigger who had caused him so much trouble was dead where he stood, he just didn't know it yet. Vincent made sure by reaching into his pocket and peeling a few notes from the roll: if the Bavenda wasn't killed for the money before he reached LM, the police would regard his wealth in only one way – the gains of violence.

'Here. This money is for food along the way.'

The Bavenda fingered the notes. He had never seen so much money together at once.

'Take it. The road will be long and hard. You will be expected to return what is left and to account for what you spent. Go now, sleep and rest.'

When the black man had gone, Vincent giggled some more. He wondered how long the Moçambique police would keep a black man alive while they beat from him the answer to his source of a thousand South African *rand*. He said sternly to the room at large 'And the wounds in your forehead. Now tell me, did you beat your employer to death and

240

steal his money after he punished you for your mis-
demeanours and insolence?' A week, ten days? The Bavenda
was tougher than he looked. 'And this cock and bull story, it
simply won't do, my good man. We have tried to trace the
people you say sent you, and there is no record of them
anywhere.' Vincent punched one fist into the palm of the
other hand while he talked. 'Come now, good Bavenda Jonas,
you cannot walk into the office of the chief of police with an
insulting message and expect your lies to be believed.
Schmack, schmack!' Of course, the Bavenda might not make
it as far as LM, a distance of more than three hundred miles
through hostile country. But if he did . . . Vincent had an
erection. He fingered it while he considered things to be done,
pain to be administered, and the time left to do it in. He had
*ime for relief and perhaps even gratification, he decided,
and pressed the bell again.

'Send in the two kennel keepers who took the Rhodesian
ridgeback away on Sunday,' he instructed his orderly.

While he waited for them to come, Vincent opened a
drawer of his desk and took from it a metal box which he
unlocked. He counted off two piles of notes of equal value
from the stock inside the metal box and replaced the box
after locking it again. From another drawer of his desk he
took a pay book and made an entry into it. He split one of the
piles of money in two. The two dog handlers came in and
stood respectfully in front of his desk.

'I persuaded Mr Chris to give you a bonus for your brave
work with the large dog on Sunday.'

Their eyes fell to the piles of notes. Vincent pushed the two
smaller piles across the desk. He spread the pay book on the
far side of the desk. 'Sign there.'

One of the handlers could read. Or perhaps the wine
steward on the veranda had carried the news of Mr Chris's
generosity. 'This is not a week's pay.'

'No. But you work for me. Our agreement is I take half.'

'Yes, but not extra, not – not bonus!' The black man finally
found the word.

'Okay. Take this then and give the half back from your
241

pocket.' Vincent touched the largest pile of money but did not push it across the desk. 'But you will have no job on Saturday, when we pay at the end of the week.' None of the servants were yet likely to know it was all over, their easy life at the base camp, the privilege of associating with Vincent.

The kennel keeper stared his hatred at the Indian for a moment with eyes red in the corners, then turned on his heel and left the room in defeat despite the defiant set of his shoulders.

The other black man bent over the pay book to make his mark. Vincent told him, 'Men must eat. Even if they are impervious to hunger the stomachs of their wives and children will growl.'

The black man finished the laborious process of making his cross and straightened. He was a fine sturdy specimen. He was all that was immediately available.

Vincent pushed the largest pile of money forward. 'Put your money on the table.'

'The money . . . ?'

'Yes, yes! Give me the half and take the whole week's wages.'

Not believing his good luck, the black man took the already sweaty thin packet of notes from his pocket and placed it on the desk. He snatched up the thicker packet and let it disappear into his pocket with the speed of a magician practising a routine. He turned to go but Vincent stopped him.

'Not so fast. Show your gratitude for my generosity first.'

The black man stared at the Indian blankly.

'I shall have my pleasure of you first.' Vincent elucidated by making a fist and banging the side of it with the palm of his other hand.

A look of revulsion crossed the black man's face, putting a keen edge on Vincent's anticipation, and he looked towards the unmade bed against the wall.

Vincent giggled again. It did not matter now that people knew he enjoyed himself as every other man did. 'No, not here. Outside in the cool, where I will not have to smell you so much.'

The black kennel keeper looked at his feet in indecision.

'Or would you rather give the thick money back and take the thin?'

The man shook his head fractionally.

'Come on then. The night waits.'

Five

In the day the boat with the compromise of her lines between seaworthiness and speed had crept slowly up the river, passing Chisselane at siesta time in the sweltering heat of the midday when prying eyes slept. At dusk she was within a mile of the South African border and seemed settled for the night, if not totally deserted. At first night, suddenly a blackness after the warm shadow of the dusk, only a very keen observer would have seen the rubber dinghy sneak away from her side, the man in it paddling with measured silence against the sluggish flow of the Limpopo until he was well past Pafuri and then running the outboard at low revolutions to keep the sound down. Only the very sharpest of observers would have been able to follow the man in his dinghy that far and even the best observer would have lost him in the blackness of the overhangs roughly, because the observer could never know, where the fence of the Kruger National Park turned inland, away from the Limpopo. Man and dinghy and outboard had simply disappeared.

The man from the dinghy moved with the tomcat ease of many victories to inspect the ground over which tomorrow or the day after or the day after that or whenever he decided suited him, regardless of some politician's infantile desires, he would lead his men to a new chapter in his own legend: an attack against white men on South African soil followed by a successful escape, the whole distorted by the international papers. He crossed the mile to the camp in twenty-five minutes, slithering through the dark as silently as a snake. White men in the bosom of White Africa were not likely to have set out guards. Nor were there likely to be any security devices, for these would be little more than a nuisance to be set off by small animals to wake weary sleepers in the middle of the night. Still, the man from the dinghy moved with care. Haste killed the cat, his father had often said. At a little past eleven he reached the camp and, as he had expected, all was in darkness. There was ample light from the full moon, which had been up for a couple of hours, to distinguish the lounge, dining-room and kitchen complex and the circle of *rondawels* curving away from it. It was the layout he had half expected, a good defensive position for soldiers. Except that the defenders would not even know what hit them or when, nor have time to organise a defence even if they knew how and had the wherewithal. He smiled whitely and moved around the circle of *rondawels*, stopping once to listen to a woman whimper softly under the stentorian snoring of her husband. If she was frustrated tonight, tomorrow his men would surely give her an excess of what she wanted. At the airstrip he lifted the tarpaulins to look at the plane and the helicopter, which called forth a short whistle. This was an affluent safari for wealthy people. He would have to watch the looting of the men he allowed to leave here after their work was done: an excess of unaccustomed and unaccountable riches adorning a black man was an invitation to questioning by the militia. He sniffed the air and walked downwind of the kennels to inspect the servants' quarters and fix their position relative to the circle of *rondawels* on his mental map. When he struck, the distance between the two points would represent a vital element of timing. He came up to the rail bordering the vegetable garden and followed it until he found the Indian sodomising the black kennel keeper. The black man stood facing the rail, his hands on it, his hips curved backward. The Indian faced the black man's back, his own body curved backwards from the ecstasy of their joined middles. The man from the dinghy was not sure whether the sucking sound was exciting or revolting. He looked down to assure himself their trousers were hobbling their ankles before he spoke:

'Enjoying yourself?'

Vincent turned his head without a break in his rhythm. The man from the dinghy had to admire the Indian's self control. Vincent did not reply.

'What is there here besides the white men's circle, the planes, the kennels and the servants' *campong*?'

'The generating house at the pool.' There was no hesitation in Vincent's answer. 'Who are you?'

The question was ignored. 'Where is the pool?'

'Beside the river. The generator is in the housing under the waterfall. Why do you want to know?'

'How many people? Men, women, children, servants?'

The phrase from the newspapers triggered Vincent's memory to the cutting from the newspaper – 'New Atrocities' – he had given Jonas to carry to the chief of police in Lourenço Marques and he giggled. 'You're a terrorist come to case the joint before an attack.'

'How many people?' the man behind him repeated patiently.

'Five white men. Three women. No children. Thirty servants, give or take a couple,' Vincent answered equitably and asked eagerly, 'Are you going to kill me?'

'No. You are too cowardly to inform the white men of my coming,' the man from the dinghy said with genuine revulsion. 'All white men deserve servants like you. You are too contemptible to die.'

It was the finest and most enjoyable humiliation of Vincent's life. He nearly came with the ecstasy of it and had to stop his thrust into the black man for a moment. Beneath the contempt of Death! It was better than the white women he had paid in Durban to pee in his face.

Vincent resumed his stroke. Then he became aware that the visitor was still standing behind him. He looked over his shoulder at the tall silhouette against the moon and knew instinctively that the man meant to kill him, disappointment at lost humiliation flushing him and almost causing him to spurt. He stopped for the space of three strokes and started again.

'You are going to kill me.'

'Do you think I am waiting for my turn with your catamite?'

'An educated nigger!' Vincent sneered. 'Will you wait until I come?'

'It is a small thing to ask in return for valuable information.'

'Thank you.'

'What do you do in the safari? Chief steward?'

'Chief steward and photographer.'

'Get any good film lately?'

He does not know the purpose of the safari! He thinks it is a camera safari! Vincent was only sorry he would not be around to see the slaughter when the unsuspecting terrorists attacked armed and determined men of the calibre of Mr Chris and Mr Bonham. That would be something to – But there would be nobody here except servants after tomorrow.

'If you're going to kill the people here, you'd better do it before noon tomorrow. They will all be gone by then.'

'You cannot buy your life.'

Vincent could hold back for only a few strokes more. He heard the terrorist come closer behind him. Even if he had wanted furiously to live, which he did not, he could not have dragged himself away from his pleasure to fight futilely for his life.

'But a favour?' the Indian strangled through a throat constricted with lust. 'Kill him first.'

The black man struggled when he grasped that his life was being bartered for a few moments of Vincent's pleasure but the Indian leant over to lock him against the rail between his arms. The black man's wriggling as the terrorist slit his throat stimulated Vincent beyond the limits of his fearful anticipation and he started spurting into the dying body.

'Who are you?' Vincent shouted as the knife sliced cleanly into his throat and a curve of blood caught the moonlight. Vincent's last coherent thought was pique at the fleet transience of the finest combination of sensations ever to pleasure him. The last words he heard through the gurgle of his own blood:

'I am Jomo Iningwe.'

THURSDAY

One

'Typical. First rat off the sinking ship,' the pilot condemned the absent Vincent while his eyes coasted professionally over the still dark eastern horizon as if to pull the sun of happier days up over it by pure willpower. From long habit, five years of habit, Curtis Bill Bonham and Chris Decker stood on the veranda in the pre-dawn dark to eat their breakfast, even on this day when there would be no hunting. But this day differed bittersweetly in that there were no clients parodying themselves with loud reassuring bravado or bloodlusting anticipation. And Vincent was not hovering in the background.

'He'll be around somewhere,' Curtis Bill said without interest. For him this was just another day; the bittersweet belonged solely to his partner.

'He didn't go with the truck last night.'

'Do you think he stole our Range Rover to make his escape?' Curtis Bill humoured his partner whimsically.

Chris Decker was appalled. 'Vincent would never steal from us!'

'And he would not walk if he can wait and ride.' Curtis Bill tired of the subject and turned to the waiter standing attentively near the lit doorway. 'Tell Vincent Mr Chris wants him.'

The waiter went inside. Decker said, 'Vincent is too frightened of you and I to steal one from us.'

The cook came from the kitchen and stood nervously twisting his hands until Curtis Bill said, 'Speak.'

'Vincent cannot come, Mr Bonham. Vincent is dead.'

'How did it happen?'

'I am having the bodies brought so that you may see for yourself, sir.' The man was very frightened. After Vincent he had been second in command over the black servants, now he would be chief. The white men might think he had killed Vincent to advance his own ambition. There was no telling what these horrible white men, who both ate so neatly and sparingly of his fine food, would do if they suspected him. 'As soon as you have finished your breakfast.'

'Now will do,' Curtis Bill said.

'We are not squeamish,' Decker added.

The cook walked to the end of the veranda and spoke sharply to the men waiting around the corner of the building, out of sight of the white men. Then he waddled back along the veranda, clucking to himself with nausea and fear. Behind him came four Bantu in blue uniforms, carrying a canvas at its four corners.

Curtis Bill recognised the pall bearers as the vegetable gardeners. 'It happened in the vegetable plot?'

'Yes, sir.'

'Let's have the lights on here,' Decker said, regretting that artificial light would spoil his natural vision and shrugging when he remembered that, with the flying he'd be doing today, taxi service for their last clients, it wouldn't really matter if his vision wasn't spot on.

The black gardeners put the canvas down and unfolded the edges. The lights came on. Chris Decker and Curtis Bill Bonham continued to eat their breakfast, the pilot waving the four Bantu away with a fork impaling toast, sausage, egg, bacon and fried tomato. The cook swallowed with difficulty and the gardeners flapped the length of the veranda on their bare feet to disappear hurriedly into the anonymous darkness beyond. Vincent and the black man lay cradled together on the canvas, obscenely locked into each other by rigor mortis, their lolling heads frozen at unnatural angles to bare the last laughter of their slit throats.

'Never suspected him of being a bumbasher.'

'He was a sadist and, I suspect, a masochist. The two often

252

go together with homosexuality,' Curtis Bill said.

'You knew and you kept him on!'

'No. I didn't know. I only suspected. Suspicion is not grounds for dismissal.' Curtis Bill waved his hand at the cook in dismissal – he did not like arguments with his partner in front of the help – and the man scuttled away gratefully.

'I wonder who did it?' Decker did not seem inclined to argue. 'Some disappointed lover?' He spat the last word out as if it tasted of aloe.

'I don't know. But I think we should get our clients out of here before we get the police in.'

'You think Pascoe did it because Vincent photographed him hurling his guts out?'

'No. Neither Pascoe nor Cameron would slit a man's throat, they would shoot him from a distance. I want them out of here because of what they may say and because their very presence makes this place newsworthy.' Curtis Bill emptied his mug and placed it on the veranda rail beside his empty plate. The black man beside the door suddenly held a coffee pot in his hand but Curtis Bill shook his head, he did not want anything else.

Decker held his mug out for more coffee. 'We could just feed them to the crocodiles and forget it all.'

'Use your head, Chris. This is South Africa, not the veld out there. Both of them – ' Curtis Bill gestured at the two headed statue on the canvas at their feet ' – have families who will make enquiries. We're going to be in trouble if we do not report a double murder. We have nothing to hide, re-member?'

'Yeah.'

'And it may hold up the sale of the property. No, the police will find their culprit quickly enough and it will be over in a few days with no fuss. But first we have to remove our clients. I'll go wake them.'

'Okay. Take-off as soon after first light as they're ready,' the pilot said, his gaze returning to the eastern horizon. 'About five minutes from now.'

A hundred yards away, at the end of the runway, the plane

253

went up in flames, whoosh! The black man who had set the explosive had done his work well but the detonator had been attached to a faulty timing device and detonated six and a half minutes before dawn, the time their new leader had asked him to set the demolition of the chopper and the plane for. He had seen the white men eating their breakfast on the veranda and had longed to kill them with his machine pistol but discipline had won ... their leader had said, *In and out, just before dawn,* and he intended to be out before dawn with five minutes in hand, having earned his share of the white women and the loot. He was on his way to the chopper to set the charge in it when the plane exploded. He went flying and came rolling upright, his knapsack under one arm, his machine pistol slung out of his way, clutching his bruised elbows. Instinctively he looked towards the veranda but the white men had disappeared and the lights had been snapped off.

Neither Curtis Bill nor Decker wasted any time asking questions. Curtis Bill fell straight to the veranda floor and was searching the flame lit area before he had finished rolling behind the heavy wooden seat of *stinkhout.* Chris Decker let the mug fall from his hand and charged through the door, taking the servant with him, snapping the lights out at the same time and without any waste motion. He used the coffee pot to smash the writing table in which his Browning target pistol was kept, locked in a drawer of which Vincent kept the key, to be taken out only on the Sunday of the hunt, one week in every month, to pique the curiosity of a baboon. As he loaded the pistol in the dark and packed his pockets with cartridges, he called out softly to Curtis Bill:

'See anything? Or was it preset?'

'He's still there. Dazed by the blast. Standing in full view. Armed with some kind of a machine pistol. Barrel's too short to have the range of us.'

'Just one?'

'I can only see one.'

Chris Decker crawled through the door on his belly, not lifting his head in response to the temptation to look.

Curiosity killed the cat. The baboon. Curtis Bill would warn him if danger should force him to abandon stealth and take the chance of charging.

'He's taking some stuff – probably explosives – from a knapsack and moving towards the chopper. The plane probably went up prematurely. Defective detonator, at a guess.'

Decker rolled over and lay beside his partner. 'We can't let him blow up the chopper. Driving over rough country roads doesn't appeal to my piles.'

'I can make a dash to my *rondawel* and get a rifle.'

'Your *rondawel*'s fifty yards. He's a hundred yards. He'd close the gap and chop you long before you reached your rifle.'

'If he saw me.'

Decker pointed. The sun was clawing its way out of the night. 'Perfect silhouette.'

'Pity we can't count on our clients to do something constructive.'

'Yeah.'

'We're going to have to go sometime. That popgun isn't much help.'

'We'll see.' Decker rested the pistol's long barrel on the rail in front of his face. 'Let's give him a mosquito bite.'

At the pilot's first shot Curtis Bill vaulted the rail. By the pilot's third shot he was twenty yards from the veranda. The man standing in the light thrown by the blazing plane looked at him in clear disbelief and let off a single burp! of his machine pistol in his direction before turning determinedly back to the helicopter. Over the crackling of the flaming plane the terrorist had not heard the modest crack of Decker's small calibre pistol and it was only when the pilot's sixth shot tugged at his clothing that he turned to the veranda to spray a single burp! at it. Curtis Bill Bonham had not even looked in his direction; he went through his *rondawel* door shoulder first, bursting the lock from inch and a half screws in solid wood. The black man had dropped the detonator when he had fired at Decker. He bent to pick it up as Curtis Bill came from his *rondawel* to stand squarely in the open out of effective range of the terrorist's machine pistol. As the terrorist rose Curtis Bill shot at the detonator in his hand, causing it to explode and take the man's fingers and half his palm along with it to the air and the ground. The black man fell to the ground, clutching what was left of his hand, a palmed stump.

'Kill the bastard,' Decker called, not doubting for a second that Curtis Bill had hit what he had aimed for.

'No. Let him use his ammunition and then we'll fetch him and have a talk to him.'

It had not occurred to either of them to kill the black man and take off in the helicopter, leaving their clients and their servants to their fate.

Curtis Bill went around the circle of *rondawels*, knocking on each door and waiting until it was opened, then saying, 'We are probably under terrorist attack. Please put on trousers and shoes over your pyjamas and come to the lounge.' In each case he resisted attempts to engage him in conversation, except at the Minowara *rondawel*, which he entered at Omo's called invitation and exited almost immediately, calling to Decker, 'Send a couple of men to carry Omo.'

The black man behind the blazing plane let off bursts at Curtis Bill and at Decker with his unhurt left hand but the range and his aim was such that they ignored him.

Curtis Bill finished his rounds and joined his partner on the veranda. They sat in chairs and shot at the black man behind what had once been their plane as he attempted for the first time since Curtis Bill wounded him to reach his target, the helicopter. To their immense satisfaction, he replied with wild bursts, wasting his ammunition.

Curtis Bill called out to the servants inside and one came cautiously to the window behind the white men. Curtis Bill sent a message to the cook and shortly afterwards they heard the cook calling all the servants to the lounge with a loud hailer. Curtis Bill looked at his watch and Decker said:

'They're late as usual. You just can't trust terrorists. They probably meant to attack at dawn, four minutes ago.'

Cameron came running across the open ground in a

crouch, a rifle in each hand and his revolver strapped around his waist. Melody walked quickly beside him, proud and erect despite a face almost obscured by livid multihued bruises. Behind them came Enoch Pascoe, bandage incongruously askew on his head, also playing movie soldiers, crouching along with an elephant gun in each hand, motioning Judith, who carried another Nitro Express 600 gingerly in both hands, to stay between him and the buildings.

Cameron stopped short when he saw the two safari owners taking their ease in chairs. Pascoe slammed into the back of the American, sending him staggering on to the veranda steps where he recovered and rose to his impressive full height.

'If this is your idea of a joke, I'll –'

Curtis Bill raised his rifle and fired past Cameron's head and the wounded black man replied immediately with a burst. Cameron froze, unfroze, looked over his shoulder at the burning plane, and rushed up the steps, heading for the door into the building. Decker reached out a massive hand and caught his arm, swinging the beefy American around effortlessly from his seated position.

'Did you keep the rest of your arms too?'

'Let me go, you fucking madman! People are shooting at me!'

'Where are the rest of your rifles?'

'Under the bed. Let me go.' Jerk as he would, the American could not loose himself from the vicelike hand of the pilot.

'And the ammunition. Under the bed too?'

'Yes!' Decker let go and Cameron ran through the door to appear almost immediately at a window and start firing into the burning plane.

The pilot stood up. He blocked Pascoe's passage. 'The rest of your guns, under the bed too, I suppose?'

Pascoe nodded and feinted to the left, then rushed around the pilot to the other side and through the door to join Cameron at the window. Decker turned to laugh at them:

'Christ, you stumblebums make me wet myself. The real attack doesn't start until I get my guns.' He called several

257

Bantu servants by name and they came very reluctantly on to the veranda. He herded them down the steps and directed them to the different *rondawels* to fetch all the arms and ammunition they could find. Once out in the open the black servants moved with alacrity to finish their tasks and regain cover. Madmen like the masters might sit on chairs on the veranda but they understood guns, something the Bantu had no desire to do.

Chris Decker bowed to Omo Minowara as the paralysed man was carried past on his bed and the Japanese inclined his head. 'May we use your arms and ammunition, please?'

'Of course. I apologise for not being of more help to you.'

'We are in need of fortitude and moral support.' Decker bowed again and preceded the two nervous Bantu, whom he had detailed to carry his own arms, into his *rondawel*. They rushed through the door as soon as he was through, shoulder by shoulder.

Bantu servants streamed up the steps and over the veranda and into the lounge with armsful of rifles and ammunition. The pilot came from his own *rondawel* and went to Curtis Bill's to fetch his partner's rifles and ammunition, the two Bantu he held with him through the force of his personality dancing their fear in involuntary little jigs. Curtis Bill's armoury and ammunition did not add much to their loaded arms: the ex-mercenary owned only three rifles – one of which he held in his hands, one racked in the helicopter out of reach – and perhaps fifty rounds of ammunition for each; Curtis Bill did not even own a pistol or a revolver. The two Bantu literally ran before the pilot's long strides. Decker laughed at their antics in genuine amusement.

It was an orderly procedure, preparing to receive a terrorist attack while already under fire, indicative of the calibre of the mercenaries Curtis Bill Bonham and Chris Decker had once been; they had not lost their experience or their natural aptitude for guerrilla fighting in five years of soft living. The only hysteria in evidence was the indiscriminate and useless firing of Pascoe and Cameron. The wounded black was not even returning their fire.

258

Curtis Bill Bonham rose as Decker ascended the steps to the veranda. 'We will not capture him now. He is saving his ammunition. He does not consider those two a threat.' He indicated the window through which the muzzles of Cameron's and Pascoe's rifles protruded modestly to spit immoderate venom at an unseen target.

The pilot looked at his watch. 'Nine minutes after dawn. If they are efficient terrorists we have one minute more.' He stood aside and Curtis Bill preceded him through the door just as the first bullets fired from the cover of the *rondawel* furthest away from the lounge crunched against the wall beside them. They stood on each side of the doorway inside the room and Decker slammed the heavy solid wood door. 'These terrorists are very efficient. Now the real thing starts.' He smiled his sincere smile, the genuine version.

Curtis Bill surveyed the large room, noting the faces. Several of the blacks were missing. They would be dead by now. One of his clients was also missing. He asked calmly:

'Where is Yodoko?'

Two

In the exact and unbreakable ritual of their marriage, Yodoko made first morning *cha* for her husband. She held his head while he drank the bitter black liquid. At the door she bowed. Not a word had been spoken. None had been necessary.

Yodoko went to the Cameron *rondawel* and knocked softly at the door. She heard someone turn over in the bed but the door remained closed. She would not knock again. Perhaps Melody felt *eta* – outcast – now that her husband was being

259

expelled from the safari and could not bear the loss of face sight of Yodoko would bring upon her. It would not be polite to knock again, especially as she would lose face through rejection of a second knock unanswered.

She walked quickly to the pool, impatient now to sink into its cool freshness. The moon lit her way. Soon there would be the dawning of another day in the east, a gift from Japan to the west. The water of the pool rippled. She undressed and folded each article of clothing neatly before placing it on the towel and bathing costume she had brought. She did not put the unnatural bathing costume on; it had been brought only because the other women considered it proper, but there would be no need for it if she was going to be alone. She walked into the water at the shallow end of the pool and let its flow wash the doubts of the night from her body and her mind. The cold water was invigorating and she swum the length of the pool several times. While she rested at the deep end she heard the boat chugging in the river Melody had told her of but paid it no attention. Never having seen the river and not knowing that a boat on it was a rare event, she did not find the sound unusual at all.

Jomo Iningwe had disregarded the toad-colonel's plan of landing upriver of the camp. It would simply add to the walking distance and he was certain the inhabitants of the base camp would not hear the sound of the boat. He had the helmsman take the boat as deep into the overhang of the trees as the man thought safe, then set the men to work camouflaging the boat while he sent the demolitions expert ahead with detailed instructions. The man would have a fifteen minute head start, more than he really needed. They would follow him. The demolitions expert went and Jomo waited seven minutes before he sent half the rest of his men to circle around the servants' *campong*, to kill all the servants and cut off the white men's line of retreat. That left him eight minutes to set the charges under the generator and the water supply plus time to lead his remaining men to the base camp for the frontal attack on the white men and their women, if you could call murdering unsuspecting and unarmed camera nuts in their beds a militay action, he mocked himself in his mind. At dawn, as the sun rose, all the explosive charges would go off at once and the attack would start. Like all the best plans, this one was of classic simplicity. There was very little that could go wrong with it.

He led his little group of men to the generating room underneath the artificial cliff built for the waterfall to tumble over. A man stepped forward eagerly with a crowbar but there was no lock on the door. Jomo told the men to wait and went into the dark room to set the charges. Packing the plastic and sticking in the detonators took only three minutes. He spent another two minutes double checking his already perfect handiwork. He emerged from the generating room looking at his watch, then at the eastern horizon through the trees. He switched off his torch and became aware for the first time that he was alone. To his right he heard the sound of excited voices over the rush of running water. His men had found the waterfall. He had not suspected them of being able to appreciate its ironic manmade beauty. Jomo followed them around the corner of the generating room.

They stood at the edges of the pool, pointing into it, laughing and talking loudly. The toad-colonel's discipline had not lasted once they were out of barracks and back into their natural savage African element. Over their heads he saw the white girl, probably a teenager, twelve, thirteen, swim the length of the pool with her hair straightening behind her on the surface of the water as she turned at the deep end. She was naked. She was obviously unaware of her audience. She swam the length of the pool again and found her feet at the shallow end to rise and stand straight and brush the hair out of her eyes and back over her ears. She was, even in the pre-dawn waning of the moon, well developed for her age.

A deep atavistic sigh shook the assembled men.

Yodoko saw the men as she cleared the hair from her eyes.

She tilted her head to each side to rid herself of the water in her ears. She heard the sigh of the wind in the cherry trees rise and turn and convulse itself into a growl of hungry wolves and looked at them from the corner of her eye. They were armed and strange, not the servants from the base camp. They were staring at her with more than rudeness, as if they had been without a pillowing for a long time.

Giving no sign of her irritation at having her bathing interrupted, Yodoko walked to where her clothing lay folded on the towel. She made no attempt to cover her breasts or genital area with her hands because the culture which had spawned her had never ascribed either prurient values or shame to their exposure.

The men watched her in the oppressive silence of many held breaths. They let her get almost as far as the clothing before one cupped his palm under her chin to send her staggering back into the arms of another. The black man held one forearm across her throat so that she could neither breathe nor call out. She heard him laughing hugely in her ear as his free hand roamed insultingly over her body, squeezing her breasts painfully, forcing her legs open to jam a large middle finger into her.

The other men fell upon her clothes and the bathing costume and the towel, smelling them, ripping them into shreds to put in their pockets. Then they turned their attention to her. She was thrown from man to man to be caught with open smacking hands which held her briefly, bruisingly, probed her piercingly, painfully, before sending her staggering or often through the air to the next pair of hands. Once she found her footing for a moment and tried to turn away but a balled fist to the side of her jaw careened her back into the humiliating merry-go-round of huge grinning black faces and pink palms. Once she found her bearings long enough to strike at one of the black men, four stiffened fingers under the shortribs into the heart. He fell over but her advantage was lost when the next man caught her by her wrist and swung her around and put his elbow into her stomach in a vicious short curve which bent her over, trying

262

to suck breath from her kneecaps. The man held her over like that by pressing her arm up behind her back. Another black man bent over the one she had struck, felt for his pulse at his wrist, wrenched open his denim blouse to place his ear on the fallen man's chest, rose to shake his head and look at her with new respect. He said something short in a strange language, perhaps what she knew already, that their comrade had suffered a complete arrest of the heart and was therefore dead. The man holding her hitched her arm up an extra notch. Yodoko looked at the black men in their upside down world between her legs and stoically accepted what she now knew would come next, heralded by a finger which appeared from the left leg edge of her vision to stroke her vagina as it peered skyward at the top of her contorted posture. Behind her the black man was opening his fly and extricating his member, already erect. Through his legs she could see fragments of other black men, seemingly all fragments of flies being opened, penises being taken out into eager hands. Her killing of their comrade and the posture of her body had excited them.

The first man entered her by the simple process of ramming until he found entry. She screamed. Then she bit her lip and felt her teeth meet through the lip; to scream was not seemly. A couple of strokes and the next man pulled him away to ram at her raised back. This one found the wrong opening and she could not contain the animal sound deep in her throat as the muscle tore and the blood started flowing down her thighs. But she did not open her mouth to scream. The next one guided himself urgently with clumsy clawed fingers and tore her genitals until he succeeded in briefly inserting his penis before the next one pulled him away. Yodoko sagged but the man holding her arm simply lifted her by it and held her in position, not interrupting his laughter at the entertainment for which he had a prime seat.

Jomo Iningwe was in a quandary. His sharp command to let the girl be was ignored by the men in their lust. His time was

263

running out and he still had to lead the men overland to the base camp on foot, to reach it and place them in position before dawn. He looked impatiently at his watch. He would let the men sport with her for five minutes, no more. They would have to make up the time by doing double speed all the way to the base camp. He stood to one side and watched them throw her about, seeming to paw her intimately in mid-air. He saw her strike at one of his men with a small hand and was surprised when the man fell woodenly forward but dismissed it as childish buffoonery. When another man inspected the fallen man and found him dead, Jomo marvelled at the singlemindedness of the South Africans who would teach their daughters fatal karate in their high schools. He did not mourn the dead man, nor feel sympathy for the girl in the punishment his men had devised for her: she had deserved it the day she was born white in an enclave of privilege.

The five minutes had gone. Jomo Iningwe drew his knife and leant over to lift the girl's head by her hair so that he could slit her throat. A machine pistol nudged threateningly at his wrist and guided his hand away. He looked up, marked the man's face.

'It is bad fortune to threaten your leader.'

The machine pistol gestured. Jomo stood back and shrugged. He looked at his watch. His choices were three: he could wait until the girl died under the assaults of his men, as she would, but it would take hours. He could unsling his own machine pistol and either fire into the ground or kill the girl but that could be heard at the base camp and alert the white men; he could also be killed by his own men in their frustration. The third choice was to submit to the enforced delay. Once more he marked the face of the man who had dared question the authority of Jomo Iningwe, thwarted and threatened him. The man would not die easily, nor quickly; his slow passing would be a lesson to others. Jomo made a mental note to make sure the man was not unnecessarily exposed in the coming action. It would be a shame if some cook slit his throat with a butcher's knife while he wasn't looking.

Jomo thought, *So much for you, toad-Colonel, and your disciplined men and your demolitions expert.* He stared at the white heat of the explosion against the deepest dark just before the dawn and listened to the whoosh of air burnt and displaced, clear even at a mile. He looked at his watch. Six minutes to dawn. He looked up at his men. The man holding the girl let her arm go and she buckled at the knees but the fully erect penis of the man behind her was buried deep in her stretched parts and held her up. Then the man reached behind his shoulder for his machine pistol and his erection lost some of its strength; she slid from him on the lubrication of her own blood.

'Double time, now!' he snapped in British drill instructor imitation and pointed at the path leading to the clear marker of white heat against the sky.

Jomo bent once more to slit the girl's throat but the same man pointed his machine pistol at him once more and Jomo rose and sheathed his knife. The girl was going nowhere. She was unconscious and would still be lying there when they returned, not more than an hour from now, half that if the white men were slow wiping the sleep from their eyes. Jomo watched the man who had threatened him kick the girl in the ribs once, twice. Then he fell in beside Jomo as they loped easily after the other men.

'You seem a man of initiative and promise,' Jomo told him. 'I want you to stay close to me, watch my back for me.' Jomo was perfectly capable of watching his own back but he did not want the man to go seeking trouble on his own account and perhaps remove himself from the scope of Jomo's wrath which he had now twice begged for.

If the men's discipline was suspect, their physical fitness left nothing to be desired. At dawn he looked at his watch and estimated they were nine minutes from the base camp. He did not urge his men to run faster: a winded, blowing man does not shoot straight. And these men were running at a faster pace than he would have set himself if he had started in the lead, instead of falling in behind at someone else's pace. He increased his pace to reach the head of the line, waving back men who tried to keep up with him as he came past them, saying, 'Nice and regular does it. We are doing well.' The man who had threatened him kept pace with him. He was a fine specimen. 'What is your name?'

'Dingane.'

'A Zulu name. But your accent is not Zulu.'

'No. My father read the white man's histories. He admired Dingane, king of the Zulus, who slayed the mighty tyrant Chaka.'

Had him killed while he himself blubbered on a woman in the dark of a hut. And then became a petty tyrant. 'Excellent!'

They heard the gunfire but did not break stride. Its direction was obvious and they would find its source soon enough. Jomo thought it was the other group attacking the servants' *campong* only minutes after the time he had set, a forgivable lapse in consideration of the understandable confusion the early demolition of the aircraft must have caused them.

They broke from the trees and Jomo saw the Bantu servants with armloads of munitions climb the steps of the veranda and enter the long building which he had identified last night as the dining-room, lounge and kitchen complex. The white men had used their time well, organising rapidly, not pausing to wipe the sleep from their eyes. He hoped his men had cut the telephone line behind the camp for this action might take longer than he had planned and reinforcements for the other side would be a complication. (Jomo would have been amused to learn that both Pascoe and Cameron had slept through the demolition of the plane and the first exchange of shots and until Curtis Bill Bonham had knocked at the door and told their wives to wake them and get them to the lounge. He would have been appalled to find out that neither Curtis Bill Bonham nor Chris Decker had even contemplated trying the phone, knowing it would be cut; this implied experience of terrorist action which no terrorist rejoices to find in his prey.) He was out of their range and kept his pace until he and his men reached the *rondawels* furthest from the lounge. He gestured at his men to spread out but did not fire. The man on the veranda and the men inside seemed to be preoccupied with the demolitions expert, who was still alive and lying between the still smouldering plane and the intact helicopter. When his men were in position, Jomo opened fire but the range was too long for accuracy with his machine pistol and his shots splattered harmlessly against the wall next to the door through which the last two white men were passing with surprising lack of hurry and with co-ordination hinting at previous experience under fire, one man even standing aside politely for the other to precede him through the door, the whole manoeuvre executed with speed and a lack of spendthrift motion and wasteful haste which caused Jomo to pause and think about tactics.

Three

'Where is Yodoko?' Curtis Bill looked around the faces once more. She was not there.

'She went to the pool,' Minowara said from his bed in the corner. Through the babel of voices following his weakened voice, Decker's stood out:

'Poor, silly, dead bitch.'

Minowara turned his head sharply to stare at Decker but the pilot did not see the Japanese glaring at him. He had turned with Curtis Bill Bonham to inspect their arms and ammunition, knowing the lead clattering against the walls outside to be a bluff which would be followed by a planning lull to be in turn followed by a renewed attack. The terrorists would have to make new plans or change existing plans to take into account the unexpected resistance they had encountered; both the ex-mercenaries knew terrorist action to be predicated upon taking unsuspecting, unforewarned and often unarmed enemies by surprise. It would be a waste of ammunition to return the fire, though Pascoe and Cameron were doing so. Everybody else kept below the level of the windowsill without being told.

'Fill all containers you can find with water, including the kitchen and laundry sinks,' Curtis Bill told the cook without looking up from his task of sorting boxes of ammunition rapidly to the rifles they were intended for. 'They may shoot at the rooftop tanks and let our water leak away.'

'Do you think they'll stick it out long enough to try and drive us out through thirst?' It was obvious Decker did not believe so.

'No. Just being careful. And make sandwiches with all the food that needs refrigeration,' Curtis Bill added to the cook. 'They will cut the electricity, if they haven't already, and there's no sense in letting everything go to waste.'

Judith Pascoe reached up to try the light switch. No lights came on. She giggled hysterically but stopped immediately when Curtis Bill turned his gaze on her. 'I'll go help in the kitchen.'

'Thank you. But stay away from the windows. And perhaps you'd care to oversee the distribution of all the canned food in equal amounts together with the necessary openers to this room, the kitchen, the laundry and the pantry.'

'Boy, are you thorough!' Decker mocked as Judith crept away to the kitchen, chatelaine with obedient servants at last.

'No more than you about your planes and your flying.'

'Ah, you command on the ground. I forgot. Sorry.'

'It's all right. What have we?'

'Enough for the siege of Mafeking. Though I must say I wish we had some of the nut cases this time round, the guys who bring gatlings and mortars with them.'

'Yes. You take the back and I'll take the front. You take Cameron, I'll keep Pascoe.'

268

'Okay. Watch out for that mother with the explosives near my chopper.'

'I'll put Pascoe on it. His eyes are very sharp.'

'And it'll keep him out of mischief?' Decker did not bother to lower his voice.

Curtis Bill smiled one of his truly rare smiles. 'There's that too.'

Melody sat against the wall and listened to them. 'How can you be so calm?' she asked through her swollen lips.

'Calm men shoot straighter,' Decker told her, avoiding looking at her face. Outside the firing had died down. Inside Cameron and Pascoe shattered the silence with their continued firing at unseen enemies.

'See if you can find out how many of the servants didn't make it.' Curtis Bill told Decker. They both knew only too well the propensity of terrorists to kill the servants of white men indiscriminately with or often before their masters.

Cameron protested, 'Enoch and me are doing okay here. You two go out back. There're no niggers there.'

'There will be,' Decker said. 'Come on.'

'No. You go.' Cameron turned back to the window. There was fear on his face as he turned back to face the man who had chipped the plaster an inch from his face. 'That shot came from inside!'

'I command here. I have shot mutineers before. I shall not hesitate to shoot you.' Curtis Bill Bonham's rifle hung loosely in his hand at his side but Cameron made no motion to raise his own rifle.

'One day, mister fucking Curtis Bill Bonham, you will go too far and I will kill you.'

'Please postpone that day until we have dealt with our common enemies. Kindly assist Chris in defending our rear.' Curtis Bill Bonham's voice was perfectly level and without inflection or emphasis, the voice of Death.

Cameron paled beneath his sunburn, took his cartridge boxes and the second rifle he had been using, and charged through the rear door without another word.

Decker looked meaningfully at his partner and followed

the American. Curtis Bill took his two rifles and their cartridges and placed the lot against a wall between two windows.

'Hey, aren't you coming to join me?'

'In a while. There will be an attack soon. Let your rifle cool down.'

'Okay.' Pascoe was reluctant.

'Timbo, will you load for me?'

'Yes, Master!'

'Good. Sala, you load for Mr Pascoe.'

'Yes, Master.' The response was a great deal less enthusiastic.

'Can you fire a rifle?' Curtis Bill asked Melody.

'No. And I have no intention of learning on living targets. People.'

Minowara said, 'If you will have your servants bring the large mirror from the wall to my side, I can watch the helicopter for you without exposing myself.'

'Thank you.' Curtis Bill nodded at two Bantu who took the mirror from the wall and arranged it next to the paralysed man.

The lull was over. Firing started at the back of the building, the burp! of automatic weapons followed immediately by the crack! of Decker's and Cameron's rifles in sharp and distinct contrast. Consistent firing also started at the front of the building, the curves of the *rondawels* spitting flame at the entrenched white men. Curtis Bill ignored the random firing and told Pascoe:

'Don't bother shooting back. Watch the *rondawel* nearest to you on the left there. That's where they'll charge from.' Curtis Bill watched the *rondawel* on their right but turned to the left when he heard the sound of an engine being raced over the rude splutter of the machine pistols. 'They've found the Range Rover. When it comes, shoot for the fuel tank. It's –'

'Yeah, yeah, I know where it is.' Pascoe took a handkerchief from his pocket and wiped the spittle from his rifle with loving care; he replaced the handkerchief in his pocket without wiping his face. 'What about my second –'

The Range Rover came racing between two *rondawels* on Pascoe's left and he raised his rifle to track with it. Two men broke from the *rondawel* nearest the lounge on the right and Curtis Bill picked them off with a single shot in the chest each. He turned his attention to the Range Rover speeding at them with men hanging on to its far, protected side, shooting over the roof at them. Pascoe fired his first shot and a gaping hole appeared in the near side of the Range Rover, followed by another large and ragged hole in the roof of the Range Rover as the bullet ricocheted from the rear axle, killing the terrorist on the back seat. His screams could be clearly heard for a brief second above the sound of gunfire and the tortured engine. Pascoe swore unintelligibly, aimed again. Curtis Bill shot twice, bursting both front tyres of the Range Rover. His third shot missed the driver as the vehicle stuck its nose down and somersaulted but it didn't matter: the Range Rover was out of control. Pascoe hit the tank as the Ranger Rover went up in the air, arresting it in mid-somersault as a ball of flame.

'Fine shot!' Curtis Bill called out. He held his hand out for his other rifle and the black man loading it for him exposed himself for the briefest moment before the window and was taken in the upper arm by a spent bullet cruising lazily through the window. 'Go get that dressed,' Curtis Bill told him, shooting at the bundles of flame rolling away from the wreck while Pascoe was still reaching for a reloaded rifle, 'and send somebody of your choice to load for me until you can return.'

'Yes, Master!' Another man took his place quickly.

'We got five of the black bastards, five!' Pascoe shouted.

'And two got away,' Curtis Bill replied levelly. 'One very tall man rolled behind the *rondawel* this side. And another has rolled up to the veranda.'

'You'd better pray he doesn't have any grenades,' Decker said. He was leaning nonchalantly against the kitchen door.

Curtis Bill shook his head. 'Not likely. What's it like back there?'

'Diversionary firing. No serious intention. Bob Cameron is

271

quite happy keeping them busy. He's even winged a couple that got too daring, he says. I came to see if you needed help but you seem to be managing.' Decker turned to go.

'Ask the cook to send us a bottle of kerosene or methylated spirits or even cooking oil and a piece of rag to make a wick.'

'One Molotov cocktail coming right up, sir.'

Pascoe licked his lips. 'You gonna burn him out?'

'Something like it.'

'If he's right up to the veranda, you could set the building on fire.'

'He could do that with a box of matches. The alternative is for one of us to go out there and kill him.'

Pascoe did not reply. He looked out of his window cautiously and saw the barrel of the machine pistol creep over the edge of the veranda. He aimed his rifle at it but Curtis Bill pushed the barrel aside and pulled Pascoe away from the window as the bullets started whining through it.

'Clear the room for a while,' Curtis Bill said calmly. 'Those who aren't in the doorways, flat on your bellies.' It was a high room and the angle of entry of the bullets was such that the ricochets were spent on the ceiling but the hot lead falling on the people inside the room could give them nasty small cuts and painful burns.

Pascoe tried to move to another window but Curtis Bill shook his head. 'Leave him be. He's doing no harm.'

A terrorist from the nearest *rondawel* on the right tried to reach the shelter of the veranda under the covering fire of the man already in position. Curtis Bill stood well back in the room, out of line of the bullets streaming through the window, and fired diagonally through the window. The man fell down, twisting this way and that in an effort to find the sanctuary of the *rondawel*'s curved wall again, the bullet having glanced off his ribs. Pascoe stood beside Curtis Bill and blasted the terrorist's head off with a single bullet from his elephant gun. The makings of the Molotov cocktail were brought by Timbo, Curtis Bill's loader, who proudly sported a white bandage on his upper arm. Curtis Bill wet the wick and stuffed it into the top of the bottle of cooking oil,

272

searched for matches in the writing-table Chris Decker had smashed only twenty minutes ago to get at his target pistol, and lit the home-made bomb. He made sure it was burning properly before casting it out of the window. It struck the edge of the veranda and rolled over. There was a muffled whoosh! and a feral scream. The bullets stopped streaming into the room. The terrorist ran away from the lounge a flaming cross, heading towards the far *rondawels*.

'Bob's gonna be furious he missed this,' Pascoe said, raising his rifle.

Curtis Bill shook his head. 'Save your bullet. They'll do it for us.' There was a *burp!* of machine pistol fire from the far *rondawel* and the flaming cross crashed to the ground writhing in agony even after life had departed it. Its smouldering form made an apt counterpoint to the burning wreck of the destroyed Range Rover.

'The man at the helicopter,' Minowara said. 'He's – '

'Shit!' Pascoe started firing but Curtis Bill struck his rifle aside.

'Do you want to blow up our helicopter yourself?'

The terrorist was under the canvas. Curtis Bill aimed carefully at the lower regions of the tarpaulin, sure that he would not hit any of the essential components of the helicopter, and fired a whole magazine in a measured row. They heard a faint scream, muffled by the tarpaulin's oppressive weight and the intervening distance. The terrorist rolled out from under the tarpaulin clutching a shattered ankle.

'All yours,' Curtis Bill said.

'Don't throw me any leftover scraps!' Pascoe snapped crossly but when Curtis Bill shrugged and raised his rifle to finish the man off, Pascoe hurriedly raised his own rifle and fired first, disintegrating the top half of the man's head.

Once more there was a lull in the firing all round.

'We've won!' Pascoe shouted jubilantly.

Curtis Bill looked at him curiously, then glanced at Decker, who had come to lean against the kitchen door again. Decker answered the Englishman:

'Not exactly. So far they've only tested our calibre, so to

speak. Next the real attack comes.'

'But all the niggers we've killed!'

'Yes, well, they are many and we are few, see. A few men doesn't matter one way or the other to them. But if we lose even one man, it could be a tragedy for us.'

Pascoe preened himself at this new evidence of his importance. Decker stepped closer to Curtis Bill and lowered his voice. 'Very efficient. Professionally trained. Soundly disciplined.'

'I've noticed. What are you getting at, Chris?'

'These squeamish motherfuckers, Cameron and Pascoe, aren't going to have the guts to kill their own women before the terrorists get at them. We're going to have to do it for them.'

Curtis Bill said flatly, 'What we have to do we will do.'

Four

Melody squatted on the floor with her back to the wall and eavesdropped dispassionately on Decker's calm judgement of the terrorists' proficiency and Curtis Bill's flat acceptance of the suggestion that they should kill her and Judith rather than let them fall into the hands of the terrorists to suffer what her mother had always called 'a fate worse than death', presumably also what the pilot had meant when he had described Yodoko as a 'poor, silly, dead bitch'. And all because she, Melody, had neglected to tell Yodoko of Decker's warning not to go to the pool alone. And this morning, when she had a chance . . .

Melody had heard the gentle knock at the door and known it was Yodoko who had come to ask her if she wanted to go swimming with her. She had turned over in the bed preparatory to rising and answering the door, had brushed against Bob, had remembered the shame of her painfully puffed and bruised face and the marks of his abuse elsewhere on her body, had also remembered what Yodoko had done the previous day, and had lain paralysed by the twin emotions of shame and revulsion until Yodoko had gone. Then she had stood at the window, watching the Japanese woman take the path for the pool in the last of the moonlight, wanting desperately to call to her to wait, she was coming, but not getting the words past frozen lips. It had not entered her mind that Yodoko was breaking the rules by going to the pool alone, not until Curtis Bill had missed Yodoko, and that she could have, should have, warned her this morning . . .

For a while Melody wallowed in self-pity, obverse side of the coin of shame, blaming herself for whatever had befallen Yodoko. Then the essential commonsense midwestern Melody rode rampant into her consciousness: she had nothing but the word of the pilot that Yodoko had been attacked by the terrorists and killed by them, and he could not have seen it happen, because he had been at the base camp having breakfast – she had noticed the dirty plates on the veranda rail as she arrived. And the terrorists need not have come from the river, they could have come from any of the points of the compass, from inland, even from some point on the river where the lush vegetation could have hidden the pool from them. Yodoko might still be swimming in the pool, unaware of the dangers awaiting her when, refreshed, she started back for breakfast.

Melody rose. At the kitchen door she met Judith, who offered her a sandwich from a huge platter loaded with an extensive variety of sandwiches. Melody took one and bit into it. It was crab. She took another sandwich to carry with her for Yodoko.

In the kitchen her husband was standing next to a window with his back to the wall, chewing out his loader for not loading his auto-ejector rifle fully: ' . . . and I can tell you haven't ever seen an automatic rifle in your miserable life, boy, so don't tell me . . . ' He didn't notice her entrance.

275

Decker was nowhere to be seen – he was in the wine cellar, selecting the least desirable bottles of brandy to be made into Molotov cocktails, but Melody did not know this – and she was glad because she did not think she would be able to fool him. Fooling Bob was a different matter, even though she had never thought of doing it before . . . She walked briskly up to the kitchen door and – surprised to find that it opened at the turn of the handle, being neither locked nor bolted – opened it to walk through erectly into the bright early morning sunlight bathing the large open unfenced backyard to the kitchen. She struck out for the trees, planning to reach them first and then circle around among them until she struck the path to the pool. She walked proudly erect, suppressing the desire to crouch or to run.

Behind her, thirty paces away in her long natural stride, Cameron shouted, 'Hey, what – where the fuck do you think you're going?'

She didn't answer him or look back and he raised his rifle but immediately lowered it again. Even here, even under these circumstances there were too many witnesses to shoot one's wife for defiance. He looked around the room. They were only black niggers but that made it all the more likely that they would rejoice in standing up in court to tell against him. Curtis Bill and Chris ought to put the whole lot of them outside so they could experience Black Brotherhood and he, Robert J. Cameron, M.D., would personally cover all bets on how soon the terrorist niggers killed them all.

Melody reached the trees. Nobody had fired at her. Since leaving the kitchen door she had not even heard any shots from the other side of the building. She turned left through the trees because the other way she would have had to expose herself by crossing the runway for the plane in order to reach the path leading to the pool; she didn't want to go far enough into the woods to be able to go around the end of the runway because she was not sure of being able to find her bearings again.

The undergrowth had been cleared by the conscientious servants and Melody's progress was as quick as if she had

276

been walking on a paved path fifteen feet from the edge of the forest. In three minutes she covered nearly two hundred and fifty yards and saw nobody. It was spooky. Where had all those shots at the building come from? 'There's not a soul here,' she said aloud to reassure herself. 'I wonder what Bob was shooting at.' As if her voice were a signal, she found out.

Black men appeared from behind the trees in front of her. With a gasp she turned around and started back, dropping the sandwich she carried in her hand for Yodoko. Two paces and grinning black faces appeared from behind the trees to stop her retreat. She realised they must have been following her while she saw and heard nothing. She turned back in the direction she had originally held and walked resolutely forward though inwardly she was shivering with fear and anticipation. A fate far worse than death.

'I am going to the pool to swim,' she said, surprised to find her voice steady. They laughed uproariously and chattered in some strange language. It occurred to her that they might not speak English. After all, this was Africa. She sighed with relief as they parted to let her pass. She quickened her step, lengthened her stride. There, she was past the last one.

The jerk on the collar of her blouse pulled her off her feet and she sat down heavily. The man who had caught her kicked her brutally in her side as she tried to rise and she fell over. He aimed his foot again and she cringed while she screamed but another black man pushed the first one away and pulled her upright only to send her back to the ground with a brutal blow to her already bruised face. Yet she thought, through her pain and fear, *It is well that he uses an open palm. A fist would make me ugly forever.* Another laughing black man pushed away the one who had slapped her and pulled her up by her hand. He began unbuttoning her blouse with clumsy fingers. Indignantly she struck his hand aside, to be rewarded with a painful blow from his fist to her stomach. Then he ripped the blouse from her by main force while she still stood with her hands clasped to her belly. He held her forearms while another pulled the strap of her bra away from her back and slit it with his knife, then pushed her to stagger backwards, her large breasts shaking, as he stood laughing with the bra in his hand.

Melody looked about wildly but there was no escape from the circle of laughing faces. She crossed her arms over her breasts but noticed that the pressure made them bulge provocatively. Before she could let go hands took her elbows from behind and forced her arms away. The man who had hit her in the belly and held her while the other cut her bra came forward slowly, licking his thick red lips. She thought he was going to strike her again and giggled with the release of the pent-up fear when he kneeled in front of her, immobilising her feet by placing his knees on them. He took out his knife while she watched fearfully, curving her body this way and that between the grip on her arms and the weight on her feet. He held the waistband of her slacks away from her body and cut through the folded material and lining, pricking her in the stomach with the sharp point of the knife when she struggled. Melody screamed continually. He ripped the slacks open and pulled them down around her knees. Then, to silence from the men in which Melody could hear her own screams, and when she stopped screaming, their breathing labouring under the suspense, he hooked his blunt fingers into the waistband of her panties and pulled them down slowly. When her blonde pubic hair appeared over the edge of the panties the men let their breath out slowly. The panties slid down her legs and they pursed their lips and smiled in appreciation of her pink vulva, which had excited Bob so, peeking through the sparse blonde hair. The man kneeling in front of her spread her knees with his elbows and forced the lips open with rough fingers for the appreciation of the others. Hands reached out to probe her and to squeeze her breasts cruelly. She started screaming again in pain and fear. A fate worse than death was not at all what she had imagined it to be. Several of the black men unbuttoned their bulging trousers to spring forth erect penises. She stopped screaming when she realised with surprise that several of them had been circumcised: who would have expected that of savages?

She also saw and noted at the back of her mind that one of the black men was eating the sandwich she had dropped, apparently with great relish. She started screaming again.

Perhaps it was the open mouth shining pinkly wet that gave the black man the idea. He came forward and pushed the others aside roughly, saying something to them which they considered funny, laughing even louder. He grabbed her by her hair and forced her to her knees. His fly was open and he was erect in front of her face. She stared fearfully at the tinsel glow and glitter of the exposed glans. He jerked her up and slapped her left and right through the face before forcing her to her knees again. He poked his member at her face and made sucking sounds with his lips to indicate what he wanted her to do. *These black bastards are as lazy as Bob* she thought and kept her mouth shut tight, not even opening it to scream when the heavy boot of a bystander anxiously trying to assist hit her in the side. A hand reached over her head from behind and held her nose closed with cruel pinching fingers. She held her breath as long as she could, until it felt as if her lungs would burst. Her bruised lips fell open to gasp for air and immediately the thing was filling her mouth, trying to enter her throat, choking her. She bit and spat the throbbing from her mouth on the ground next to her and looked in horror at the tip of the man's penis on the ground next to her, still throbbing: had she done that, bitten off in her mouth, with her teeth, part of this man's proudest possession? Was that why he was screaming a pure *basso profundo* above her, letting her hair go with a tearing jerk?

A rifle butt crashing into her neck sent Melody to merciful oblivion.

'Inept idiot can't even take his pleasure of a white woman without getting his cock bitten off!' Jomo was laughing so much that his first shot took the man in the side of his chest, sending him crashing to the ground but not killing him. Jomo walked over and put another shot through his ear and his jerking ceased. None of the others expressed surprise at the summary execution; they all knew that they had no medical facilities and a man incapacitated or even only in pain could be a danger to them all; they also knew that they themselves would be shot by their comrades if they should be wounded — it was preferable to being captured by the white men.

Jomo had come up in time to see the last scene of the drama, the big white woman spitting out the valuable piece of living flesh on the ground. He looked at her body and noted that his men had handled her roughly, then reconsidered. Some of the bruises were yellow and purple, not new. Was she the one he had heard whimpering last night, the one he had assumed to be in need of the solace only a black cock could give her? In that case he had made a serious mistake then. A husband who beat his wife, or at least a man who beat his woman, and a girl who knew enough karate to kill a man and was not afraid to use it, plus a determined defence of some ingenuity did not definitely not conform to the pattern he would expect of a camera safari. It was a pity he couldn't ask the woman . . . He thought back over the events of the attack while his men watched him respectfully.

One, the girl (woman?) who had killed one of his men with a single blow of her bare hand, expertly placed. Plus the man who had beaten his woman. Two, the speed with which a defence had been arranged. Three, he himself could not have made a better choice of a defensive position anywhere else in the camp. Four, the fact that these men did not rush for the helicopter at first sign of trouble and try to take off — getting themselves caught in the open and killed while still warming the machine up or killing themselves by taking off with an unchecked cold machine — indicated that they did not panic, and probably that they were experienced soldiers or at least had an experienced soldier in command. Five, the range and calibre of their armoury was too extensive for a camera safari, probably even too extensive for a group of game poachers. Jomo wished he had some hand grenades and a mortar. Six, and worst of all, the manner in which the beleaguered men had beaten off the attack with the Range

Rover. Jomo had gone with his men to the garage and noted how the men headed for the mini tractor: *Fucking peasants always go straight towards the agricultural implements.* He had chosen the Range Rover because it would afford his men more protection. As they had come into the open he had found himself approving the manner in which the men inside held their fire. When the first shot ricocheted off the axle he knew their chances of completing their plan – driving the Range Rover up the steps of the veranda and then bursting bodily into the room where the defenders would by then be cowering in a corner to be executed like mad dogs – were not high; men who knew enough and were cool enough to account for the vehicle before attending to the men on it who were firing at them, would not cower in corners. And when the front tyres went *before* the man behind the rifle started shooting at the driver, Jomo jumped from the baulking Range Rover and rolled under its cover towards the safety of a *rondawel*. As he rolled he was aware of the fine marksmanship of the man with the big bore rifle as he shot the tank into a vicious explosion while the Range Rover turned in mid-air. Seven, the Molotov cocktail which had dealt so convincingly with the only man from the Range Rover to come near their target by rolling under the protection of the raised veranda: Jomo was well aware that the making and casting of a live bomb like a Molotov cocktail is a dangerous process attempted only by those with steady nerves and certainly not the kind of defence somebody on a camera safari was likely to conjure up. The burning man had fallen near enough to him for Jomo to smell the household cooking oil from which the Molotov cocktail had been made. The men in the house were not the innocents to be slaughtered that the toad-colonel had assured him of.

On the other hand, there were only four rifles in their hands, only one of them auto-fire and none continuous-fire, while his own men, superior in numbers, had fully automatic weapons. And the Molotov cocktail had given him an idea ...

'Four of you stay here,' he told the waiting men. 'Fire occasionally at the house to let them know you are still here.

Do not expose yourselves needlessly. If they try to escape this way, cut them down in the open space between the building and the forest. The rest of you,' he pointed at the biggest and strongest men, 'you come with me. We have heavy work to do.'

Five

'Nothing but the best at Ultimate Test, Incorporated,' Decker told Cameron as he came up the cellar steps with his arms full of brandy bottles. 'It's a shame to burn good stuff but we haven't any second-rate Molotov cocktail type brandy in our cellar.'

Cameron opened his mouth to tell Decker about Melody's escape – which was how he thought of it, escape – but the pilot was already passing through the door to the lounge, saying, 'Keep up the good work, Bob-oh. Watch our back, boy, watch our back.' Cameron wondered if Decker had been sampling the brandy in the cellar.

Decker put the bottles in a row against the outer wall and took the kitchen towels the black man who had followed him handed him one by one as he made the Molotov cocktails.

'I'll do that if you like.' Curtis Bill did not take his eyes from the window he was looking through.

'It's all right. There's nothing happening out back anyway. Too much open space for the blighters to cross. Here, up front, is the only place with any decent cover. And, frankly, I never did like hiding behind the round walls of *rondawels*. No sort of cut-off point, y'know. Very insecure.'

Curtis Bill Bonham nodded his agreement.

'What's happening?'

'He's pulled out all but two or three of his men.'

'I told you we'd beaten the shit out of them!'

They ignored the Englishman. His wife said, 'Shh, Enoch. Have a sandwich.'

'Planning new mischief,' Decker said as a statement. 'What?'

'I don't know. But those Molotov cocktails of ours . . . ' Curtis Bill pointed at the orderly row standing beside his and Decker's feet.

'Burn us out?'

'How many full drums of fuel in the garage?'

'More than enough. If you're thinking of making a break for it in the helicopter, forget it. I couldn't get it into the air in time.'

'No. They'd slaughter the servants. Our only chance is to break out now, across the open circle, into the forest. But . . . ' Curtis Bill let the sentence trail off. Decker completed it for him:

'Many of the servants would be killed by the automatic weapons. Perhaps even some of our clients and ourselves. In the bush, on foot, Cameron and Pascoe will become liabilities instead of the assets they are now, while sandwiches are being served.'

'We have to stay.'

'I have never envied land commanders. Give me the skies any day.'

'Yes. We may want your help here when they attack. Timbo, fetch Mr Chris' rifles and ammunition.'

'Yes, Master!'

'Cameron's going to squeal.'

'Let him.'

'You could put Enoch in the kitchen for a while and bring –'

'I've earned my right to stay here,' Pascoe interrupted truculently.

'Has he?'

'Yes.'

Decker shrugged. It was useless arguing with Curtis Bill

283

once he had made up his mind. He ignored the hatred
Pascoe stared at him and checked his firearms thoroughly.
These highly trained terrorists would not take long to
organise their next and probably decisive attack. He found
himself looking forward to hand to hand combat. He'd go
out as he had lived, fighting. 'How about some coffee?' he
suggested to Judith Pascoe, not because he wanted coffee but
to irritate the sweating English inventor. Judith scuttled out
to oblige. Pascoe took a step forward towards Decker with
blood in his eyes but Curtis Bill said:

'Here it comes,' in his usual calm and colourless voice.

'I don't like me wife going around offering sandwiches to
niggers,' Pascoe muttered as he turned away to his window.
'And I like it less when some sky-taxi jockey orders her
around for coffee.'

'Fuckoffhere,' Decker mimicked the Englishman's accent.
'Don't shoot that drum, you silly motherfucker! That's
exactly what they want us to do.'

Pascoe glared at him balefully but took his finger from
the trigger and watched the rolling drum pass by his window.
The little tractor had darted out of the protection of a
rondawel only long enough for the drum to be rolled from
the two thin prongs of the drum lift attached to its rear.
The drum stopped near the middle of the veranda. The
terrorists obviously realised the improbability of puncturing
it with their machine pistols because they did not fire and
the next drum rolled out with the bung out, the little tractor
not appearing at all, frustrating the three men at their
windows as they waited for a shot at the driver and his
assistant. Another drum came out of the protection of the
rondawels with the bung out, then another, then three more
all at one shove, drowning the area in front of the veranda,
already saturated with dog and monkey blood, with fuel.
Several more drums rolled forward with the bungs out as the
white men watched powerlessly, the only sound their breathing interrupted by the occasional shot from the kitchen. Far
off they could also hear the commands called out casually to
the black men handling the drums and their excited laughter

in anticipation of the slaughter of the white men.

The flaming torch which came from behind the *rondawel* was a branch broom used by the Bantu for sweeping the yard. Decker hit it in the air with his first shot, worked the bolt, aimed and blew it beyond the flow of the fuel with his second shot.

'Jesus! That's faster than Bob's automatic!'

Chris Decker looked at Pascoe as he handed the rifle to his loader, who had followed him, to reload. 'Auto-ejectors may jam and fail but the hand of Chris Decker never falters.' He was laughing so much he could hardly get the words out. 'You chaps are actually both outstanding shots but I am a professional. The difference is like between Sunday and Monday.'

Pascoe was already regretting his admiring remark. This fucking safari driver never failed to make him feel small. He turned his back on the laughing pilot, not knowing why the man mocked him but determined to find out as soon as they had shot the remainder of the idiot terrorists the equally dumb safari organisers seemed to rate so highly.

The terrorists set the fuel aflame by lighting it with a match where it flowed around the nearest *rondawel* and jumping away quickly. The three men stood watching the flames spread.

'What're they trying to do? Burn us out or smoke us out?' Pascoe shouted.

'Neither,' Curtis Bill answered him. He and Chris Decker each picked up a bottle of brandy and lit the wicks. They looked at each other and their arms came over in co-ordinated motion to dash the bottles on the veranda steps. The two explosions ran into one long crash of yellow and blue violence.

'Hey! Are you mad? You'll set the building alight.'

'Shut up,' Decker said pityingly. 'Your ignorance is showing.'

'Huh? Was that –'

'Terrorists pay themselves in kind. They would burn us but not the women. If they wanted to burn us, they could

285

have let the drums roll up against the building, couldn't they?'

'They're creating a screen to run behind. The veranda is too high to vault cleanly at the ends. We'd kill them while they were clambering up or in the clear field of fire we have down the veranda's length. Watch the steps.' Curtis Bill spoke easily.

The first terrorist came through the flames his comrades had made, expecting to breathe clean air on the steps. He inhaled deeply, flaming brandy burning his throat and lungs. His scream died as Curtis Bill shot him without raising his rifle from his hip. Decker accounted for the second and third terrorists as they stumbled in the flames and fell over the body of the first. Curtis Bill shot the next one in the stomach and he went reeling back. They could hear him screaming on the far side of the wall of flame, though they could not see him.

Pascoe said, 'Nothing for me,' his voice orphaned.

'You have to be quick for your thrills,' Decker told him brutally. He lifted up his sleeve to look at a long weal raised on his wrist by a bullet fired by one of the burnt men as they came through the fire with their fingers on the triggers of their machine pistols.

'Coffee's brewing on the primus,' Judith Pascoe said, returning with her tray of sandwiches.

'Hurt?' Curtis Bill asked his partner, without looking up from lighting another Molotov cocktail.

'No. The main pain is going to be deciding whether to burst the blood blister or not.'

'Can I put a dressing on it for you?' Judith Pascoe put the tray of sandwiches, hardly depleted, on the smashed writing desk.

'No, thank you. But you can hold two of those bottles for me, then hand them to me one at a time after I've lit them.'

Pascoe glared at the pilot but said nothing. Judith picked up the bottles with their wet sagging rag tops and stood behind Decker, waiting patiently. Curtis Bill watched the ends of the veranda alternately. Pascoe kept his eyes on the flam-

286

ing steps to the veranda but Curtis Bill did not disillusion him of his hope and his dream that more terrorists would follow their comrades through the fatal flames; he was not running a schoolroom course in guerrilla tactics. He saw the fuel drum being raised onto the veranda from the protection of the blank side of the building and glanced at the other end of the veranda: another drum was placed on the veranda equally carefully. The terrorists wanted to make no noise to attract attention, they wanted the white men to watch the nice display of fireworks they had arranged for them. Curtis Bill decided that whoever led them would be a good man to have on your side. He nodded to the pilot as the drums started rolling towards the door. He wondered how many men were behind each drum. He'd find out soon enough.

Chris Decker lit both the wicks as Judith held the bottles at arm's length from her frail body. She was shivering with fear. He smiled reassuringly at her but she dropped her eyes, remembering how he had smiled the day he had killed the baboon. She wasn't having any. Well, that was her privilege. He took one of the burning bottles from her and swung his arm through the window. The bottle smashed on top of the drum and splattered its burning contents over the man pushing the drum along. He rose to dance a jig in the flames, his machine pistol spurting useless death against the wall beside him. A ricochet sliced through four of his ribs into his heart at the same moment that another took out both of his eyes and the bridge of his nose. He died of massive trauma – pure shock – before his heart had pumped even a pint of his life into the nothingness.

One man behind each drum. Now he knew. Where were the rest? 'Away from the end walls, away.' Curtis Bill gestured at the Bantu servants cowering on the floor. 'Get away!'

The explosions as the end walls imploded killed his last sentence. Murallo and plaster and brick and mortar and bits of flying flesh caused everybody to duck reflexively and Judith to scream. Then Curtis Bill killed the two men who came through the hole nearest to him with a single shot each, followed by a second shot each to make sure only a second later. Their machine pistols had been blazing into the Bantu servants nearest to them and several were wounded and some would be dead or dying, Curtis Bill knew. Machine pistols were designed for massacres at close range, as he well knew.

Decker hefted the rifle he still held in his free hand and shot past Pascoe's back at the two terrorists coming through the gaping hole swathed in swirling dust at the far end of the room, narrowly missing Pascoe and the servants in between. He hit one of the men in the face. Then there were servants between him and the remaining terrorist, falling as the terrorist swung his machine pistol in a short, vicious arc, holding it down to prevent its endemic built-in climb, thereby betraying his thorough training. His magazine empty, he stepped back to reload or retreat and from the far side of the room Curtis Bill shot him through the throat as the terrorist stepped back on to the rubble caused by the explosion which had first permitted him entry. Pascoe was still turning to see what had caused the disturbance but it was all over.

Judith looked at the live bomb in her hand and retreated away from it. It followed her at arm's length. She was holding it! She opened her fingers to drop it and caught it before it had fallen an inch: she'd go up with it. She ran to the window, passing behind Decker as he waited for a clear shot at the second terrorist. The terrorist, lying flat on his stomach, gave the drum a vicious push with both hands to clear his field of action, then looked up startled into her eyes as she leant out of the window. His hand scrabbled frantically beside him on the veranda for his machine pistol which he had put down to have both hands free for the drum. She dropped the Molotov cocktail on the veranda in front of his nose and stepped back into the room. The bomb exploded immediately, sending a hot blast into the room to singe her hair and burn her eyebrows from her face. The burning man danced his torment in the frame of the window. 'Eric, Joan. Eric, Joan,' Judith repeated her children's names in her mind. 'Eric, Joan.' Decker shot the man in the chest and the force of the bullet sent him backwards across the veranda until he crashed into the rail to totter for a century on top of it while Judith could not take her eyes from the man she had killed. 'Eric. Joan. Oh, my God . . . ' Then he fell out of sight.

Decker leant over without moving his feet to squeeze a nerve on her stringy neck, just under the ear, almost affectionately. 'Stop screaming,' he said softly and she stopped immediately.

'Christ, I'm bleeding,' Pascoe bleated, ripping his shirt open to look incredulously at the wound the 7.62mm bullet had made. 'Some bastard shot me!'

Decker stared at him in disbelief. 'What – what did you think was going on here?' For once he was incapable of adding sarcasm.

Pascoe did not answer him. He looked trustingly down into his wife's face as she stood on tiptoe to look at the wound. Over her shoulder she said commandingly, 'Melody, fetch me some hot water please. And boil a couple of kitchen towels.'

'Melody went into the kitchen earlier,' Curtis Bill told her. 'I'll go tell her.'

'Don't bother.' Cameron was leaning against the kitchen door as nonchalantly as he had seen Decker do earlier. 'She came to the kitchen and went straight through and into the forest.'

Decker picked up a box of cartridges and opened the lid to make sure it was full. He stuffed it in his pocket and went past Cameron in the silence. To Cameron he said, 'You motherless fuckwit.'

'He's gone after her!' Cameron said with surprise as the shooting started at the back of the building. Curtis Bill ran past him and fired a few shots. After thirty seconds, before anybody thought of going to see, he came back, carrying his rifle slackly in his hand.

'He's dead,' Pascoe stated with relish.

'No,' Curtis Bill said without surprise at the Englishman's

assumption. 'There was only one man in the trees and Chris got him before I even opened fire. I just shot off a few rounds for moral support.'

'Why'd he go after her?'

Curtis Bill looked at the Bantu servants carrying out their dead and wounded. 'Because you didn't.'

'Are you implying I'm a coward just because I didn't – '

'No! I am simply observing that Chris went after your wife and you did not. Please return to your post. This action is not over yet.'

'Well, just you look here, mister fucking Curtis – '

'We can settle our differences later. Return to your post!'

Cameron stared at the slim tanned man. He fingered his rifle where it hung at his side. It would be so easy. So easy.

'Better go back to the kitchen, Bob,' Pascoe said, frightened that Curtis Bill might allow the American to stay and send him to the kitchen where nothing seemed to happen.

'Yeah,' Cameron said. 'Yeah. But just you wait. Just you wait. Robert J. Cameron, M.D., does not forget.'

Curtis Bill ignored the American. To Pascoe he said, 'Watch the hole in the wall. Forget the veranda.'

Cameron went into the kitchen to nurse his grudge.

Chris Decker killed the terrorist with two shots before he came into the range of the man's machine pistol. Or, as the pilot thought of it, the man killed himself by opening fire before his enemies were within effective range. He stopped to pick up the man's machine pistol. A glance told him what it was: Pistolet-Pulemet Shpagina Obrazets 1941G type, exactly as he had thought, and probably in one of the Czech manufacturing variants, though he couldn't be sure without a thorough examination he had no time for now; all the identifying marks had been ground out. He took the weapon and the man's remaining magazines and carried it in his right hand, after making sure it had a full magazine in it, as he instinctively turned left through the trees. He ran easily, watching every tree, ready for instant action, yet having a corner of his mind free to speculate on the arms. Russian. Or Russian inspired, same thing. Close quarters stuff. Not even a Kalishnikov assault rifle amongst the lot to give them any range at all. Obviously meant for this job only. And they had expected to take somebody – Ultimate Test, Incorporated? – by surprise and without resistance or they would have had longer range arms and grenades. Conclusion: They had come specifically for them, for this safari, but they knew nothing about the histories of the men involved or there would have been at least a sniper's rifle to winkle men out of entrenched and determinedly defended positions, grenades and perhaps even a mortar. Decker smiled as he ran. It was rather funny that the terrorists should pick on him and Curtis Bill Bonham. Even this terrorist group, which had proven itself disciplined and ingenious in its attacks, had fallen victim to a planning fuckup. It only went to prove what he had often said, that the efficiency of terrorists was more a creation of the newspapers than of reality. And of course they had let themselves be distracted from their main task by the white women ...

He heard them long before he came within line of sight of them through the trees. They were laughing. Decker turned away noiselessly, into the trees. He would come up on them from the direction they least expected a threat to arise from, a nice little surprise for the black bastards who'd had the bloody cheek to attack his safari base camp simply because it was geographically convenient for them. Well, he was going to teach them convenience ...

He stood between two tree trunks fifteen feet from the terrorists and watched them sport over the rigid and naked bruised body of Melody on the ground between them. They would stand on one side of her, hunch themselves up, bend and jump over her, landing within a fraction of an inch of her body on her far side. They were taking bets on who could get closest without touching her. At first Decker thought she was dead, but then he saw her eyes moving with the jumping men and knew her unearthly stillness to be inspired by fear. One of the terrorists had his machine pistol standing against a tree, the other two carried theirs slung across their shoulders. Chris Decker flicked the selector lever to single fire, and listened to the sound with a connoisseur's appreciation. It was not a loud sound. But it was the wrong kind of sound under the men's laughter. There was silence – Melody screamed as a startled terrorist landed on her belly with both his feet and all his weight but nobody listened to the irrelevant distraction, nobody heard her scream – for a long moment. The rustle of clothing as the two terrorists tried for the machine pistols slung against their backs. The smack of hand against wood and plastic and metal and cloth.

Decker let them get the machine pistols off their shoulders before he shot them, one shot each in the hollow at the base of the throat.

The third terrorist stood staring at the pilot. He looked away at his machine pistol where it rested against a tree. He looked back at Decker, grimaced at him, took a step forward towards the white man with open arms as if to embrace him in welcome to some civil ceremony, then broke away towards his rifle.

Decker flicked the lever to automatic fire. He let the terrorist pick up his machine pistol. He knew there would be thirty-three rounds left in the magazine. He waited until the terrorist started rising and turning at the same time. He wanted to know whether the man would turn to his left or his right. When he was certain, he aimed at the terrorist's right ankle and held the trigger as the man turned to his left, the torque of the 900 rpm cyclic rate lifting the muzzle to cut a neat spiral around his body. On the man's face as he turned to face his killer was comic surprise. He fell forward on his face, full length to Decker, head pointing the way. His two companions gurgled in their blood.

Decker fitted a new magazine to the machine pistol in his hand. He set the lever to single fire. He dispatched the two gurgling men with a shot each between glazed eyes. They didn't stop gurgling immediately. Decker shrugged at the wilful persistence of the heart. He turned towards Melody's screams.

She lay flat on the ground, rigidly unmoving, only her mouth open and her tongue ululating to indicate life still skulked in her battered body.

'It's all right now. Uncle Chris is here to take care of everything that's bothering Melody.' He squatted on his haunches beside her and pressed the nerve under her ear gently. 'It's all right now.'

She looked at him in silence, her eyelashes fluttering over her innocent blue eyes. Her voice had the tone of drawing-room farce rising inappropriately in it. 'Oh, Chris, it was so terrible!' Her arms went around his neck and she pulled him down on her. Her tongue probed his ear while her arms clasped him to her fiercely.

Decker already had an erection to celebrate his very satisfactorily professional killing of the three terrorists and his daring rescue of the fair maiden. He thought, *Why not a quickie? She wants it, so why not? One up on that bastard Cameron. And she's just rewarding me for saving her life.* He laughed joyfully as he zipped open his fly. Melody giggled in response and held him tighter.

Six

'War, military action, is a formalised game.'

Jomo Iningwe sat with his back to the wall of a *rondawel*. He looked up into the sun, an hour above the horizon, to see if Dingane was listening. He was not. He was staring in disbelief at the building from which he had seen the legendary Jomo Iningwe repulsed several times in the space of an hour.

Jomo shrugged. It didn't matter whether the man listened. He had only a limited number of choices of attack open to him. And each one had been anticipated and met and defeated by the numerically inferior group of men trapped in the building. In there a man commanded, a man of considerable expertise in this kind of fighting, a man who seemed able to read his mind and anticipate and outplan him. Such men were not many. He knew the names of all, and their reputations, though he had never met any of them. Mad Mike Hoare. The fanatic, Peters. The calculating iceman, Bonham. The disciplinarian, Steiner. The gimpy braggart, Theron. The best mercenary leaders. Chances of one of them being here without the toad-colonel being aware of it were a million to one. He looked at his watch. He would rest for another minute. Fifteen minutes to plan and execute another attack. Then he would have to retreat with the remainder of his men – if any remained. He smiled wryly to himself: he would not have to kill any of his men to leave behind as mute testimony of an atrocity, he had his atrocity already in the bodies shot and burnt and with their throats slit. Only it wasn't white men, women and children being slaughtered. This was White Men Massacre Black African Freedom Fighters. The toad-colonel was not going to be pleased. Well, fuck the colonel and his goddamn lousy intelligence and his *bolle de mendego* – balls of butter – for not having done his minor part of the job better. *Merde!* Jomo pulled himself up against the wall by holding on to the windowsill.

Jomo Iningwe stood transfixed, staring idiotically through the window. Of course! He nodded at the head under its hygienic plastic cover. It explained everything by simply staring at him with unblinking eyes from which the eyelids had been pinned back by dressmaking pins. This was no camera safari, nor did these men creep around in the night poaching animals. No, they went out, probably in broad daylight – they would have to for the late Indian photographer to perform his obscene recording activities – and shot black men. It explained the firearms and their ability

294

and inclination to use them against men. It explained the quality of their leadership, for men would not embark on such dangerous hunts without competent leadership, not if they intended to survive the revenge of the hunted and the prosecution of the law. And men who would shoot another man and then cut his head off as a trophy were obviously not above teaching their daughters how to kill a man with a single blow, nor would such men hesitate to beat women who irritated them.

Jomo had made a number of mistakes in his judgements and his men had paid for his errors with their lives. Idi Amin had hired him to provide a cause for gloating over the discomfiture of the South Africans. The killing of the white men was really incidental to the main purpose, icing on the cake to give it extra newspaper mileage. Jomo considered the mixed metaphor, concluded it had no holes of logic. Now he had found Big Daddy's *cause macabre* his duty was clearly to get out alive with his news. To attempt to punish the arrogant white men for their crimes against Africa would be hubris. He was tempted to disregard his own good sense and lead one last charge even if he perished in it. But he knew no purpose would be served.

'We have found what we have come for,' he told Dingane as he smashed the window with the barrel of his machine pistol. 'Go, get that head on the table for me. Then we can leave. Our work here is finished.'

Dingane climbed through the window, eager to see what it was that had held their leader's attention so raptly. While Dingane was inside the *rondawel*, Jomo heard the dogs.

Melody jerked to a stop. 'I'm not going in there!'

'Come on!' Decker dragged her along by her arm. 'It's the only place you'll be safe for the time being.' He had to shout to be heard above the howling the dogs had set up as they approached the kennels.

She went reluctantly with him. He had a very firm hold on her arm. And he had proved he knew what he was doing when he had saved her from the terrorists. The dogs yowled at them, jumped up against the fencing, snarling their yellow fanged fury. Decker led her around the largest kennel, in which the smaller dogs were kept communally. He gripped her by the waist and lifted her onto the roof. The corrugated iron cladding burned her bottom – her own clothing had been in tatters so the pilot had given her his shirt and it was her only piece of clothing – enraging the weals Bob had raised with his belt the night before.

'Stay here until somebody comes to fetch you. Understand?'

'Yes. Where are you going?'

'You'll see.' Decker cast around until he found one of the *knopkieries* the kennel keepers used to assure the dogs' good behaviour. He opened the kennel gates for the smaller dogs first and let them stream out to mill around his ankles, then the bigger dogs which he hit on their noses to stop their snapping at him, then the Rhodesian ridgeback which gazed at him contemplatively from a distance. 'Hamba! That way. Baboon!' Decker pointed the way with his *knopkieries*. After a moment of hesitation the large yellow dog headed for the circle of *rondawels* and was followed by the raggle taggle of the assorted crossbreeds and evolutionary accidents. Decker looked vastly relieved as he started to run after them. Melody called after him:

'Hey, what about me?'

'Just stay there. If you get down, some of the dogs might get ideas about you.' He turned and ran on, *knopkierie* in one hand, machine pistol in the other, his rifle slung across his back. He knew his tanned bare chest made a good impression and kept himself erect as he ran. Nobody was going to shoot at him any more. Far ahead of him the dogs rounded the corner of the lounge. Decker ran up to the kitchen door and opened it. Inside Cameron turned to him from his window:

'What's happening?'

'Your wife's at the kennels. She needs medical attention.' Decker marched briskly into the lounge, leaving Cameron behind him in the kitchen nursing a hundred questions.

'We beat the shit out of them!' Pascoe told him before he could ask. 'They're in full retreat, but sourface won't go after them yet.' He looked venomously at Curtis Bill, who was still in position beside his window.

'Shh, Enoch,' Judith said. 'Hold still.' The bandages around the shoulder and upper arm were taking on Frankenstein proportions for what was after all only a flesh wound.

Decker joined Curtis Bill at the window. 'That right?'

'Perhaps. They've certainly ceased firing. Probably to plan new mischief.'

'You're worried?'

'Yes. Their time must be running out. I do not like having to fight desperate men. They are unpredictable.'

'Any chance they'll break and run?'

'No. They might try for an orderly retreat though. Did you let the dogs loose?'

'Yes.' Decker looked at the dogs milling around in the open yard in front of the lounge, snapping at each other, smelling the charred corpses, trying to dig the baboon from the earth in which they could smell its blood. 'Not helping much, they aren't.'

'No. Not yet. But if the dogs get in their way . . . '

'How many men have they left?'

'Seven, eight. Not many.' Curtis Bill did not need to ask his partner whether he had killed the men at the back of the lounge.

'Still superior numbers. What about a break by the back door?'

'No. We have too many wounded we would have to leave behind.' Curtis Bill gestured at the Bantu servants moaning on the floor. 'There are more in the pantry.'

They stood silently looking out of the window at the mess in front of them. Both of them knew there would be only one more attempt and it would be decisive. They had won all the battles so far but that would be no consolation if they were killed in the last desperate onslaught by blood-crazed men. Neither of them was inexperienced enough to count their victory yet. And neither would consider deserting their retainers, leaving them to be tortured by the terrorists. Nor were they anxious to take to the bush with the likes of Pascoe and Cameron; battered as their fort the lounge was, it was still better protection than trees and natural conformations.

'Jesus! Wish for a thing and it happens.' They watched through the space between the far *rondawels* as Jomo Iningwe and his men melted into the forest. Decker raised his rifle but had no opportunity to fire.

'Now they're retreating,' Curtis Bill said to Pascoe.

'Are you going to go after them or shall I?' the pilot asked.

'You go. I'll stay and start clearing up here.'

As he passed through the kitchen, Decker noticed Cameron still keeping his vigil by the window, firing now and again at a shadow moving. 'It's all over. You can go fetch your wife now.' He did not wait for the American's reply but ran on.

'Patronising shit!' Cameron called out but the pilot did not hear him.

Chris Decker kicked out at the dogs milling around him as he rounded the corner cautiously. He found the mini-tractor behind the Pascoe *rondawel* and climbed up on it. It started immediately. He drove it in the direction of the river, calling to the dogs, 'Baboon. That way,' pointing in the direction the terrorists had run. But the dogs were disinclined to leave the vicinity of the strong smell of baboon blood. Decker turned the tractor around and drove it back past the lounge. Cameron came running from the kitchen door and he stopped to wait for him.

'Where are you going?'

'I'll drop you at the kennels so you can look after Melody. Then I'm chasing the terrorists.'

'Don't worry about Melody. I've told Judith Pascoe to go fetch her,' Cameron lied. 'I'll come with you.'

'Okay,' Decker said reluctantly. 'Hop on.'

Cameron jumped on to the towbar of the tractor and

clung precariously to the back of the seat Decker was occupying. 'Hey! They must have gone the other way. I didn't see them at all.'

Decker didn't answer. He stopped the tractor and reversed so that it had its back to the trees. He jumped off and grabbed a length of rope from a hook on the inside of one mudguard. Cameron followed him curiously. They came through the trees and Cameron almost stumbled over one of the three dead terrorists.

'Jesus!' The American put his hand against a tree to steady himself. 'What happened here?'

'They were attacking your wife.'

'You killed them?'

'Yeah. And their lookout, about two hundred yards that way.' Decker turned his head to indicate the direction. His hands were busy tying together the ankles of the man he had perforated spirally with a nearly full magazine of the burp gun.

'What're you gonna do with him?'

'Remember the big live baboon and the little dead baboon and the dogs?' Decker asked, knowing full well that Cameron did not.

'No. I missed that.' Cameron was sullen. He had missed much. 'Just another piece of anti-Americanism, favouritism, like today, letting Enoch have all the fun and leaving me at the back where nothing happened.'

Decker put the rope over his shoulder and dragged the corpse through the trees to the tractor. 'Come on, big boy. Now's your chance to be a hero too.' He tied the rope to the towbar and jumped up on the seat and had the tractor started and moving while Cameron was still scrabbling for a foothold on the towbar. He looked at his watch. Two minutes and five seconds since he had first found the tractor. The terrorist leader was not going to let his men do more than about a mile every ten minutes or even twelve minutes for fear of tiring them out in case they had to fight again. He would catch them before they reached the river. He drove the tractor with its riddled towed cargo through the

299

space between the lounge and the Pascoe *rondawel*. Enoch Pascoe came running along the veranda, his naturally clumsy gait turned into a stumbling comedy by the weight and bulk of the bandages Judith had festooned his flesh wound with.

'Hey! Wait for me!' When it became clear to him that Decker was not going to stop, he arrested his forward momentum by grabbing at the rail just before he crashed over it. He shouted bitterly after the tractor, 'I deserve to come along. I've earned the right.' He was sobbing in frustration. He had been short changed on almost everything. All they'd let him shoot, Curtis Bill and Chris, was the Range Rover. Then they'd taken everything else for themselves, giving him the consolation prize of flattering words. Even Judith had had a better chance than he, bombing that terrorist right outside the window. And now Decker was taking Cameron to hunt down the fleeing terrorists while he, Enoch Pascoe, who had paid as much for this safari and had, in addition, been wounded in their defence, was left behind. He stopped sobbing as the tractor made a wide turn in the open circle between the *rondawels* and headed for him. But Decker was only dragging the bloody corpse around to give the dogs a smell of it. He turned the tractor away and disappeared between the two far *rondawels* and down the path through the forest to the pool, Cameron holding on for grim life, the pack of dogs yapping behind, led by the large yellow Rhodesian ridgeback. Enoch Pascoe shook his fist at them, spluttering his words orgasmically in incomprehensible uncontrollable foamy rage. He turned and saw the corpses of Vincent and the black frozen together on their canvas and kicked the prone double statue viciously until Judith came and led him away.

The little tractor was shaking along at its top speed, barely twenty miles an hour, but Decker was content to ignore Cameron's shouted commands for more nonexistent speed. He looked at his watch and calculated that he would catch up with the fleeing terrorists while they were still six hundred yards from the river, a very, very long distance to flee under fire and harassed by vicious dogs. He laughed to him-self: the last day of Ultimate Test, Incorporated was turning out to be a very good day indeed. He turned in his seat to look at the corpse they were dragging behind them. The rope had worn through the perforated ankle but held on the other ankle. The corpse no longer looked even remotely like what had once been a man. It turned on the ankle, thumping the earth, grazing along, bloody all over and streaming a smear of red for the dogs to follow. As he looked, the large yellow Rhodesian ridgeback bit off a flying hand in midair, severing it so quickly that the revolution of the corpse was not checked at all, the arm flinging on its way without a break. The dog swallowed once, twice and loped on, followed by the lesser breeds also straining for a piece of the flesh so tantalisingly out of reach. Then the big dog lost interest in the corpse, its nose to the ground, confirm-ing the *spoor* of a live sample of whatever was being dragged behind the machine. Decker sighed as he waited for its training to remind it that the live ones were more fun . . . He looked back at his steering and the Rhodesian ridgeback streaked past him, nose to the ground. He laughed as he slowed down to let the rest of the pack follow its leader: he didn't want to trample any of the dogs under the tractor's wheels. Cameron pointed backwards and shouted something in his ear. Decker looked. A tiny dog was sitting on the corpse with its teeth dug in, twisting and turning with it but not letting go despite being bashed unmercifully against the ground. Decker laughed and stopped the little tractor. He climbed down, picked the tiny dog up and handed it to Cameron. The little animal looked at the men with trusting red eyes and did not attempt to bite them as the tractor once more sped on its way.

The pack, running before the tractor, and the men on the tractor saw the fleeing terrorists at the same time. The dogs renewed their baying, the tiny dog in Cameron's arms join-ing the cacophony as a boy soprano. Cameron reached up with it and threw it far in front of the tractor where it fell in the middle of the pack and was running with the pack as its feet touched ground. Cameron raised his rifle but Decker put his hand on the muzzle and forced it down.

'Not yet. Give the dogs a chance first and you'll see what you missed on Sunday.'

Cameron reluctantly lowered his rifle. 'It'd better be good,' he slurred.

There were five terrorists, glancing fearfully over their shoulders at the dogs and the tractor fast closing the three hundred yards between them. One slowed, obviously with the intention of turning around to face the threat, but a tall, light skinned man turned his head to snap something at him and they all increased their pace.

Decker laughed jubilantly. 'They're going to try and outrun us,' he shouted over the minitractor's tortured scream.

'I reserve the big white nigger for myself. Okay?' Cameron shouted in his ear.

'Yeah. Okay. But wait first, you hear?'

Cameron nodded his understanding.

The terrorists had spread out in their desperate burst of speed. In front ran the tall, light-skinned leader and with him a broader man carrying something under his arm: it occasionally caught the glint of the sun to send a defiant message to the men on the speeding tractor.

'That nigger stole Omo Minowara's head!' Cameron shouted. 'Goddamn thief!'

The large yellow dog closed on the rearmost of the three men strung out behind the leaders. Its jaws closed on the man's wrist pumping past its nose. The man jerked around and the dog's teeth closed into his throat and ripped it out without a break in stride. The man was still falling to the ground when the ridgeback was already ten yards away after the remaining four fleeing terrorists. Decker cheered.

'Jesus! Jesus! Jesus! I wouldn'ta believed it if you hadn't shown me!' Cameron whistled.

The small dogs and the big dogs tore at the dead man briefly before running on after the large yellow dog. The ridgeback reached the second terrorist of the group of three, looked over its shoulder to see if the pack was following, and

302

left the man for the lesser dogs. Decker groaned. The large dog had made a serious strategic mistake. As it went past the man, the terrorist unslung his machine pistol and raised it to fire at the ridgeback speeding towards the back of his comrade. Before he could fire, he heard the lesser dogs behind him and turned on them. He sprayed a one second burst into the main body of the pack when it was ten paces from his feet. When the pitifully depleted remainder of the pack were five paces from him he emptied his magazine with another one second burst. Decker shot him in the chest and again in the head while he was falling. The four dogs surviving from the pack jumped over his body.

'Sly bastard killed my dogs,' Decker raged as he drove the tractor straight over the corpse.

The man running before the large yellow dog unslung his machine pistol as he ran. Suddenly he turned and faced the way he had come, ready to defend himself against the threat which had caused his comrade to fire a burst. The ridgeback rose into the air and closed its teeth around and into the man's neck as the second burst sounded. A jerk and the head severed to roll away as Decker's two shots rang out. The ridgeback would not be distracted from its prey by the sound of gunfire. It was already at full speed and gaining on the man with the parcel, who had fallen behind the long-legged pace of the light-skinned leader. Before them all the Limpopo flowed calmly.

Slowly at first, and then with gathering speed, a large section of the green overhang of the river broke away towards the middle of the black water. The helmsman had lost his nerve. The tall terrorist leader shouted at the boat, then dived into the water to swim after it. Cameron fired at him from the bumping and swaying tractor but missed as the wheels went over a root just as he fired.

The man who had followed the leader and nearly kept pace with him might have heard the breathing of the ridgeback close behind him over his own tortured breathing or might have known instinctively about the death on his track. He turned on the river bank, took the head from under his arm and threw it accurately into the open jaws of the monster dog. While the dog crushed the skull to rid its mouth of the encumbrance and blockage, the man dived into the river. The lesser dogs stemmed a moment, afraid to pass the big yellow dog, then jumped into the river to swim after the black man.

Decker brought the minitractor to a halt on the river bank. While Cameron ran forward swearing to kneel on the bank, Decker ripped the rope from the mangled hunk of flesh behind the tractor and tied one end securely to the end of a hoe he had found clipped to the side of the tractor's engine covering. He walked up behind the Rhodesian ridge-back and tied the rope to the ring on its collar. As the dog crunched the skull and spat it out, he stepped back to hold it at a distance with the handle of the hoe. It snarled at him but he held it away with ease.

Cameron couldn't get a clear shot at the terrorist leader. The man and the dogs had churned the water into waves and now the crocodiles were adding to the confusion as they took the dogs struggling down to drown them.

'Come help me, you bastard!' Cameron screamed at Decker.

Decker laughed. 'No need to waste bullets, man. Wait for a clear shot.'

The terrorist leader reached the boat, which was now reversing towards him, the helmsman having regained his nerve when he had seen that the commotion was caused only by dogs and two white men on a lawn mower tractor. The boat shielded both helmsman and terrorist leader from Cameron's fire. The terrorist leader appeared again briefly as he crawled through the rail on the far side but Cameron pulled the trigger only to hear the click of an empty magazine.

Decker swore and started for the tractor, to fetch his rifle and complete the job Cameron had botched, but the dog dug in and restrained him and he would not let it go because it would go into the water and get taken by the crocodiles. He dragged it inch by inch towards the tractor. Then he stopped and watched the water in fascination.

The bulge of water, tons of it, could only mean one thing as it closed on the terrorist who had foiled the ridgeback so cleverly and was now swimming for his life with a powerful over-arm stroke, totally unaware of the danger in the water with him, trying only to escape the guns of the white men behind him.

The eyebrow ridges broke the water at the same time as the obscene ear stubs and the malformed nostrils. The hippopotamus had its mouth open, the teeth large stumps threatening the disturbance of its territorial waters, yet dwarfed by the vastness of the cavernous mouth. A moment before the jaws took him the terrorist became aware of a large body in the water next to him. He looked up into the open jaws and screamed. His head-half continued screaming as the hippopotamus bit him cleanly in two, continued screaming as the two halves of his body floated away separately, the open mouth drowning its scream only as a crocodile took the upper half of his body under the surface to store it under a muddy overhang to rot for later consumption.

'What happened?' Cameron swung his rifle up.

'A hippo bit the nigger clean in two,' Decker said.

'Where? Where?' Cameron saw only the river smoothing out the waves of disturbance, flowing perhaps a little pinkly twenty feet from them. He looked again and the pinkness was gone, unconfirmed.

'Just get the bloody boat's fuel tanks before it gets away, you goddamn fuckwit!' Decker started dragging the dog towards the tractor again.

The boat's engines whirled into high revolutions and Decker stopped dragging the dog towards the tractor. The nose of the boat lifted and in seconds it was planing, disappearing down the river at speed. Cameron fired a full magazine after it but to no effect, though they saw his first three shots strike white paint from the boat. They stood watching until the boat's wake had been calmed by the flow of the river. It did not take long. Decker smiled around the epitaph to the terrorist attack:

'Only one got away.'

Seven

They were an incongruous trio climbing the steps of the veranda, stepping over the charred crop of dead men sprung up since dawn: Decker, barechested, tanned, leading his dog at the end of a hoe; Cameron, equally barechested but pasty white and blazing red from sunburn in contrasting blotches, carrying his rifle in his hand; Yodoko, wearing Cameron's shirt down to her knees, refusing all assistance, walking by herself, her short attire and the pain of her torn loins robbing her walk of delicacy and exaggerating the natural bowleggedness of Japanese women.

Melody met them just inside the door. 'How many black men did the conquering hero of Africa shoot on his last expedition?' she enquired silkily of her husband. She still wore Decker's shirt.

'We got four,' he replied, taken unawares.

'To be precise,' Decker said behind him, half his attention on the restless dog outside the door at the end of the hoe's length, 'the dog got two, a hippo got one and I got one, while Doctor Fuckwit here let the other one get away, trying all the time to perfect his magic trick of firing bullets out of an empty magazine.'

'Yeah. You didn't give me much of a chance, did you? And when it came to the crunch, you were more concerned with your fucking precious lap dog than with fighting terrorists.'

306

'You asked for him, the terrorist leader. In my mistaken generosity I let you have him. You missed him. He got away. That's that. Now go see to the women and then to the wounded servants.'

'Nobody speaks to –'

'He just has, hasn't he?' Cameron's wife cut softly but incisively across his outburst. 'But you needn't examine me. I just got raped by a lot of blacks, I don't know how many. I lost count after the tenth one because I was enjoying it so much, thinking how badly your limp little thing compared to real men's cocks.' She told her lies convincingly.

Cameron raised his hand and slapped her backhanded through the face. 'Slut!'

Decker smiled at her across Cameron's shoulder as he caught the man's arm from behind on the return swing. He knew none of the blacks had taken her, that he had been the first to enter her. And she had rather enjoyed it, hadn't she?

'Okay, okay. She doesn't want you. Go see to Yodoko then and after that to the wounded servants.'

'You don't give me –'

'Shut up!' Decker's eyes were caught in the drama in the room.

Yodoko stood in the middle of the room, her eyes on the floor. But now she looked at her husband on his bed. He turned his face away from her. She shook her head.

'My wife and I both know what happened. We do not need an examination.'

The strained syllables of Omo Minowara's words hung on the air and dropped one by one with a heavy thud of sinister premonition. Cameron's voice was low and persuasive as he caught the last thud:

'She is torn and bleeding and as a doctor I –'

'No!'

It was the first time any of the men had heard Yodoko speak even one word. The emphatic negative froze Cameron and Decker in a strange tableau, hands locked together above their heads. Pascoe lowered the glass he was drinking from, pushed it away as Judith tried to return it to his lips.

307

Curtis Bill Bonham looked up from the floor where he was bandaging the arm of a wounded Bantu servant.

Yodoko shook her head again. Nobody replied to her. There was no reply to her husband's rejection or to her abject agreement with it.

Curtis Bill Bonham, his hands sure on the wounded man's arm, broke the spell. 'As soon as you can get the chopper radio going, Chris, I'd like to speak to the police.'

'Yeah.' Decker pushed the American away from him. 'Neither of the women want you to look up them, Sport. Go see to the wounded servants in the pantry.'

Cameron stumbled to the kitchen door and turned, cocking his rifle as he turned. When he had described a full circle, the rifle was level and menacing Decker's chest. Decker, hampered by having the end of the hoe by which he was holding the dog in one hand, raised his rifle and curled his finger around the trigger.

'There's no bullet in the chamber,' Cameron told him. 'There's no way a proper little soldier, like you pretend to be, will walk into a room full of people with a loaded rifle, is there? Come on, squeeze the trigger and find out how death feels when I squeeze my trigger on my nice loaded gun.'

Decker lowered his rifle, let it hang slackly by his side.

'Drop it.'

Decker dropped the rifle. 'I'm going to kill you for this, you realise that, of course?' he said conversationally.

Curtis Bill had not even looked towards his own rifle, leaning against a wall twenty feet away. He knew exactly where it was and how long it would take to get there. Too long. 'What's the melodrama in aid of?' he asked Cameron. If the American swung his rifle away from Chris for just a second it would be enough time and to spare for Chris to reach his rifle and kill him.

Cameron refused to let his temper betray him. 'I haven't had the hunting I've paid for yet. No police until I've had my money's worth.'

'You're mad,' Melody said softly, without surprise.

308

'And best to hunt the man who soiled your honour and mine,' Minowara said from his bed. Cameron nodded at the support from an unexpected quarter without looking at the Japanese on his bed.

'Yeees,' Enoch Pascoe let out his breath slowly. 'I haven't had my money's worth either.'

'Yeah, but you been favoured while I got stuck in the kitchen.'

'Shit, I saw more but all the fun I got was leftovers and scraps their lordships threw me, niggers they'd already drilled.'

Cameron considered. 'Okay. Go pick up the sky taxi driver's gun.'

Judith Pascoe said, 'Enoch, you –'

'Shut up,' he told her caressingly as he lumbered forward.

'I wouldn't if I were you,' Decker said casually. 'It is no small thing to be on my shit list or Curtis Bill's. Often it is quite fatal.'

Pascoe stopped to look at the pilot's face. Decker smiled at him like a shark. Pascoe stood indecisive while the assembly held its collective breath.

'He is bluffing,' Omo Minowara assured the hesitant Englishman. His calm tone, more than the words, encouraged Pascoe to dart forward and grab the rifle. As he scuttled away with it Decker planted his large boot on the Englishman's broad posterior with impressive force while not taking his defiant smiling eyes from Cameron. Pascoe walked deliberately to where his own rifles rested against the wall and exchanged Decker's for one of his own rifles. He made sure it was loaded, then aimed it at the pilot. His finger was whitening at the knuckle over the trigger when Cameron stopped him:

'No. We cannot hunt without a jockey for the chopper. Him.'

Melody sighed. Decker smiled his gratitude for her concern at her. His breathing was even, undisturbed.

'I warned you once about underrating Enoch,' Cameron said to Decker. He watched Pascoe turn the elephant gun on

Curtis Bill's still kneeling form. 'We need him too, to operate the camera. Where is it?'

'What?' Decker asked languidly.

'The camera.'

Decker was silent. The cook snapped a word at one of the Bantu and the man went scuttling out. Pascoe swung his rifle around but the man was gone.

'What was that?' Cameron asked the cook.

'I send man for camera, Master.' The cook could barely articulate the words through his terror. 'Mister Chris and Mister Bonham will never tell you.'

'Is that so?'

The cook stood dumb.

'Okay. You did well. Does he know to bring film as well?'

'Yes, Master. He was Vincent's orderly.'

'Orderly?'

'Houseboy.'

'If he does not return, you will be shot to teach you deceit.'

'He will return, Master,' the quaking man said with a return of the assurance of command and some of the pay-master's relish, 'or he loses a week's pay.'

'Perhaps you could have me carried to the helicopter while you wait,' Minowara suggested.

'What for?' Pascoe demanded.

Minowara turned his head to look at the Englishman. 'To see you kill the man who soiled my wife,' he said at last, his voice barely audible.

'Why not,' Cameron ruled, grateful for the support the Japanese had already given him. 'Have him carried out and tied into one of the canvas chairs in the helicopter,' he ordered the cook.

The cook snapped some more instructions and four black servants carried Omo Minowara's bed out to the airfield. He did not nod or look at Yodoko as he was carried past her. She stood with downcast eyes until he was gone, then remained so.

The servant who had been Vincent's orderly came back

310

with the camera and its black bag and several boxes containing reels of film. Cameron said, 'Take it all out and put it in the chopper.' The man left with his load.

Cameron looked at the end of the hoe Decker was still holding, the hoe a live thing in the pilot's hand as the dog moved restlessly outside. 'Is there a muzzle for that dog?'

'Yes, Master. I'll have it fetched.'

While they waited, Cameron explained to Pascoe. 'That nice little doggie is going to do our tracking for us if Chris and Curtis Bill prove unwilling to give us value for our money.'

The muzzle was brought and put on the dog, but not until one Bantu servant, slow in removing his hand from the dog's reach, had been severely bitten. Cameron told him to put iodine on his wounds. The dog was taken away and tied up inside the helicopter, growling at the constriction of the muzzle.

'You go outside, Enoch,' Cameron told the Englishman, 'and cover the door as they come out. If there's any funny business, blast them.'

Pascoe left. Through the door they could see him take up position ten feet from the bottom of the steps, out in the open circle.

'Out, you two,' Cameron gestured with his rifle. To the women he added, 'Back in a couple of hours,' and followed Decker and Curtis Bill through the doorway.

'Oh, god,' Judith Pascoe sobbed, 'those terrible men are going to kill my Enoch.'

'And my late Bob and Yodoko's Omo, as soon as they take their guns from them,' Melody added calmly. 'Let's hope it's before they take off so we can watch.'

Yodoko watched her husband strapped into his chair for the journey from which there was no return and started thinking of the preparations she would have to make to take the course she had first considered in Johannesburg and which Omo-san had so clearly indicated when he had refused medical attention for her and which she so dearly desired to take herself.

311

Decker ducked under the tail of the helicopter, glaring at the servants who had obligingly removed the tarpaulin before the white men had reached the helicopter. He transferred his attention from their frightened downcast looks to the whitish grey of the plastic explosive under the engine.

'Come on,' Cameron said with irritation, 'you're flying it, not pushing it.'

Pascoe laughed but his words were perfectly intelligible. 'The detonator was left out of that bomb. It's harmless.'

'So leave it,' Cameron ordered the pilot. Decker left the bomb where it was only after probing it carefully with his forefinger to make sure there was no detonator hidden in it but it was as Enoch said, harmless. He took his pilot's seat and started the warmup procedure. Cameron had Curtis Bill sit on the lip of the helicopter and strapped him into the harness system to immobilise him as a threat. Cameron took the other canvas seat, the one not occupied by Minowara, for himself and Pascoe stood behind them, resting his bottom on the dog's back, quipping about the steady rest the shoulders of Cameron and Minowara in front of him would provide. They all put on their headsets and Cameron warned Decker not to 'try any funny business' or they would shoot Curtis Bill first and then Decker himself as soon as they had landed again.

The helicopter was ready and with a jerk they were airborne.

Eight

Jomo Iningwe shuddered at his mental picture of what would happen to a boat speeding along the river at forty knots if it hit a submerged log. The boat he was on. The helmsman leant forward and touched the throttles to make sure they had both been set at the very last notch and could be advanced no more. He turned to look anxiously at Jomo.

'Watch the river,' Jomo reassured him and added to his back, 'They have no boat. And there's nothing on this river to touch your boat for speed.' Except the safari's chopper and the planes of the police, but Jomo did not speak out on these thoughts. It was unlikely that the safari's perverts would chase him with their helicopter. What was very likely indeed was that they would call the police on the radio in the chopper and the police were likely to mobilise very quickly indeed. He should have sent a man to fire his machine pistol into the tanks of the helicopter and so blow it up. What if he would have lost the man in the attempt? Didn't he lose all the men anyway? And his head of proof. But that was not so important. The story of the head hunting added to the successful penetration of terrorists to South African soil – though not their successful escape, he admitted ruefully to himself – would provide ample basis for investigative reporters to build an international hullabaloo on.

But first Jomo Iningwe had to escape with his story.

He watched the river banks carefully, but more from long habits of vigilance and care than any expectation of opposition to their flight. For a wild moment he thought on the uniqueness of border rivers, split down the moment of time flowing liquidly through their exact middles, one half to one country, one half to another, and considered telling the helmsman to keep to the left, Rhodesian side of the river. He restrained himself from the hysterical foolishness just in time; the South Africans were not likely to honour such a minor technicality.

When they passed Pafuri he heaved a sigh. They were still on the same river, the Limpopo, but now they were in Moçambique, South Africa and Rhodesia behind them. They were in another country.

Without a word to the helmsman Jomo walked across the deck to the rail. He slung his machine pistol across his back, sat on the rail with his back to the water exactly as if he were in full scuba gear, diving off Inhaca Yacht Club, and let his body fall backwards into the rushing water, holding his nose as a private joke with himself. The thrash of water churned by the boat's racing propellers buffeted him cruelly but he allowed his body to float to the surface without moving his arms. He did not fear the crocodiles, who rarely took men and then only from the river banks. But he did not want some shortsighted hippopotamus thinking he had been responsible for the aggravating disturbance of its territorial waters; he'd rather not share Dingane's fate of being bitten into two pieces by a hippopotamus, two halves much more convenient for the crocodiles, who would be the only beneficiaries of his death. And the bank in Zurich where he kept his money, on second thought.

He looked up at the clear blue sky as he floated easily, waiting for the wake of the boat, the crocodiles, the hippopotami and the tasty but dangerous eels found in these parts, all to settle back into peaceful rest. The vapour trails were thin and high but very clear. He knew the South Africans were not even going to honour the major technicality of the terrorists now being in another country. He heard the supersonic *crack!* and turned over lazily in the water. The Mirage screamed down the valley of the river at the receding boat and fired its two rockets before ascending sharply. The boat lifted clear out of the water, as if it were a log some child had shot from a stream with a twenty-two, he thought. The second *crack!* was followed by the two rockets of the second Mirage which struck the boat in midair. Jomo looked at the boat and waited for the third Mirage. *Crack!* The boat was just starting to explode when the rockets of the third Mirage crashed into its already destroyed frame.

Jomo paddled lazily in the backash of the explosion half a mile away and wondered whether the fourth Mirage, keeping watch from on high, was going to come down for another bash at the splinterwood. But no, the three Mirages which had fired the rockets rejoined the lookout and streaked westwards towards South Africa in perfect formation. From their appearance on the horizon to their disappearance over the horizon had taken fourteen seconds.

'Overkillers!' Jomo shouted at them. He turned over and struck out for the shore, using a gentle and effeminate breast stroke even though he knew that crocodiles, hippopotami and eels alike would now be fully occupied with the carnage caused within the narrower radius of the explosion: hundreds, perhaps thousands of animals dead with all their vessels burst from the compactive force of the many thousands of tons of water displaced by the explosion.

He had run steadily along the river in a south-eastward direction for an hour when he became convinced he was being hunted. There was no one thing he could name though he knew the dread of being watched by many unseen eyes. He stopped and climbed a tree hastily, not unslinging his machine pistol which would be worse than useless – dangerous to him even – after its immersion in the river. He drew his knife instead and clenched it in his teeth. Two men ran past underneath his tree. The only word he caught of their carefree banter was to be translated, in his imperfect knowledge of their language, as 'turban'. Turban? Indians or Arabs? Ridiculous! But they were not hunting him and that helped.

He struck out inland, intending to keep pace with them on a parallel course, but found more black warriors running along after an unseen quarry. He waited five minutes behind a tree and counted twelve men loping past in easy pursuit of whatever it was they were hunting. It was evidently a major communal effort. All the men he had seen had been running in pairs.

They were protective covering. He joined the hunt, a hundred yards to the rear of it, covering the miles easily in his longer stride. When the hunt turned north-east Jomo went after it. He would not find such perfect camouflage anywhere else.

Nine

Yodoko carried the first firewood in her arms. The servants, grateful for a reassuring routine initiated by someone else, brought more firewood. Yodoko laid out a rectangle twelve feet by twenty and indicated the height she wanted the fire laid to by holding her hand over her head. The servants nodded their eager understanding. A wheelbarrow appeared, laden with firewood. Then another. Yodoko went to cleanse herself with a bath, to be able to attend to the ritual to come, the most important in her life, in the proper state of bodily purification, as far as such a state was still possible for her. She made no distinction between being soiled by black men or white, one man or many. As Omo-san had so incisively distinguished, she had been soiled and both he and she knew it. That was enough. She was proud of the force of his rejection of her, glad that the paralysis had not sapped the indomitable strength of his uniquely Japanese will, now so contrasted by the self indulgent behaviour of the soft barbarians who understood neither life nor death. It was regrettable that she would have to ask Judith and Melody to assist in the ritual but they were all that were available. Judith had asked her – commanded her – to help with the wounded but Yodoko had shaken her head resolutely, she had more important things to do; it was an honour to die in battle but a disgrace to return wounded and maimed: Yodoko had never questioned the Japanese policy of honouring soldiers who fell in battle but providing no pensions for those returning wounded, leaving the maimed to beg for their bread or to die. And what she had not questioned for others would apply equally to her. With the exception that, being the daughter of an honourable family brought up in the worthy tradition and now of the house of Minowara, she would act decisively to expunge the shame she had brought to the name and the family of her husband. She was proud that it would also be her last act of obedience to her husband, Minowara Omo-san. The highest compliment he had ever paid her had been to leave in the helicopter for his own joyous meeting with the mystical Death he had so long stalked, certain in his knowledge that she would do what was necessary without let or fail.

Yodoko soaked and soaped with care, ignoring the painful sting of soap on torn and bleeding muscle and irritated skin surfaces rasped raw by uncaring hands and rough denim cloth. She resisted the temptation to let the hot water carry her fatigue away on its soothing stability, leaving her in healing sleep. Instead she rose and dried herself, once more ignoring the pain as even the luxuriously soft towels supplied by Ultimate Test, Incorporated to soothe the skin of its favoured clients rubbed her painfully awake with even the gentlest touch. Yodoko gritted her teeth and persevered, her movements slowing in her fatigue but none the less deliberate and ordered to her single goal. Dry, she applied perfume and powder, then dressed in all the garments a Japanese woman should wear on such a day. Last of all she washed her ceremonial dagger in hot water with soap, being careful not to let her slow movements become clumsiness to cut her hands on its razor edges or to prick herself with the needle sharp point. She dried the dagger with a soft cloth and put it in its sheath at her waist. She was ready.

She left the *rondawel*, not looking around at her possessions, carrying with her only a large white cloth and a small rock. The rock, hardly larger than a big gnarled stone, was her favourite from her garden in Tokyo. It had been given into her care on the day of her wedding by Omo-san. It was a very old and honourable rock, having been in the Minowara family for more centuries than she could remember now. It was called Third Generation Rock and passed in the Minowara family from grandfather to grandson. Minowara Omo-san, last recipient of Third Generation

317

Rock, had no children and no grandchildren therefore but there had still been hope on their wedding day. Now the hope had not been realised and it was too late for the union ever to bear man-fruit to father another manchild to receive Third Generation Rock in his turn. It was fitting that Third Generation Rock should be with her today, when she expunged the insult to and the shame on the house of Minowara.

The minitractor had been fetched from the river and the trailer hooked up to it to carry the great volume of firewood required to build the large pyre Yodoko had wanted. The stack of firewood was complete and the minitractor stood beside it. The machinery offended Yodoko's aesthetic sense and she waved it away; servants jumped to obey.

Judith and Melody were drawn onto the veranda by the premonition which hung silently in the air over the base camp. Yodoko walked to the bottom of the steps and looked up to them as she explained what had to be done and what was expected of them. Judith was inclined to argue but Melody looked straight at Yodoko and nodded, admitting to the logic and the necessity even though it was strange and new to her. Yodoko turned her back on the Englishwoman's futile words, after bowing to each of the women, and went with dignity to the foot of the pile of good dry wood.

Yodoko spread the white cloth and went around to each of the corners to pull the wrinkles from it. Then, holding Third Generation Rock in both hands, she stepped on to the cloth and kneeled with rediscovered grace, her fatigue swirled away in the conquering stream of her conviction, in her singleness of purpose. She placed Third Generation Rock in front of her and well away and bowed to it. She took the dagger from her waist-sheath and placed it before her, between her and Third Generation Rock. She bowed to the dagger. Then she waited for the disturbing voices from the veranda to cease.

'She's serious!'

'Of course she's serious,' Melody replied. 'Why should she not be serious?'

318

'But – we must restrain her!'

'What she does not do here today she will do elsewhere tomorrow and curse you with it.'

'But –'

'Shut up, will you!'

In the silence Yodoko turned and bowed to the women. Melody came and stood at one corner of the white cloth, behind Yodoko. Judith came reluctantly to stand at the other corner. Yodoko bowed to each of them once more, then faced forward, faced Third Generation Rock and her dagger.

It would not be easy without proper seconds but those who delight in finding obstacles should not attempt *seppuku*. She should not be too long or the seconds available would lose their nerve and perhaps interfere in their barbaric ignorance.

She took the ceremonial dagger, refined through an aeon for exactly this ceremony, in her hand and composed herself, completing the process started in her bath. She had no guilt and no regret and the shame would soon be duly paid and expunged. And she had had much joy in Omo-san, in the pride of being his wife and part of his family and of him.

She brought the ceremonial dagger to the side of her throat, its point at the junction of jaw and throat. She let the point rest there for a moment to savour the rightness of it and then, not to indulge immoderately, she pressed the three inches home into her jugular. Quickly she pulled the knife out and placed it against the other side of her throat and pressed it home again after only the briefest pause. She looked indifferently at the blood first splashing and then streaming on to the sheet between her and Third Generation Rock. Her hand, holding the knife, came slowly into her view. She was proud as she had never been proud in her life.

Melody looked for a moment at Judith's fainted form before stepping onto the sheet. She reached for the knife in the already limp hand beside Yodoko but a spiral of blood fell on it and she pulled her hand away in instinctive revulsion. She stood up then, reached forward to pull Yodoko back into a kneeling position. She had both her hands around Yodoko's forehead to avoid the blood spurting everywhere else. She put her knee to the back of Yodoko's neck and jerked strongly with both hands to break Yodoko's neck.

Ten

'We should destroy the radio.' In the throat microphone and amplifier system Omo Minowara's voice no longer sounded tired and old.

'You'd hear if I said it,' Decker protested.

'Yeah,' Cameron said and turned his rifle towards the pilot. 'Which is it?' he asked the Japanese.

Decker said, 'I'll show you. For chrissake don't go blasting away and destroy one of our other vital systems!' He put his hand out to indicate the radio.

'He is being honest,' Minowara said.

Cameron unbuckled himself and took Curtis Bill's rifle from the rack above the hole in the side of the helicopter. He smashed the radio with its butt, ignoring the sparks flying at him. Decker winced. Cameron returned to his seat and threw Curtis Bill's rifle into the river below them. 'Just so's Curtis fucking Bill doesn't get any ideas, eh,' Pascoe laughed uproariously. Nobody paid any attention to him. Cameron had misunderstood Decker's gesture of pointing out the radio to him. The pilot had calculated it preferable to sacrifice a part of their survival equipment than to let a maniac loose smashing systems at random and probably bringing them down in the Limpopo below them. Cameron generalised from his misconception:

'Chris, you're not such a bad guy and we all know you're one hell of a pilot.' He waited for the response, received

320

none. 'Look, co-operate with us just this once, make it a good hunt for us. In return, I'll let you have Melody. Free and clear.'

'Thanks. But I do not ever accept payment in kind for my services. Especially not payment in secondhand goods. And you'll be giving me nothing I haven't got already.'

'Why, you glorified tourist guide, when we get back – '

'I shall kill you, if Curtis Bill doesn't do it first, you poor, silly, misguided, motherless fuckwit. You are dead where you sit.'

Once more Cameron refused to be angered. He chuckled into his throat microphone. 'What do you say, Curtis fucking Bill?'

Curtis Bill did not reply. Threats served no purpose except to warn those you were about to punish. But it might be just to let Chris have the American; there had been no need to throw an expensive rifle into the river in addition to the other aggravations the man had already brought upon them. For such a man a quick bullet might be too easy.

Decker said, 'We may as well turn back. There's what's left of their boat. An oil spot and some matchwood.'

They looked down at the river as Decker held the helicopter steady. The oil spot flowed away from them, carrying with it the debris, pitifully little of it, which had once been a sizeable boat.

'A very big bird came out of the sky and did that,' Decker said. He turned the helicopter around and headed for the base camp up the river. He looked up when he felt Pascoe's elephant gun in the nape of his neck. 'Look man, this isn't just the coppers any more. That was a Mirage jet, more than one of them, that blasted their boat with great big rockets. It means the South African police will be waiting for us when we get back to the base camp.'

'South African law doesn't operate here,' Cameron said. 'You guys told me that yourselves.'

'The planes that blew that boat up could only have been South African Airforce,' Curtis Bill said. 'And they could only have been called in by the police.'

'We'll deal with the police later. Now we're doing their job for them, teaching terrorists a lesson. Enoch, I'm going to count to three. If we're not flying north-east by that time, shoot our co-operative friend dead. One –'

'You'll all go down with me.'

'You wouldn't know about it, would you?' Pascoe chuckled obscenely.

'Look, we're running out of fuel. I'm not joking about going down.'

'Two.'

Decker turned the helicopter north-east. 'Why north-east?'

'Because that's the way he went.'

'You're stupider than I thought if you think anybody survived that –' Decker pointed over his shoulder at the river.

'The white nigger, the big bastard, he would have jumped overboard as soon as they left South African waters. Logical, huh, Curtis Bill?' Cameron jabbed his foot into the safari organiser's back.

Curtis Bill turned to look at him. 'Don't kick me,' he said calmly. 'And yes, leaving the boat as soon as possible would be logical. But north-east is only an inspired guess.'

'Inspired is better than perspired or even expired,' Pascoe gurgled his wit.

When they found him, he stood waving at them. He carried the message stick upright in one hand and his food for the day, cooked maize, in a satchel slung over his shoulder. In his other hand he carried *assegai* and shield clasped together. He waved with both loaded hands, his white shirt and white shorts flapping in the downthrust of the helicopter's motive power.

'A wounded black bastard terrorist,' Cameron judged.

'Are you blind?' Decker exploded. 'He's wearing Ultimate Test, Incorporated uniform, clothing issue.'

'He's a kitchen helper by name of Jonas,' Curtis Bill said.

'So why's he got a bloody bandage around his head?' Pascoe demanded triumphantly.

'Because Vincent beat him about the forehead last Saturday.'

'What's he doing here if he isn't running away?' Cameron asked.

'I don't know. But that is a message stick he's carrying.'

'He's a nigger messenger for the terrorists,' Pascoe gurgled. 'Let's shoot him.'

'You cannot go around killing our servants,' Curtis Bill said, anger tinging his voice ever so faintly.

'Man, you just aren't for real,' Cameron told him. 'He's a nigger or is he a nigger?'

Pascoe laughed again. 'Let's make him run.'

'No. I have an idea we would do well to give him a lift to wherever he's going to carry that message. Chris, put the chopper down.'

'Look, he's not the kind of nigger who would have anything to do with terrorists. Leave –'

'Put the chopper down!'

Decker put the helicopter down a good fifty feet from the black kitchen helper to give him a chance to disappear into the grass and the trees. Instead the black man came running towards the helicopter, his face split with the joy of recognition and the prospect of no longer having to run, of being transported mechanically in his masters' whirling machine. Curtis Bill and the pilot watched him come with trepidation at what the Englishman and the American would do to him. It was thus that they did not hear or sense Cameron and Pascoe scuffling behind them until it was too late and the loosened dog was pushed over Curtis Bill by Pascoe as Cameron simultaneously removed the muzzle in one fearful lunge.

Curtis Bill sighed. Decker shouted, 'No, damnit, no!' They watched helplessly, gun muzzles in their necks reminding them of their powerlessness.

The Rhodesian ridgeback landed surely on all four feet and then it was in the air towards the man charging joyfully towards it, laughing and waving his arms. Jonas died with a smile on his face, not realising that the dog had been set on him, his last words a shout of welcome to his masters. The dog paused to see if there were any other fleeing figures and found none; it worried Jonas's body for a while, then looked up at the men in the helicopter.

'Go get it back for us,' Cameron said to Curtis Bill, thrusting the muzzle over his shoulder, kicking him in the back once more.

Curtis Bill undid the quick release catch and stood up. He turned to Cameron and looked at him searchingly.

'Frightened, little man?' the American mocked him, poking his rifle at Curtis Bill's stomach.

Curtis Bill stepped back from the rifle. 'No, I am not afraid of you.' He turned his back on the man and the rifle, leaving his headset on his seat.

'Hey! What about the muzzle?' Pascoe shouted after him.

Curtis Bill ignored the question. He took his suede jacket off and rolled it around his left arm. The dog watched him intently. He took two paces towards the dog. The dog took three short paces and launched itself at him. Curtis Bill put up his roughly padded arm and the ridgeback sank his teeth into it, swinging Curtis Bill this way and that as it tried to dislodge its teeth to try again for the more productive purchase to be had on the throat of the man.

Each time Curtis Bill swung past the chest of the monster he would kick out with his neatly polished but highly serviceable heavy boot, angling the kick upwards under the animal's shortribs into its heart. The dog grunted each time Curtis Bill kicked it and renewed its efforts to free its teeth in order to defend itself. Finally its teeth came free and Curtis Bill fell to the ground under its massive head.

The ridgeback opened its slavering jaws as its head dived towards the throat of the man underneath it, defenceless and open. A swung arm took its legs from under it as Curtis Bill rolled away, sending the dog crashing into the ground on its nose. It was up immediately, yelping with pain and growling in rage. Curtis Bill was also up, rolling effortlessly into an upright position without putting his hands on the earth under the flattened grass. The dog circled the man warily; it was not going to let pain and anger goad it into an unwise attack.

Curtis Bill stood in the same place and turned as the dog growled its way around him. He adjusted the padding the suede jacket afforded his arm and wrapped his handkerchief around his other hand. The dog came in fast as both his hands were down.

Curtis Bill smiled faintly as he brought up his padded arm. The dog feinted at the arm, then struck cobra-like to the other side past it at the man's throat. Incredibly, the handkerchief-wrapped hand was there to protect the throat and take hold of the dog's lower jaw in a grip which would not relent even when it closed its jaws and shook its head. And then the man had one foot flatly on the ground and the dog's head in the air so that its forefeet were off the ground and he was kicking it under the shortribs, again and again and again, his heavy boot moving with force and speed. The man watched the dog's eyes as he held its head above his own head and listened to its breathing. The dog's breathing was becoming ragged as its lungs laboured to provide its bruised heart with oxygen; its eyes were rolling wildly with the repeated agonising rupture of each blow from the boot.

Curtis Bill judged the dog severely weakened. He took a deep breath and let it out slowly through three more kicks curving viciously under the dog's shortribs. Then suddenly he changed his handhold on the now open and gasping jaw and forced the dog's head down to the ground. He put his boot on the lower jaw and grasped the upper jaw with both hands. He inhaled deeply as he rose with the dog's upper jaw, all his weight on the foot in its lower jaw. The dog whinnied painfully when the jaw broke out of its socket, the crack of splintering bone testifying that the operation had not been cleanly executed. It tried to snap at Curtis Bill as he stood back but its jaws were slack. It no longer had any control over the functioning of its only weapon. It lay down on its side.

Curtis Bill turned to the helicopter.

'I'd be grateful if one of you gentlemen would dispatch the dog.'

He did not wait to see his request fulfilled. He walked to his late servant Jonas and bent down to turn him over on his back.

Curtis Bill Bonham did not look up when the single shot rang out and the dog's whinnying stopped.

In the helicopter the four men sat stunned by Curtis Bill's virtuoso performance in killing the Rhodesian ridgeback with his bare hands. Decker said, 'I could have kept that dog.' Nobody else spoke.

'Perhaps that's how Curtis Bill will kill you, Bob-oh,' the pilot said in a bantering tone which did not take flight, earthbound by the weight of his hatred. 'Take you in the mouth and kick you in the stomach until you lie down and beg for mercy. And then he will put his foot in your mouth and break your jaw so that you can no longer swill and spout shit like the pig you are.'

'Shut up!' Cameron screamed, a high cutting edge of hysteria in his voice.

'But truly Curtis Bill is a dangerous man,' Omo Minowara said into the throat microphone, his lips not moving but his words clear. 'Now that he has killed the dog our chances of finding the tall man who led the terrorist attack have been reduced.'

'Yeah,' Pascoe said quietly, 'and we only told him to catch the dog, not to kill it.'

'Nobody on these safaris has ever hunted a white man,' Minowara added conversationally.

'You are stark raving mad,' the pilot protested, not raising his voice. 'Bonkers. Nuts.' His breathing was hoarse.

'Shut up,' Pascoe told him. Cameron grunted.

Minowara continued as if there had been no interruptions. 'He neglected to protect us from terrorist attack. In consequence two of us were dishonoured by having our wives soiled and another was wounded. He has reneged on his promise to let Enoch hunt again. He has no intention of letting Bob have the hunt Bob has paid for and has the right to expect. He failed to save my life as is his responsibility. He has –'

'We have no fuel!' Decker shouted.

They ignored him.

'He has cheated us. And he is a Jew,' Cameron concluded. He shouted, 'Hey! Curtis Bill!'

Eleven

The servants had all gone, not wishing to be embarrassed with the masters' and mistresses' killing of themselves and each other. Melody rose and filled her glass and Judith's once more from the bottle on the windowsill behind them. There was no ice or mixers. She handed Judith her glass and resumed her seat, holding her own glass to the front of Decker's shirt which she still wore.

The two women watched the activity incuriously. Ten minutes ago the helicopter had landed. On its side it proclaimed its owners to be the SA Special Security Police. The men streaming from it wore paramilitary combat fatigues and carried submachine pistols and FN automatic rifles. They spread out and their eyes seemed to observe everything while their bodies were never exposed for more than a very brief period. The men came back to the helicopter in groups and went inside one by one to report. A man Melody and Judith had not seen before came from the helicopter and climbed the steps to the veranda to stand in front of them.

'My name is Rocco Burger, Colonel Rocco Burger.' He was slight and near retirement age. His hair was thin and greying and must once have been wavy. He was deeply tanned and had the coldest blue eyes Melody had ever seen. Except Curtis Bill's. He wore a brown suit and highly polished brown shoes. His shirt was cream and his tie striped in three shades of brown. 'What happened here?'

'Atrocity week ended with a bang.'

The policeman waited.

'Colonel, neither of us knows all of it. Ask us specifics and we'll tell you.'

'There are a lot of corpses here.'

'Terrorists attacked us.'

'Sodomy and murder. Who by?' Colonel Burger pointed at the nearby canvas on which the rigor mortis statue of Vincent and his catamite still lay.

'I don't know. The Indian was the chief servant and also photographer of the safari.'

'Ah, Vincent.'

'You knew him?'

'Only by reputation. There is a man with his private parts bitten off, lying dead in the wood behind the camp.'

'I did that. He was trying to rape me.'

The policeman looked at her silently for a moment. 'Did you kill the others as well?'

'No. A gallant knight on a white horse did that.'

'Why doesn't she speak?' He indicated Judith with a nod of his head.

Judith mouthed, 'Eric, Joan. Eric, Joan,' silently at him.

'She's in shock. She bombed a man with a bottle of burning brandy. That one.' Melody pointed at the burnt corpse behind the policeman and he turned to look at it.

'Only one?'

'The men mostly killed the others. Though Yodoko also killed one with her hand. Near the pool.'

'Where's this Yodoko now? She is a woman, I presume?'

'Yes.' Melody pointed at the smouldering remains of Yodoko's funeral pyre.

'She did not survive the . . . ' He let the sentence trail away.

328

'She survived. She committed *seppuku*. For the shame of being raped, if I understood the situation.'

'*Seppuku?*'

'Ritual suicide.'

'*Hara kiri?*'

'I suppose so. She stuck a short knife into both sides of her throat.'

'And you stood by and let her?'

'We didn't let her bleed to death. I broke her neck.'

'Uh. And then you burnt the body?'

'Yes. It was her last request.'

The policeman looked for a chair and sank wearily into it. One of his men ran up the veranda steps and bent to whisper in his ear. He nodded and the man went away.

'And the men dead on the way to the river?'

'The dogs.'

'And the crushed severed head of a man, wrapped in household plastic?'

'I don't know about the crushing. Yodoko cut the head from a man she shot yesterday.'

The policeman looked curiously at her for a long time before he asked his next question.

'And your men? Did you burn their bodies as well?'

'No. They are all alive. They went after the last of the terrorists, the one that got away.'

The policeman rose, then sat down again. 'They'll return as soon as they've found the wreckage of the boat. That was the first thing we did, have the Air Force shoot it up a bit. I'll wait here for your men.'

'While you wait, have a drink. I'm sorry there's no ice.'

Twelve

Curtis Bill Bonham looked up at the rifles pointing at him. Behind the rifles the faces of the men had changed. Curtis Bill did not need to be told what the different expressions presaged. He had seen the faces of too many bloodlusting primitives from the affluent society to misread the omens. They were going to kill him.

Curtis Bill was not afraid. He laid the head of his late servant Jonas, who had depended on him and had come running with open arms to welcome him, who had been maliciously and unnecessarily killed by men whose food he had prepared, carefully back on the grass and the earth. He rose to look at the helicopter and the men in it, calculating ways and means of staying alive until he had made them pay for the death of the innocent Jonas.

Curtis Bill Bonham looked at his shadow on the ground for his bearings and at his watch for the time. The helicopter had fifteen minutes of fuel remaining. Then it would fall from the sky. He was twelve minutes on foot from the fuel depot. They would not wish to lose him. Nor did he want Cameron and Pascoe to have a chance to reconsider and try to remove themselves from the scope of his wrath, though he did not think such intelligence likely in their present state of blood-intoxication. But once out of his sight, who knew whether they might not sober up? His icy resolve was to kill them and men logically considering their survival would flee from such as himself, he knew.

He unwound the tattered suede jacket from his arm and dropped it on the ground without bothering to take his wallet from it. There was nothing in the wallet he would need; he did not carry even a picture of Julia or his son in it.

On second thoughts he picked up the coat and spread it over the face of what had once been his servant. Then he turned and started walking briskly towards the fuel depot, ignoring the shots striking the ground on either side of him and behind him, not looking back once. Soon he was out of the trampled circle and into the tall grass and he heard the helicopter ascend behind him.

He did not hurry. The helicopter could outrun him to the fuel depot and by hurrying he might give his intention away. It was essential to his plan that he reach the fuel depot before or simultaneously with the helicopter. It was simple, his plan, like all good plans and needed no further conscious thought. He occupied his mind with other things.

It was conceivable that he might not survive the day, as had been true of every single one of his working days for many years now. He had lived intimately with death and did not fear it, his sole concern to meet it with dignity. At least as much dignity as some of the men he had killed or helped to kill. Perhaps even as much dignity as the brave black man who had brought the helicopter down with his *assegai*. For a moment Curtis Bill regretted that the men killing him would not be worthy of his last salute; he put the petty thought from him: such primitivism was not for him. The dignity he sought was an inner thing, for himself, for his son, who would know instinctively that his father had died with his will intact, fighting with his last breath.

His plan and the odds against its success and the nature of the materials he would have to construct his defence from and the superior armoury of the opposition, all these things made it more probable that today would be his last, rather than any of the days of his violent past.

He had been brought up a Catholic and now he smiled into the blazing African sun as the thought of confession and repentance entered his head. He had lived without God and would die without Him. He had always risked as much as he had taken and fairer than that no man could be spoken of. And he had always distrusted a god who would stay his justice in the face of the remorseful tears of men.

He thought back, searching for guilt or shame or debts unpaid in his thirty-five years and found none. He put other men's values firmly from him then and concentrated on his own.

He had one regret: he would have liked to have talked to his wife Julia and his son once more.

Then he emptied his mind of all else to enjoy the Africa he loved as he walked towards the fuel depot.

Chris Decker had seen his partner look at his watch and knew the significance of the gesture. He glanced at his own dials. Sixteen minutes of fuel remaining. Then they were going to fall out of the sky. Crunch!

The pilot also noted the direction Curtis Bill took and smiled his sincere smile, genuine edition, to himself. This was going to be very interesting. Very interesting indeed.

'Motherfucker's going for a walk on his lawn,' Cameron screamed his rage as Curtis Bill walked away from them.

'Let's hurry him up a little,' Pascoe suggested hoarsely. He raised his rifle but Cameron reached up and pushed it away.

'He's mine!'

'Bullshit!' Pascoe pulled his rifle back until the muzzle was behind Cameron's head though still pointing past it. 'Ours. We are in this together.' Suddenly his words were crystalline.

Cameron shrugged. 'Okay. But don't shoot any nearer than two feet to him yet. We're going to make the nigger-loving Jew bastard run yet. He's going to wish he was never born.'

Decker turned in his seat to watch them. He had no fear that they would hit his partner yet. They started firing and the pilot's smile grew broader in potent scorn and direct proportion to their frustration. He had no need to look to know that Curtis Bill was unconcerned by the shots. When the shots stopped, he knew Curtis Bill had entered the grass wall. Curtis Bill was in a class of his own.

'Take us up! After him.'

'We're running out of fuel. Really.'

'Yeah? I can hear the motor running.'

'Sure. And in a couple of minutes it's going to stop running and we're going to drop like a stone.'

'Is that right, Omo?'

'Perhaps. But we should chase Curtis Bill until that happens. We are very near the fuel stockpile, I think.'

'Christ, you know as well as I do, you Jap bastard, that if we come down with a bang the fuel vapour in the tanks will explode and send us all to hell.'

With amazing speed for one so lumbering Pascoe swung his rifle around to hit Decker a stunning blow over the ear with the muzzle. 'Are you calling our friend Omo a liar?'

Decker took the helicopter up and after Curtis Bill Bonham. It was their funeral and they were sitting a lot nearer to the fuel tanks than he was. And as for Pascoe, something special and very, very lasting would have to be devised.

They shot desultorily at Curtis Bill, preoccupied with the thought of having to chase Curtis Bill on foot through the veld. To prevent them having second thoughts, Decker said, 'He's heading for the depot. We'll just reach it with the last of our fuel at the same time he does, maybe a couple of minutes to spare.'

The pilot knew now what his partner's plan was and was impressed with its daring conception and its brilliant simplicity and its vital directness. Curtis Bill was going towards the fuel depot. Once there with or without the hunters in the helicopter he would let the fuel out of the drums. With no fuel for the helicopter the hunters would be reduced to waiting at the helicopter for someone to come – unlikely, understatement, hahaha! – or take to the grass either in search of Curtis Bill or in an attempt to return home. At the helicopter they would die of thirst. In the grass Curtis Bill would kill them with ridiculous ease if they didn't die of heart attacks at the unaccustomed exercise long before he got tired of stalking them. And, of course, they would not want to shoot at Curtis Bill to kill or wound him seriously because then they would miss out on their sport of making him beg for mercy. And if they shot at him once he had a fuel drum open or, for that matter, they themselves had a fuel drum open, well . . . Even these fuckwits wouldn't, couldn't be so dumb as even to have nightmares about the results.

Curtis Bill might have betrayed him to a lifetime of poverty and insulted him by offering him money but Decker had known him for many years and no bunch of idiot play-boy maniacs was going to kill his partner while he was around.

Ah! And Curtis Bill's plan included a certain amount of confusion in which he, Chris Decker, could easily escape the doubtful vigilance of the American and the Englishman – the paralysed Jap counted for nothing except aggravation – and join Curtis Bill in their revenge on these morons. Curtis Bill was in a class so superior other men had never even considered it, not to mention aspired to it. Decker licked his lips in anticipation.

'Perhaps we should shoot ahead with our fuel and wait there for him,' Cameron suggested.

'Daisy, you're stupider than I thought. What's in it for me?'

Cameron replied immediately, so confirming his disin-clination to honour any promise he made. 'Ten thousand dollars, American.'

'And the same from me,' Pascoe added.

You can't collect from dead men. 'That's peanuts.'

'I'll make it up to one hundred thousand American dollars and give you a cheque on my bank under my own signature for the full amount as soon as we get back to the base camp,' the Japanese financier said.

Just now he wanted us to drop out of the sky in flames. He has no intention of returning. That is what the whole rigmarole with his wife was about. 'Soiled.'

Decker said, 'The whole hundred thousand?'

'Yes.'

'Okay. That's exactly what he wants us to do, go ahead to the fuel depot. He'll disappear into a clump of trees and we'll never find him again.'

'Diabolically clever,' Pascoe said.

'So?' Cameron.

'We just let him go ahead of us to the fuel depot. When we have refuelled, we know where he is.'

'Ah!' Minowara's short breath was admiring.

'And we'll have fuel to make him run a long time,' Cameron concluded.

Decker waited.

'Meanwhile, let's not scare him off by shooting at him,' Cameron said. Decker resisted the temptation to sigh; the mike would pick it up and relay it to the others. Anybody that stupid deserved to die.

Curtis Bill Bonham walked into the burnt circle, aware of the helicopter above and three hundred yards behind him. He felt no temptation to run to the fuel drums and execute his plan immediately. There had been no further shots. Chris had divined his plan and somehow deceived the others. There was no urgency now. He kept his pace until he reached the first drum, the helicopter now a hundred yards behind him. He walked past the first drum until there were fuel drums lying on their sides all around him. The helicopter was fifty yards away.

Now.

'Now the no-good nigger-loving Jew tries to crawl behind drums,' Cameron said with satisfaction.

'But we'll soon winkle him out.' Pascoe.

The pilot smiled his joy in their fatal stupidity to himself and let the helicopter drift nearer to the drums from where he had deftly let it slide to a standstill in the air, fifty yards away.

'He's wiggling through those drums like a worm in a gorgonzola just before you slice its head off,' Pascoe said.

Cameron made a yech in his throat at the degenerate image.

Omo Minowara said nothing.

He has a death wish. He is neither blind nor stupid and he is a pilot, he knows all about fuel.

Enoch Pascoe brought his rifle to his shoulder and sighted through his telescope at the flashes of Curtis Bill's body seen infrequently, briefly, between drums.

'Don't shoot him, huh?'

Pascoe did not reply to Cameron's admonition. Instead he said, 'He's letting the fuel out of the drums. If we got no fuel in the chopper's tanks and he's let the fuel out of the drums, how do we get home?' His tone was calm but the pitch bordered on high hysteria.

Cameron raised his rifle grimly, without saying a word.

'Don't shoot!' Decker shouted and sent the helicopter upwards to throw their aim off. 'You'll set everything aflame!'

The shots rang out behind him, Pascoe's elephant gun sending a vibration through the helicopter as he steadied it against Vincent's camera pole. Both Pascoe and Cameron corrected instinctively for the movement of the helicopter. Neither of them hit Curtis Bill but it did not matter. Decker fancied he could hear the zing! of the bullet – one of Cameron's – as it ricocheted from the curve of a drum split open a fraction of a second before by a heavier bullet – Pascoe's – to send a stream of sparks into the vapour still compressed in the drum. There was only a small explosion at first, then a bigger one, then a raging fire over a hundred square yards of the fuel bath Curtis Bill Bonham had run. Conception through consumption within a second.

'You cheated us,' Minowara said to Decker, satisfaction creeping into his tone.

You expected to be cheated. 'You had no intention of paying me, did you?'

The Japanese did not answer the obvious. To Cameron and Pascoe he said, 'You can make some pretty novas by shooting at the red-hot drums you can see in the flames.'

'Fucking useless old fart,' Pascoe mumbled but nevertheless added to the conflagration by puncturing one of the

336

drums. It made a satisfying explosion and he reloaded while Cameron shot at another drum.

The mistake Curtis Bill and I made was to think any of these people wanted to live, ever.

Curtis Bill came from the edge of the inferno, a dancing dervish limned in flame, holding his nose resolutely with one hand while his other arm and his legs shot out a futile syncopation as he moved towards them.

Pascoe gurgled spittle as he giggled, 'Guy Fawkes!'

'He sure learns better than any nigger we ever taught. Whoopee!'

'For Christ's sake, shoot him!'

They ignored Decker's plea, shooting at the drums nearer to Curtis Bill's slowly advancing form to spread the fire ever closer to his uncoordinated heels. Omo Minowara sighed his satiation deep in his throat.

'Please! You can't let a man burn to death! Tell them, Omo, you're a pilot too.'

Minowara was quiet. Cameron said, 'Can't we? He's a nigger-lover and a Jew.'

'He's neither!'

'Want to climb out and ask him?' Pascoe giggled.

The flaming man jerked his hand from his nose and half his face was unfleshed, the bone of his skull and his white teeth glaring through the flames flickering at the edges of the raw wound where there was still flesh to consume. Suddenly his feet took on rhythm and his arms started pumping as he ran, the flesh of his face swinging grotesquely in one hand; the flesh of his hand had been fused to the flesh of his face by the flames as he had held his nose to protect his lungs from the searing mortality of the fire. His efforts to break the unbalancing fusion had caused the lack of co-ordination in his body; rid of the distraction, he ran towards them fast enough to make the flames stream behind him.

'His lungs are still okay,' Cameron said professionally. 'That's what kills most of them, shock and burnt lungs. Skin you can always graft back on, a nose, lips, etcetera.'

'Kill him now, please!'

'Shut up, sky jockey.'

'Can we still make him run?' Pascoe breathed eagerly.

'That's what old Doc Bob's here for, to make him run.'

If he does not kill you first. Yet. Decker set the helicopter down. There was perhaps a minute and a half of fuel left. As he turned in his seat to disable one of the hunters while Curtis Bill Bonham's flaming form took the other, his knee brushed the pocket beside it and he felt the hardness of his revolver in it. He sank back in his seat and opened the small flap in the plexiglass bubble beside him. He turned the intercom to full volume and screamed as loudly as he could into it, partly to disorient Pascoe and Cameron but mostly to prevent the quick-thinking Japanese from giving them orders. He took the revolver from the pocket and checked that it was loaded, ignoring his shouting, postponing the anguish he knew he would carry with him for the rest of his life for not having remembered it sooner. He put his hand and the revolver through the open flap.

Curtis Bill Bonham was running jerkily towards the helicopter, only fifteen paces away now, his clear blue eyes cold as ever against the burnt black of his hair and forehead, incongruously intelligent and untouched above the bare skull of his middle face. His eyes flicked to the pilot's bubble and he came to a shuffling halt. He stood erect and the flames blowing behind him caught up with his flesh again.

He does not wish to be a skin graft pitied by his wife and feared by his son. Decker aimed carefully and squeezed the trigger with painful gentleness.

Even as the bullet took him in the chest, Curtis Bill Bonham's teeth parted in his skull and the tongue between them moved twice, languorously sticking behind the lower teeth for the first word, then forming a chute to roll the second word from. *Thank you.* Incredibly, hit in the chest with a bullet from a heavy-calibre firearm at short range, he steadied himself and stood erect, his arms at his sides.

Tears rolled down Chris Decker's cheeks as he squeezed the trigger again and again to send the bullets crashing into the standing corpse of the only friend he had ever had.

338

Every man should die standing straight up like Curtis Bill.
He fired the last bullet as the muzzle of Pascoe's empty rifle
smashed into his arm, breaking it in the wrist, the force
of the sixteen and a half pounds of dead weight of the rifle
moved by Pascoe's considerable venom easily overcoming
the resilience of the bones. The revolver dropped from his
powerless fingers outside the helicopter.

Almost lazily Chris Decker reached over his shoulder with
his good hand to take the muzzle as it came swooping down
towards his head. One jerk and it was in his hands. He
smashed the butt repeatedly into Pascoe's face until the
Englishman slid down the rear firewall of the helicopter,
conscious but bloody and dazed and totally unable to think
straight or act through the pain of his smashed skull, cheek-
bones, nose, teeth and jaw.

Chris Decker looked around for the other man he intended killing, but not yet, not before he could do it properly
and at length. Cameron. Decker realised he was still screaming and stopped. He turned the intercom's volume switch
back to its previous low setting. Cameron.

'Well done, Mr Decker!'

'I'll deal with you later, you traitorous Japanese snake.'
Decker was watching Cameron.

The American stood for a moment beside the body of
Curtis Bill Bonham, prodding it with his Abercrombie and
Fitch boot as if he expected it to jump up and start running.
Then he turned the body over with his foot and leant forward to inspect it closely, trying to find one last shred of life
lurking in it to be extracted and tortured. But the mutilated
crumbling thing was dead, only the staring blue eyes coolly
commanding as they had been in life. Cameron kicked the
corpse away from him, char flying from the streak cut by his
boot.

Cameron turned to the helicopter to face the man who'd
taken his prey from him once more, once too easily, at last
too often. He raised his rifle slowly, savouring the immobi-
lised helicopter before him.

Decker laughed softly to himself. Perhaps a minute of

339

fuel left. If he miscalculated he was dead. If he remained here he was dead. He would lead Cameron a short hop into the grass, land and then ... *Let's see how Doctor Loudmouth survives in the veld without food or water or transport when he is being hunted by an unarmed one-handed man.*

Decker took the helicopter straight up.

Thirteen

Jomo Iningwe felt first the man's body, then the dog's. Both were warm. The dog was familiar, the man was not. But the blood-stained bandage around the man's head had the shape of a turban. It was easy to deduce from the marks on the grass and from prior knowledge what had happened here. The men had brought the dog in the helicopter. The black man had run towards the helicopter. The dog had taken the black man from the front. Someone had then killed the dog with his bare hands, shielded from its fangs only by his expensive Gucci suede jacket. The natives who had been chasing the 'turbaned' man were now on the *spoor* of something else a couple of minutes ahead of him. Jomo took the time to take the wallet from the jacket and look inside. The card said the owner was Curtis Bill Bonham, gave his name and his address as well as his blood group, A-positive. It was very stupid of the white man to follow him, Jomo thought as he lengthened his stride in pursuit of the natives, hoping to overtake them before they took whatever it was they were hunting, perhaps one of the white men, perhaps another man-killing dog. Whatever it was, Jomo Iningwe wanted it as proof of his incredible tale. Preferably alive rather than dead, especially if it was a man who could be persuaded to

340

articulate his sins and the sins of his friends for the devouring mass media and later at a show trial.

He crashed through the long grass into the cleared circle in time to see Curtis Bill Bonham run burning from the spreading fire towards the helicopter. Because he was behind the helicopter, Jomo stayed where he was. Soon a number of black men came out of the grass to stand beside him and gaze at the spectacle. He nodded at those closest to him. They raised their shields to him.

'Why did you hunt the turban?'

'Bavenda not welcome in our land.'

Jomo turned back towards the helicopter. He saw it sink to the ground. He ran thirty paces along the inner perimeter of the grass circle to get a clear view past the pilot's perspex bubble. The natives ran with him, apparently willing to accept him as one of them since he had hunted with them. Or perhaps, of all the people on earth, they objected only to the Bavenda. Jomo did not really care.

Jomo was too late to see more than the crumpling of Curtis Bill Bonham's flaming form as a pistol fired by a dismembered hand stuck on the perspex mercifully killed him. Then Cameron came running from the helicopter to prod the smouldering corpse with his boot. He seemed disappointed that it was dead. He turned it over with his boot and glared at it with hatred clear to Jomo's eyes even across the intervening distance. Then Cameron rose and turned his rifle on the helicopter or those in it. The gloating on his face was not pleasant to see.

Jomo was split between pleasure at dissent between the white men and his own powerlessness – his machine pistol useless because of wet ammunition – to prevent them killing each other to the last man. He needed at least one of them alive. He breathed his relief as he saw the helicopter ascend. He saw the star in the plexiglass and wondered at the idiocy of a man who would shoot at the pilot of a helicopter when its tanks were plainly, pitifully, obscenely exposed. And not hitting the pilot, the man continued firing into the fast receding cockpit at an impossible angle. *How did these men ever beat me and kill all my men?*

Cameron stood clicking the trigger long after the magazine was empty, range contorting his face. Then he started laughing and threw his rifle on the ground and jumped on it as he pointed a derisory finger at the sky.

Jomo tore his eyes away from the mad man and looked upwards where his finger pointed. The helicopter hung still in the air for one long moment, its rotor drooping quietly without motive power. Then the machine fell from the sky, not straight down to earth in decency but obliquely, obscenely towards the infernal holocaust at the back of its accuser who turned to laugh his insane triumph directly at it. The helicopter twisted so the hole in one side was towards Jomo and the silent black men flanking him. A tall blond man appeared in the hole and cast another burly man struggling from the machine, not quite managing to hurl him clear of the edge of the fiery circle the helicopter was heading for. When the helicopter was thirty feet above the flames, the blond man came to the edge of the hole with another man in his arms, steadied himself against the side of the hole with his foot, and jumped. They did not clear the flames either. Jomo admired the pilot's persevering sense of duty as he ran towards the bulky man who was now scratching in his pockets for cartridges. It would not do if the man reloaded his rifle. Jomo was glad when the *crump!* of the helicopter's arrest by the earth was followed by the excruciating tearing of metal being violently torn apart in an explosion, distracting Cameron for two full seconds.

Jomo Iningwe needed only two seconds to run around Cameron. He stood in front of the man, pointed his machine pistol at him.

Cameron bent quite slowly to pick up his rifle, unwilling to tear his eyes from the flames into which Decker had thrown first Pascoe and then himself and Minowara.

'It is not loaded.'

Cameron dropped the rifle, seemed to see his captor for the first time. 'Look, I killed your enemies for you.'

Jomo Iningwe changed hands on his machine pistol and

smashed the white man through the face with the back of his hand. Cameron stumbled backwards and fell. He made no attempt to rise, his eyes riveted to the edge of flame behind Jomo. Jomo turned around, his back contemptuously to the white man.

Pascoe crawled from the flaming earth on to the scorched earth of an earlier fire. He screamed dementedly, no longer aware of his surroundings. Jomo Iningwe stood aside to let him crawl past, a hunched-up flaming form on its way to oblivion. Behind Jomo the American giggled. The shot crashed into the ground six inches from Jomo's foot and nine inches from Pascoe's nose. Jomo turned and kicked the revolver from Cameron's hand.

'Just give me one more shot at him,' Cameron whined, then started giggling again. If he had not been giggling he would have killed Pascoe. And then the nigger, of course. Jomo once more turned his back on him. Cameron drew the hunting knife from his belt.

Jomo Iningwe stuck out a long leg and tripped the American as he tried to rush past him towards Pascoe crawling away from them. Cameron fell heavily on his face, the knife flying out of his reach. Cameron lay still where he fell, listening to the sound of somebody coming slowly through the flames.

Behind them, no longer holding their attention, the hunched thing which had been Enoch Pascoe fused itself into a ball of fire and ceased screaming. They did not hear the silence, their eyes taken by the flaming multiple form approaching them, slowly, doggedly through the inferno.

Decker carried the Japanese in his arms as he had jumped from the falling helicopter with him. Underneath Omo Minowara's body Decker's broken wrist sagged, a separate flaming stump, behind him a broken ankle dragged an upside down foot through the fire, to leave its caress last of all. But not yet, for both bodies were burning.

Cameron rushed past the terrorist leader before he could stop him. 'I'll take him. I'm a doctor.' He tried to take Minowara from the pilot but Decker would not let go, lashing out with his good foot at the American. He fell forward and Cameron took Minowara's flaming form from his arms as he fell.

Cameron retreated a few paces from the heat of the main fire, ignoring the small heat generated by the burning body in his arms. Jomo Iningwe turned curiously to see what the doctor intended doing for the man who was smiling so serenely content through the flames devouring his ascetic face.

Cameron laid Minowara tenderly on the ground, kneeled beside him and took the narrow face lovingly in his hands, quashing the fire without care for the blisters raised on his own skin.

'Look at me, Omo,' Cameron said. He waited until the Japanese turned his warm brown eyes towards him, then curved his thumbs over and through Minowara's eyes into his brain.

The unexpected attack left the Japanese no time for prepared stoicism and he screamed with pain, his lips tearing apart their fused flesh to emit the thin sound. He screamed only briefly, therefore not losing much face, then he was dead.

Jomo watched Cameron as he rose and dusted himself down. This was fascinating.

'I am an American citizen. I demand to see my consul immediately.'

Jomo shook his head and turned to attend to the tugging at his trousers leg. He looked down.

Decker lay where he had fallen but somehow he had laboriously and painfully turned his ruined body over on its back. He was burning, broken, clearly dying. He opened his mouth to speak and a conversational tone came from it. The words were not quite comprehensible and Jomo leant forward to listen again, careful not to come within reach of the burnt claws which had once been hands. The pilot had a great deal of determination and if he succeeded in digging those claws into your neck he would not let go until the sinews were cut after he was dead.

344

'...clean death...'tween eyes...please.'

Jomo stayed in his bent position and worked his mouth. Then he spat sizzlingly between the pilot's eyes, regretting immediately dousing even that much of the flame. He watched the pilot's eyes as Decker realised that there would be no quick death, no merciful shot between the eyes. It took three long seconds, then the pilot started screaming his fear. Jomo, who knew it was fear and not pain for the pilot was beyond pain, listened for half a minute.

Then Jomo Iningwe turned to his duty, to the American doctor, but the natives had taken him. Jomo shuddered.

Fourteen

The arrival of the helicopter proudly proclaiming its owner-ship by the SA Special Security Police in foot-high letters on its side coincided with the death of Decker, his last breath a frightened whimper turning halfway through into a wel-coming sigh. The contortion on his dead face could have been a smile or a grimace or a start of surprise. Jomo was not disappointed. In the last half hour the pilot's weakening screams had palled on him, his attention taken by adversity elsewhere.

Jomo had tried to recover the American doctor from the natives but the *assegais* had turned against him. He had tried in his imperfect version of their language to explain why he needed the man alive but they had shaken their heads politely, stubbornly. He was welcome to hunt with them but must not interfere with their pleasure or with punishment of the captured prey. He stood by and watched, fuming with the anger of helplessness, while they stripped

345

the American, smeared him with honey and then tied him over an empty fuel drum which had escaped the conflagration. While a few of them laid a trail of honey to the edges of the cleared circle and into the grass, others delicately cut the American's eyelids from his head. The American was getting the treatment intended for the dead Bavenda but Jomo's frustrated anger kept the irony from him.

The policemen started jumping smoothly from the helicopter before it had even touched ground, lining up to the left and the right, machine pistols and assault rifles at the ready, every man with a clear field of fire. Professionals. Jomo sighed for such men.

The natives looked at the policemen and carried on with what they had been doing as soon as it became apparent that the white men intended no aggressive action nor interference.

An ageing man in a neat brown suit came from the helicopter, looked around unhurriedly and walked up to Jomo. He was unarmed.

'You certainly have some very destructive habits,' he said conversationally, waving his hand at the fire and the corpses and the sections of white hot metal from the drums and the exploded helicopter littering the circle.

'You are well into Moçambique territory,' Jomo said, for want of anything else to say.

'Oh, are we? Slight navigator's error.'

A navigator would have to be blind to miss the Limpopo. 'Same navigator's error your jet pilots made when they blew up my boat well into Moçambique?'

The slim man with the thinning grey hair which had once been wavy and the clear cold blue eyes ignored the question. 'I am Rocco Burger and you must be Jomo Iningwe.' There was no question in his voice.

'I am honoured that a white full colonel is sent after me.'

'I just happened to be in the vicinity and thought I'd drop in.' There was no trace of sarcasm in the policeman's voice.

Jomo smiled carefully. The dandy before him was one of Africa's most dangerous men.

346

'We have known for a while of the activities of Bonham and Decker, the atrocity week – ' Colonel Burger smiled in recognition of the phrase stolen from Melody, ' – they ran once a month. They were making a great deal of money and competitors were starting up. The greedy scum of Africa. We didn't want them but we don't like scandals either. So, to set them an example, I was going to drop in on Bonham and Decker at noon today. Decker and Bonham would have been shot while resisting arrest on drug smuggling charges and their foreign playmates sent home with the fright of their lives. But you went in first with your fires of purification.'

'They burnt all the men. I only burnt some fuel as a screen for my men to run behind.'

'Ah.' The South African turned towards the drum on which the naked and honey-sticky body of the American doctor was spreadeagled. The first of the ants had just reached him and he renewed his screaming. 'Which one is he?'

'American. Says he's a doctor.'

'Cameron. He is. Can't we do something about his screaming?'

'You could kill him. Then your men would have to kill all the natives too. International scandal. Invasion of foreign soil with paramilitary troops. Mass murder.'

'And you'd like him alive? He is your proof.'

Jomo nodded. His fate was in this man's hands anyway.

'I'm afraid not. We are glad to be rid of him but we do not want an embarrassment, as I have said. And, besides, my government never interferes in the simple pastoral rites of Bantu.'

Jomo laughed easily. 'There's that to say for your government. It might be a long wait, though.'

'I have patience and my men are paid to wait. Perhaps, while we wait, I could interest you in the advantages of retirement.'

'I have been convinced already. Tell me instead about Bonham and Decker.' Jomo slung his machine pistol around his shoulder and turned to stand beside the South African so they both had a clear field of view at the drum with its spread of misery. He listened as the other man talked and marvelled at his good fortune in escaping alive.

A black man wearied of Cameron's screaming. He looked around for something to stuff in the open mouth and spied the torn clothing beside the drum. He picked some of it up but cast it immediately from him and rubbed his hands together squashing dead the ants that had been on the honey-impregnated clothing in his hands. He looked around once more and found nothing. He leant over Cameron's head and gestured to another man, who held the American's nose while he cut out his tongue. The open mouth did not seem right to his aesthetic sense. He lifted Cameron's genitals by pulling the testicles up around the flaccid penis. His knife flashed in the African noonday sun as he cut the genitals from the loins with a single slash and stuffed them pulsing into the gaping silent mouth.

FRIDAY

On the seventh day the god of war and other atrocities rests.

*In New York, death has no meaning for the seed repro-
ducing itself in Melody's womb as she walks again on the
American soil which will be its false fatherland.*

*In Kent, on their estate, Judith tells her children Eric and
Joan that she will be able to devote much more time to
them now their father is dead; they seem signally unmoved
by either the news or the promise.*

*In Pretoria, Colonel Rocco Burger buries the potentially
embarrassing file, confident that the women will be too
ashamed of their husbands' activities or their own to talk
and knowing that nobody would believe the surviving black
servants anyway.*

*In Lourenço Marques, a squat black British-trained army
officer dreads his return to Kampala where they will no
doubt blame him for their own stupidity in hiring an
incompetent and a thief to perform a simple task.*

*In Zurich, Jomo draws his money from a bank and
enquires about the price of a villa in the south of France.*

Africa continues as before.